THE SMURFS
3 IN 1

Peyo

PAPERCUTZ

PEYO GRAPHIC NOVELS AVAILABLE FROM PAPERCUTZ

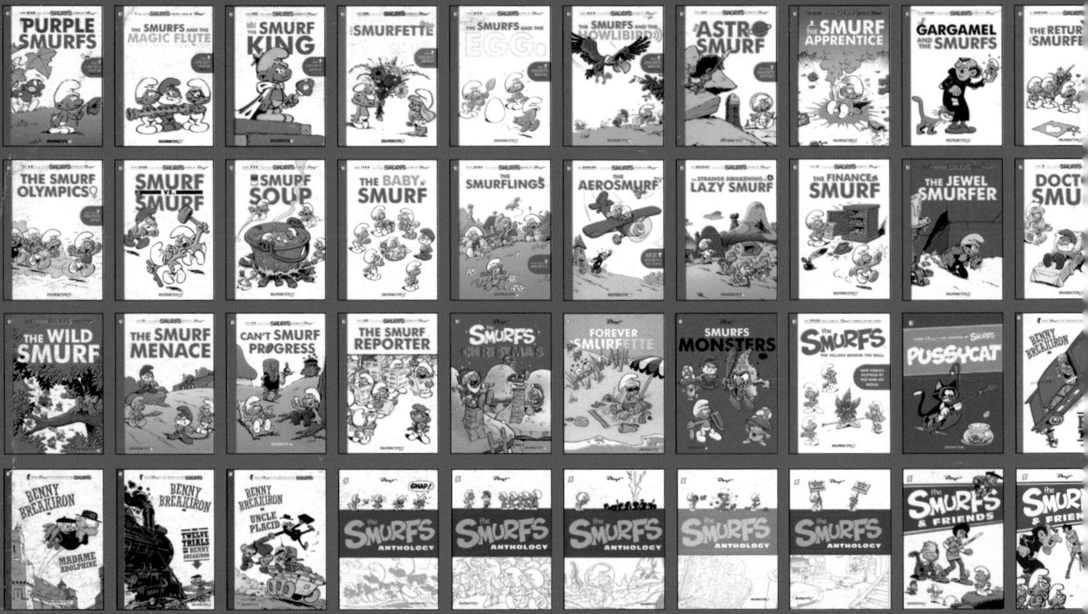

PURPLE SMURFS
THE SMURFS AND THE MAGIC FLUTE
THE SMURF KING
THE SMURFETTE
THE SMURFS AND THE EGG
THE SMURFS AND THE HOWLIBIRD
THE ASTROSMURF
THE SMURF APPRENTICE
GARGAMEL AND THE SMURFS
THE SMURF OLYMPICS
SMURF VS SMURF
SMURF SOUP
THE BABY SMURF
THE SMURFLINGS
AEROSMURF
THE STRANGE AWAKENING OF LAZY SMURF
THE FINANCE SMURF
THE JEWEL SMURFER
THE WILD SMURF
THE SMURF MENACE
CAN'T SMURF PROGRESS
THE SMURF REPORTER
SMURFS CHRISTMAS
FOREVER SMURFETTE
SMURFS MONSTERS
the SMURFS
PUSSYCAT
BENNY BREAKIRON
MADAME ADOLPHINE
TWELVE TRIALS
UNCLE PLACID
GNAP!
the SMURFS ANTHOLOGY
the SMURFS & FRIENDS

THE SMURFS

1. THE PURPLE SMURFS
2. THE SMURFS AND THE MAGIC FLUTE
3. THE SMURF KING
4. THE SMURFETTE
5. THE SMURFS AND THE EGG
6. THE SMURFS AND THE HOWLIBIRD
7. THE ASTROSMURF
8. THE SMURF APPRENTICE
9. GARGAMEL AND THE SMURFS
10. THE RETURN OF THE SMURFETTE
11. THE SMURF OLYMPICS
12. SMURF VS. SMURF
13. SMURF SOUP
14. THE BABY SMURF
15. THE SMURFLINGS
16. THE AEROSMURF
17. THE STRANGE AWAKENING OF LAZY SMURF
18. THE FINANCE SMURF
19. THE JEWEL SMURFER
20. DOCTOR SMURF
21. THE WILD SMURF
22. THE SMURF MENACE
23. CAN'T SMURF PROGRESS
24. THE SMURF REPORTER

- THE SMURFS CHRISTMAS
- FOREVER SMURFETTE
- SMURFS MONSTERS
- THE SMURFS THE VILLAGE BEHIND THE WALL

PUSSYCAT

BENNY BREAKIRON

1. THE RED TAXIS
2. MADAME ADOLPHINE
3. THE TWELVE TRIALS OF BENNY BREAKIRON
4. UNCLE PLACID

THE SMURFS ANTHOLOGY

– VOLUME ONE
– VOLUME TWO
– VOLUME THREE
– VOLUME FOUR
– VOLUME FIVE

THE SMURFS AND FRIENDS

– VOLUME ONE
– VOLUME TWO

THE SMURFS (#1-20), THE SMURFS CHRISTMAS, FOREVER SMURFETTE, SMURFS MONSTERS, graphic novels are available in paperback for $5.99 each a hardcover for $10.99 each; THE SMURFS #21, #22, #23, #24 and THE SMURFS THE VILLAGE BEHIND THE WALL graphic novels are available in paperback for $ each and in hardcover for $12.99 each. BENNY BREAKIRON graphic novels are available in hardcover only for $11.99 each; and THE SMURFS ANTHOLOGY and THE SMURFS & FRIENDS #1 are available in hardcover only for $19.99 each. THE SMURFS ANTHOLOGY #5 and THE SMURFS & FRIENDS #2 are availal hardcover only for $24.99 each at booksellers everywhere. Order online at papercutz.com. Or call 1-800-886-1223, Monday through Friday, 9 – 5 EST. MC, Visa AmEx accepted. To order by mail, please add $4.00 for postage and handling for first book ordered, $1.00 for each additional book and make check payable to Publishing. Send to: Papercutz, 160 Broadway, Suite 700, East Wing, New York, NY 10038.

SMURFS, BENNY BREAKIRON, and PUSSYCAT graphic novels are also available digitally wherever e-books are sold.

PAPERCUTZ.COM

SMURFS™

3IN1 #2

3 SMURFS GRAPHIC NOVELS BY Peyo IN 1

PAPERCUTZ™

New York

THE SMURFS 3 IN 1 #2

© *Peyo* - 2018 - Licensed through Lafig Belgium - www.smurf.com

"The Smurfette"
BY YVAN DELPORTE AND PEYO

"The Hungry Smurfs"
BY YVAN DELPORTE AND PEYO

"The Smurfs and the Egg"
BY YVAN DELPORTE AND PEYO

"The Fake Smurf"
BY YVAN DELPORTE AND PEYO

"The Hundredth Smurf"
BY YVAN DELPORTE AND PEYO

"The Smurfs and the Howlibird"
BY PEYO AND GOS

"The Smurf Express"
BY PEYO

"You Can't Smurf in the Way of Progress"
BY YVAN DELPORTE AND PEYO

Joe Johnson, *SMURFLATIONS*
Janice Chiang, *LETTERING SMURFETTE*
Adam Grano, *ORIGINAL SMURFIC DESIGN*
Dawn Guzzo, *SMURFIC DESIGN*
Michael Petranek, *ORIGINAL ASSOCIATE SMURF*
Matt. Murray, *SMURF CONSULTANT*
Jeff Whitman, *ASSISTANT MANAGING SMURF*
Jim Salicrup, *SMURF-IN-CHIEF*

ISBN: 978-1-5458-0164-2

Printed in China
November 2018

Papercutz books may be purchased for business or promotional use.
For information on bulk purchases, please contact Macmillan Corporate
and Premium Sales Department at (800) 221-7945 x5442.

Distributed by Macmillan
First Papercutz Printing

INTRODUCTION

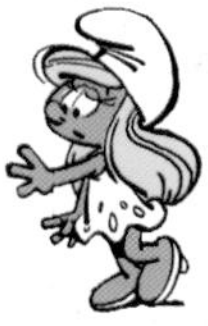

THERE'S A BLUE GIRL IN TOWN

By Jim "Smurftastic!" Salicrup

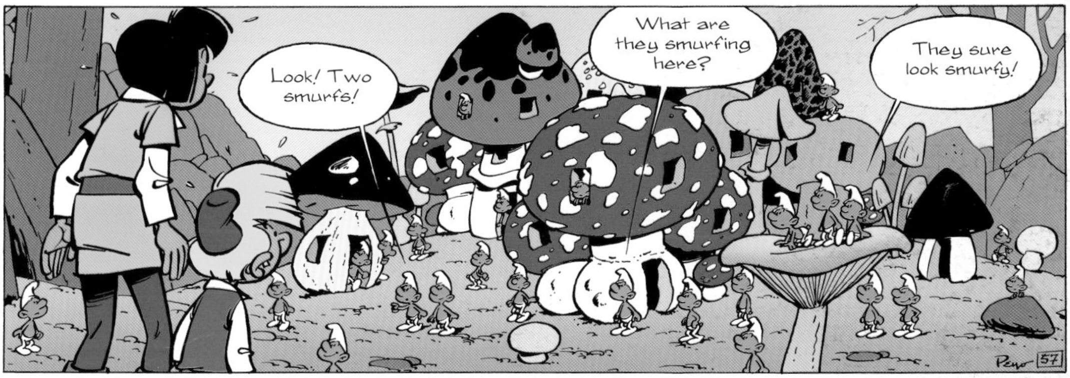
Look! Two smurfs!
What are they smurfing here?
They sure look smurfy!
Peyo
57

The world's first look at the Smurf Village.

Pierre Culliford, the cartoonist better known as Peyo, was on a winning streak. First, he was working on his humorous medieval adventure comics series called *Johan and Peewit*, about a young knight-in-training and a court jester, and in their ninth story, "The Flute with Six Holes," the heroes encountered a village filled with magical blue gnomes called *les Schtroumpfs*, or as we've come to call them in North America, the Smurfs. That story was re-titled "The Smurfs and the Magic Flute" and has been republished many times as the official first appearance of the Smurfs, most recently in THE SMURFS 3 IN 1 #1.

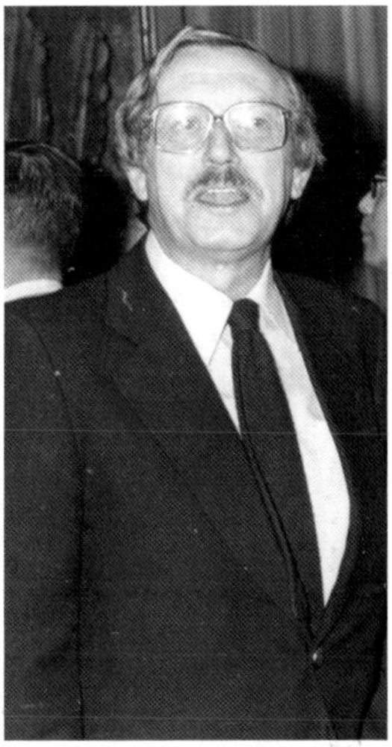

"Peyo"

To say that the Smurfs were a big hit, would be an understatement. *Johan and Peewit* were being serialized in the Belgian comics magazine *Le Journal de Spirou*, and the audience demanded to see more Smurfs. And Peyo delivered. He created Smurfs mini-comics that were featured in *Spirou*, and had the Smurfs return in the *Johan and Peewit* stories in either cameo appearances or as guest stars. But still there was demand for more Smurfs stories, and that's when THE SMURFS graphic novels (called albums in Europe) started up, publishing new stories along with revised and expanded versions of the stories from the mini-comics.

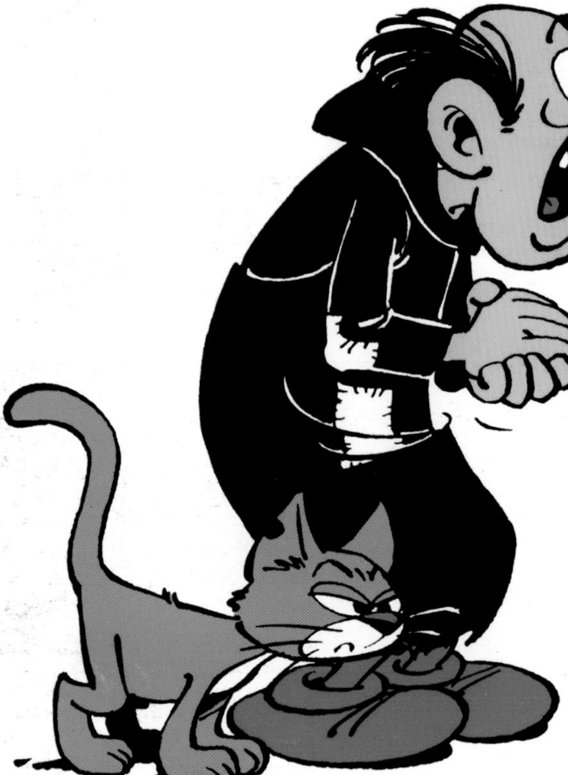

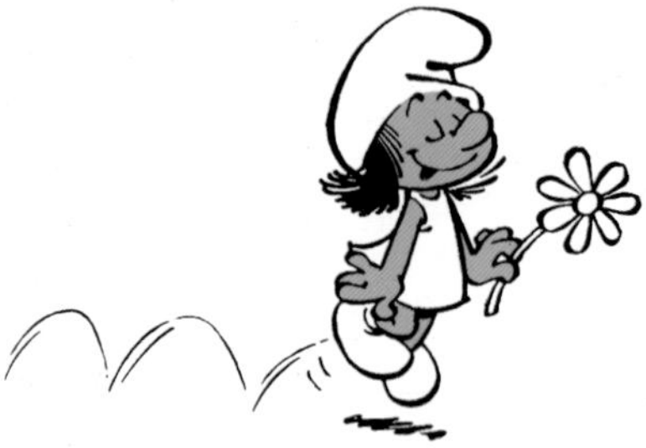

It's really not that uncommon in Pop Culture for characters introduced in an ongoing series to become so popular that they wind up with a series of their own. In American comic strips, way back in 1929, *Thimble Theatre* was in its tenth year when cartoonist Elzie Crisler Segar introduced a new character who became the new star of the strip: Popeye the Sailor.

Peyo probably didn't expect the Smurfs to become as world-famous as they eventually became when he originally introduced them in that *Johan and Peewit* story. Chances are he didn't expect the characters that he and writer Yvan Delporte created for "The Smurfnapper," the evil wizard Gargamel and his pet cat Azrael to return either. And when that dastardly duo returned, Peyo and Yvan Delporte introduced yet another character that was destined to forevermore be a Smurfs super-star: The Smurfette.

Smurfette has since become such a vital part of THE SMURFS that it's hard to believe that she wasn't there since the very beginning. Equally unbelievable, after her debut in "The Smurfette," she didn't return until several albums later. In fact, many years later, when the Smurfs were adapted into Saturday morning cartoons, Hanna-Barbera decided to retroactively work her into all the stories that she didn't appear in originally.

More recently, Smurfette, along with Papa Smurf, Brainy Smurf, Astro Smurf, GNAP! Smurf, and even Gargamel with Azrael, were made into a Funko Pops, a true sign of her iconic Pop Culture status.

Now, without further smurfy ado, may I present to you, on the following page, the one and only... "The Smurfette."

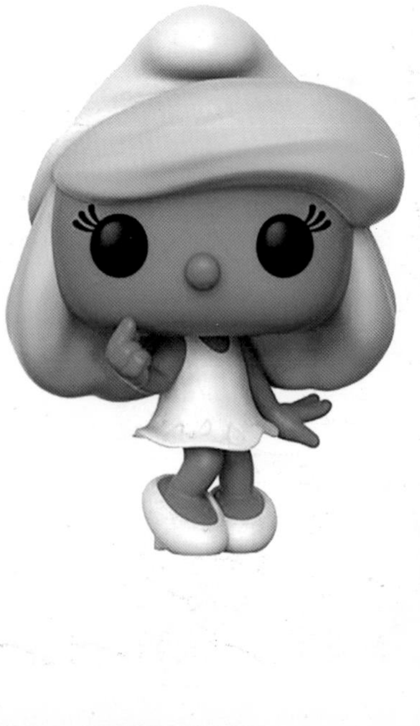

THE SMURFETTE

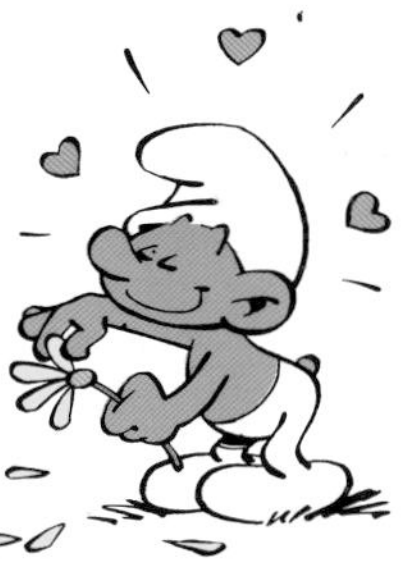

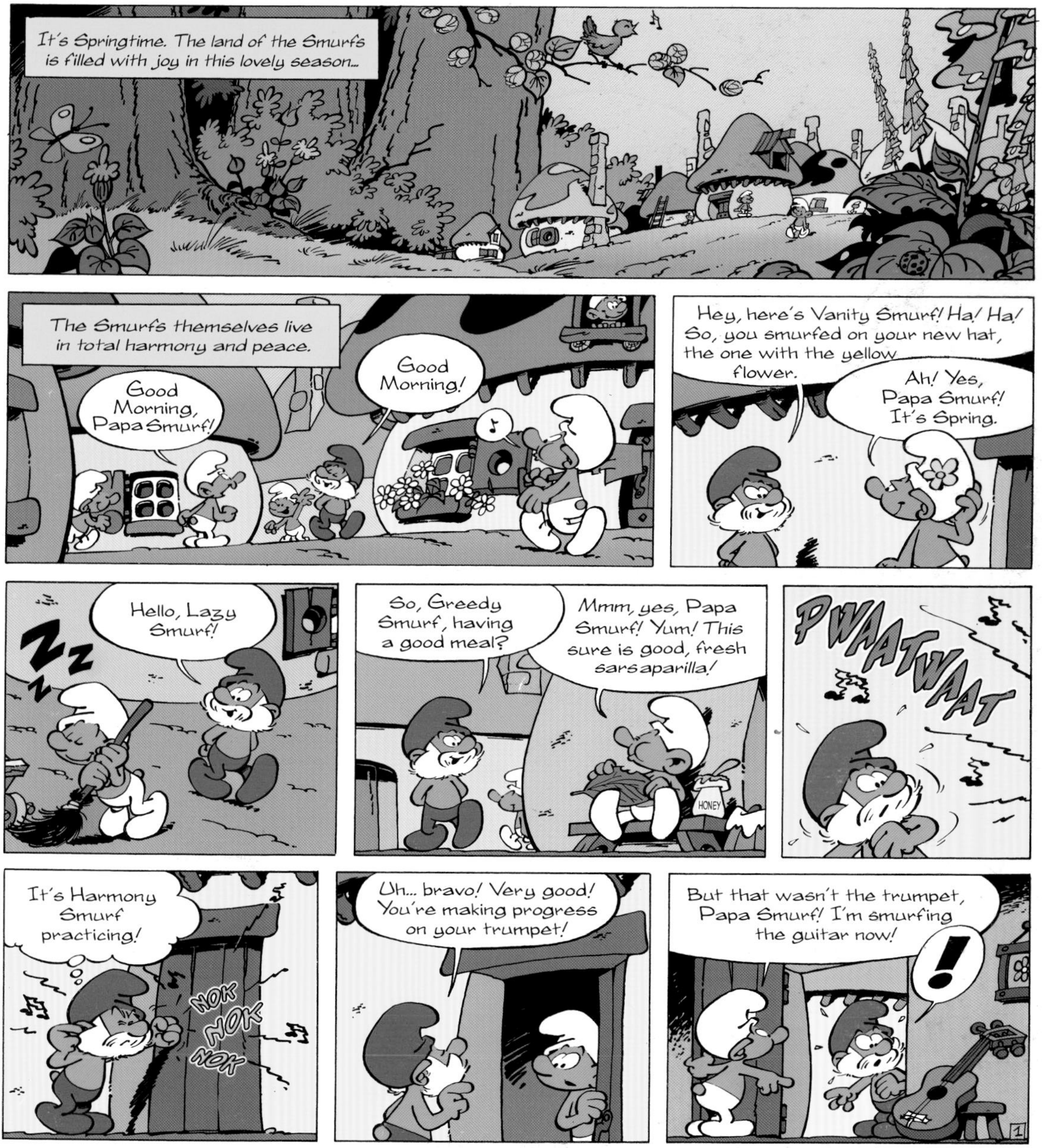
It's Springtime. The land of the Smurfs is filled with joy in this lovely season...
The Smurfs themselves live in total harmony and peace.
Good Morning, Papa Smurf!
Good Morning!
Hey, here's Vanity Smurf! Ha! Ha! So, you smurfed on your new hat, the one with the yellow flower.
Ah! Yes, Papa Smurf! It's Spring.
Hello, Lazy Smurf!
So, Greedy Smurf, having a good meal?
Mmm, yes, Papa Smurf! Yum! This sure is good, fresh sarsaparilla!
HONEY
PWAATWAAT
It's Harmony Smurf practicing!
NOK NOK NOK
Uh... bravo! Very good! You're making progress on your trumpet!
But that wasn't the trumpet, Papa Smurf! I'm smurfing the guitar now!
!
1

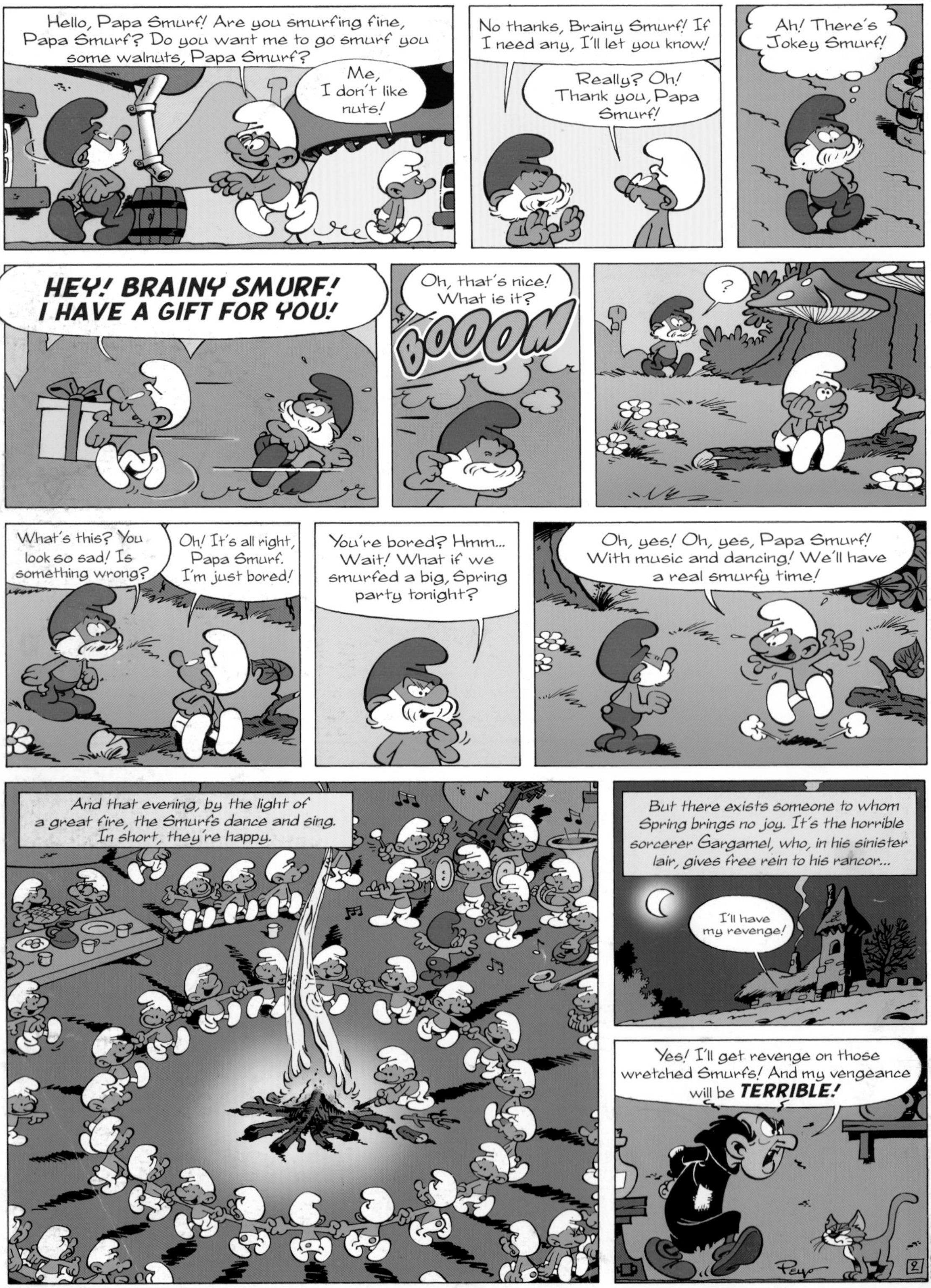

Hello, Papa Smurf! Are you smurfing fine, Papa Smurf? Do you want me to go smurf you some walnuts, Papa Smurf?
Me, I don't like nuts!
No thanks, Brainy Smurf! If I need any, I'll let you know!
Really? Oh! Thank you, Papa Smurf!
Ah! There's Jokey Smurf!
HEY! BRAINY SMURF! I HAVE A GIFT FOR YOU!
Oh, that's nice! What is it?
BOOOM
?
What's this? You look so sad! Is something wrong?
Oh! It's all right, Papa Smurf. I'm just bored!
You're bored? Hmm... Wait! What if we smurfed a big, Spring party tonight?
Oh, yes! Oh, yes, Papa Smurf! With music and dancing! We'll have a real smurfy time!
And that evening, by the light of a great fire, the Smurfs dance and sing. In short, they're happy.
But there exists someone to whom Spring brings no joy. It's the horrible sorcerer Gargamel, who, in his sinister lair, gives free rein to his rancor...
I'll have my revenge!
Yes! I'll get revenge on those wretched Smurfs! And my vengeance will be **TERRIBLE!**
Peyo
2

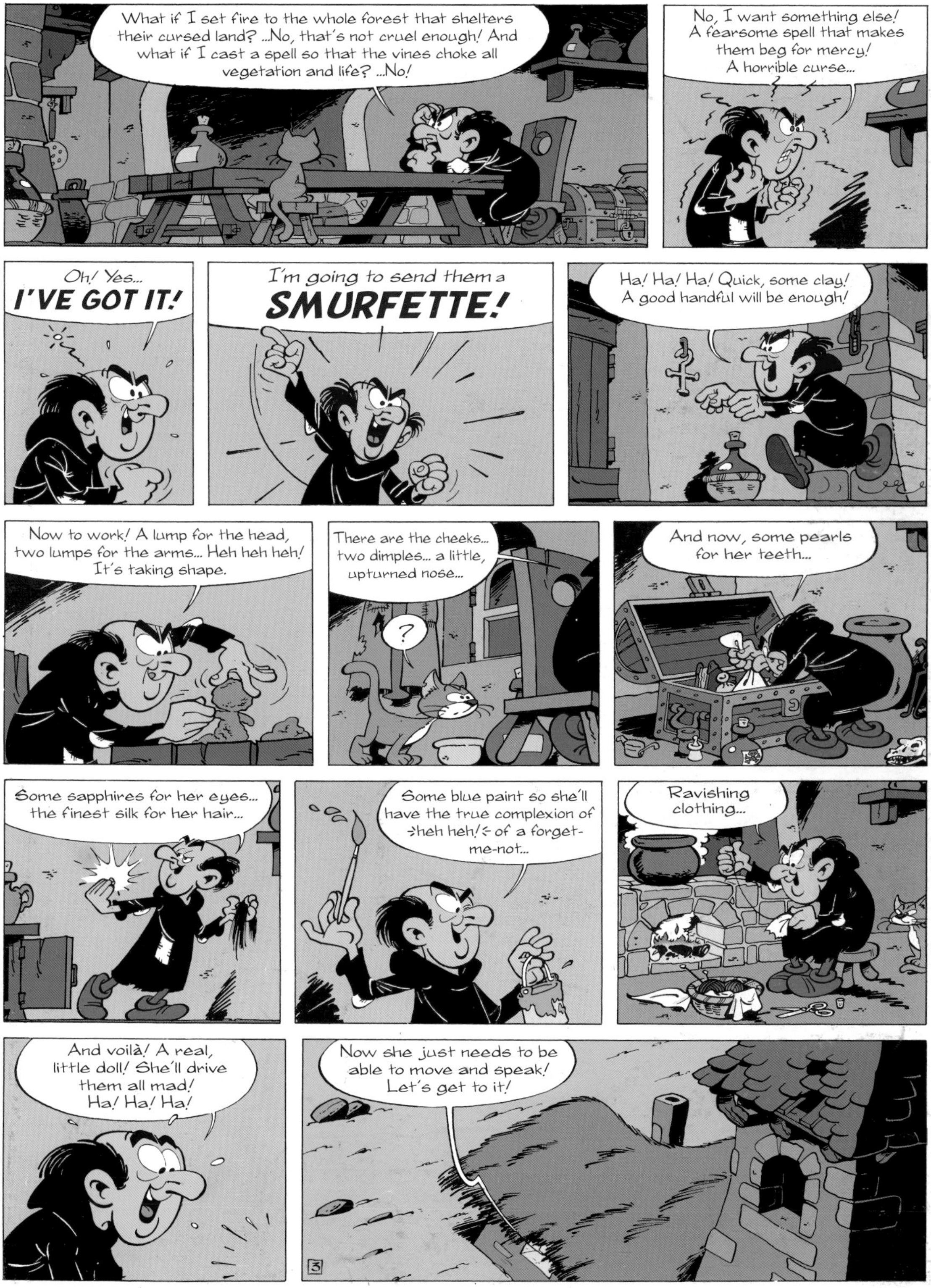

What if I set fire to the whole forest that shelters their cursed land? ...No, that's not cruel enough! And what if I cast a spell so that the vines choke all vegetation and life? ...No!
No, I want something else! A fearsome spell that makes them beg for mercy! A horrible curse...
Oh! Yes... I'VE GOT IT!
I'm going to send them a SMURFETTE!
Ha! Ha! Ha! Quick, some clay! A good handful will be enough!
Now to work! A lump for the head, two lumps for the arms... Heh heh heh! It's taking shape.
There are the cheeks... two dimples... a little, upturned nose...
?
And now, some pearls for her teeth...
Some sapphires for her eyes... the finest silk for her hair...
Some blue paint so she'll have the true complexion of -heh heh!- of a forget-me-not...
Ravishing clothing...
And voilà! A real, little doll! She'll drive them all mad! Ha! Ha! Ha!
Now she just needs to be able to move and speak! Let's get to it!
3

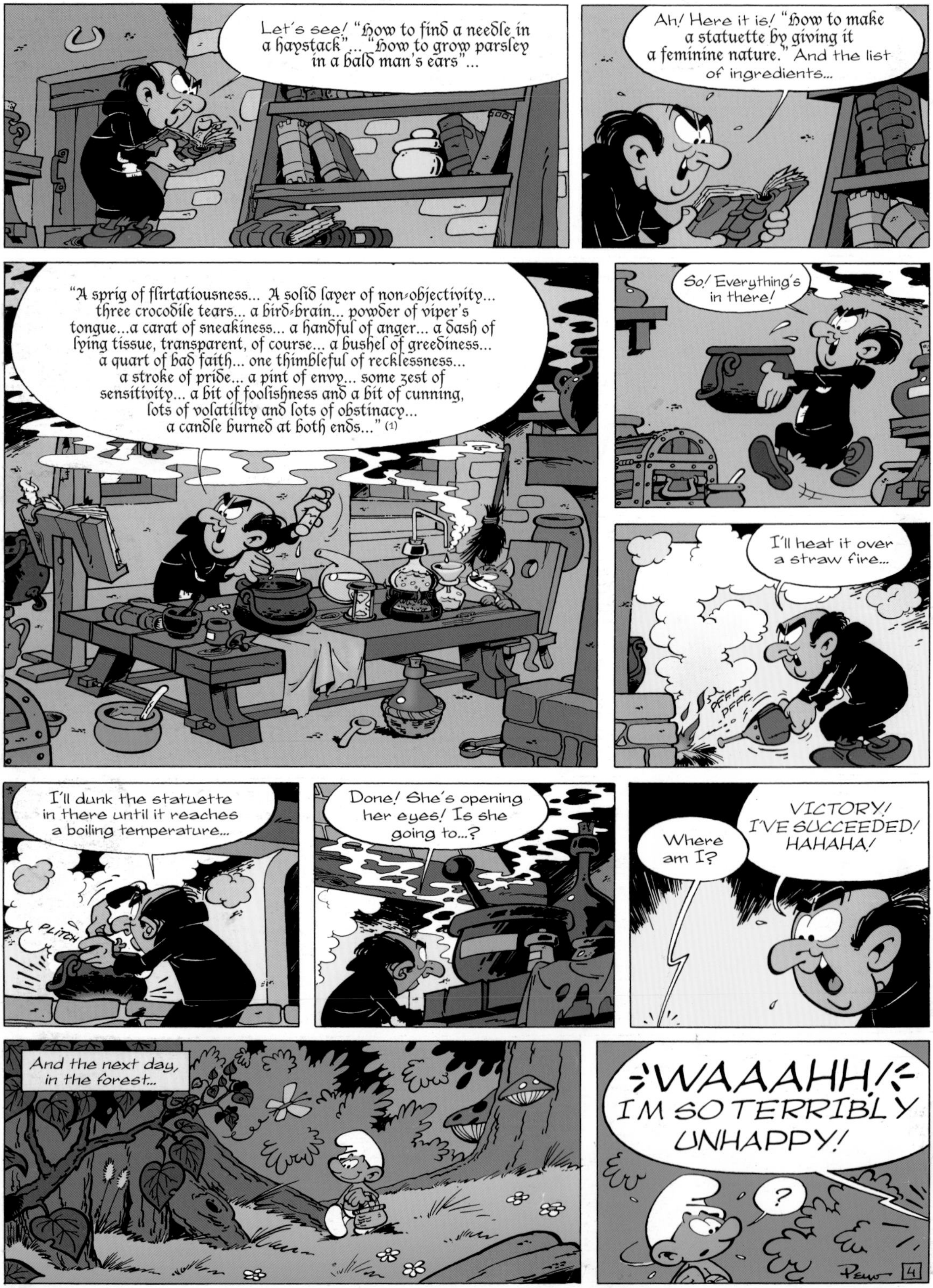
Let's see! "How to find a needle in a haystack"... "How to grow parsley in a bald man's ears"...
Ah! Here it is! "How to make a statuette by giving it a feminine nature." And the list of ingredients...
"A sprig of flirtatiousness... A solid layer of non-objectivity... three crocodile tears... a bird-brain... powder of viper's tongue...a carat of sneakiness... a handful of anger... a dash of lying tissue, transparent, of course... a bushel of greediness... a quart of bad faith... one thimbleful of recklessness... a stroke of pride... a pint of envy... some zest of sensitivity... a bit of foolishness and a bit of cunning, lots of volatility and lots of obstinacy... a candle burned at both ends..." (1)
So! Everything's in there!
I'll heat it over a straw fire...
PFFF PFFF
I'll dunk the statuette in there until it reaches a boiling temperature...
PLITCH
Done! She's opening her eyes! Is she going to...?
VICTORY! I'VE SUCCEEDED! HAHAHA!
Where am I?
And the next day, in the forest...
WAAAHH! I'M SO TERRIBLY UNHAPPY!
?
4

(1) This text is the sole responsibility of the author of the spell-book "Magicae Formulae," Beelzebub Editions.

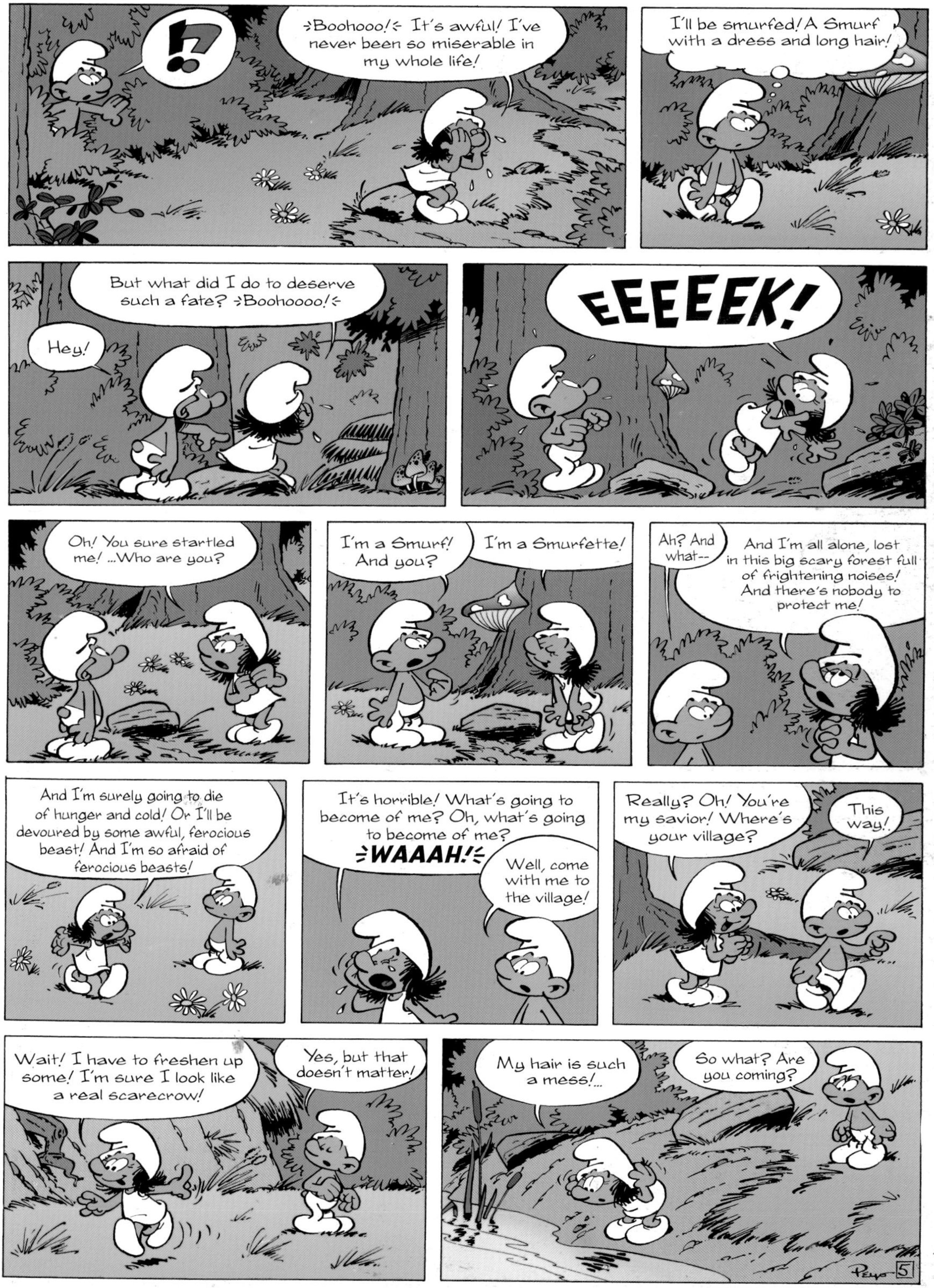

!?
Boohooo! It's awful! I've never been so miserable in my whole life!
I'll be smurfed! A Smurf with a dress and long hair!
But what did I do to deserve such a fate? Boohoooo!
Hey!
EEEEEK!
Oh! You sure startled me! ...Who are you?
I'm a Smurf! And you?
I'm a Smurfette!
Ah? And what--
And I'm all alone, lost in this big scary forest full of frightening noises! And there's nobody to protect me!
And I'm surely going to die of hunger and cold! Or I'll be devoured by some awful, ferocious beast! And I'm so afraid of ferocious beasts!
It's horrible! What's going to become of me? Oh, what's going to become of me?
WAAAH!
Well, come with me to the village!
Really? Oh! You're my savior! Where's your village?
This way!
Wait! I have to freshen up some! I'm sure I look like a real scarecrow!
Yes, but that doesn't matter!
My hair is such a mess!...
So what? Are you coming?
Peyo
5

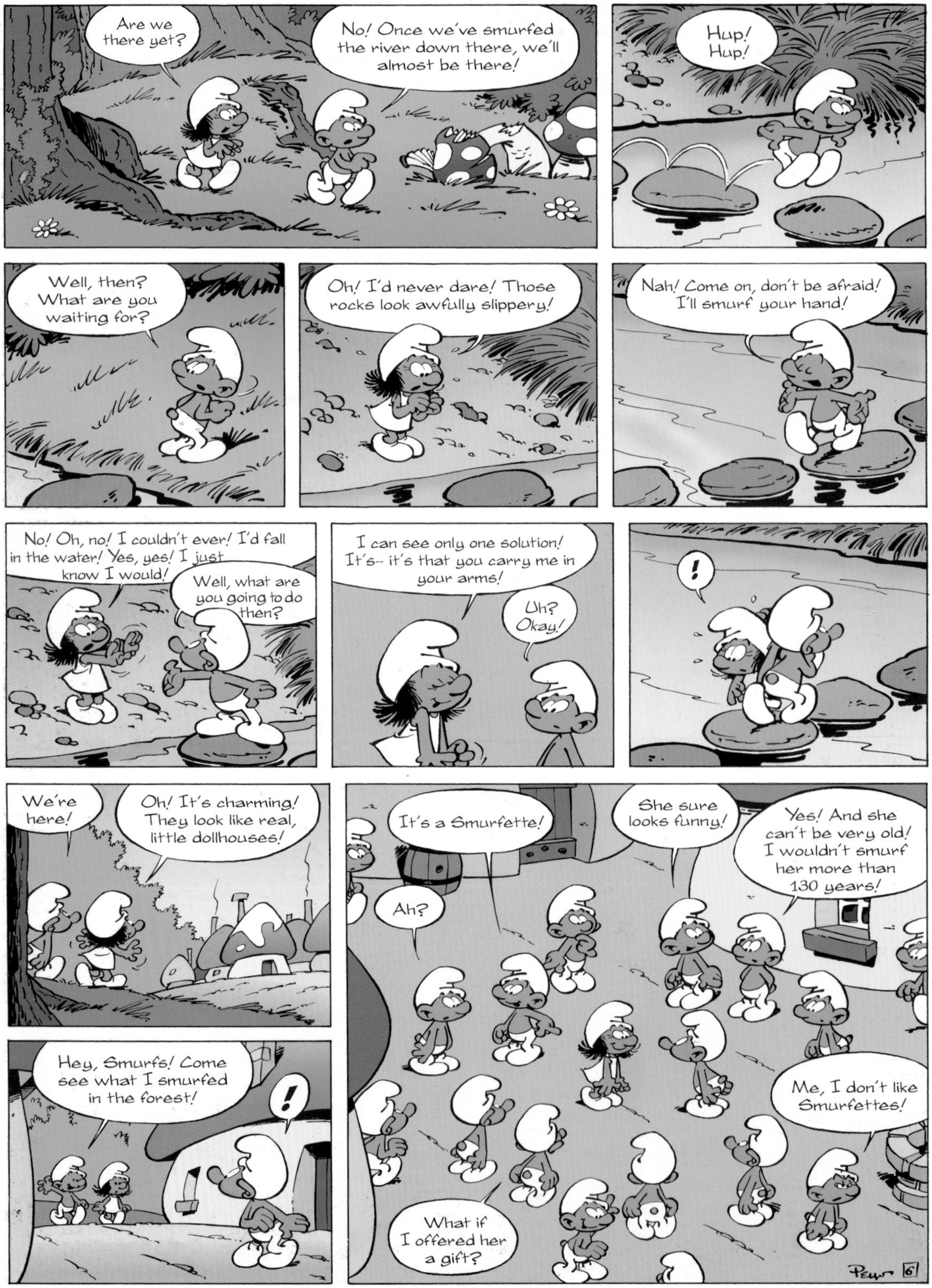

Are we there yet?
No! Once we've smurfed the river down there, we'll almost be there!
Hup! Hup!
Well, then? What are you waiting for?
Oh! I'd never dare! Those rocks look awfully slippery!
Nah! Come on, don't be afraid! I'll smurf your hand!
No! Oh, no! I couldn't ever! I'd fall in the water! Yes, yes! I just know I would!
Well, what are you going to do then?
I can see only one solution! It's-- it's that you carry me in your arms!
Uh? Okay!
!
We're here!
Oh! It's charming! They look like real, little dollhouses!
Hey, Smurfs! Come see what I smurfed in the forest!
!
It's a Smurfette!
She sure looks funny!
Yes! And she can't be very old! I wouldn't smurf her more than 130 years!
Ah?
Me, I don't like Smurfettes!
What if I offered her a gift?
Peyo 6

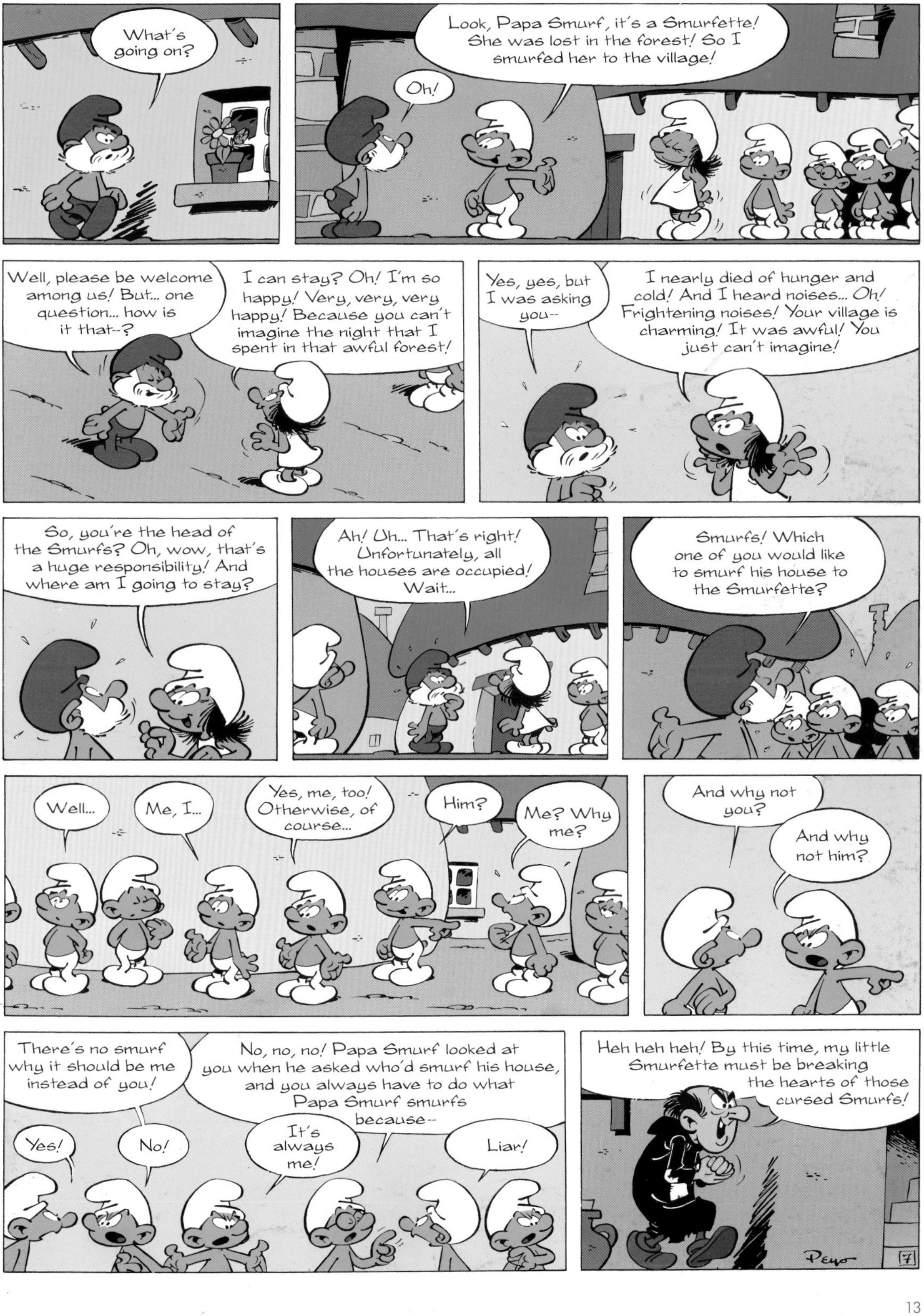

What's going on?
Look, Papa Smurf, it's a Smurfette! She was lost in the forest! So I smurfed her to the village!
Oh!
Well, please be welcome among us! But... one question... how is it that--?
I can stay? Oh! I'm so happy! Very, very, very happy! Because you can't imagine the night that I spent in that awful forest!
Yes, yes, but I was asking you--
I nearly died of hunger and cold! And I heard noises... Oh! Frightening noises! Your village is charming! It was awful! You just can't imagine!
So, you're the head of the Smurfs? Oh, wow, that's a huge responsibility! And where am I going to stay?
Ah! Uh... That's right! Unfortunately, all the houses are occupied! Wait...
Smurfs! Which one of you would like to smurf his house to the Smurfette?
Well...
Me, I...
Yes, me, too! Otherwise, of course...
Him?
Me? Why me?
And why not you?
And why not him?
There's no smurf why it should be me instead of you!
No, no, no! Papa Smurf looked at you when he asked who'd smurf his house, and you always have to do what Papa Smurf smurfs because--
Yes!
No!
It's always me!
Liar!
Heh heh heh! By this time, my little Smurfette must be breaking the hearts of those cursed Smurfs!
Peyo
7

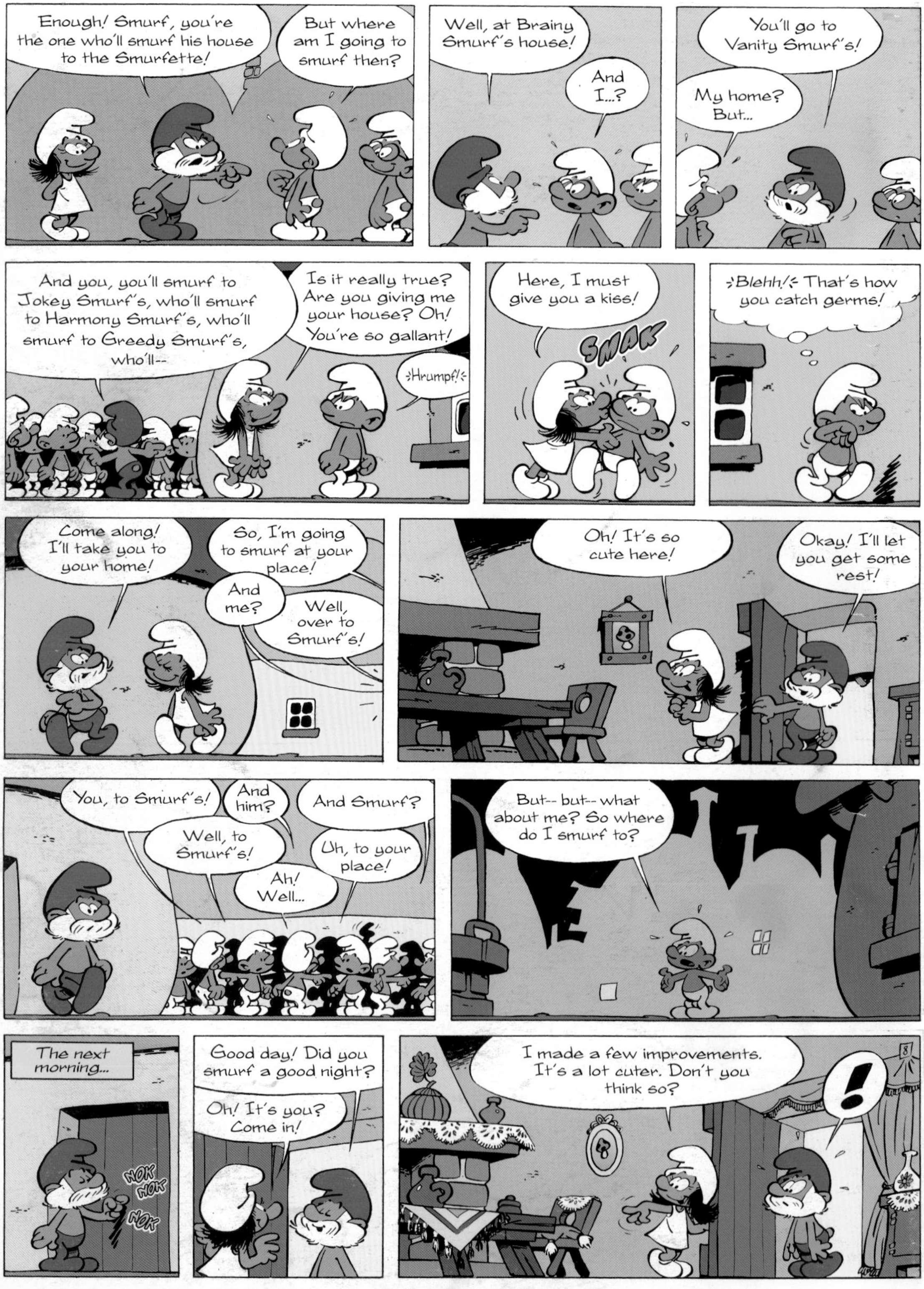

Enough! Smurf, you're the one who'll smurf his house to the Smurfette!
But where am I going to smurf then?
Well, at Brainy Smurf's house!
And I...?
You'll go to Vanity Smurf's!
My home? But...
And you, you'll smurf to Jokey Smurf's, who'll smurf to Harmony Smurf's, who'll smurf to Greedy Smurf's, who'll--
Is it really true? Are you giving me your house? Oh! You're so gallant!
Hrumpf!
Here, I must give you a kiss!
SMAK
Blehh! That's how you catch germs!
Come along! I'll take you to your home!
So, I'm going to smurf at your place!
And me?
Well, over to Smurf's!
Oh! It's so cute here!
Okay! I'll let you get some rest!
You, to Smurf's!
And him?
Well, to Smurf's!
And Smurf?
Uh, to your place!
Ah! Well...
But-- but-- what about me? So where do I smurf to?
The next morning...
NOK NOK NOK
Good day! Did you smurf a good night?
Oh! It's you? Come in!
I made a few improvements. It's a lot cuter. Don't you think so?
!

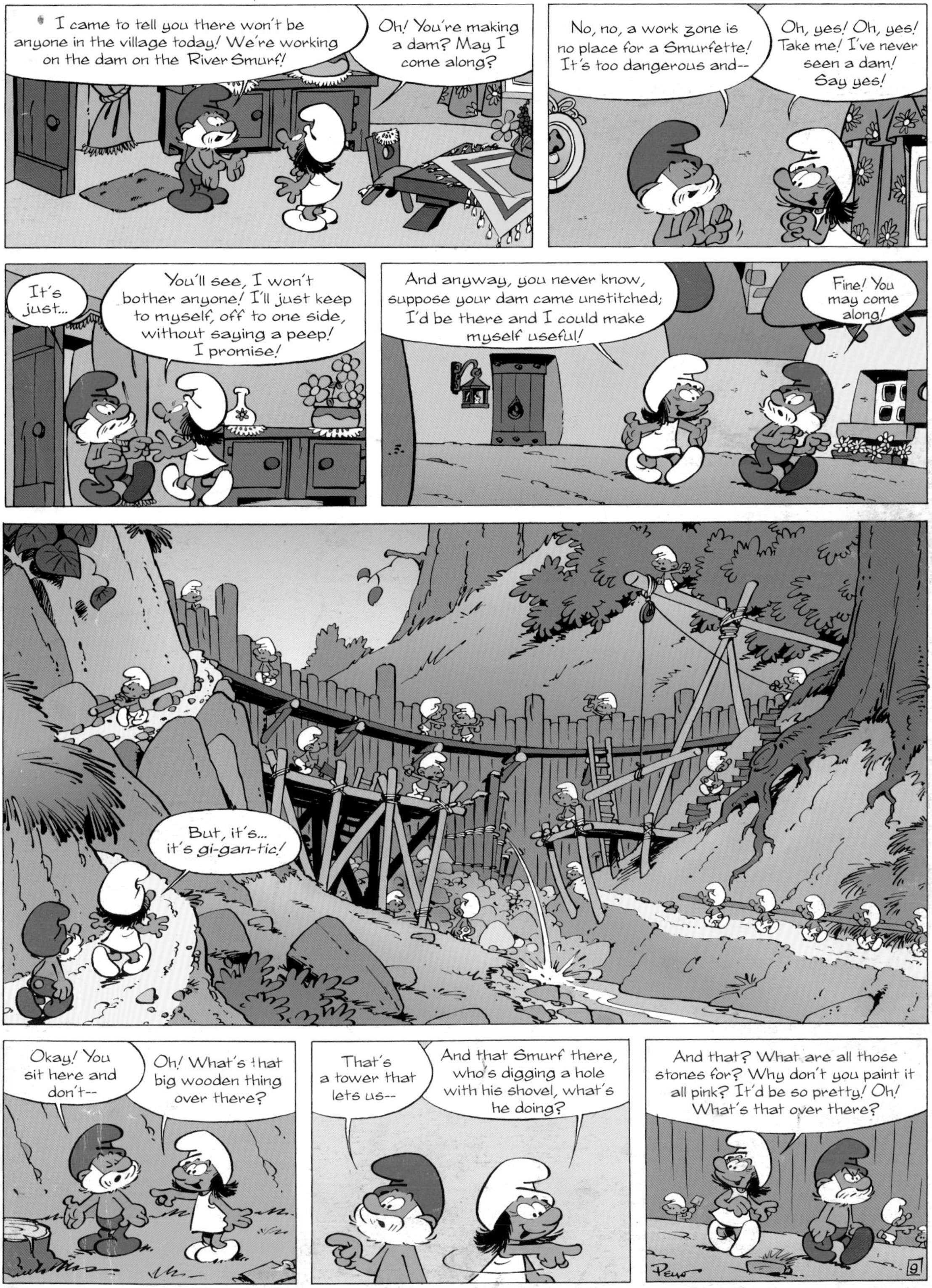

I came to tell you there won't be anyone in the village today! We're working on the dam on the River Smurf!
Oh! You're making a dam? May I come along?
No, no, a work zone is no place for a Smurfette! It's too dangerous and--
Oh, yes! Oh, yes! Take me! I've never seen a dam! Say yes!
It's just...
You'll see, I won't bother anyone! I'll just keep to myself, off to one side, without saying a peep! I promise!
And anyway, you never know, suppose your dam came unstitched; I'd be there and I could make myself useful!
Fine! You may come along!
But, it's... it's gi-gan-tic!
Okay! You sit here and don't--
Oh! What's that big wooden thing over there?
That's a tower that lets us--
And that Smurf there, who's digging a hole with his shovel, what's he doing?
And that? What are all those stones for? Why don't you paint it all pink? It'd be so pretty! Oh! What's that over there?
9

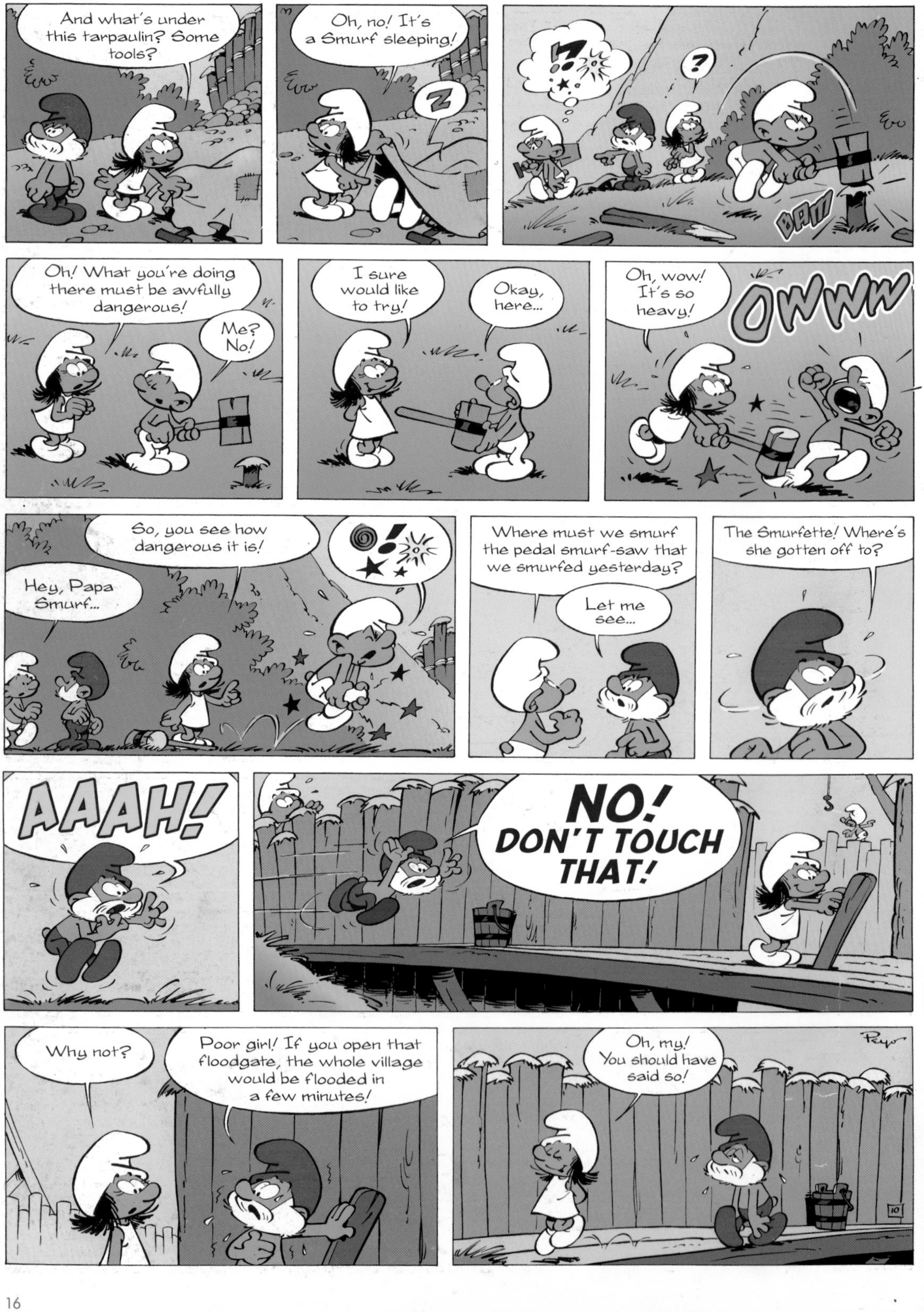
And what's under this tarpaulin? Some tools?
Oh, no! It's a Smurf sleeping!
Z
?
BAM!
Oh! What you're doing there must be awfully dangerous!
Me? No!
I sure would like to try!
Okay, here...
Oh, wow! It's so heavy!
OWWW
So, you see how dangerous it is!
Hey, Papa Smurf...
Where must we smurf the pedal smurf-saw that we smurfed yesterday?
Let me see...
The Smurfette! Where's she gotten off to?
AAAH!
NO! DON'T TOUCH THAT!
Why not?
Poor girl! If you open that floodgate, the whole village would be flooded in a few minutes!
Oh, my! You should have said so!
Peyo
10

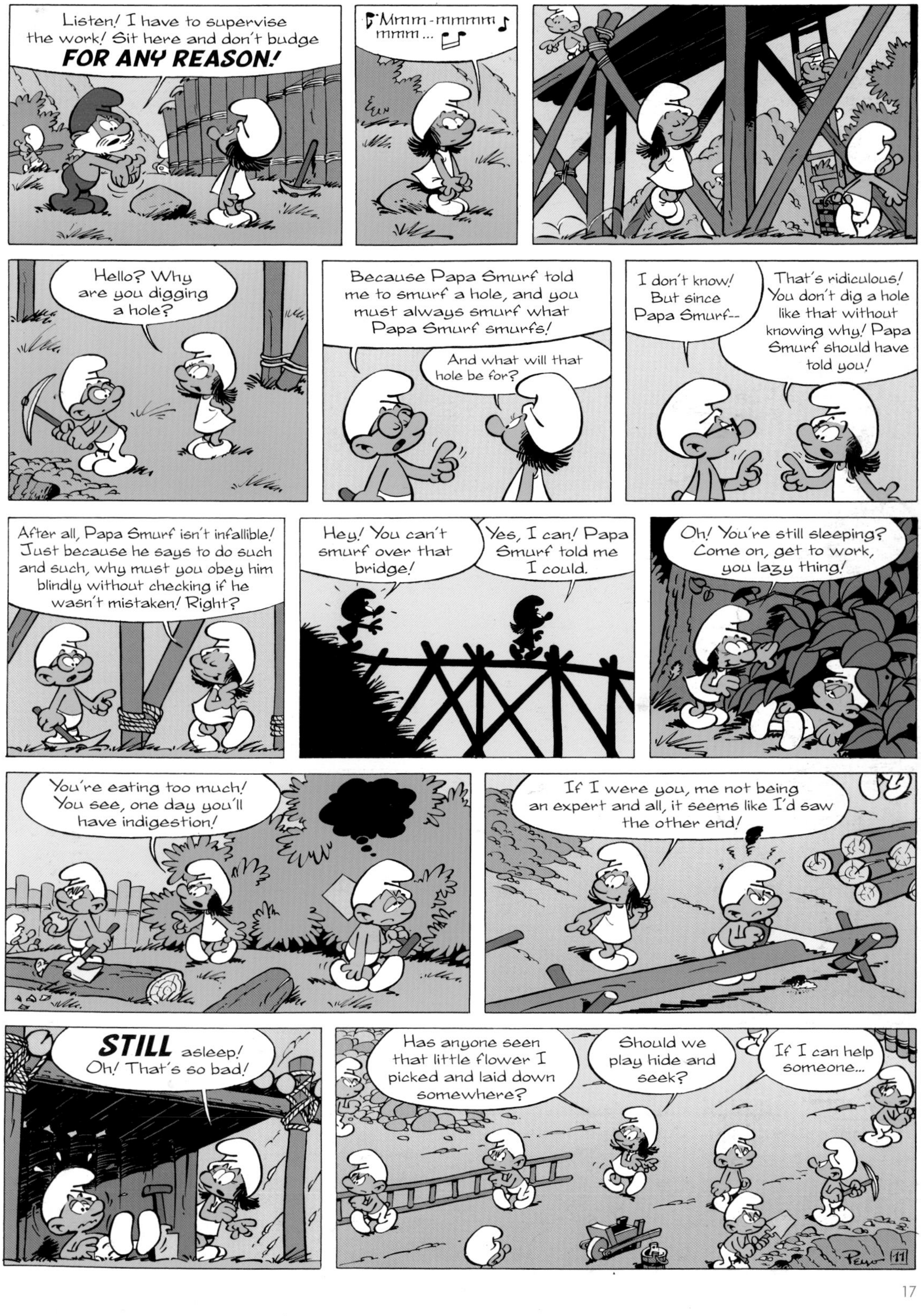
Listen! I have to supervise the work! Sit here and don't budge **FOR ANY REASON!**
Mmm-mmmm mmm...
Hello? Why are you digging a hole?
Because Papa Smurf told me to smurf a hole, and you must always smurf what Papa Smurf smurfs!
And what will that hole be for?
I don't know! But since Papa Smurf--
That's ridiculous! You don't dig a hole like that without knowing why! Papa Smurf should have told you!
After all, Papa Smurf isn't infallible! Just because he says to do such and such, why must you obey him blindly without checking if he wasn't mistaken! Right?
Hey! You can't smurf over that bridge!
Yes, I can! Papa Smurf told me I could.
Oh! You're still sleeping? Come on, get to work, you lazy thing!
You're eating too much! You see, one day you'll have indigestion!
If I were you, me not being an expert and all, it seems like I'd saw the other end!
STILL asleep! Oh! That's so bad!
Has anyone seen that little flower I picked and laid down somewhere?
Should we play hide and seek?
If I can help someone...

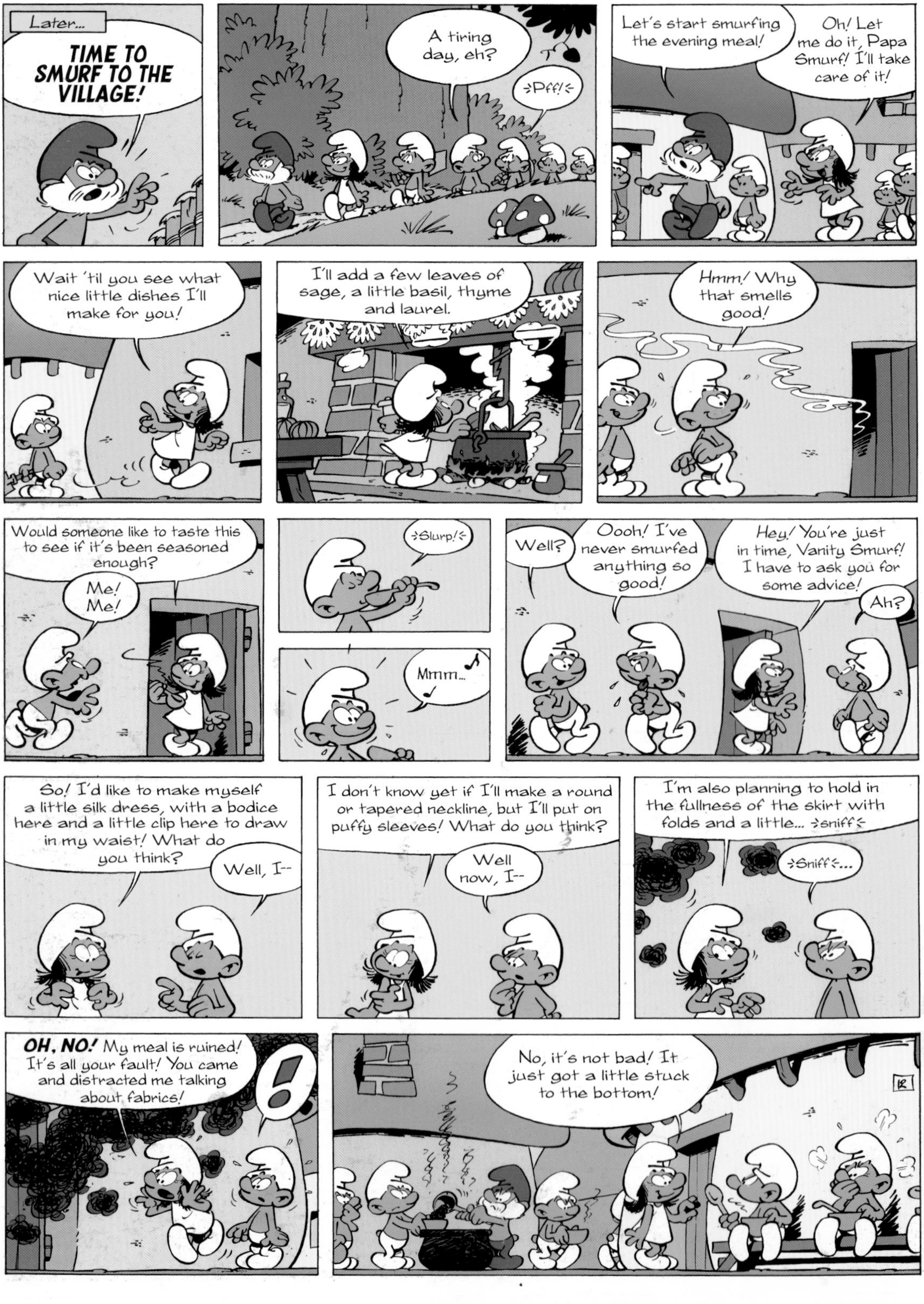
Later...
TIME TO SMURF TO THE VILLAGE!
A tiring day, eh?
Pff!
Let's start smurfing the evening meal!
Oh! Let me do it, Papa Smurf! I'll take care of it!
Wait 'til you see what nice little dishes I'll make for you!
I'll add a few leaves of sage, a little basil, thyme and laurel.
Hmm! Why that smells good!
Would someone like to taste this to see if it's been seasoned enough?
Me! Me!
Slurp!
Mmm...
Well?
Oooh! I've never smurfed anything so good!
Hey! You're just in time, Vanity Smurf! I have to ask you for some advice!
Ah?
So! I'd like to make myself a little silk dress, with a bodice here and a little clip here to draw in my waist! What do you think?
Well, I--
I don't know yet if I'll make a round or tapered neckline, but I'll put on puffy sleeves! What do you think?
Well now, I--
I'm also planning to hold in the fullness of the skirt with folds and a little... sniff
Sniff...
OH, NO! My meal is ruined! It's all your fault! You came and distracted me talking about fabrics!
!
No, it's not bad! It just got a little stuck to the bottom!

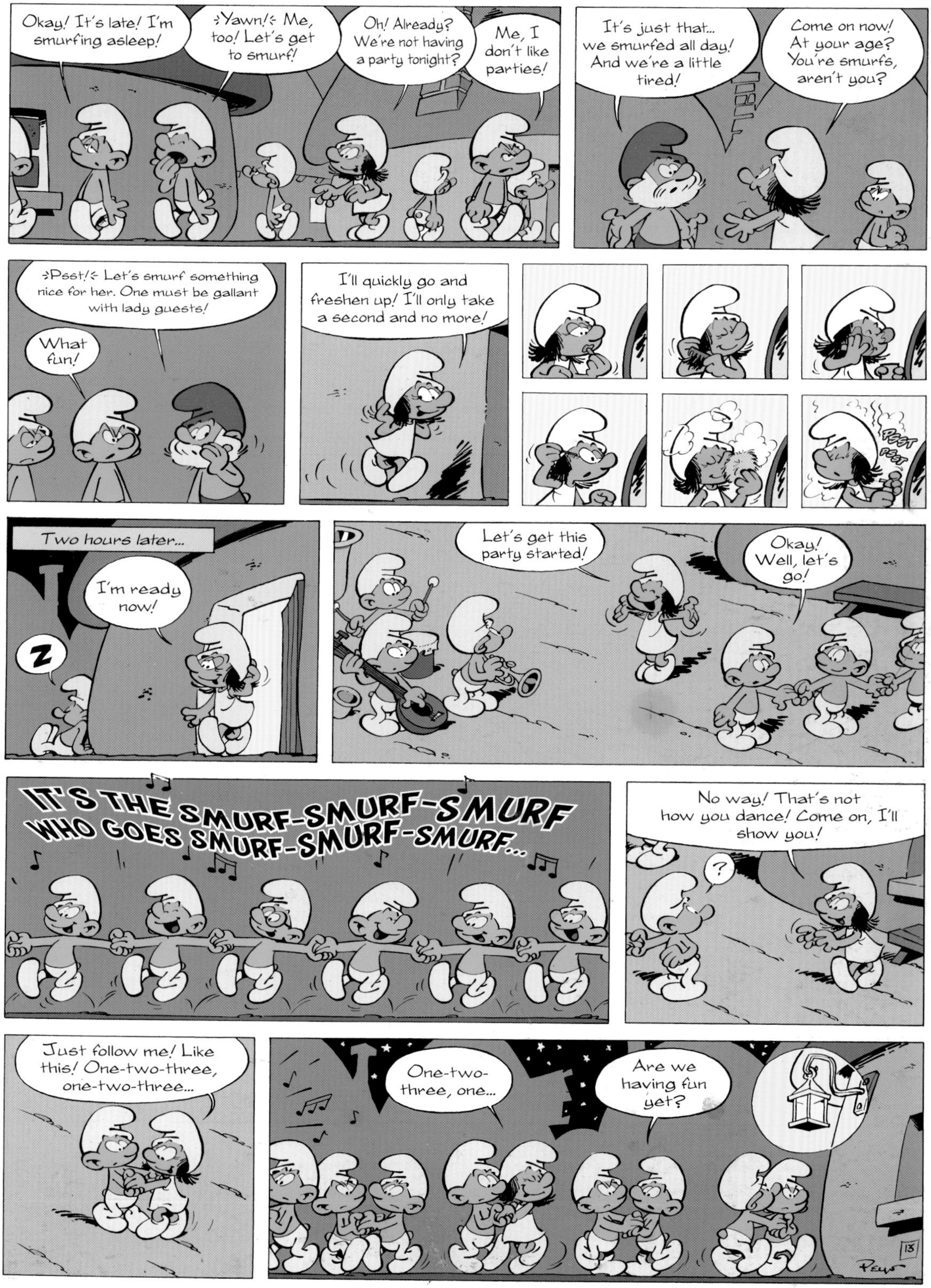
Okay! It's late! I'm smurfing asleep!
:Yawn!: Me, too! Let's get to smurf!
Oh! Already? We're not having a party tonight?
Me, I don't like parties!
It's just that... we smurfed all day! And we're a little tired!
Come on now! At your age? You're smurfs, aren't you?
:Psst!: Let's smurf something nice for her. One must be gallant with lady guests!
What fun!
I'll quickly go and freshen up! I'll only take a second and no more!
PSST PSST
Two hours later...
Z
I'm ready now!
Let's get this party started!
Okay! Well, let's go!
IT'S THE SMURF-SMURF-SMURF WHO GOES SMURF-SMURF-SMURF...
No way! That's not how you dance! Come on, I'll show you!
?
Just follow me! Like this! One-two-three, one-two-three...
One-two-three, one...
Are we having fun yet?
13

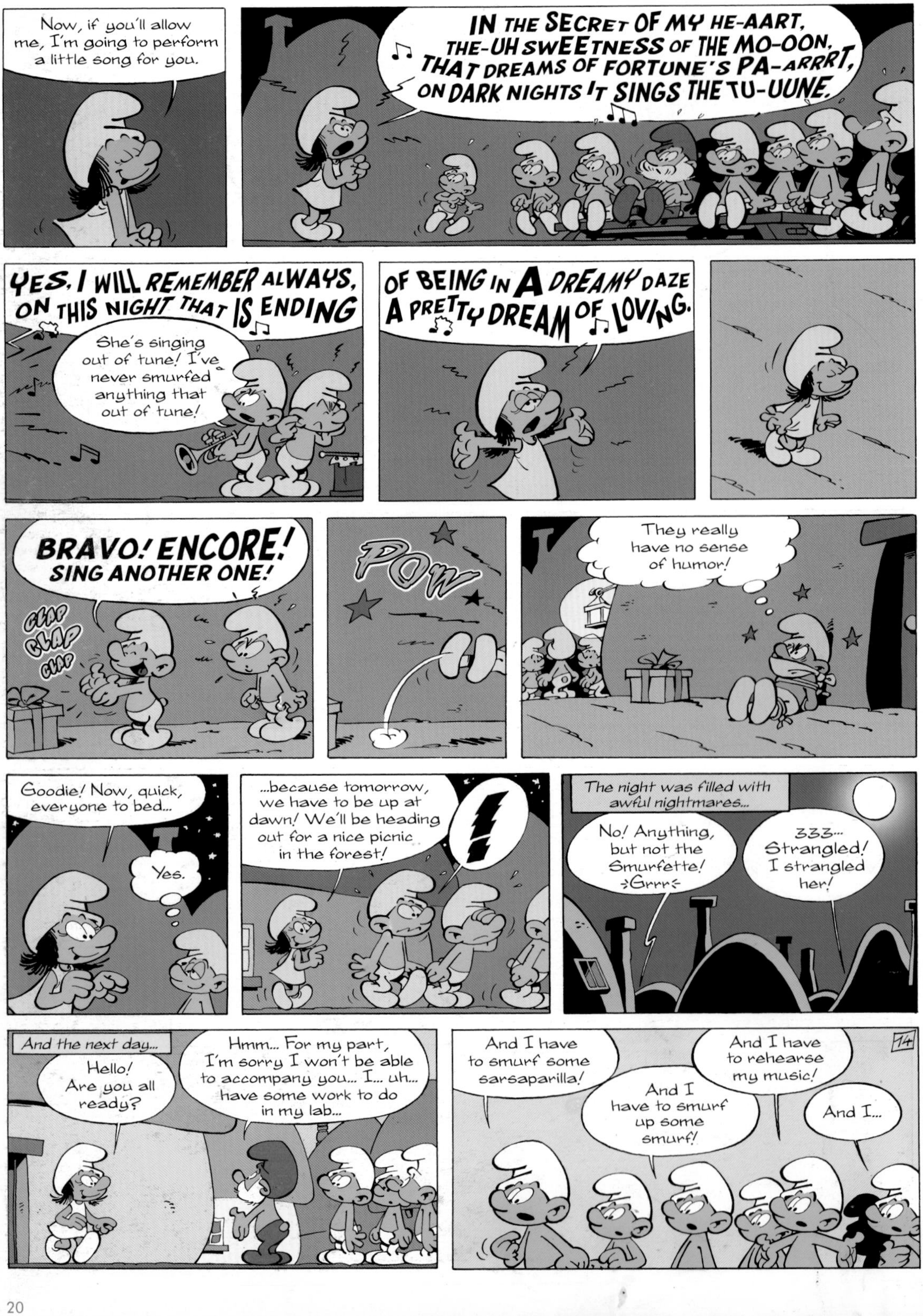
Now, if you'll allow me, I'm going to perform a little song for you.
IN THE SECRET OF MY HE-AART, THE-UH SWEETNESS OF THE MO-OON, THAT DREAMS OF FORTUNE'S PA-ARRRT, ON DARK NIGHTS IT SINGS THE TU-UUNE.
YES, I WILL REMEMBER ALWAYS, ON THIS NIGHT THAT IS ENDING
She's singing out of tune! I've never smurfed anything that out of tune!
OF BEING IN A DREAMY DAZE A PRETTY DREAM OF LOVING.
BRAVO! ENCORE! SING ANOTHER ONE!
CLAP CLAP CLAP
POW
They really have no sense of humor!
Goodie! Now, quick, everyone to bed...
Yes.
...because tomorrow, we have to be up at dawn! We'll be heading out for a nice picnic in the forest!
The night was filled with awful nightmares...
No! Anything, but not the Smurfette! Grrr
ZZZ... Strangled! I strangled her!
And the next day...
Hello! Are you all ready?
Hmm... For my part, I'm sorry I won't be able to accompany you... I... uh... have some work to do in my lab...
14
And I have to smurf some sarsaparilla!
And I have to smurf up some smurf!
And I have to rehearse my music!
And I...

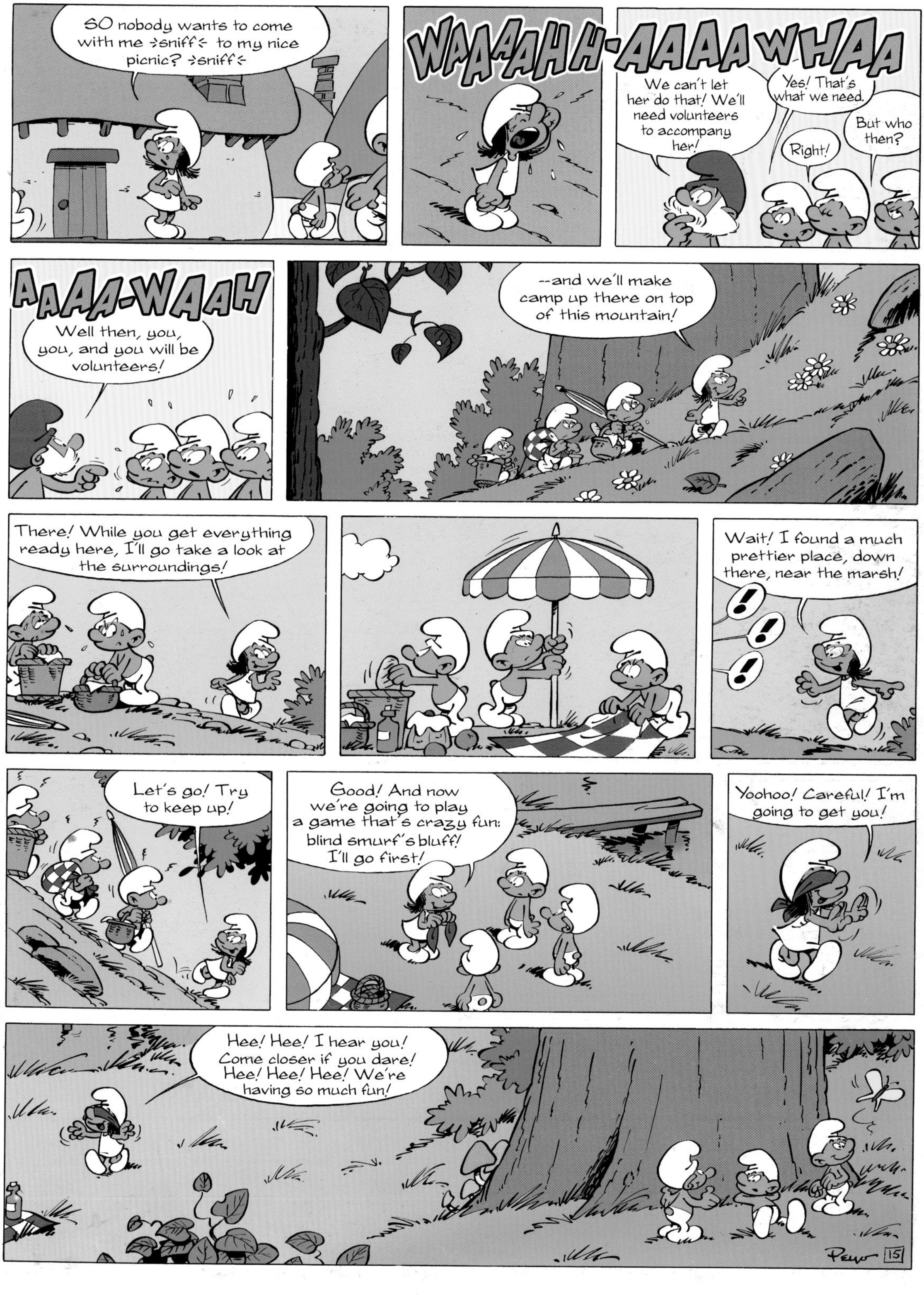

SO nobody wants to come with me ⇢sniff⇠ to my nice picnic? ⇢sniff⇠
WAAAAHH-AAAAWHAA
We can't let her do that! We'll need volunteers to accompany her!
Yes! That's what we need.
Right!
But who then?
AAAA-WAAAH
Well then, you, you, and you will be volunteers!
--and we'll make camp up there on top of this mountain!
There! While you get everything ready here, I'll go take a look at the surroundings!
Wait! I found a much prettier place, down there, near the marsh!
!
!
!
Let's go! Try to keep up!
Good! And now we're going to play a game that's crazy fun: blind smurf's bluff! I'll go first!
Yoohoo! Careful! I'm going to get you!
Hee! Hee! I hear you! Come closer if you dare! Hee! Hee! Hee! We're having so much fun!
Peyo 15

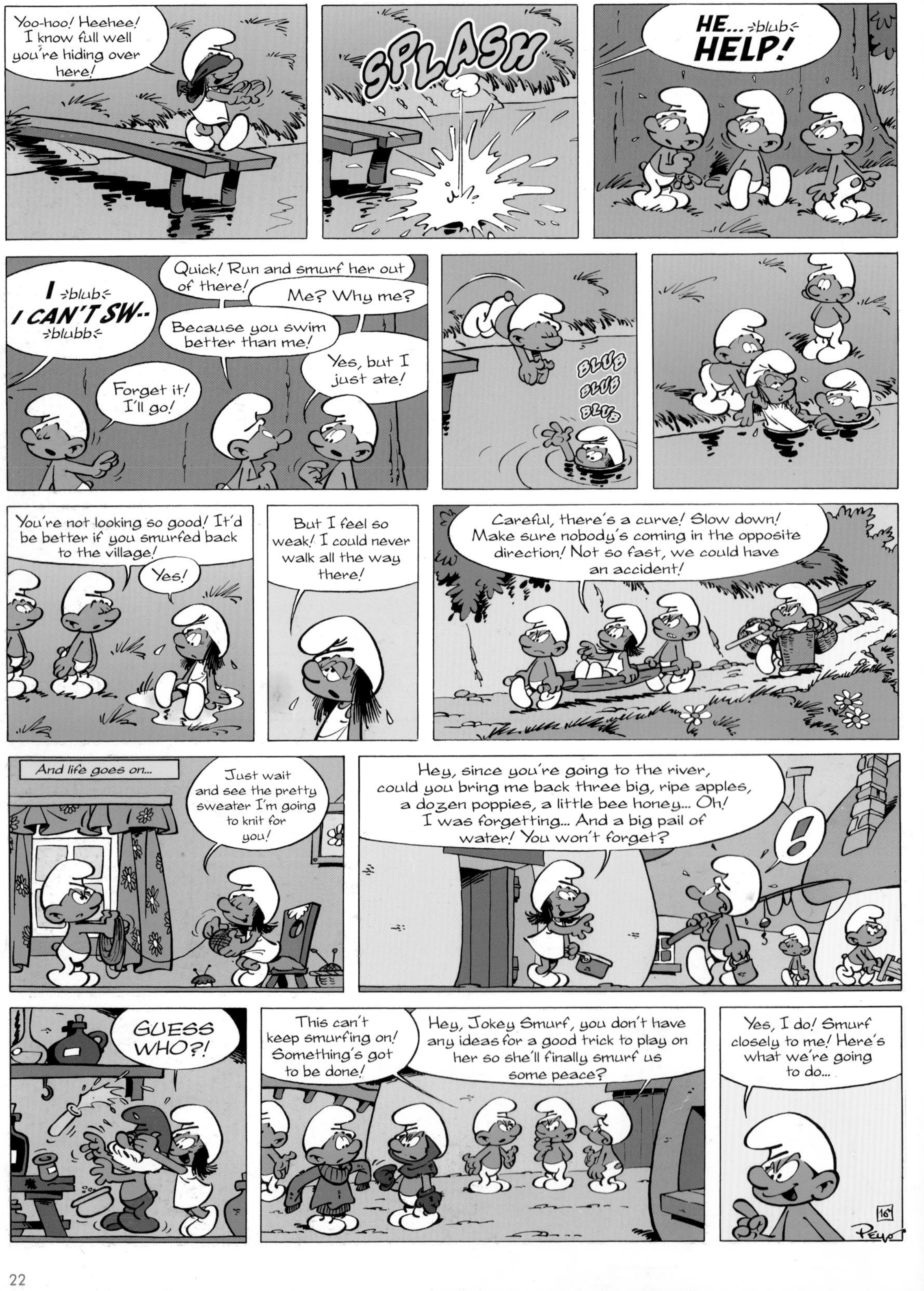
Yoo-hoo! Heehee! I know full well you're hiding over here!
SPLASH
HE... ‹blub› HELP!
I ‹blub› I CAN'T SW-- ‹blubb›
Quick! Run and smurf her out of there!
Me? Why me?
Because you swim better than me!
Yes, but I just ate!
Forget it! I'll go!
BLUB BLUB BLUB
You're not looking so good! It'd be better if you smurfed back to the village!
Yes!
But I feel so weak! I could never walk all the way there!
Careful, there's a curve! Slow down! Make sure nobody's coming in the opposite direction! Not so fast, we could have an accident!
And life goes on...
Just wait and see the pretty sweater I'm going to knit for you!
Hey, since you're going to the river, could you bring me back three big, ripe apples, a dozen poppies, a little bee honey... Oh! I was forgetting... And a big pail of water! You won't forget?
!
GUESS WHO?!
This can't keep smurfing on! Something's got to be done!
Hey, Jokey Smurf, you don't have any ideas for a good trick to play on her so she'll finally smurf us some peace?
Yes, I do! Smurf closely to me! Here's what we're going to do...

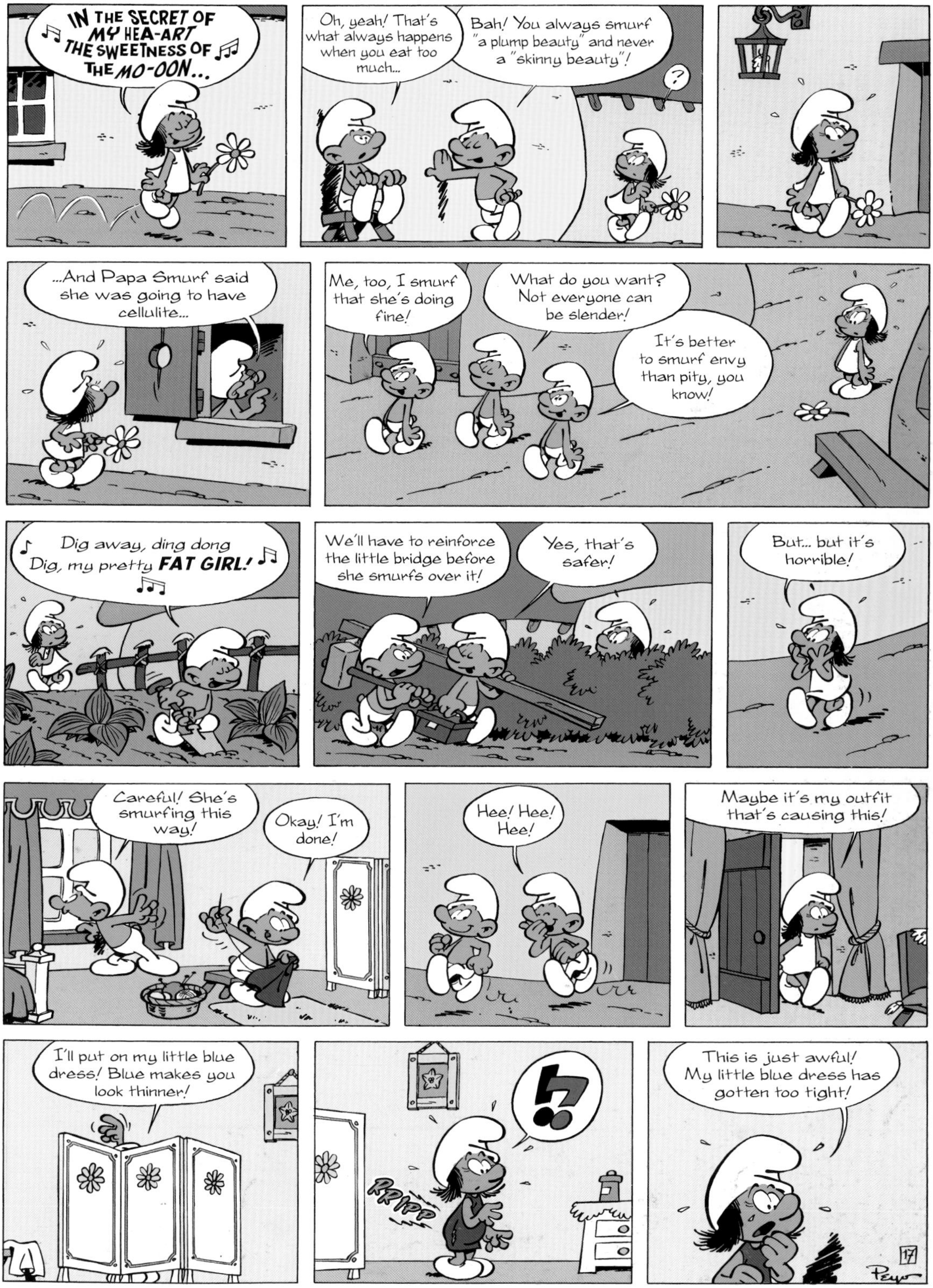

IN THE SECRET OF MY HEA-ART THE SWEETNESS OF THE MO-OON...
Oh, yeah! That's what always happens when you eat too much...
Bah! You always smurf "a plump beauty" and never a "skinny beauty"!
?
...And Papa Smurf said she was going to have cellulite...
Me, too, I smurf that she's doing fine!
What do you want? Not everyone can be slender!
It's better to smurf envy than pity, you know!
Dig away, ding dong Dig, my pretty FAT GIRL!
We'll have to reinforce the little bridge before she smurfs over it!
Yes, that's safer!
But... but it's horrible!
Careful! She's smurfing this way!
Okay! I'm done!
Hee! Hee! Hee!
Maybe it's my outfit that's causing this!
I'll put on my little blue dress! Blue makes you look thinner!
RRIPP
This is just awful! My little blue dress has gotten too tight!
17
Peyo

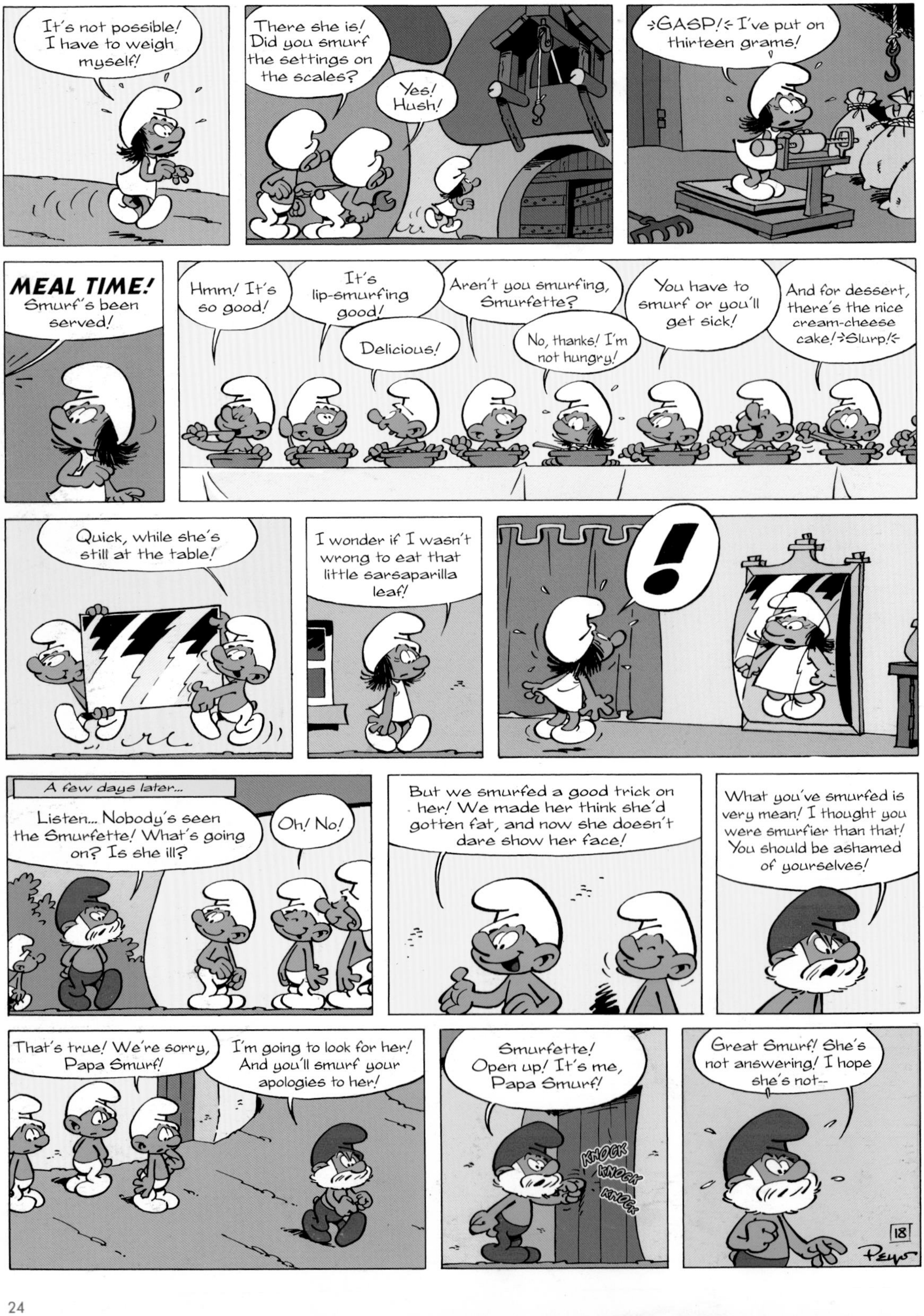
It's not possible! I have to weigh myself!
There she is! Did you smurf the settings on the scales?
Yes! Hush!
GASP! I've put on thirteen grams!
MEAL TIME! Smurf's been served!
Hmm! It's so good!
It's lip-smurfing good!
Delicious!
Aren't you smurfing, Smurfette?
No, thanks! I'm not hungry!
You have to smurf or you'll get sick!
And for dessert, there's the nice cream-cheese cake! Slurp!
Quick, while she's still at the table!
I wonder if I wasn't wrong to eat that little sarsaparilla leaf!
!
A few days later...
Listen... Nobody's seen the Smurfette! What's going on? Is she ill?
Oh! No!
But we smurfed a good trick on her! We made her think she'd gotten fat, and now she doesn't dare show her face!
What you've smurfed is very mean! I thought you were smurfier than that! You should be ashamed of yourselves!
That's true! We're sorry, Papa Smurf!
I'm going to look for her! And you'll smurf your apologies to her!
Smurfette! Open up! It's me, Papa Smurf!
KNOCK KNOCK KNOCK
Great Smurf! She's not answering! I hope she's not--
18

Stand back! I'll have to break in the door!

BAM

SMURFETTE! WHERE ARE YOU?

Well? Well? What's wrong?

~*Boohooo!*~... I'm so unhappy!

I'm too fat! And I'm ugly! My hair looks just terrible! My complexion's awful! Nothing looks good on me! **I WANT TO DIE!**

Oh, now, now!

There's nothing wrong with her! I should smurf something to cheer her up!

Come along! We'll try to make everything better!

~*Sniff?*~

I warn you: It'll probably take a while!

LABORATORY NO SMURFING

Hey! Smurf...

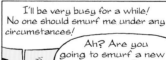

I'll be very busy for a while! No one should smurf me under any circumstances!

Ah? Are you going to smurf a new experiment, Papa Smurf?

Yes!

SLAM

He didn't tell me anything else...

Maybe he's smurfing the recipe for a new cake!

Or maybe the way to smurf up some smurf?

If Papa Smurf conducts an experiment and he doesn't want to smurf what kind of experiment it is, it's because that experiment...

Me, I don't like experiments!

Wait! I'll find out what he's smurfing up!

Peyo [19]

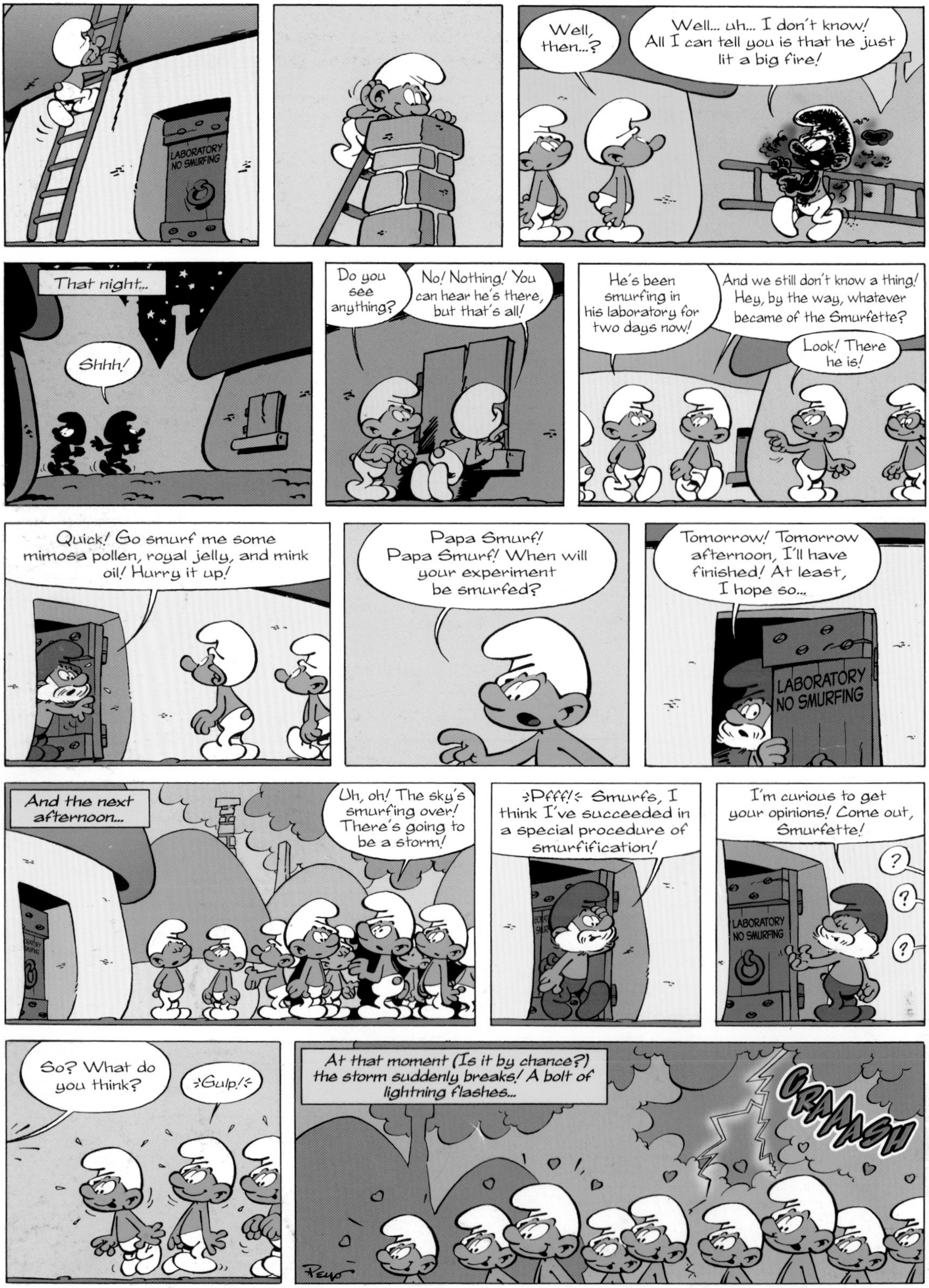
LABORATORY NO SMURFING
Well, then...?
Well... uh... I don't know! All I can tell you is that he just lit a big fire!
That night...
Shhh!
Do you see anything?
No! Nothing! You can hear he's there, but that's all!
He's been smurfing in his laboratory for two days now!
And we still don't know a thing! Hey, by the way, whatever became of the Smurfette?
Look! There he is!
Quick! Go smurf me some mimosa pollen, royal jelly, and mink oil! Hurry it up!
Papa Smurf! Papa Smurf! When will your experiment be smurfed?
Tomorrow! Tomorrow afternoon, I'll have finished! At least, I hope so...
LABORATORY NO SMURFING
And the next afternoon...
Uh, oh! The sky's smurfing over! There's going to be a storm!
Pfff! Smurfs, I think I've succeeded in a special procedure of smurfification!
I'm curious to get your opinions! Come out, Smurfette!
?
?
?
LABORATORY NO SMURFING
So? What do you think?
Gulp!
At that moment (Is it by chance?) the storm suddenly breaks! A bolt of lightning flashes...
CRAAASH
Peyo

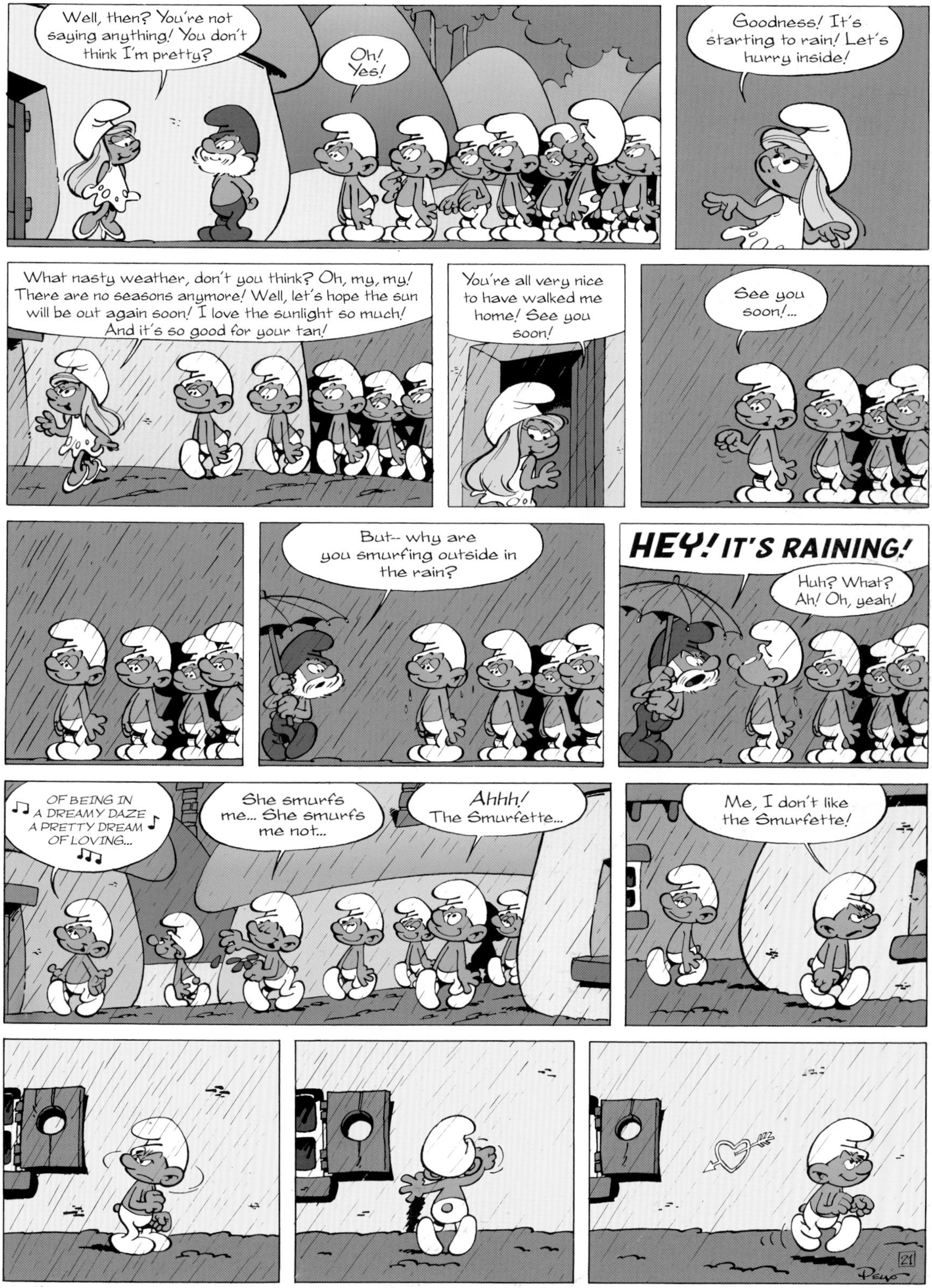
Well, then? You're not saying anything! You don't think I'm pretty?
Oh! Yes!
Goodness! It's starting to rain! Let's hurry inside!
What nasty weather, don't you think? Oh, my, my! There are no seasons anymore! Well, let's hope the sun will be out again soon! I love the sunlight so much! And it's so good for your tan!
You're all very nice to have walked me home! See you soon!
See you soon!...
But-- why are you smurfing outside in the rain?
HEY! IT'S RAINING!
Huh? What? Ah! Oh, yeah!
OF BEING IN A DREAMY DAZE A PRETTY DREAM OF LOVING...
She smurfs me... She smurfs me not...
Ahhh! The Smurfette...
Me, I don't like the Smurfette!
21

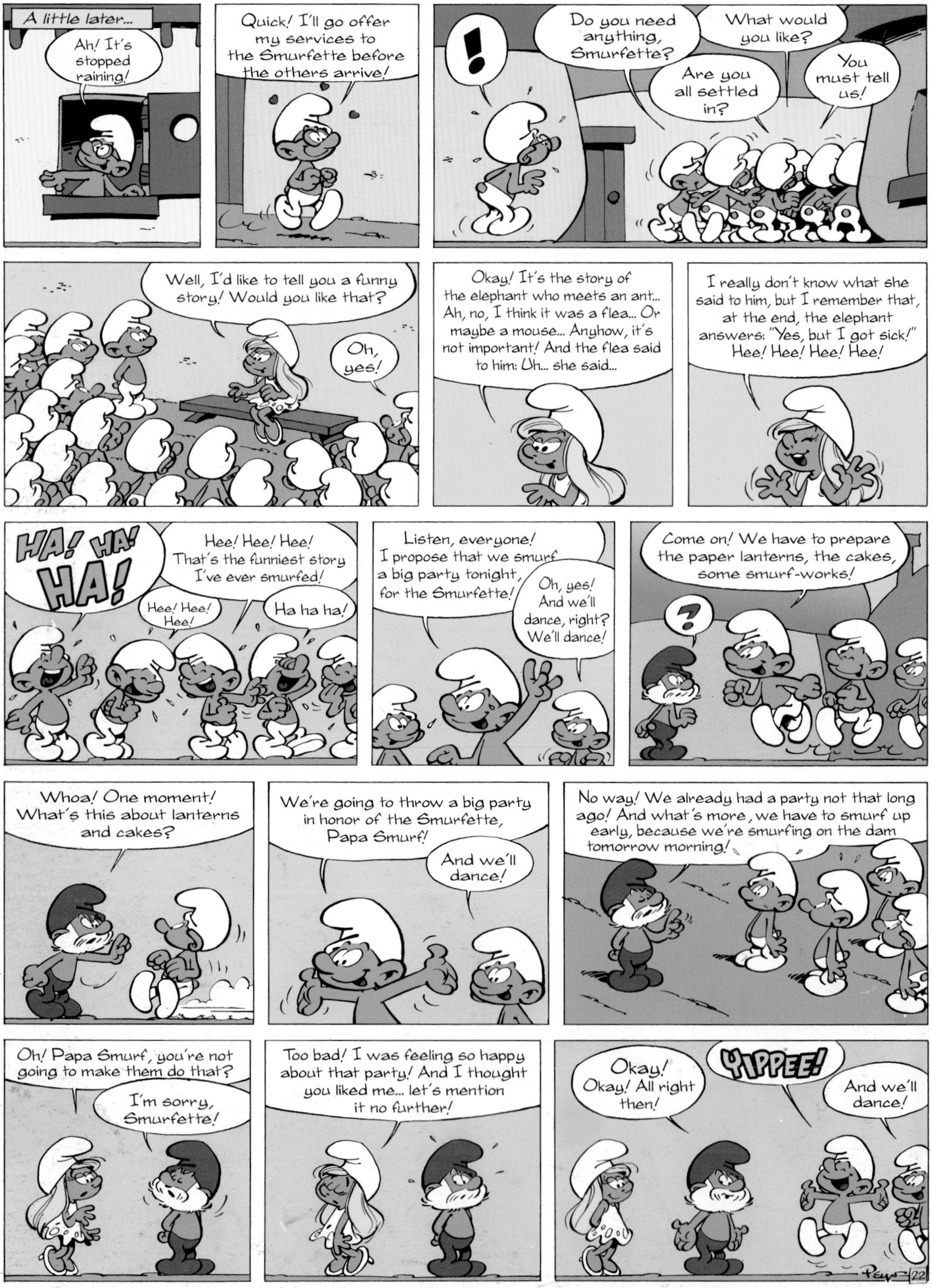
A little later...
Ah! It's stopped raining!
Quick! I'll go offer my services to the Smurfette before the others arrive!
!
Do you need anything, Smurfette?
What would you like?
Are you all settled in?
You must tell us!
Well, I'd like to tell you a funny story! Would you like that?
Oh, yes!
Okay! It's the story of the elephant who meets an ant... Ah, no, I think it was a flea... Or maybe a mouse... Anyhow, it's not important! And the flea said to him: Uh... she said...
I really don't know what she said to him, but I remember that, at the end, the elephant answers: "Yes, but I got sick!" Hee! Hee! Hee! Hee!
HA! HA! HA!
Hee! Hee! Hee! That's the funniest story I've ever smurfed!
Hee! Hee! Hee!
Ha ha ha!
Listen, everyone! I propose that we smurf a big party tonight, for the Smurfette!
Oh, yes! And we'll dance, right? We'll dance!
Come on! We have to prepare the paper lanterns, the cakes, some smurf-works!
?
Whoa! One moment! What's this about lanterns and cakes?
We're going to throw a big party in honor of the Smurfette, Papa Smurf!
And we'll dance!
No way! We already had a party not that long ago! And what's more, we have to smurf up early, because we're smurfing on the dam tomorrow morning!
Oh! Papa Smurf, you're not going to make them do that?
I'm sorry, Smurfette!
Too bad! I was feeling so happy about that party! And I thought you liked me... let's mention it no further!
Okay! Okay! All right then!
YIPPEE!
And we'll dance!
22

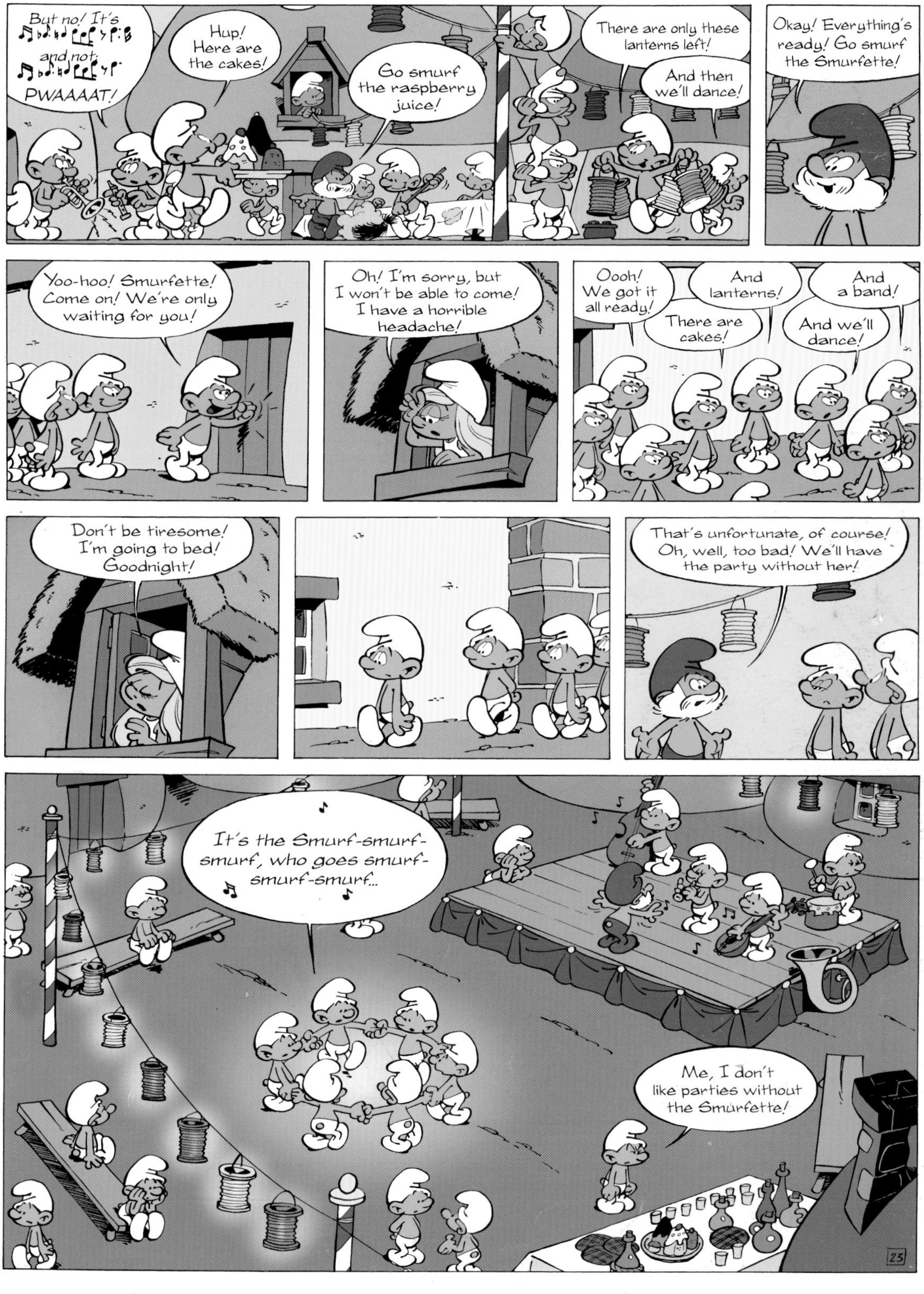
But no! It's
and not
PWAAAAT!
Hup! Here are the cakes!
Go smurf the raspberry juice!
There are only these lanterns left!
And then we'll dance!
Okay! Everything's ready! Go smurf the Smurfette!
Yoo-hoo! Smurfette! Come on! We're only waiting for you!
Oh! I'm sorry, but I won't be able to come! I have a horrible headache!
Oooh! We got it all ready!
And lanterns!
There are cakes!
And a band!
And we'll dance!
Don't be tiresome! I'm going to bed! Goodnight!
That's unfortunate, of course! Oh, well, too bad! We'll have the party without her!
It's the Smurf-smurf-smurf, who goes smurf-smurf-smurf...
Me, I don't like parties without the Smurfette!
25

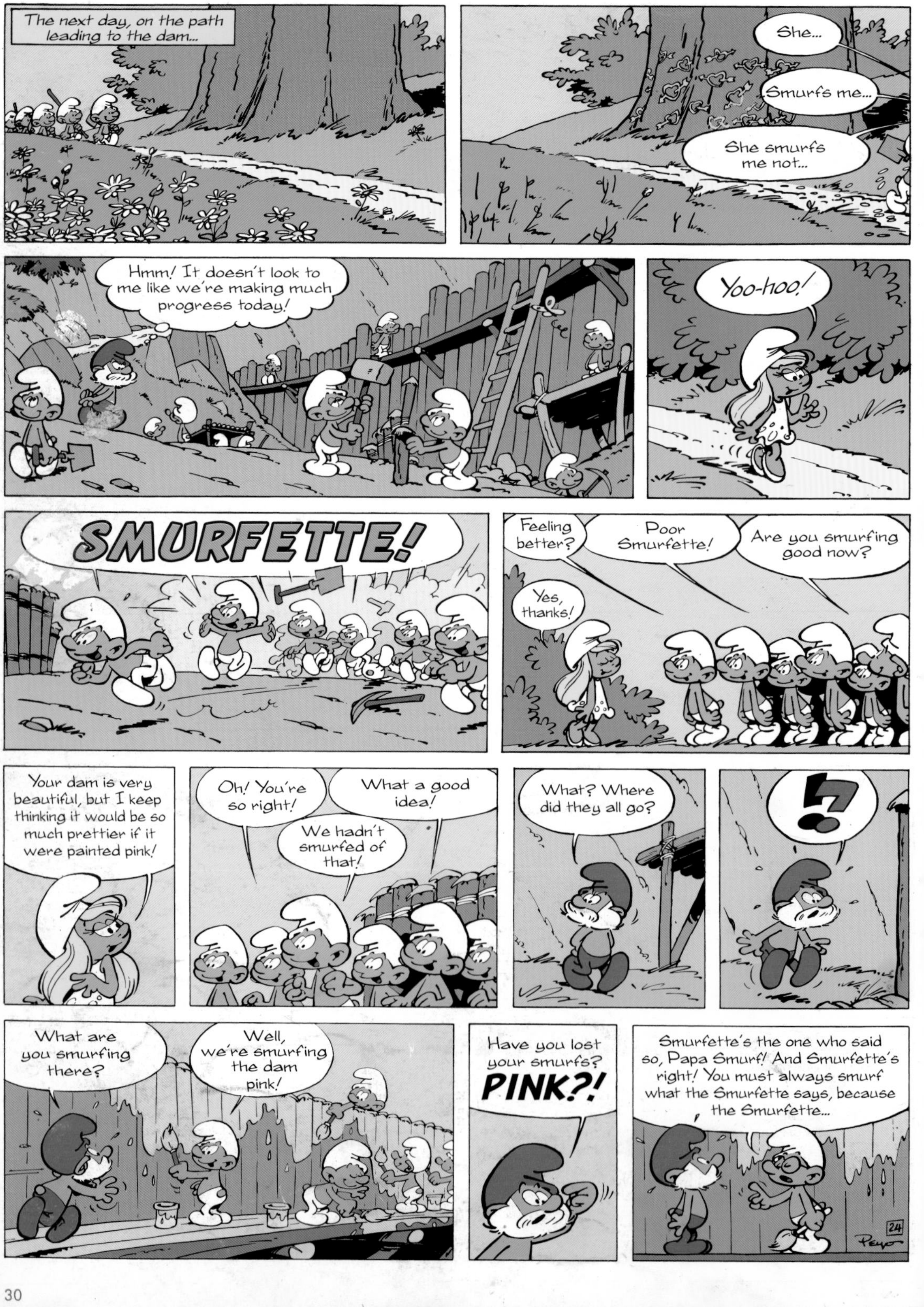

The next day, on the path leading to the dam...
She...
Smurfs me...
She smurfs me not...
Hmm! It doesn't look to me like we're making much progress today!
Yoo-hoo!
SMURFETTE!
Feeling better?
Poor Smurfette!
Are you smurfing good now?
Yes, thanks!
Your dam is very beautiful, but I keep thinking it would be so much prettier if it were painted pink!
Oh! You're so right!
What a good idea!
We hadn't smurfed of that!
What? Where did they all go?
What are you smurfing there?
Well, we're smurfing the dam pink!
Have you lost your smurfs? PINK?!
Smurfette's the one who said so, Papa Smurf! And Smurfette's right! You must always smurf what the Smurfette says, because the Smurfette...
24
Peyo

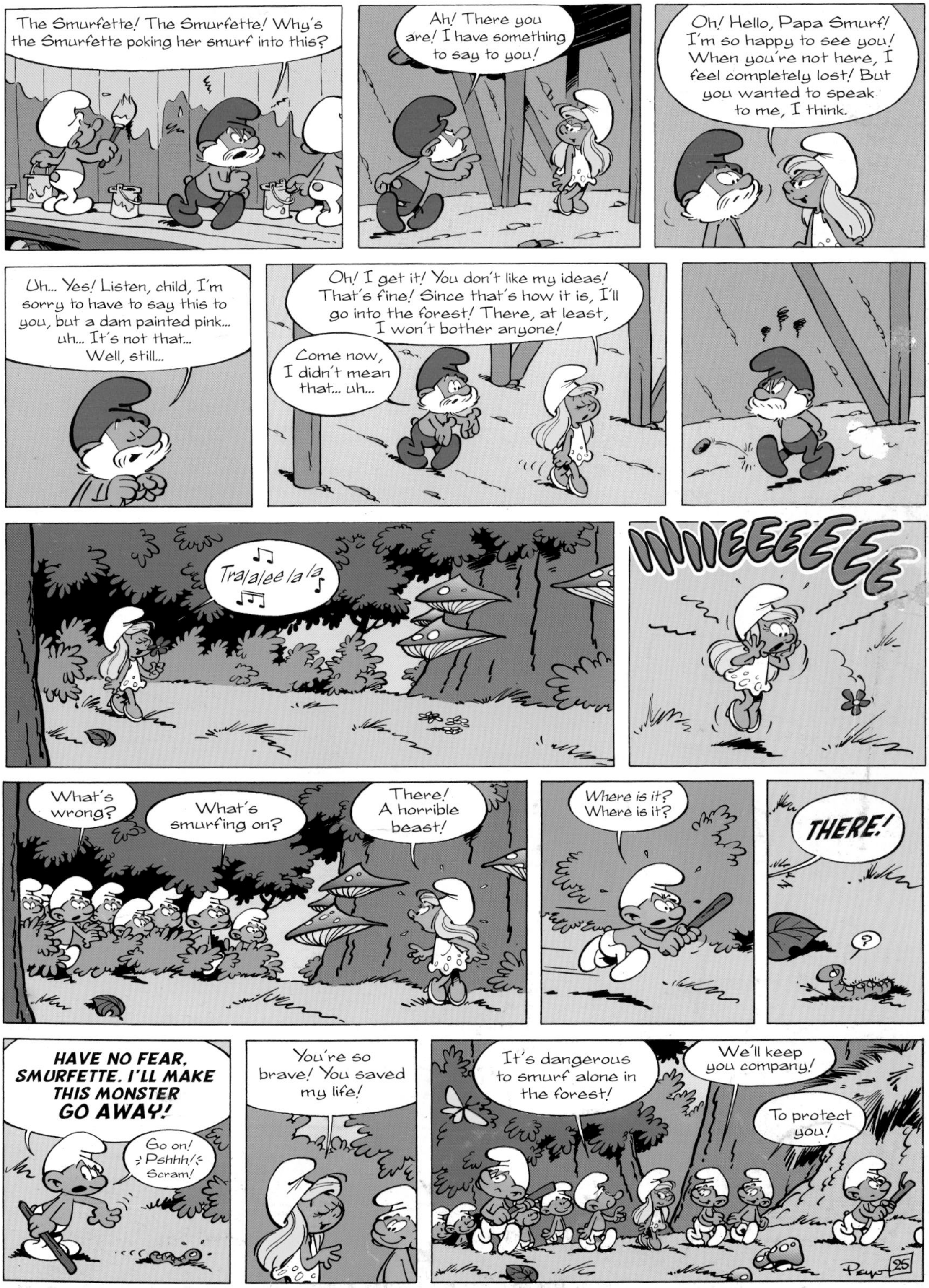

The Smurfette! The Smurfette! Why's the Smurfette poking her smurf into this?
Ah! There you are! I have something to say to you!
Oh! Hello, Papa Smurf! I'm so happy to see you! When you're not here, I feel completely lost! But you wanted to speak to me, I think.
Uh... Yes! Listen, child, I'm sorry to have to say this to you, but a dam painted pink... uh... It's not that... Well, still...
Oh! I get it! You don't like my ideas! That's fine! Since that's how it is, I'll go into the forest! There, at least, I won't bother anyone!
Come now, I didn't mean that... uh...
Tralalee la la
WIIIEEEEEEE
What's wrong?
What's smurfing on?
There! A horrible beast!
Where is it? Where is it?
THERE!
?
HAVE NO FEAR, SMURFETTE. I'LL MAKE THIS MONSTER GO AWAY!
Go on! Pshhh! Scram!
You're so brave! You saved my life!
It's dangerous to smurf alone in the forest!
We'll keep you company!
To protect you!
Peyo
25

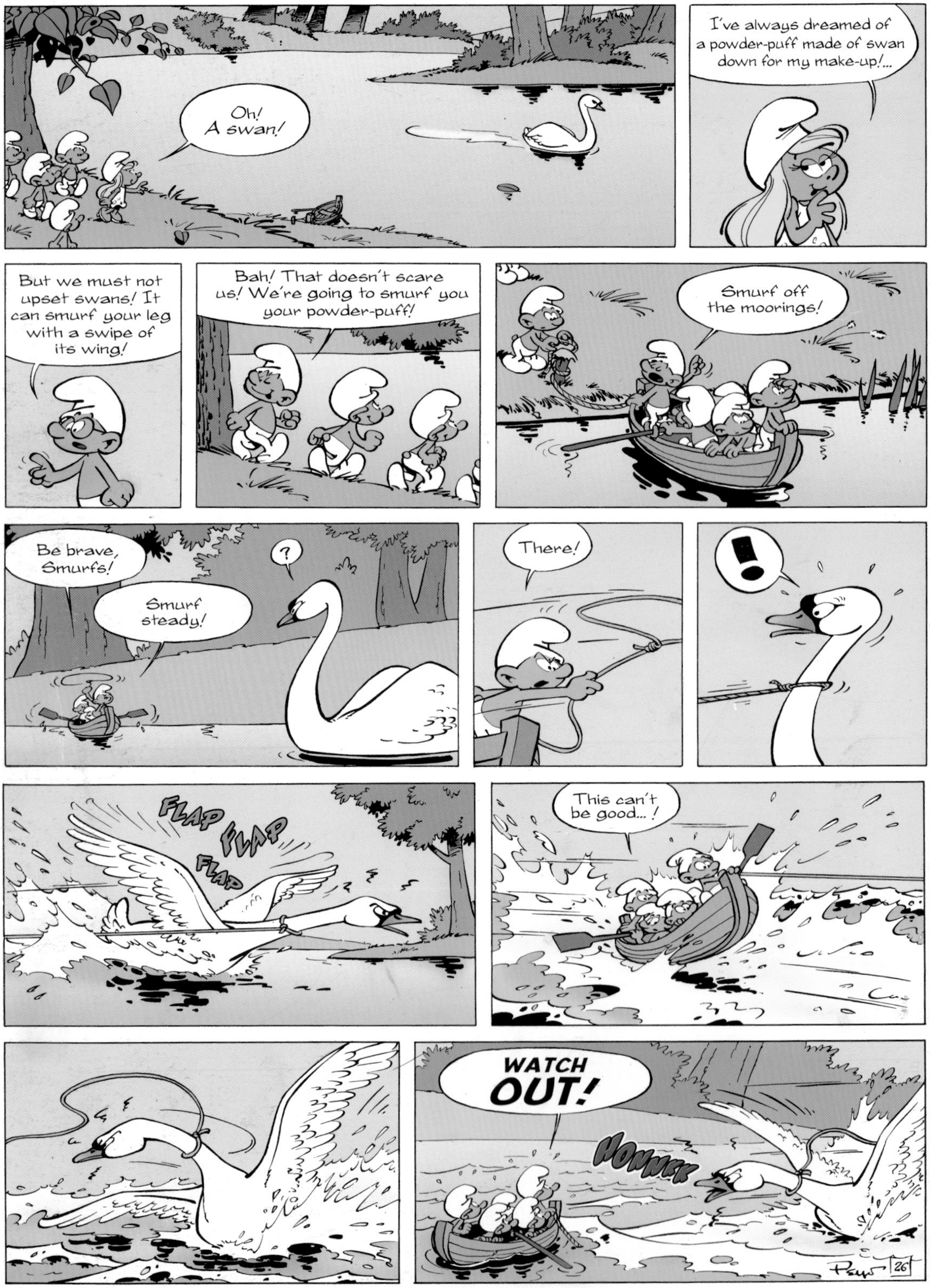
Oh! A swan!
I've always dreamed of a powder-puff made of swan down for my make-up!...
But we must not upset swans! It can smurf your leg with a swipe of its wing!
Bah! That doesn't scare us! We're going to smurf you your powder-puff!
Smurf off the moorings!
Be brave, Smurfs!
Smurf steady!
?
There!
!
FLAP FLAP FLAP
This can't be good... !
WATCH OUT!
HONNKK
26

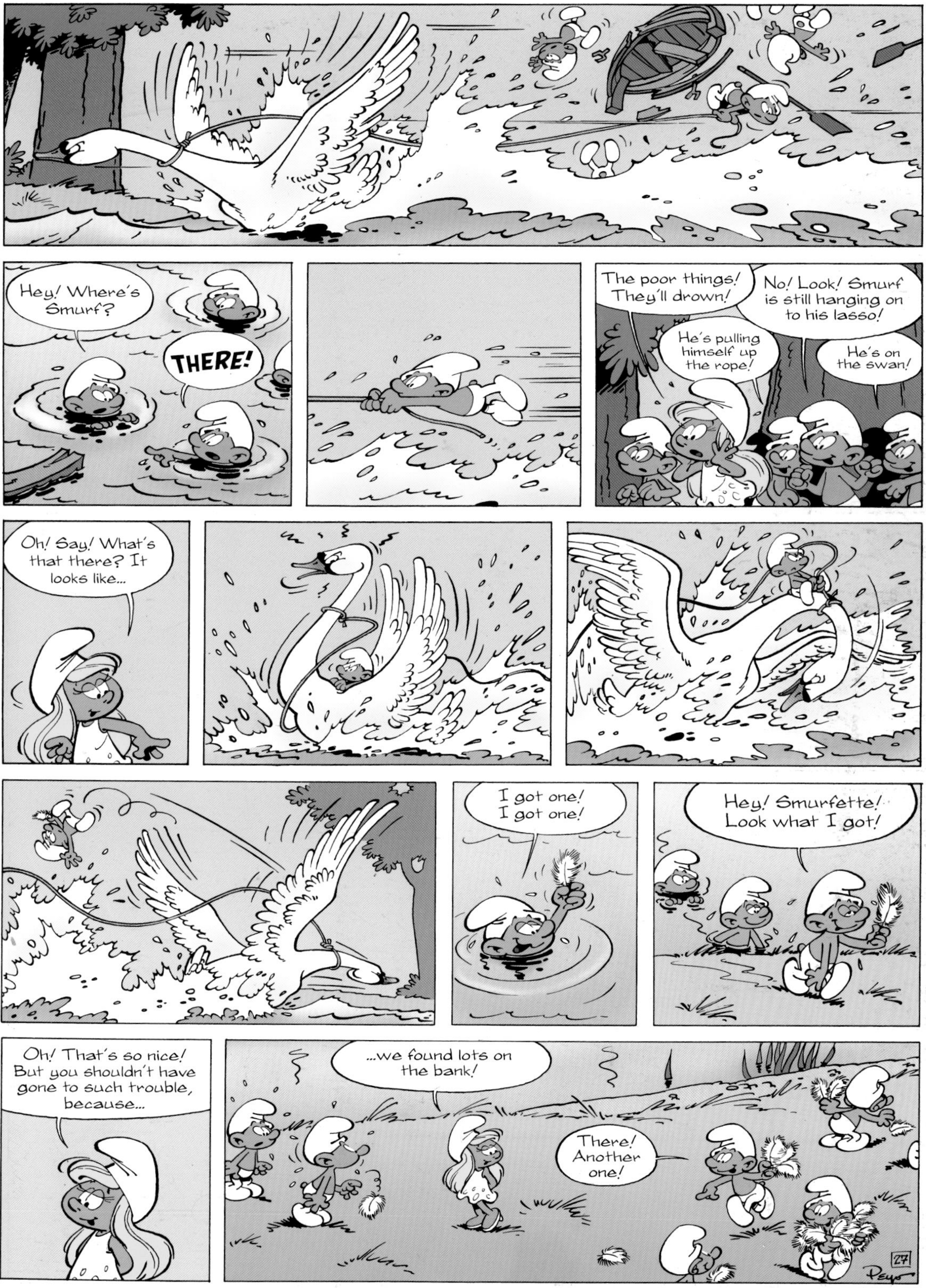

Hey! Where's Smurf?
THERE!
The poor things! They'll drown!
No! Look! Smurf is still hanging on to his lasso!
He's pulling himself up the rope!
He's on the swan!
Oh! Say! What's that there? It looks like...
I got one! I got one!
Hey! Smurfette! Look what I got!
Oh! That's so nice! But you shouldn't have gone to such trouble, because...
...we found lots on the bank!
There! Another one!
27
Peyo

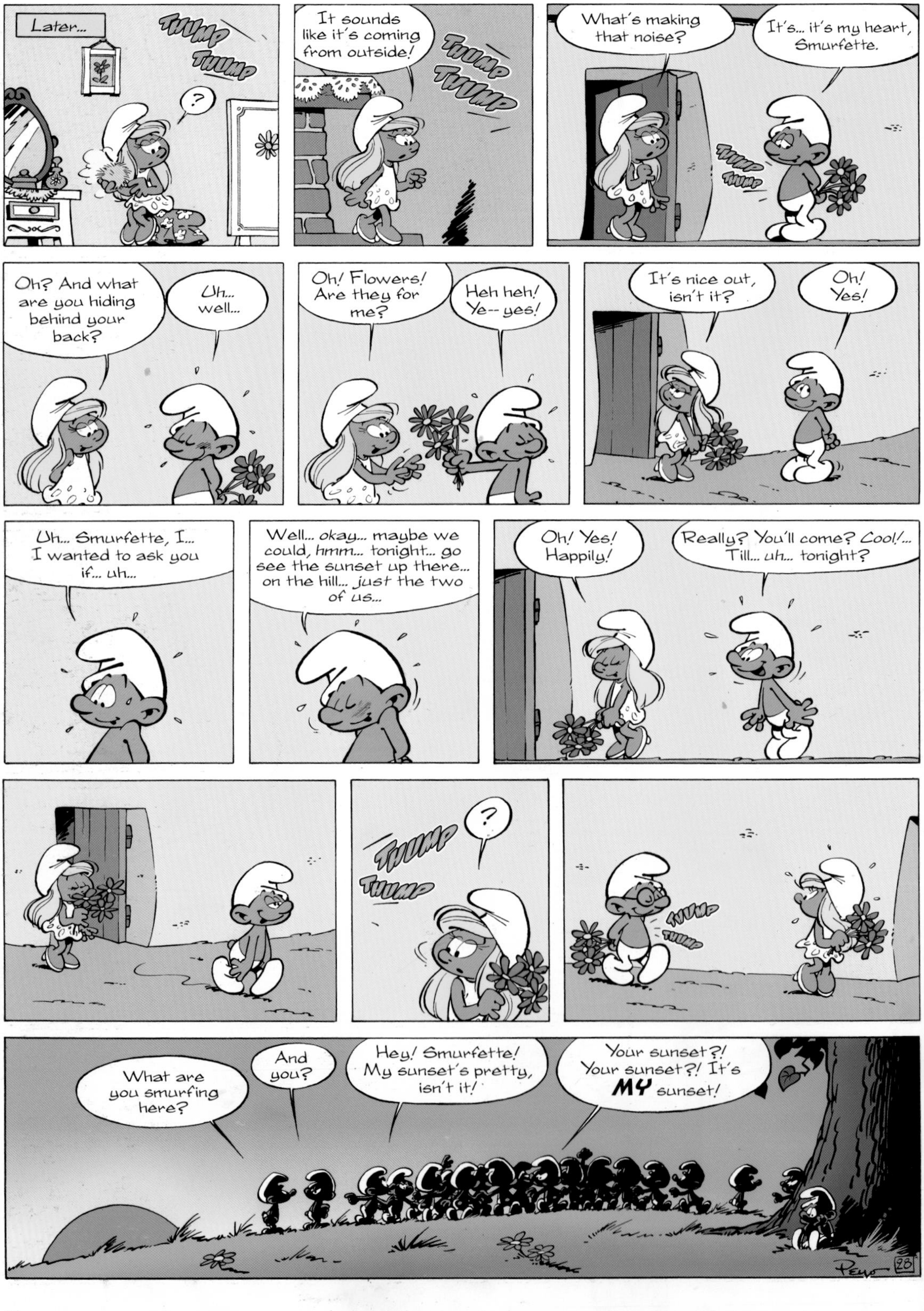
Later...
THUMP
THUMP
?
It sounds like it's coming from outside!
THUMP
THUMP
What's making that noise?
It's... it's my heart, Smurfette.
THUMP
THUMP
Oh? And what are you hiding behind your back?
Uh... well...
Oh! Flowers! Are they for me?
Heh heh! Ye-- yes!
It's nice out, isn't it?
Oh! Yes!
Uh... Smurfette, I... I wanted to ask you if... uh...
Well... okay... maybe we could, hmm... tonight... go see the sunset up there... on the hill... just the two of us...
Oh! Yes! Happily!
Really? You'll come? Cool!... Till... uh... tonight?
THUMP
THUMP
?
THUMP
THUMP
What are you smurfing here?
And you?
Hey! Smurfette! My sunset's pretty, isn't it!
Your sunset?! Your sunset?! It's MY sunset!

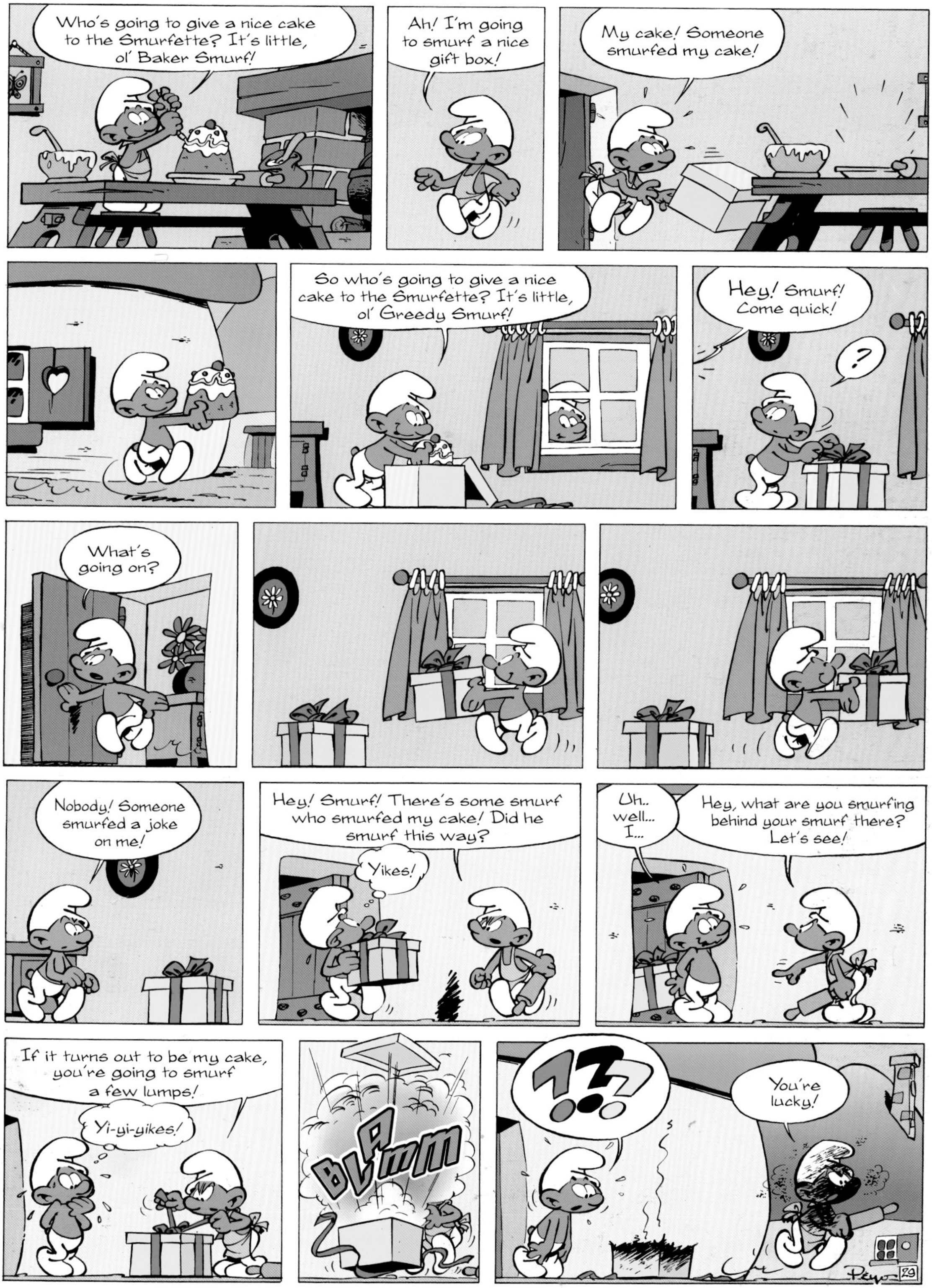
Who's going to give a nice cake to the Smurfette? It's little, ol' Baker Smurf!
Ah! I'm going to smurf a nice gift box!
My cake! Someone smurfed my cake!
So who's going to give a nice cake to the Smurfette? It's little, ol' Greedy Smurf!
Hey! Smurf! Come quick!
?
What's going on?
Nobody! Someone smurfed a joke on me!
Hey! Smurf! There's some smurf who smurfed my cake! Did he smurf this way?
Yikes!
Uh.. well... I...
Hey, what are you smurfing behind your smurf there? Let's see!
If it turns out to be my cake, you're going to smurf a few lumps!
Yi-yi-yikes!
BLAMM
You're lucky!

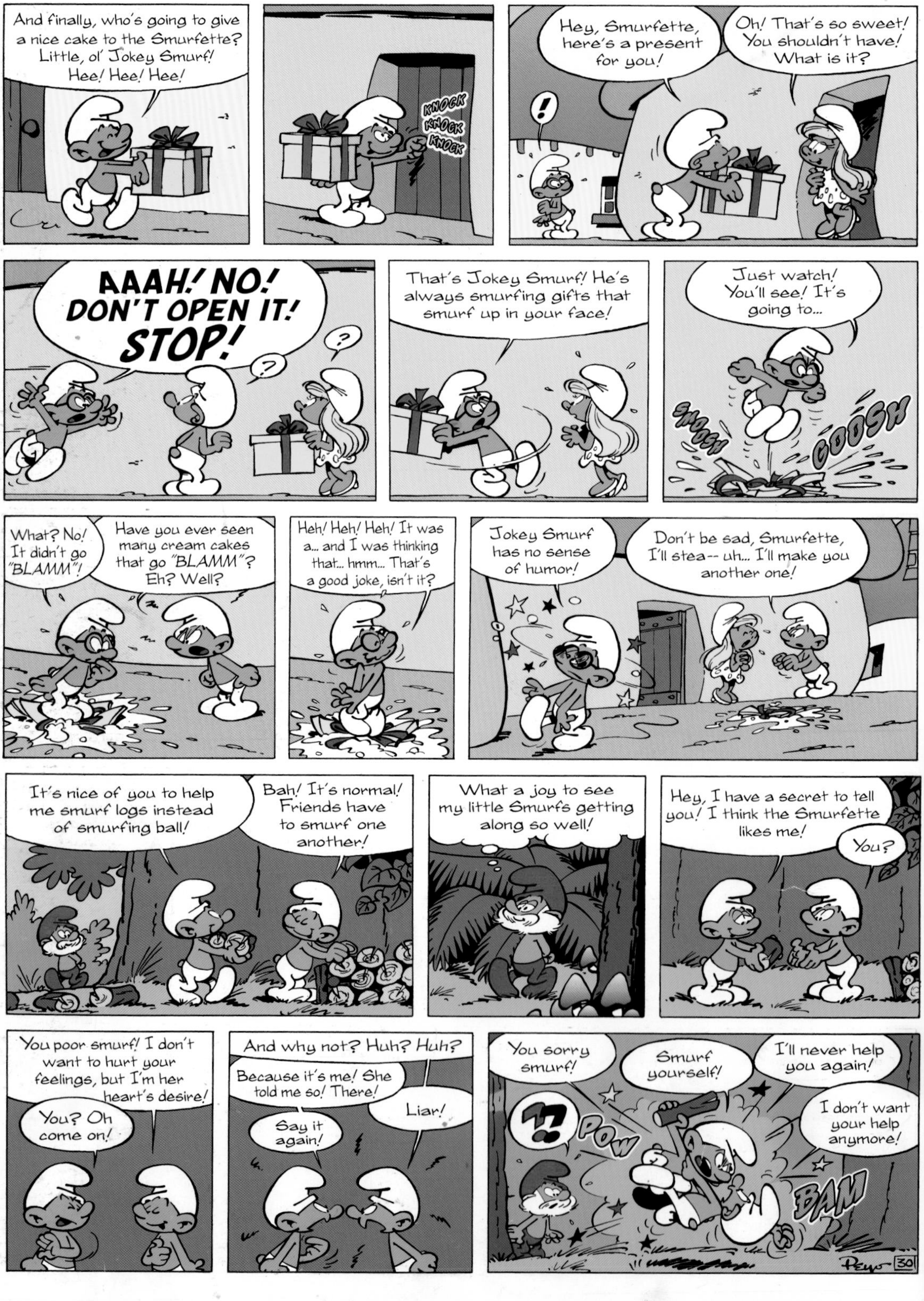
And finally, who's going to give a nice cake to the Smurfette? Little, ol' Jokey Smurf! Hee! Hee! Hee!
KNOCK KNOCK KNOCK
Hey, Smurfette, here's a present for you!
Oh! That's so sweet! You shouldn't have! What is it?
!
AAAH! NO! DON'T OPEN IT! STOP!
?
?
That's Jokey Smurf! He's always smurfing gifts that smurf up in your face!
Just watch! You'll see! It's going to...
SHOOSH
GOOSH
What? No! It didn't go "BLAMM"!
Have you ever seen many cream cakes that go "BLAMM"? Eh? Well?
Heh! Heh! Heh! It was a... and I was thinking that... hmm... That's a good joke, isn't it?
Jokey Smurf has no sense of humor!
Don't be sad, Smurfette, I'll stea-- uh... I'll make you another one!
It's nice of you to help me smurf logs instead of smurfing ball!
Bah! It's normal! Friends have to smurf one another!
What a joy to see my little Smurfs getting along so well!
Hey, I have a secret to tell you! I think the Smurfette likes me!
You?
You poor smurf! I don't want to hurt your feelings, but I'm her heart's desire!
You? Oh come on!
And why not? Huh? Huh?
Because it's me! She told me so! There!
Liar!
Say it again!
You sorry smurf!
Smurf yourself!
I'll never help you again!
I don't want your help anymore!
POW
BAM
Peyo
30

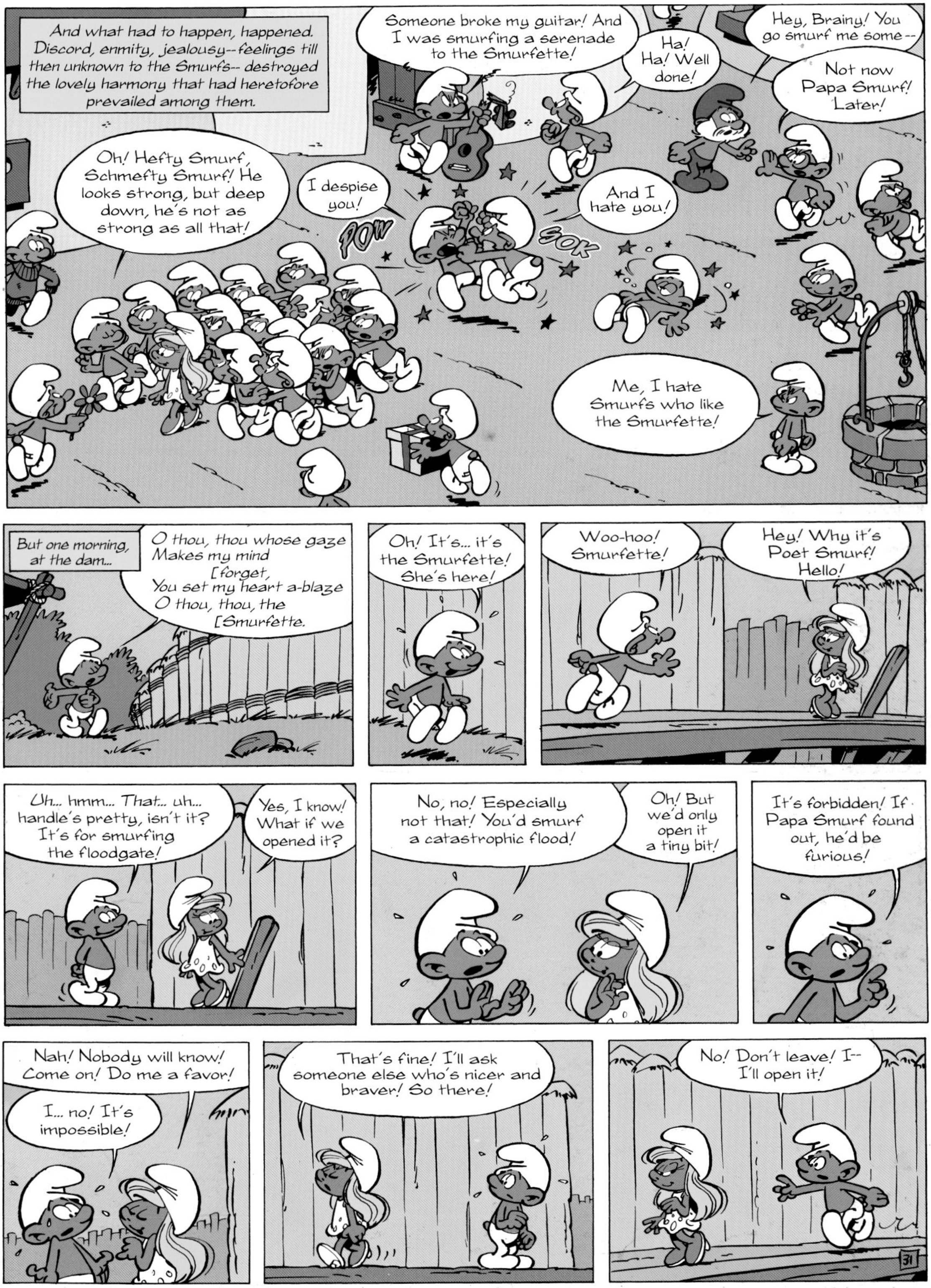

And what had to happen, happened. Discord, enmity, jealousy--feelings till then unknown to the Smurfs-- destroyed the lovely harmony that had heretofore prevailed among them.
Someone broke my guitar! And I was smurfing a serenade to the Smurfette!
Ha! Ha! Well done!
Hey, Brainy! You go smurf me some--
Not now Papa Smurf! Later!
Oh! Hefty Smurf, Schmefty Smurf! He looks strong, but deep down, he's not as strong as all that!
I despise you!
POW
And I hate you!
SOK
Me, I hate Smurfs who like the Smurfette!
But one morning, at the dam...
O thou, thou whose gaze Makes my mind [forget, You set my heart a-blaze O thou, thou, the [Smurfette.
Oh! It's... it's the Smurfette! She's here!
Woo-hoo! Smurfette!
Hey! Why it's Poet Smurf! Hello!
Uh... hmm... That... uh... handle's pretty, isn't it? It's for smurfing the floodgate!
Yes, I know! What if we opened it?
No, no! Especially not that! You'd smurf a catastrophic flood!
Oh! But we'd only open it a tiny bit!
It's forbidden! If Papa Smurf found out, he'd be furious!
Nah! Nobody will know! Come on! Do me a favor!
I... no! It's impossible!
That's fine! I'll ask someone else who's nicer and braver! So there!
No! Don't leave! I-- I'll open it!
31

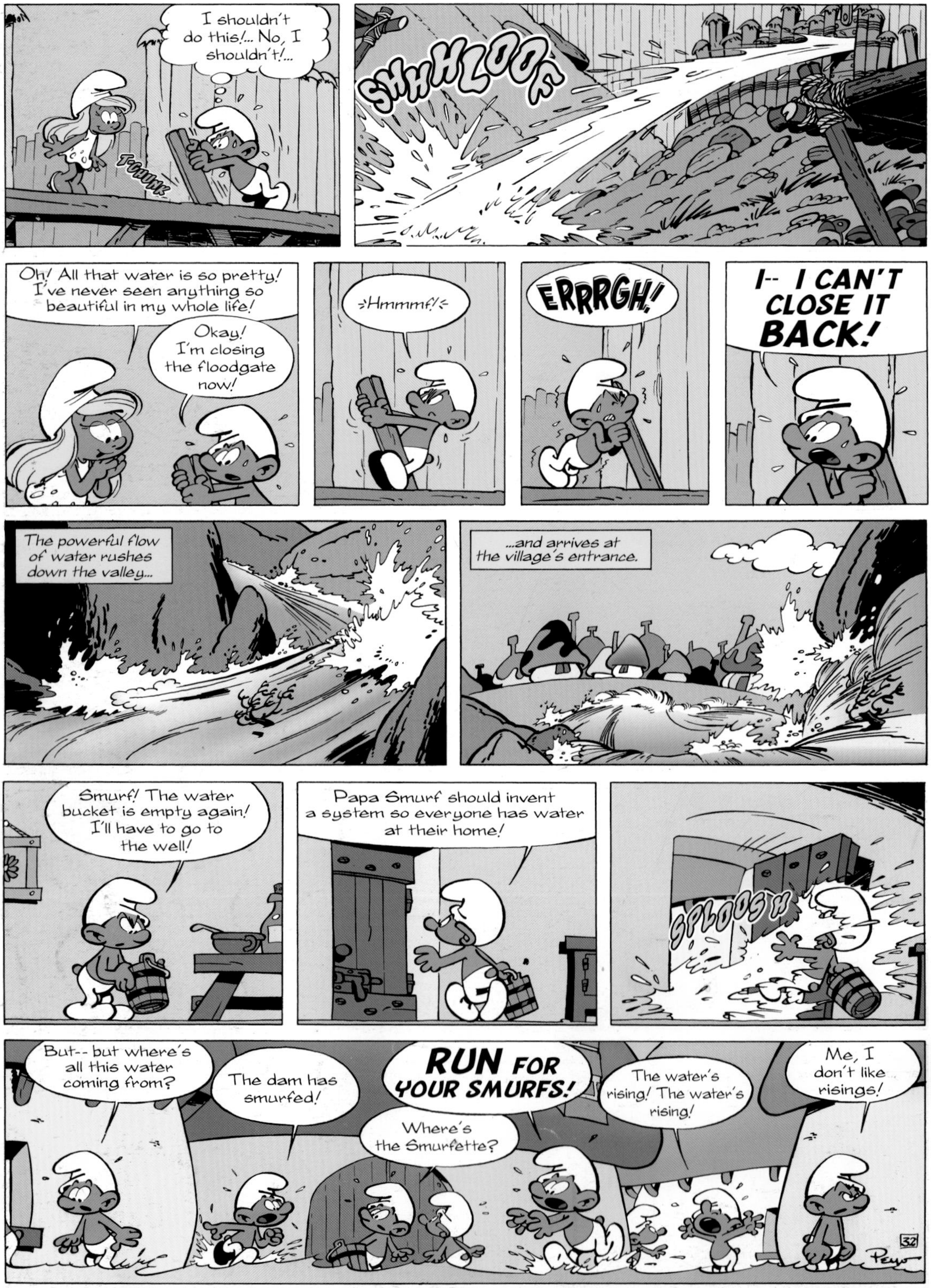

I shouldn't do this!... No, I shouldn't!...
T-CHUNK
SHHHLOOF
Oh! All that water is so pretty! I've never seen anything so beautiful in my whole life!
Okay! I'm closing the floodgate now!
Hmmmf!
ERRRGH!
I-- I CAN'T CLOSE IT BACK!
The powerful flow of water rushes down the valley...
...and arrives at the village's entrance.
Smurf! The water bucket is empty again! I'll have to go to the well!
Papa Smurf should invent a system so everyone has water at their home!
SPLOOSH
But-- but where's all this water coming from?
The dam has smurfed!
RUN FOR YOUR SMURFS!
Where's the Smurfette?
The water's rising! The water's rising!
Me, I don't like risings!
32
Peyo

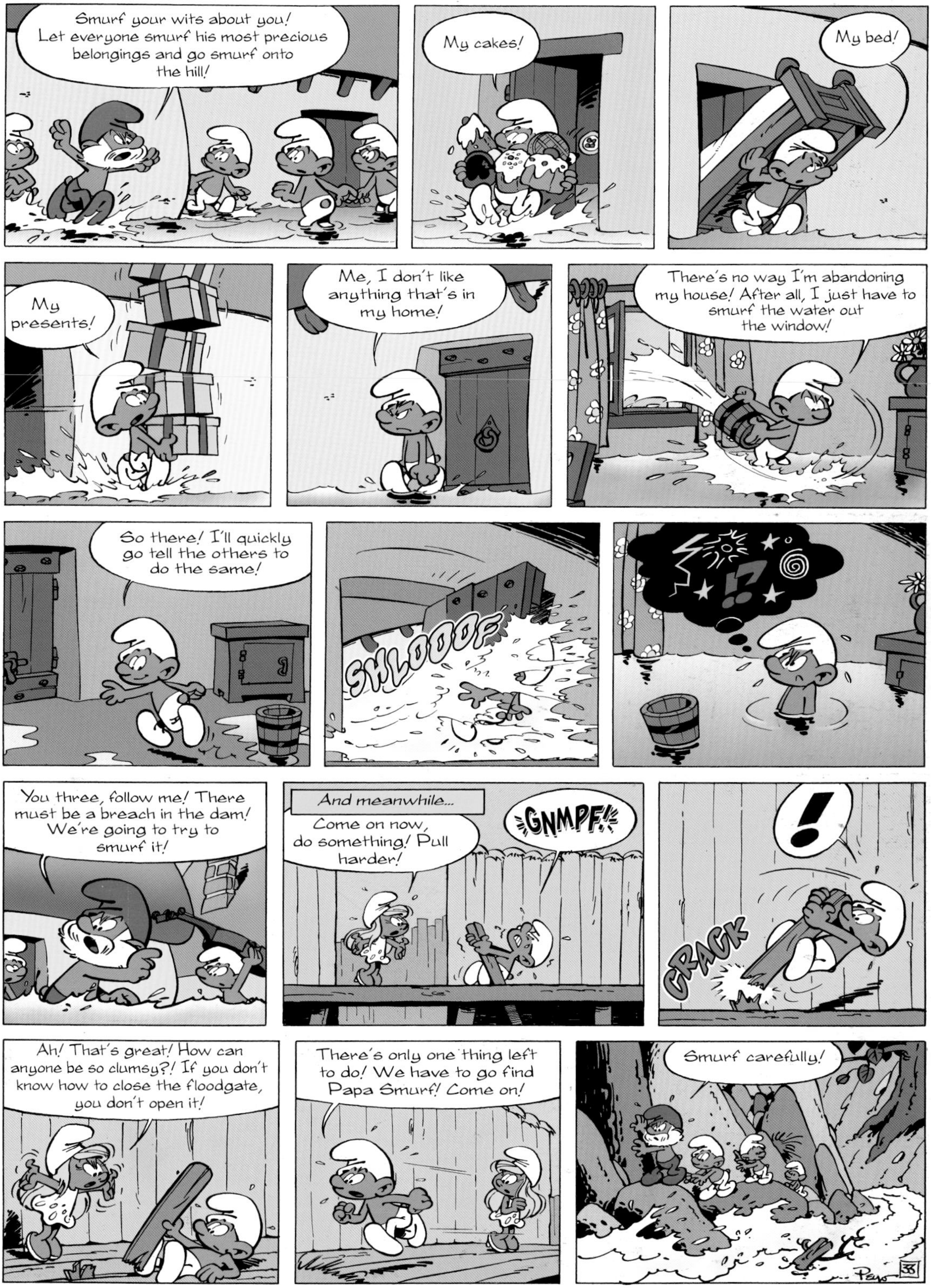
Smurf your wits about you! Let everyone smurf his most precious belongings and go smurf onto the hill!
My cakes!
My bed!
My presents!
Me, I don't like anything that's in my home!
There's no way I'm abandoning my house! After all, I just have to smurf the water out the window!
So there! I'll quickly go tell the others to do the same!
SHLOOOF
You three, follow me! There must be a breach in the dam! We're going to try to smurf it!
And meanwhile...
Come on now, do something! Pull harder!
GNMPF!
!
CRACK
Ah! That's great! How can anyone be so clumsy?! If you don't know how to close the floodgate, you don't open it!
There's only one thing left to do! We have to go find Papa Smurf! Come on!
Smurf carefully!
Peyo
38

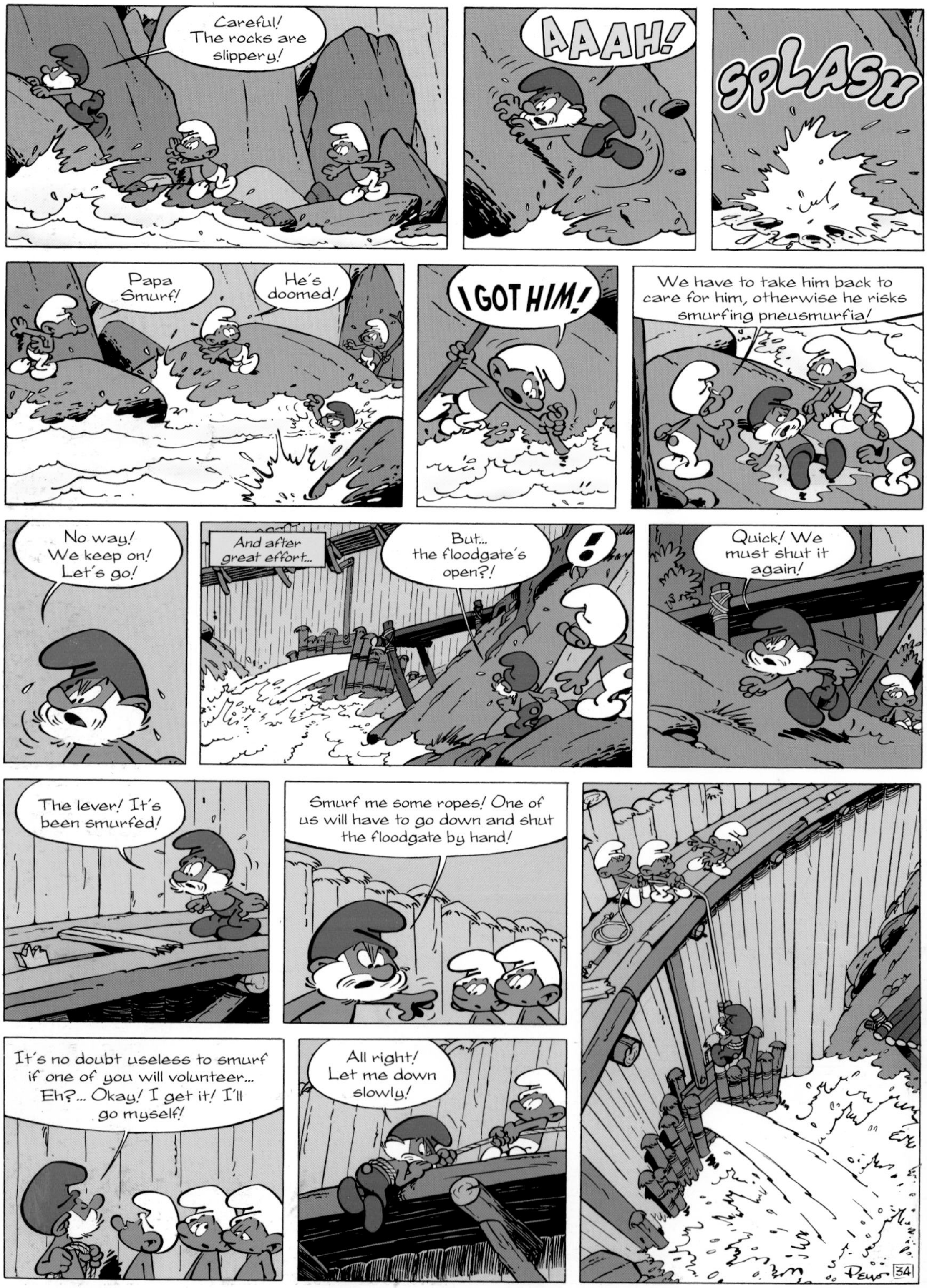

Careful! The rocks are slippery!
AAAH!
SPLASH
Papa Smurf!
He's doomed!
I GOT HIM!
We have to take him back to care for him, otherwise he risks smurfing pneusmurfia!
No way! We keep on! Let's go!
And after great effort...
But... the floodgate's open?!
!
Quick! We must shut it again!
The lever! It's been smurfed!
Smurf me some ropes! One of us will have to go down and shut the floodgate by hand!
It's no doubt useless to smurf if one of you will volunteer... Eh?... Okay! I get it! I'll go myself!
All right! Let me down slowly!
Peyo
34

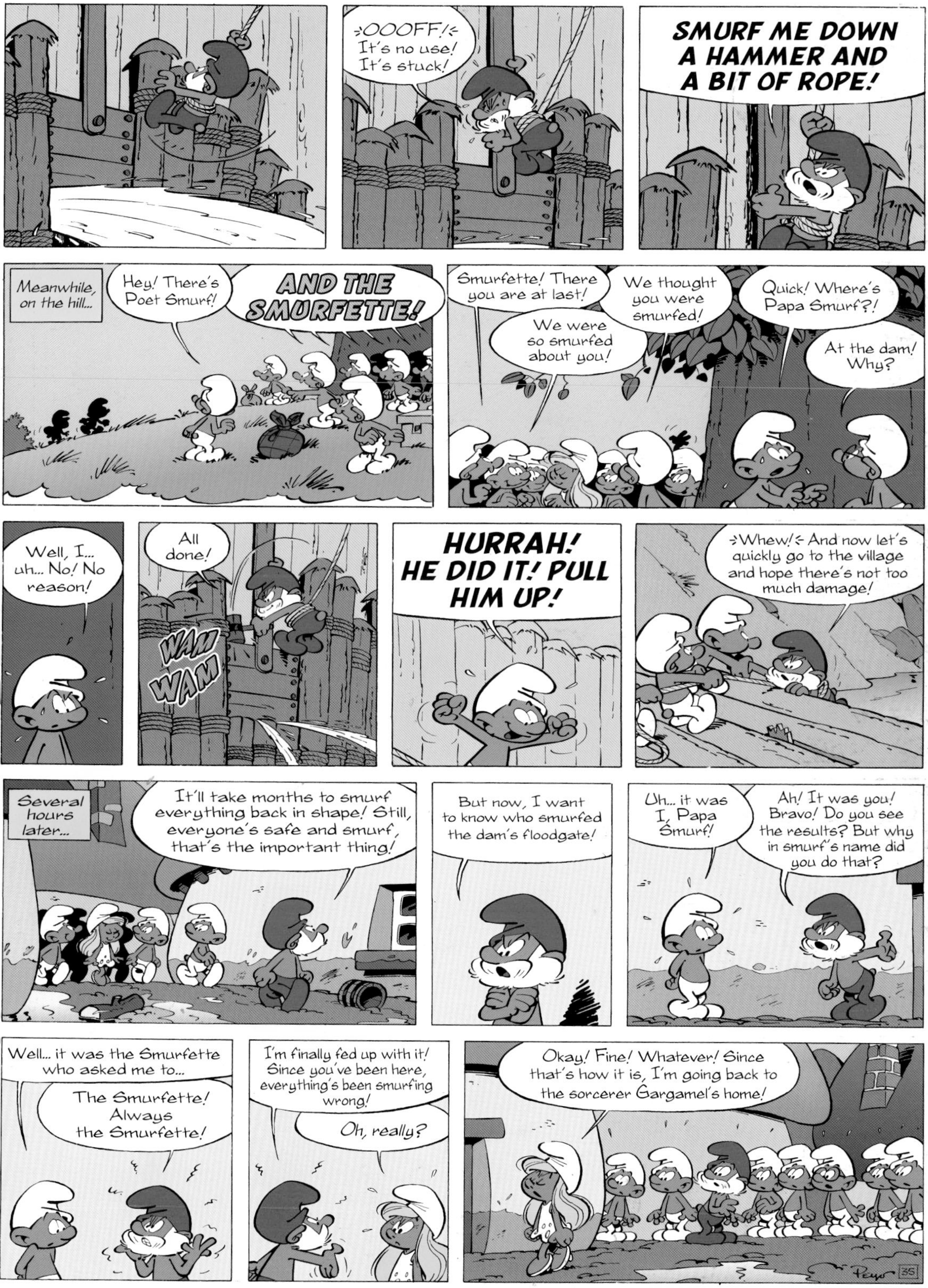

OOOFF!
It's no use! It's stuck!
SMURF ME DOWN A HAMMER AND A BIT OF ROPE!
Meanwhile, on the hill...
Hey! There's Poet Smurf!
AND THE SMURFETTE!
Smurfette! There you are at last!
We were so smurfed about you!
We thought you were smurfed!
Quick! Where's Papa Smurf?!
At the dam! Why?
Well, I... uh... No! No reason!
All done!
WAM WAM
HURRAH! HE DID IT! PULL HIM UP!
Whew! And now let's quickly go to the village and hope there's not too much damage!
Several hours later...
It'll take months to smurf everything back in shape! Still, everyone's safe and smurf, that's the important thing!
But now, I want to know who smurfed the dam's floodgate!
Uh... it was I, Papa Smurf!
Ah! It was you! Bravo! Do you see the results? But why in smurf's name did you do that?
Well... it was the Smurfette who asked me to...
The Smurfette! Always the Smurfette!
I'm finally fed up with it! Since you've been here, everything's been smurfing wrong!
Oh, really?
Okay! Fine! Whatever! Since that's how it is, I'm going back to the sorcerer Gargamel's home!
Peyo
35

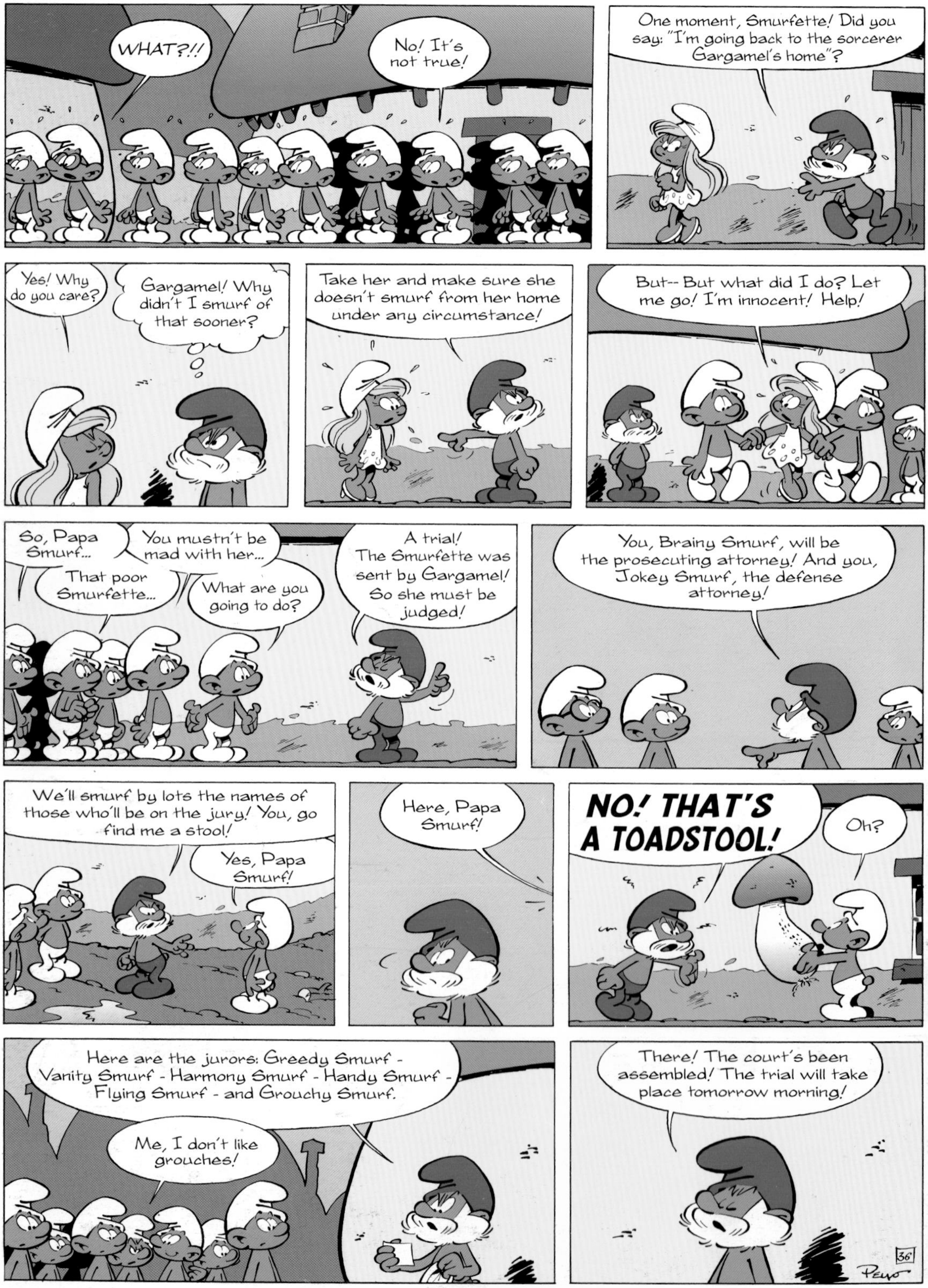
WHAT?!!
No! It's not true!
One moment, Smurfette! Did you say: "I'm going back to the sorcerer Gargamel's home"?
Yes! Why do you care?
Gargamel! Why didn't I smurf of that sooner?
Take her and make sure she doesn't smurf from her home under any circumstance!
But-- But what did I do? Let me go! I'm innocent! Help!
So, Papa Smurf...
You mustn't be mad with her...
That poor Smurfette...
What are you going to do?
A trial! The Smurfette was sent by Gargamel! So she must be judged!
You, Brainy Smurf, will be the prosecuting attorney! And you, Jokey Smurf, the defense attorney!
We'll smurf by lots the names of those who'll be on the jury! You, go find me a stool!
Yes, Papa Smurf!
Here, Papa Smurf!
NO! THAT'S A TOADSTOOL!
Oh?
Here are the jurors: Greedy Smurf - Vanity Smurf - Harmony Smurf - Handy Smurf - Flying Smurf - and Grouchy Smurf.
Me, I don't like grouches!
There! The court's been assembled! The trial will take place tomorrow morning!
36
Peyo

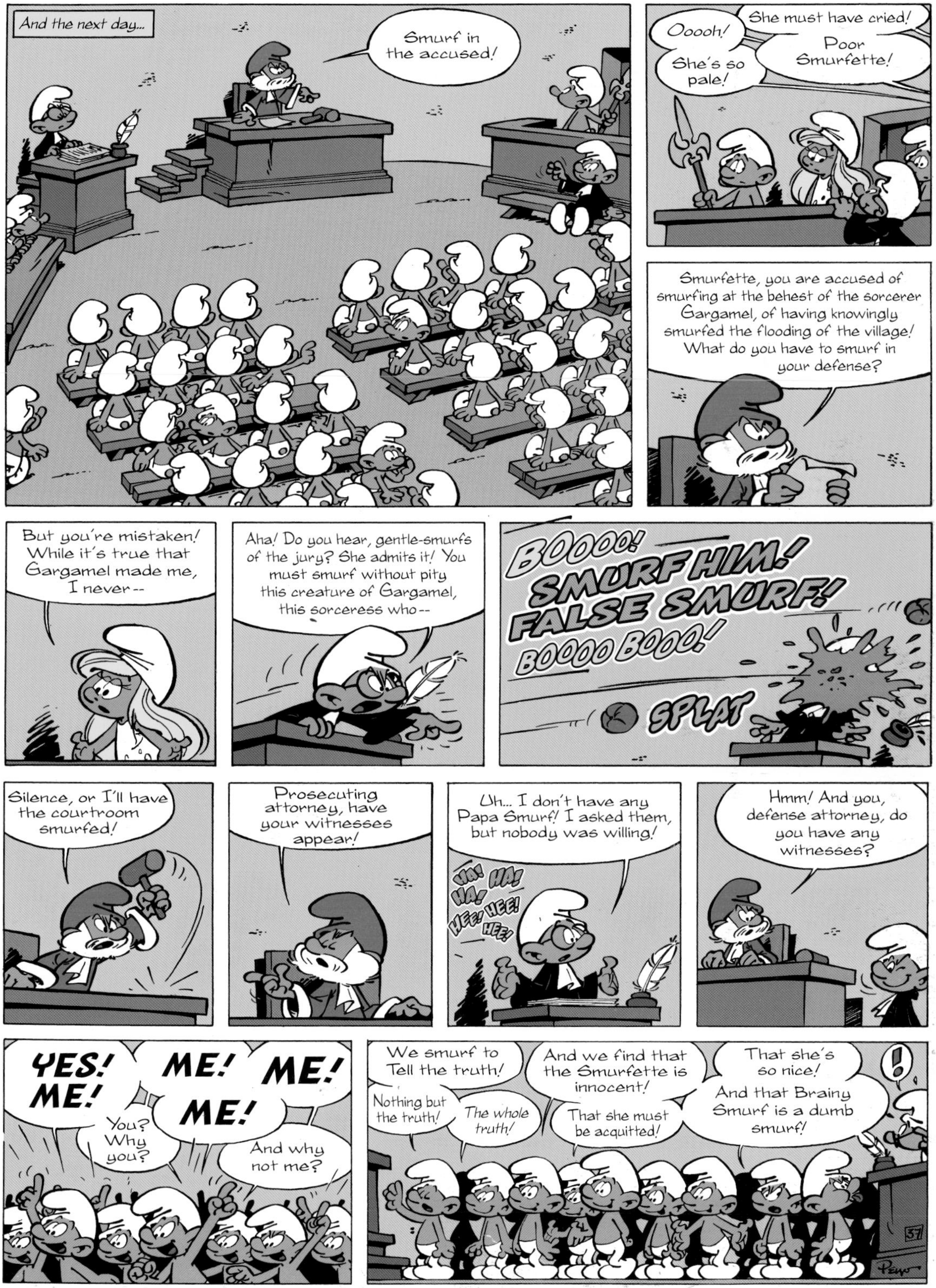

And the next day...
Smurf in the accused!
Ooooh!
She's so pale!
She must have cried!
Poor Smurfette!
Smurfette, you are accused of smurfing at the behest of the sorcerer Gargamel, of having knowingly smurfed the flooding of the village! What do you have to smurf in your defense?
But you're mistaken! While it's true that Gargamel made me, I never--
Aha! Do you hear, gentle-smurfs of the jury? She admits it! You must smurf without pity this creature of Gargamel, this sorceress who--
BOOOO! SMURF HIM! FALSE SMURF! BOOOO BOOO!
SPLAT
Silence, or I'll have the courtroom smurfed!
Prosecuting attorney, have your witnesses appear!
Uh... I don't have any Papa Smurf! I asked them, but nobody was willing!
HA! HA! HA! HEE! HEE! HEE!
Hmm! And you, defense attorney, do you have any witnesses?
YES! ME!
ME!
ME!
ME!
You? Why you?
And why not me?
We smurf to Tell the truth!
Nothing but the truth!
The whole truth!
And we find that the Smurfette is innocent!
That she must be acquitted!
That she's so nice!
And that Brainy Smurf is a dumb smurf!
!
37

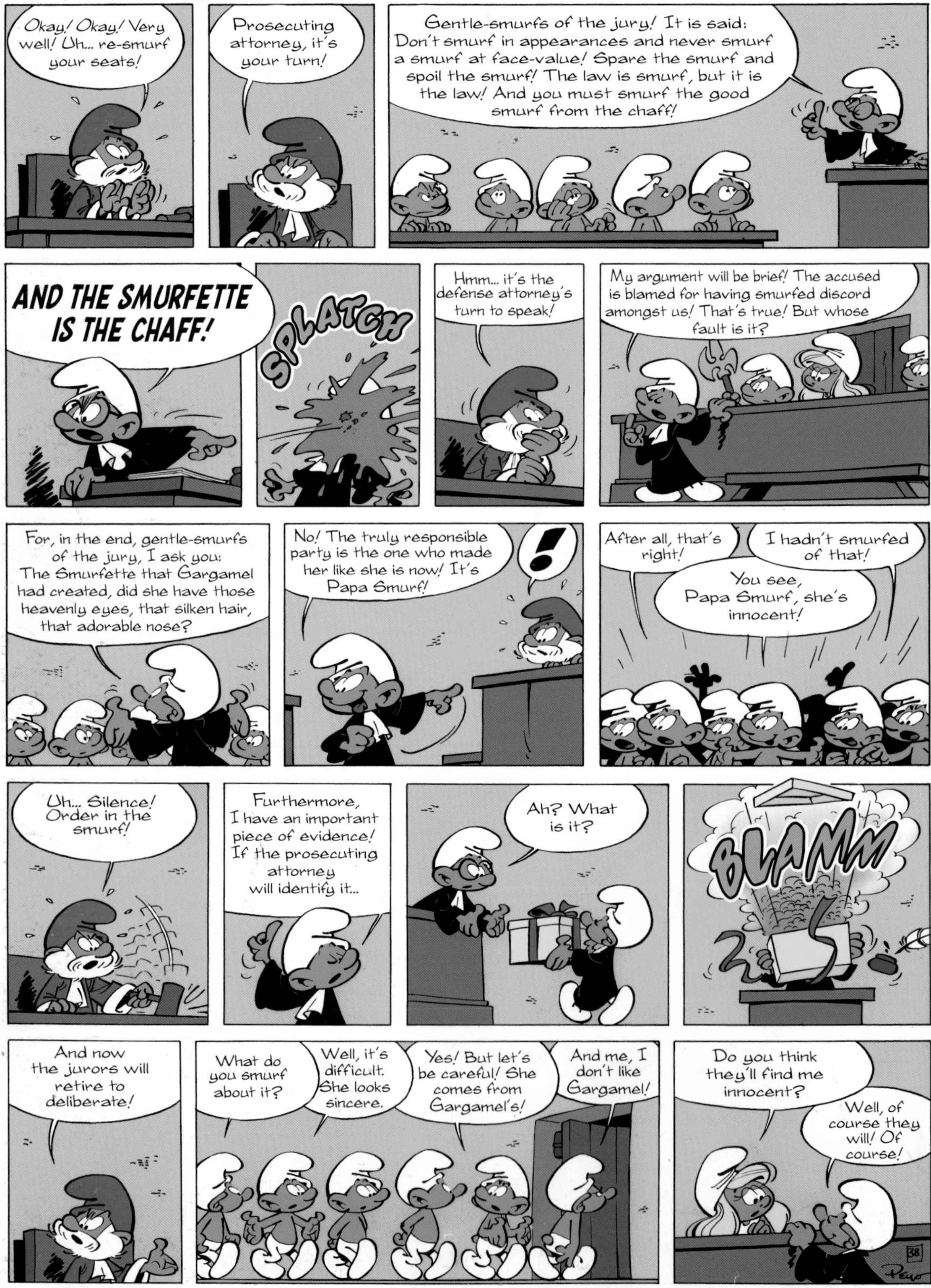
Okay! Okay! Very well! Uh... re-smurf your seats!
Prosecuting attorney, it's your turn!
Gentle-smurfs of the jury! It is said: Don't smurf in appearances and never smurf a smurf at face-value! Spare the smurf and spoil the smurf! The law is smurf, but it is the law! And you must smurf the good smurf from the chaff!
AND THE SMURFETTE IS THE CHAFF!
SPLATCH
Hmm... it's the defense attorney's turn to speak!
My argument will be brief! The accused is blamed for having smurfed discord amongst us! That's true! But whose fault is it?
For, in the end, gentle-smurfs of the jury, I ask you: The Smurfette that Gargamel had created, did she have those heavenly eyes, that silken hair, that adorable nose?
No! The truly responsible party is the one who made her like she is now! It's Papa Smurf!
!
After all, that's right!
I hadn't smurfed of that!
You see, Papa Smurf, she's innocent!
Uh... Silence! Order in the smurf!
Furthermore, I have an important piece of evidence! If the prosecuting attorney will identify it...
Ah? What is it?
BLAMM
And now the jurors will retire to deliberate!
What do you smurf about it?
Well, it's difficult. She looks sincere.
Yes! But let's be careful! She comes from Gargamel's!
And me, I don't like Gargamel!
Do you think they'll find me innocent?
Well, of course they will! Of course!
38

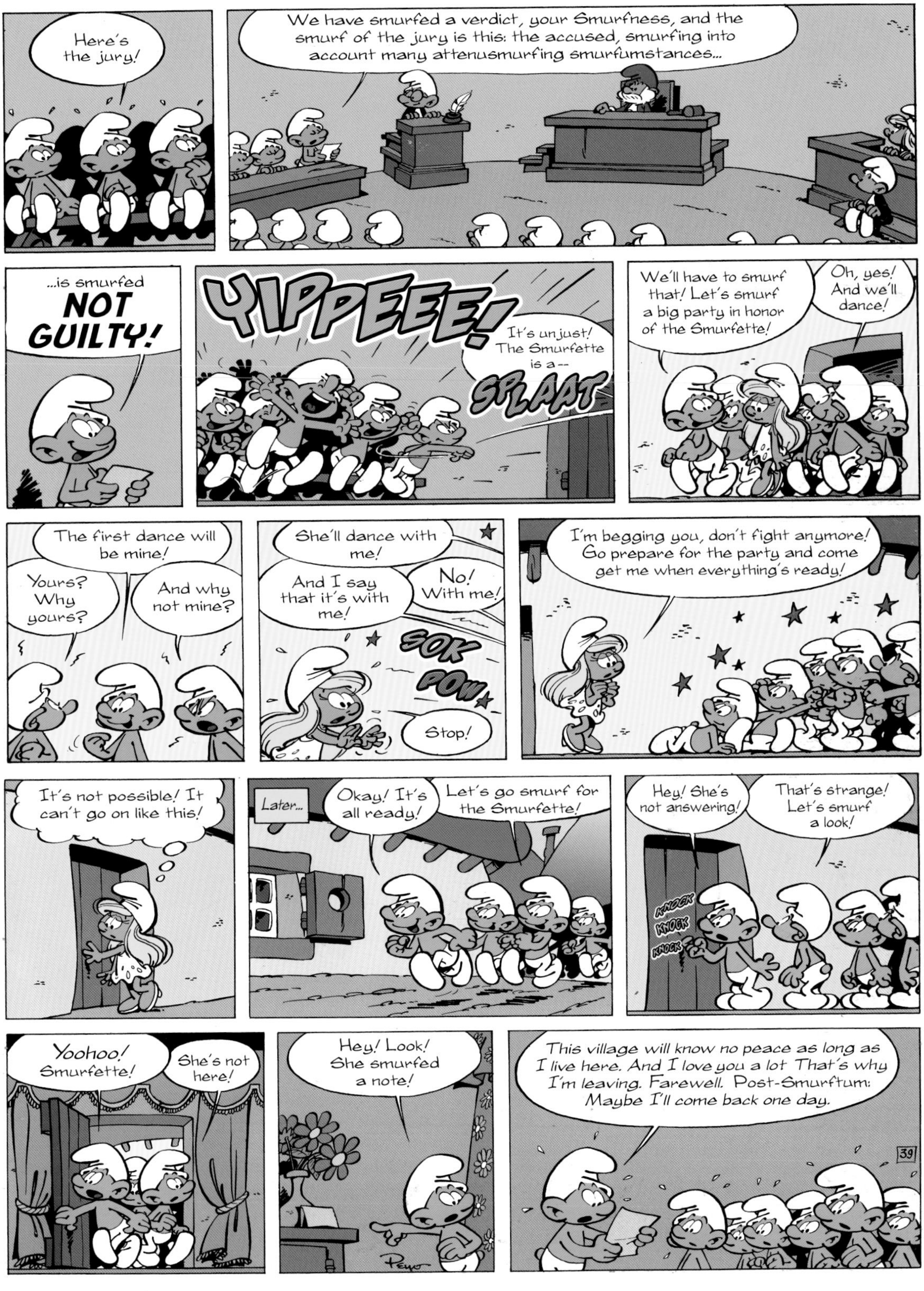
Here's the jury!
We have smurfed a verdict, your Smurfness, and the smurf of the jury is this: the accused, smurfing into account many attenusmurfing smurfumstances...
...is smurfed NOT GUILTY!
YIPPEEE!
It's unjust! The Smurfette is a--
SPLAAT
We'll have to smurf that! Let's smurf a big party in honor of the Smurfette!
Oh, yes! And we'll dance!
The first dance will be mine!
Yours? Why yours?
And why not mine?
She'll dance with me!
And I say that it's with me!
No! With me!
SOK
POW
Stop!
I'm begging you, don't fight anymore! Go prepare for the party and come get me when everything's ready!
It's not possible! It can't go on like this!
Later...
Okay! It's all ready!
Let's go smurf for the Smurfette!
Hey! She's not answering!
That's strange! Let's smurf a look!
KNOCK
KNOCK
KNOCK
Yoohoo! Smurfette!
She's not here!
Hey! Look! She smurfed a note!
This village will know no peace as long as I live here. And I love you a lot That's why I'm leaving. Farewell. Post-Smurftum: Maybe I'll come back one day.
39
Peyo

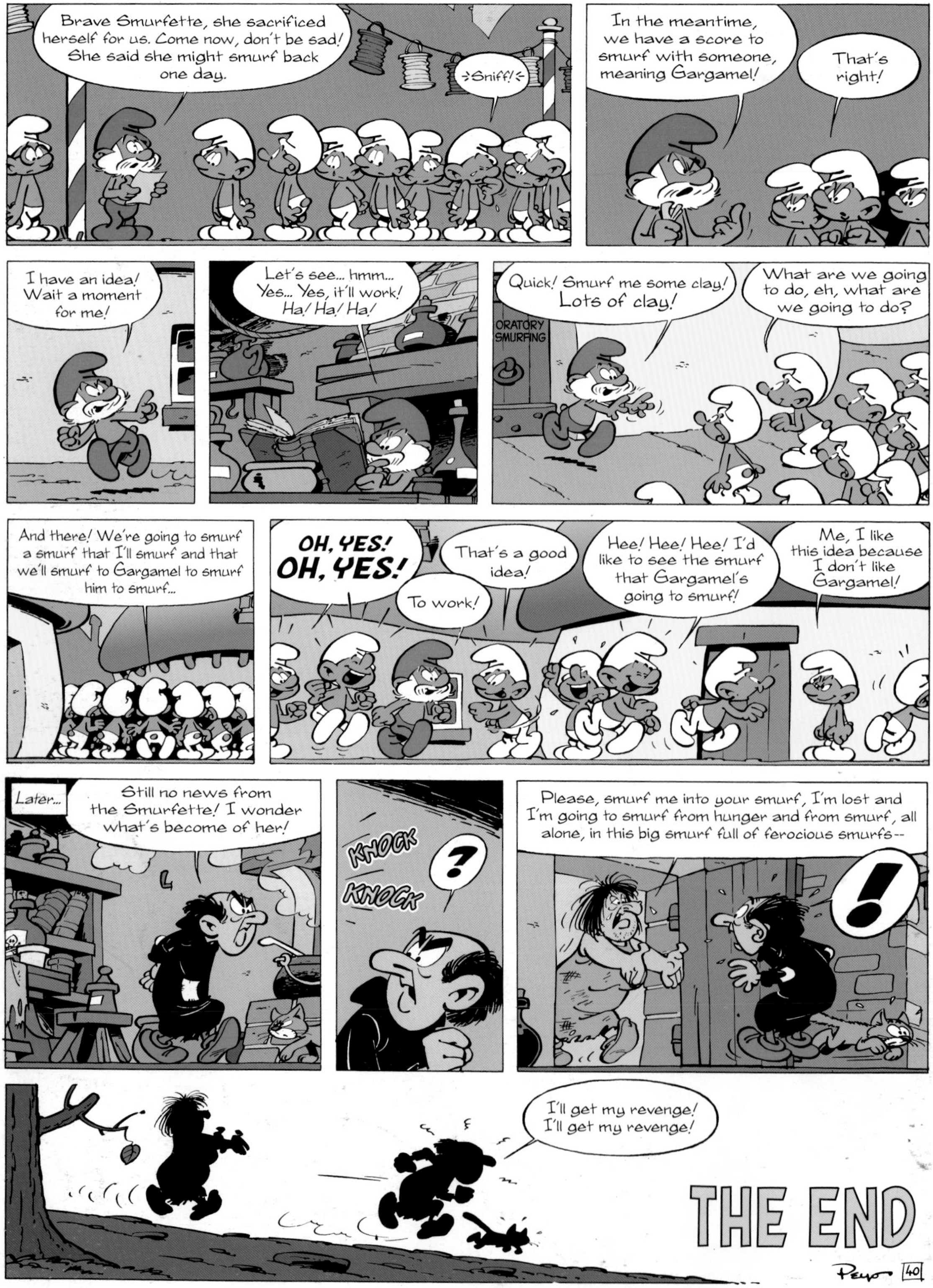

Brave Smurfette, she sacrificed herself for us. Come now, don't be sad! She said she might smurf back one day.
Sniff!
In the meantime, we have a score to smurf with someone, meaning Gargamel!
That's right!
I have an idea! Wait a moment for me!
Let's see... hmm... Yes... Yes, it'll work! Ha! Ha! Ha!
ORATORY SMURFING
Quick! Smurf me some clay! Lots of clay!
What are we going to do, eh, what are we going to do?
And there! We're going to smurf a smurf that I'll smurf and that we'll smurf to Gargamel to smurf him to smurf...
OH, YES! OH, YES!
To work!
That's a good idea!
Hee! Hee! Hee! I'd like to see the smurf that Gargamel's going to smurf!
Me, I like this idea because I don't like Gargamel!
Later...
Still no news from the Smurfette! I wonder what's become of her!
KNOCK
KNOCK
?
Please, smurf me into your smurf, I'm lost and I'm going to smurf from hunger and from smurf, all alone, in this big smurf full of ferocious smurfs--
!
I'll get my revenge! I'll get my revenge!
THE END
Peyo
40

THE HUNGRY SMURFS

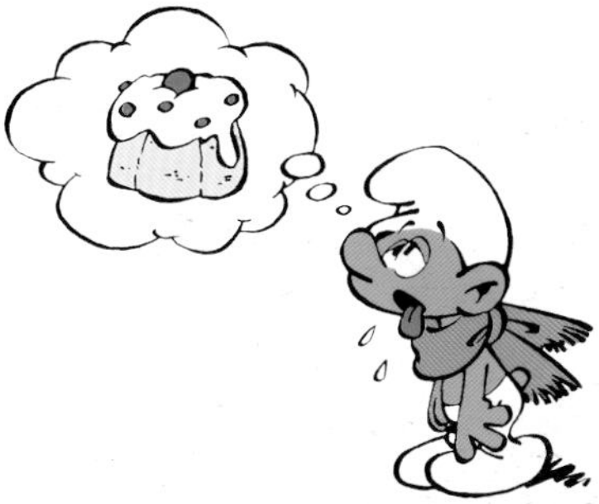

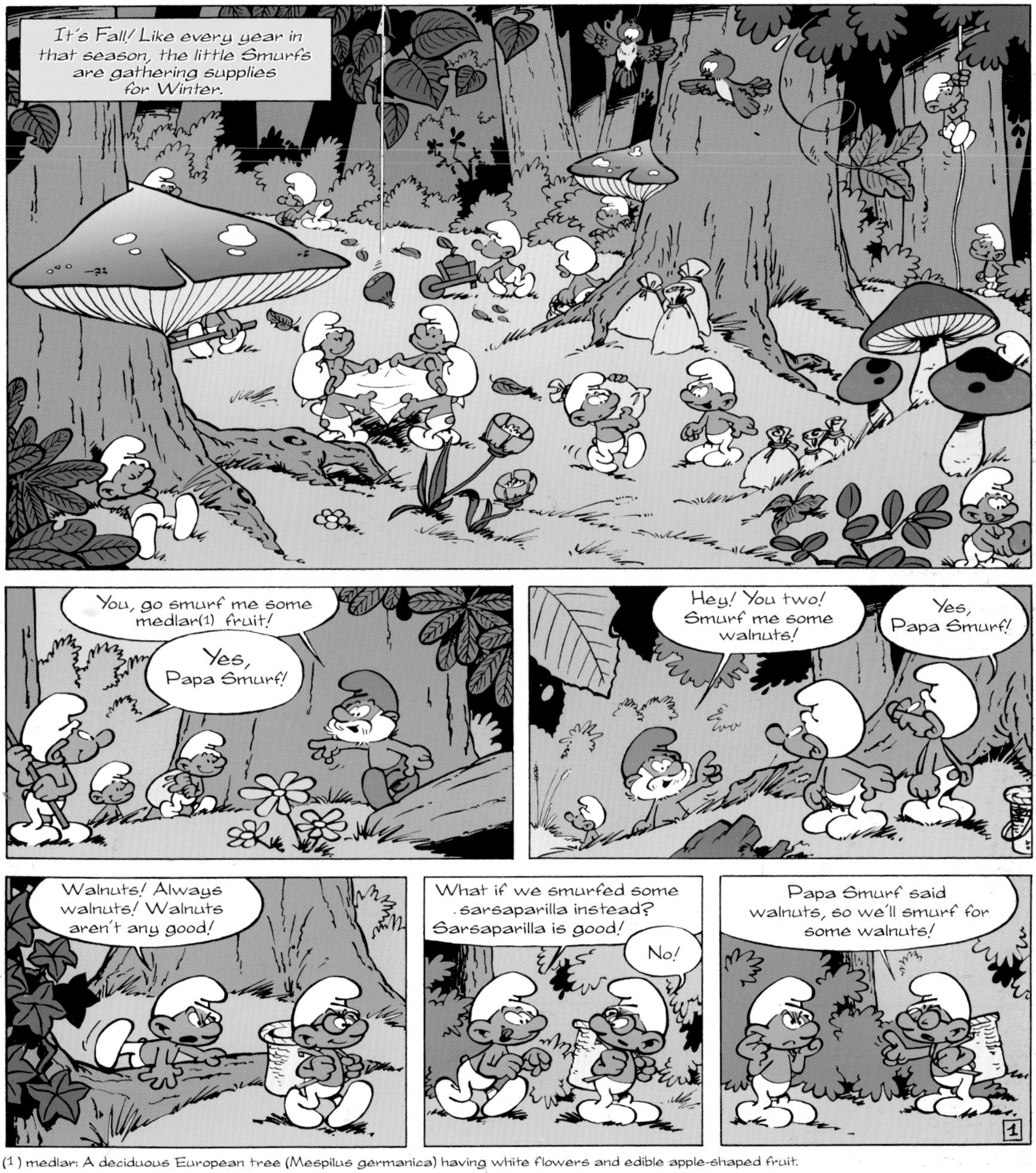

It's Fall! Like every year in that season, the little Smurfs are gathering supplies for Winter.
You, go smurf me some medlar(1) fruit!
Yes, Papa Smurf!
Hey! You two! Smurf me some walnuts!
Yes, Papa Smurf!
Walnuts! Always walnuts! Walnuts aren't any good!
What if we smurfed some sarsaparilla instead? Sarsaparilla is good!
No!
Papa Smurf said walnuts, so we'll smurf for some walnuts!
1

(1) medlar: A deciduous European tree (Mespilus germanica) having white flowers and edible apple-shaped fruit.

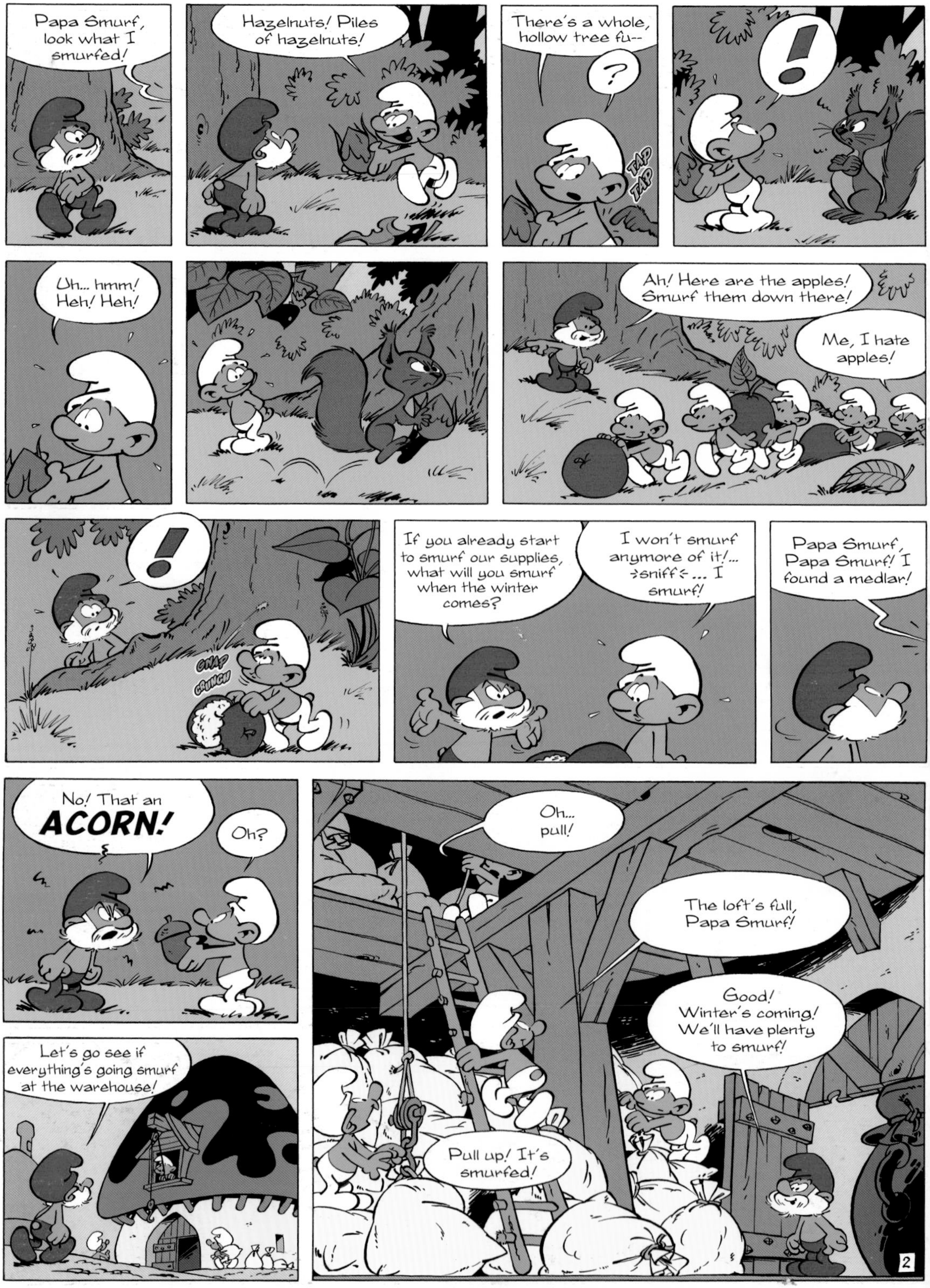
Papa Smurf, look what I smurfed!
Hazelnuts! Piles of hazelnuts!
There's a whole, hollow tree fu--
?
TAP TAP
!
Uh... hmm! Heh! Heh!
Ah! Here are the apples! Smurf them down there!
Me, I hate apples!
!
GNAP
CRUNCH
If you already start to smurf our supplies, what will you smurf when the winter comes?
I won't smurf anymore of it!... >sniff< ... I smurf!
Papa Smurf, Papa Smurf! I found a medlar!
No! That an ACORN!
Oh?
Let's go see if everything's going smurf at the warehouse!
Oh... pull!
The loft's full, Papa Smurf!
Good! Winter's coming! We'll have plenty to smurf!
Pull up! It's smurfed!
2

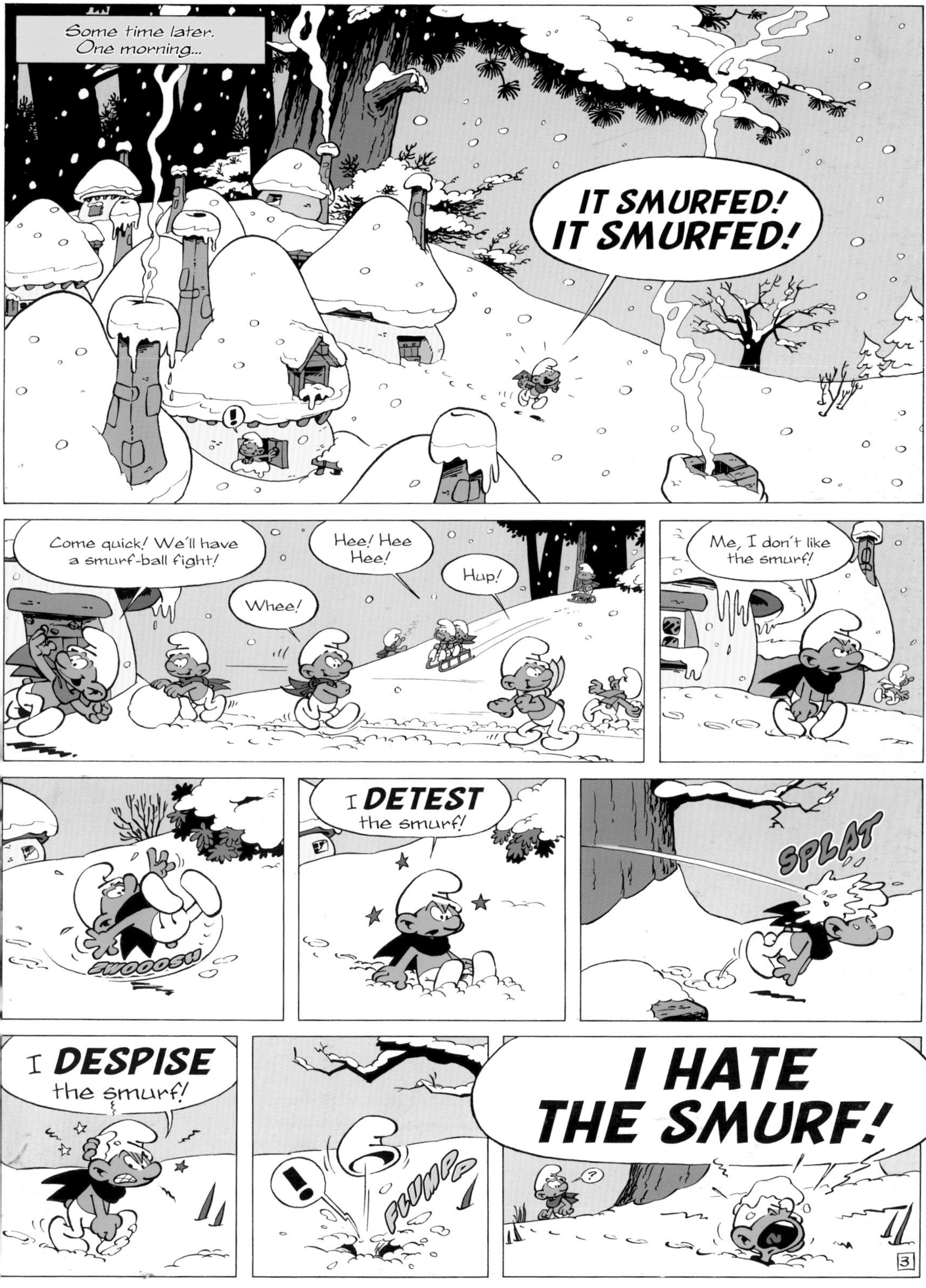

Some time later. One morning...
IT SMURFED! IT SMURFED!
Come quick! We'll have a smurf-ball fight!
Whee!
Hee! Hee Hee!
Hup!
Me, I don't like the smurf!
ZWOOOSH
I DETEST the smurf!
SPLAT
I DESPISE the smurf!
!
FLUMPP
?
I HATE THE SMURF!
3

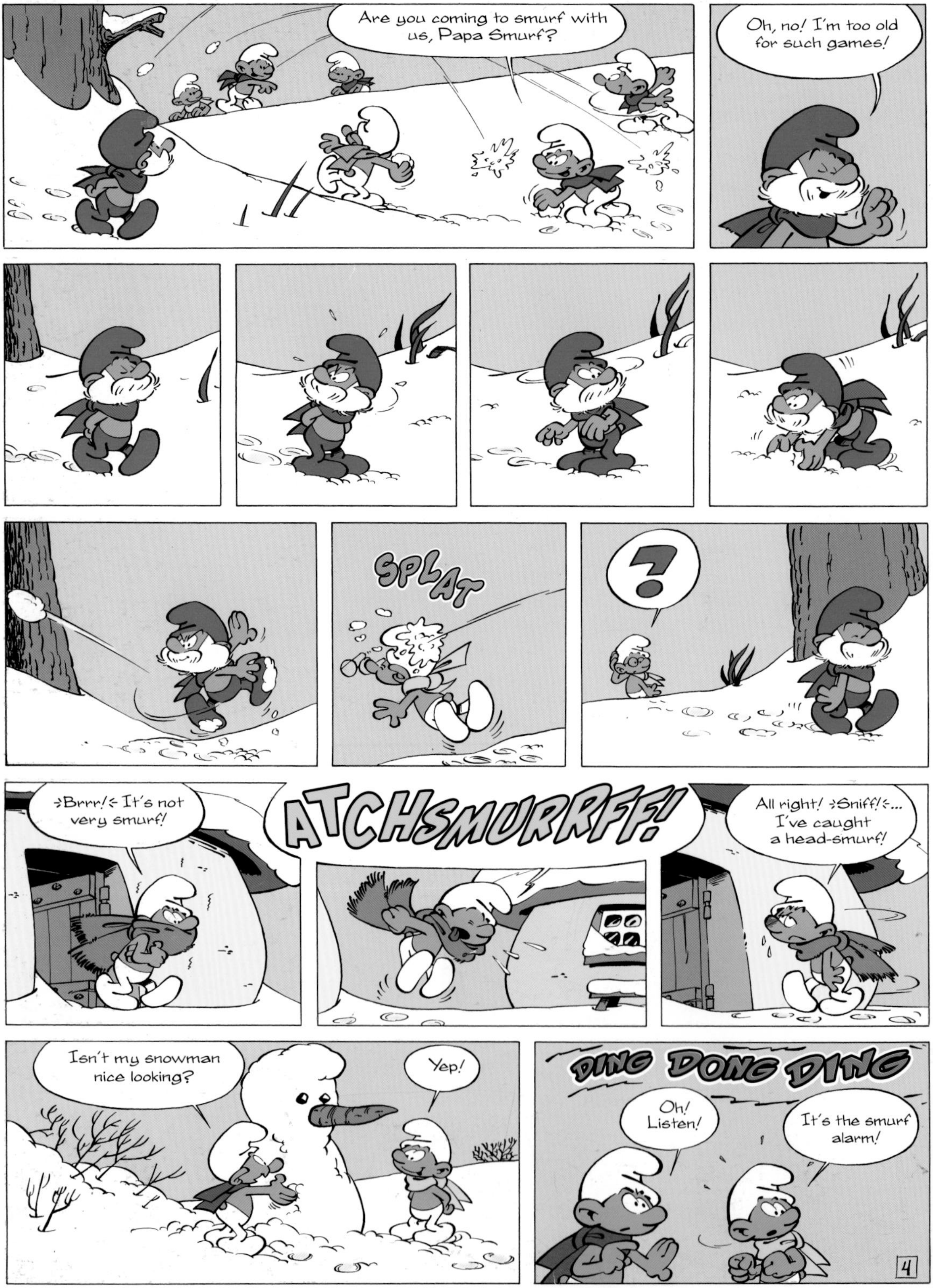
Are you coming to smurf with us, Papa Smurf?
Oh, no! I'm too old for such games!
SPLAT
?
⊰Brrr!⊱ It's not very smurf!
ATCHSMURRFF!
All right! ⊰Sniff!⊱... I've caught a head-smurf!
Isn't my snowman nice looking?
Yep!
DING DONG DING
Oh! Listen!
It's the smurf alarm!
4

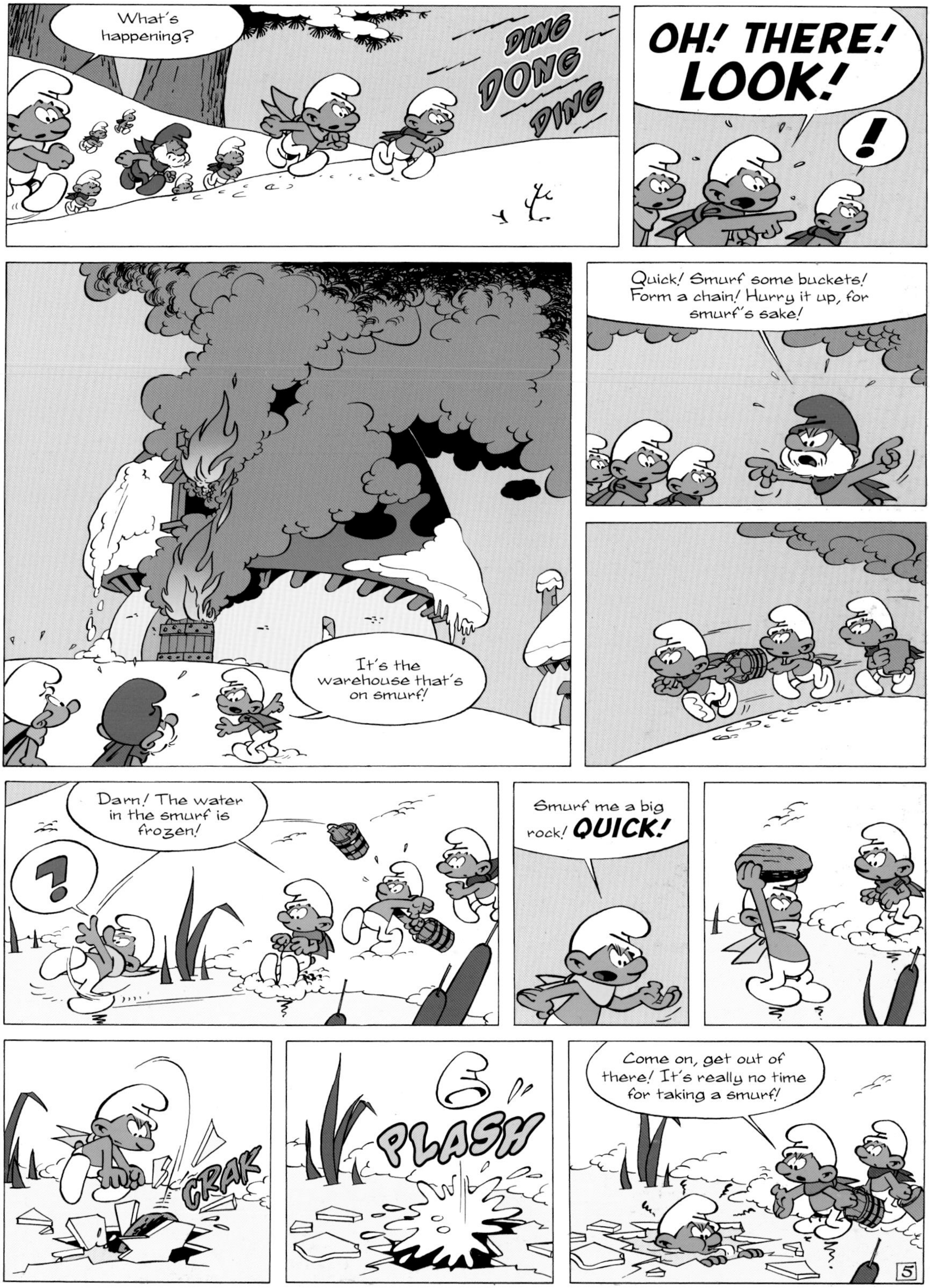
What's happening?
DING DONG DING
OH! THERE! LOOK!
!
It's the warehouse that's on smurf!
Quick! Smurf some buckets! Form a chain! Hurry it up, for smurf's sake!
Darn! The water in the smurf is frozen!
?
Smurf me a big rock! QUICK!
CRAK
PLASH
Come on, get out of there! It's really no time for taking a smurf!
5

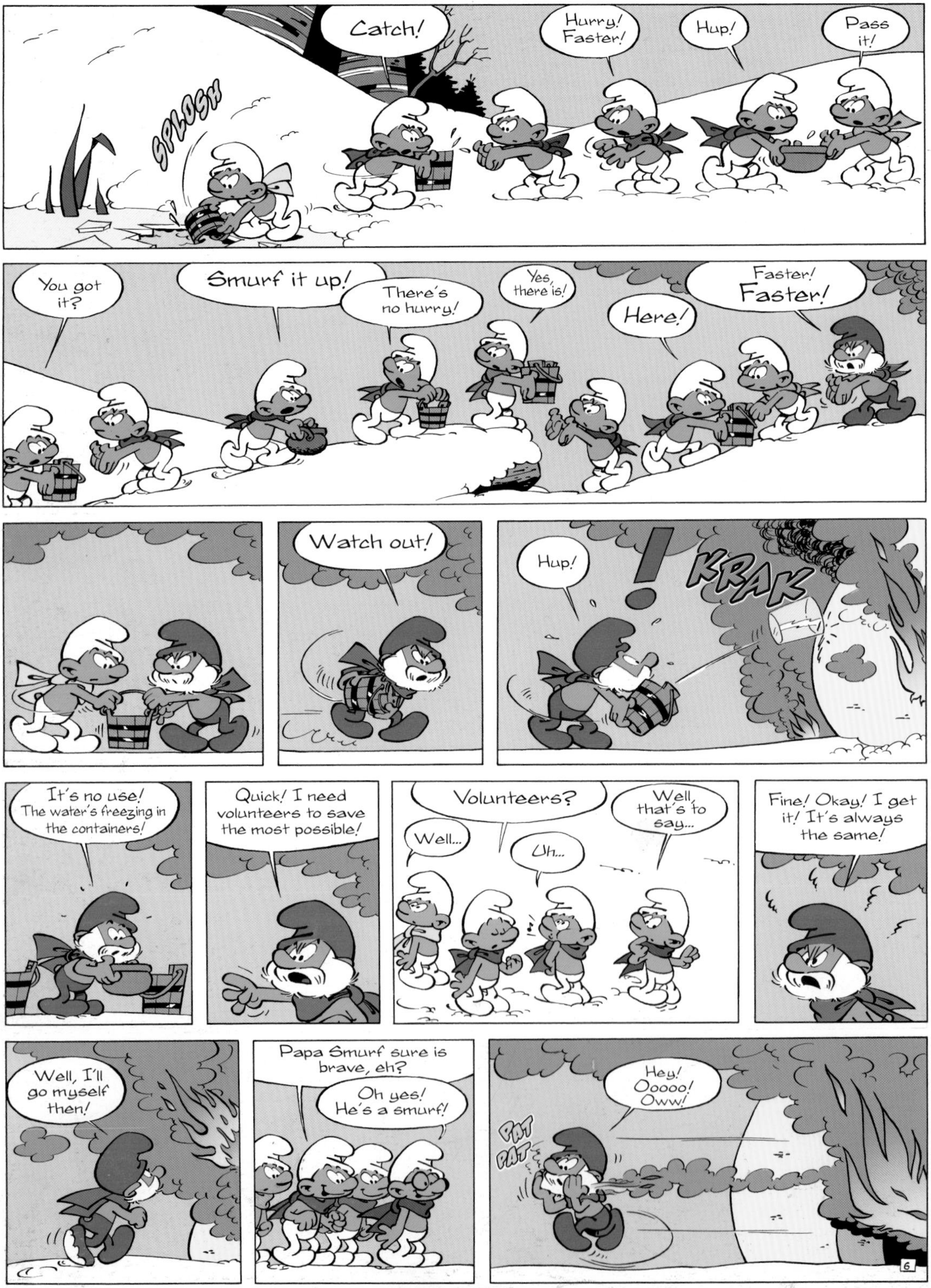
SPLOSH
Catch!
Hurry! Faster!
Hup!
Pass it!
You got it?
Smurf it up!
There's no hurry!
Yes, there is!
Here!
Faster! Faster!
Watch out!
Hup!
!
KRAK
It's no use! The water's freezing in the containers!
Quick! I need volunteers to save the most possible!
Volunteers?
Well...
Uh...
Well, that's to say...
Fine! Okay! I get it! It's always the same!
Well, I'll go myself then!
Papa Smurf sure is brave, eh?
Oh yes! He's a smurf!
Hey! Ooooo! Oww!
PAT PAT

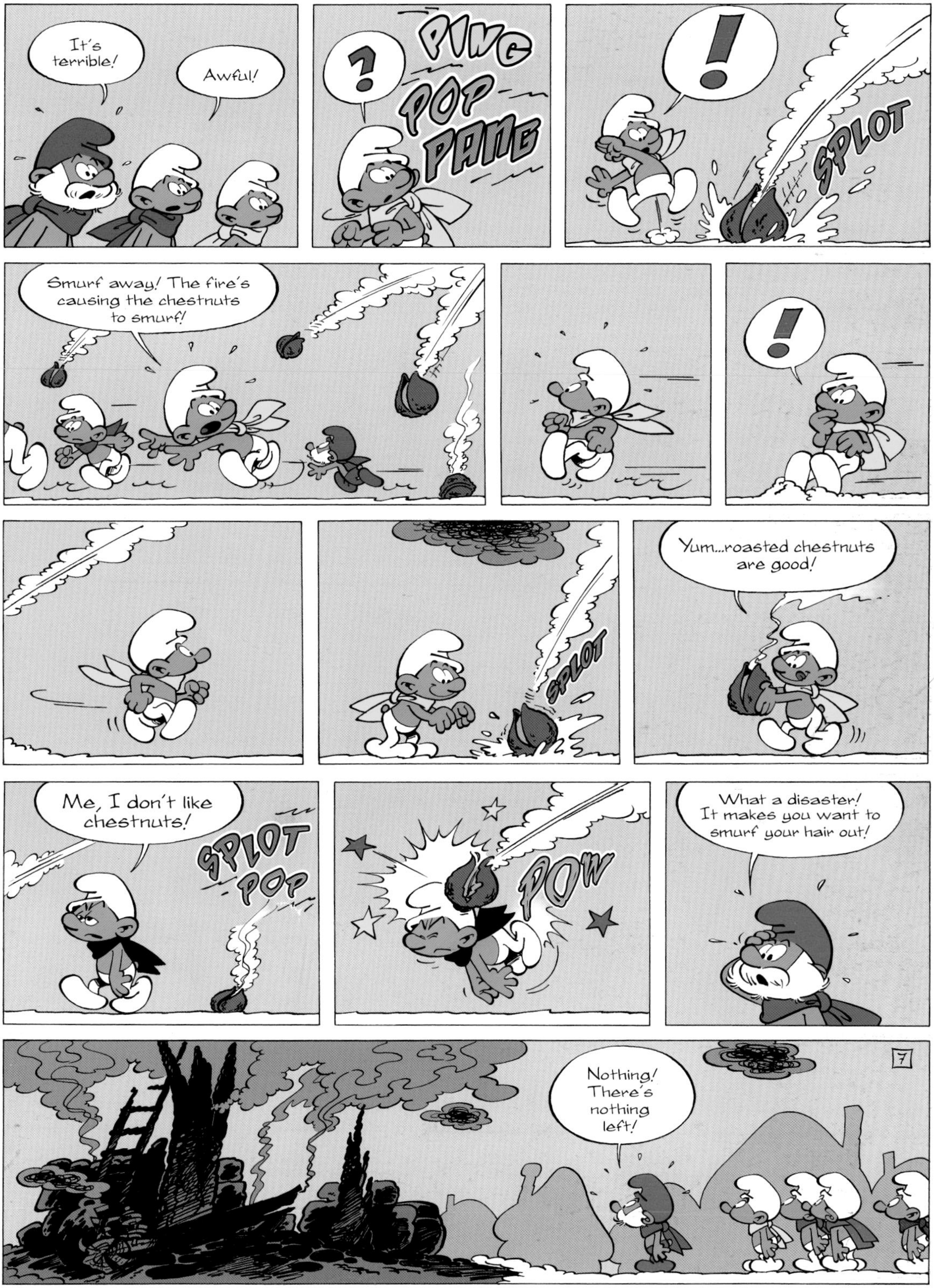
It's terrible!
Awful!
?
PING
POP
PANG
!
SPLOT
Smurf away! The fire's causing the chestnuts to smurf!
!
SPLOT
Yum...roasted chestnuts are good!
Me, I don't like chestnuts!
SPLOT
POP
POW
What a disaster! It makes you want to smurf your hair out!
7
Nothing! There's nothing left!

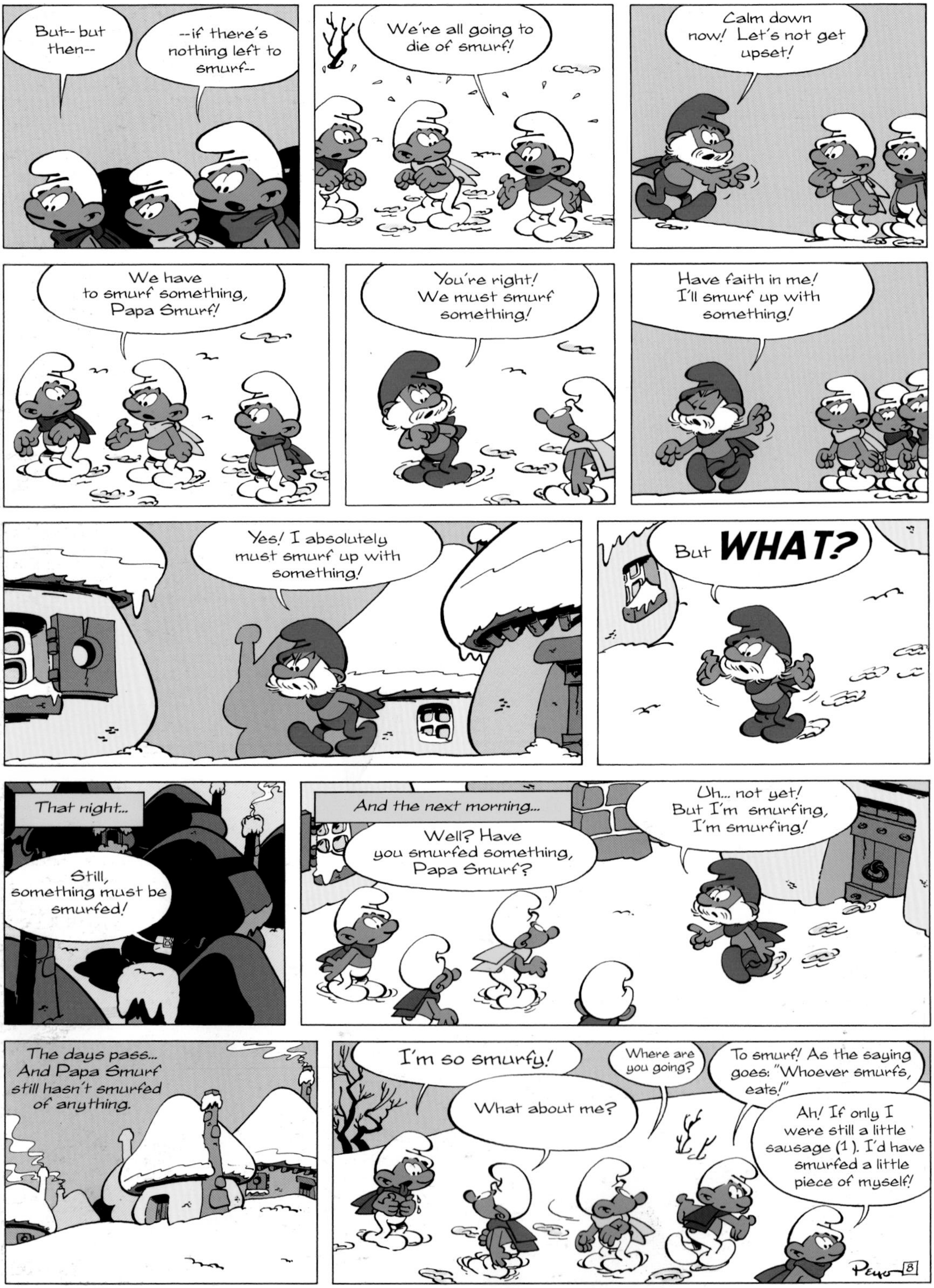

But-- but then--
--if there's nothing left to smurf--
We're all going to die of smurf!
Calm down now! Let's not get upset!
We have to smurf something, Papa Smurf!
You're right! We must smurf something!
Have faith in me! I'll smurf up with something!
Yes! I absolutely must smurf up with something!
But WHAT?
That night...
Still, something must be smurfed!
And the next morning...
Well? Have you smurfed something, Papa Smurf?
Uh... not yet! But I'm smurfing, I'm smurfing!
The days pass... And Papa Smurf still hasn't smurfed of anything.
I'm so smurfy!
What about me?
Where are you going?
To smurf! As the saying goes: "Whoever smurfs, eats!"
Ah! If only I were still a little sausage (1). I'd have smurfed a little piece of myself!
Peyo 8

(1) See "The Smurfs and the Egg," starting on page 67.

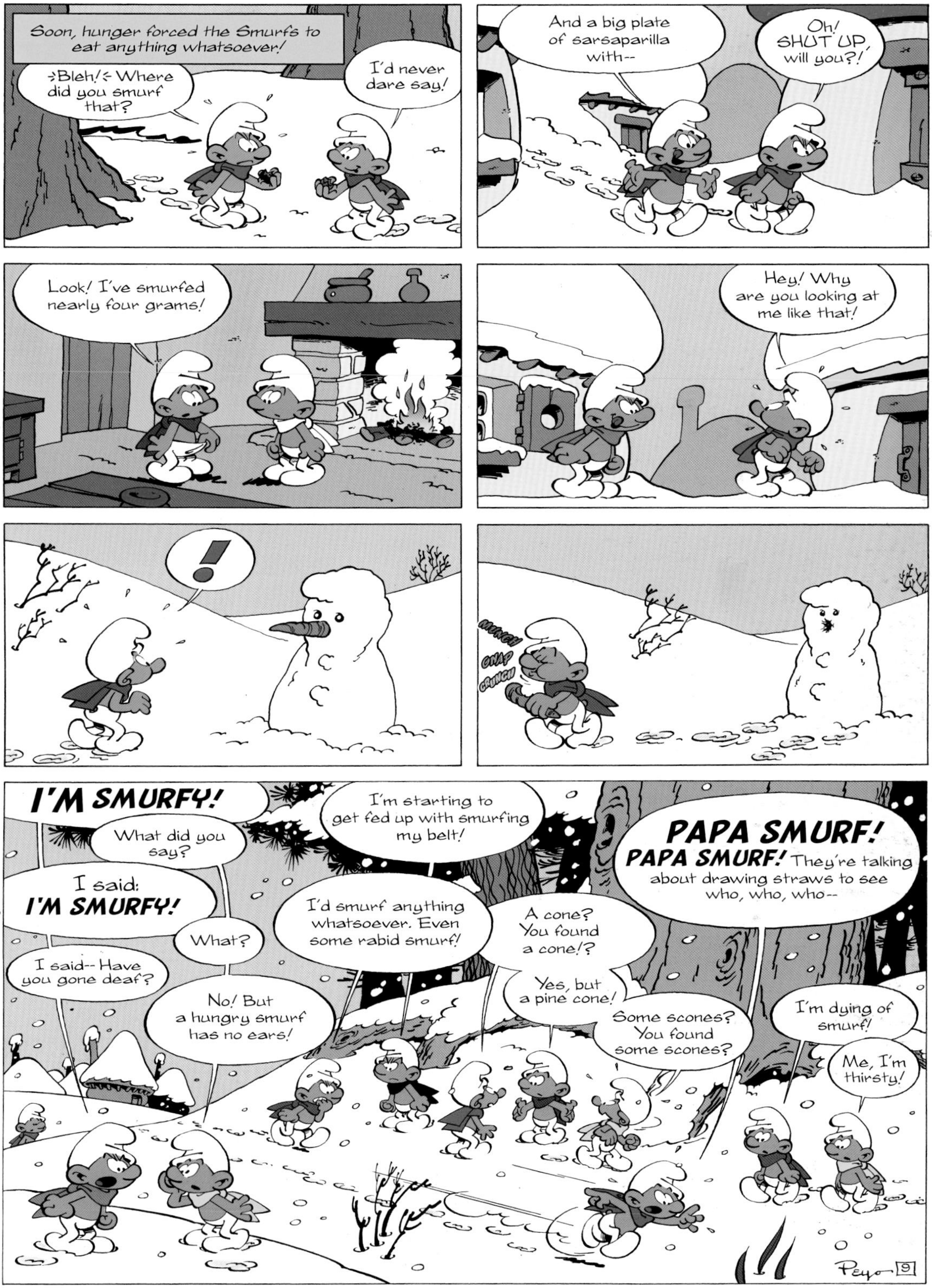
Soon, hunger forced the Smurfs to eat anything whatsoever!
-Bleh!- Where did you smurf that?
I'd never dare say!
And a big plate of sarsaparilla with--
Oh! SHUT UP, will you?!
Look! I've smurfed nearly four grams!
Hey! Why are you looking at me like that!
!
MUNCH
CHAP
CRUNCH
I'M SMURFY!
What did you say?
I said: I'M SMURFY!
What?
I said-- Have you gone deaf?
No! But a hungry smurf has no ears!
I'm starting to get fed up with smurfing my belt!
I'd smurf anything whatsoever. Even some rabid smurf!
A cone? You found a cone!?
Yes, but a pine cone!
Some scones? You found some scones?
PAPA SMURF! PAPA SMURF! They're talking about drawing straws to see who, who, who--
I'm dying of smurf!
Me, I'm thirsty!
Peyo
9

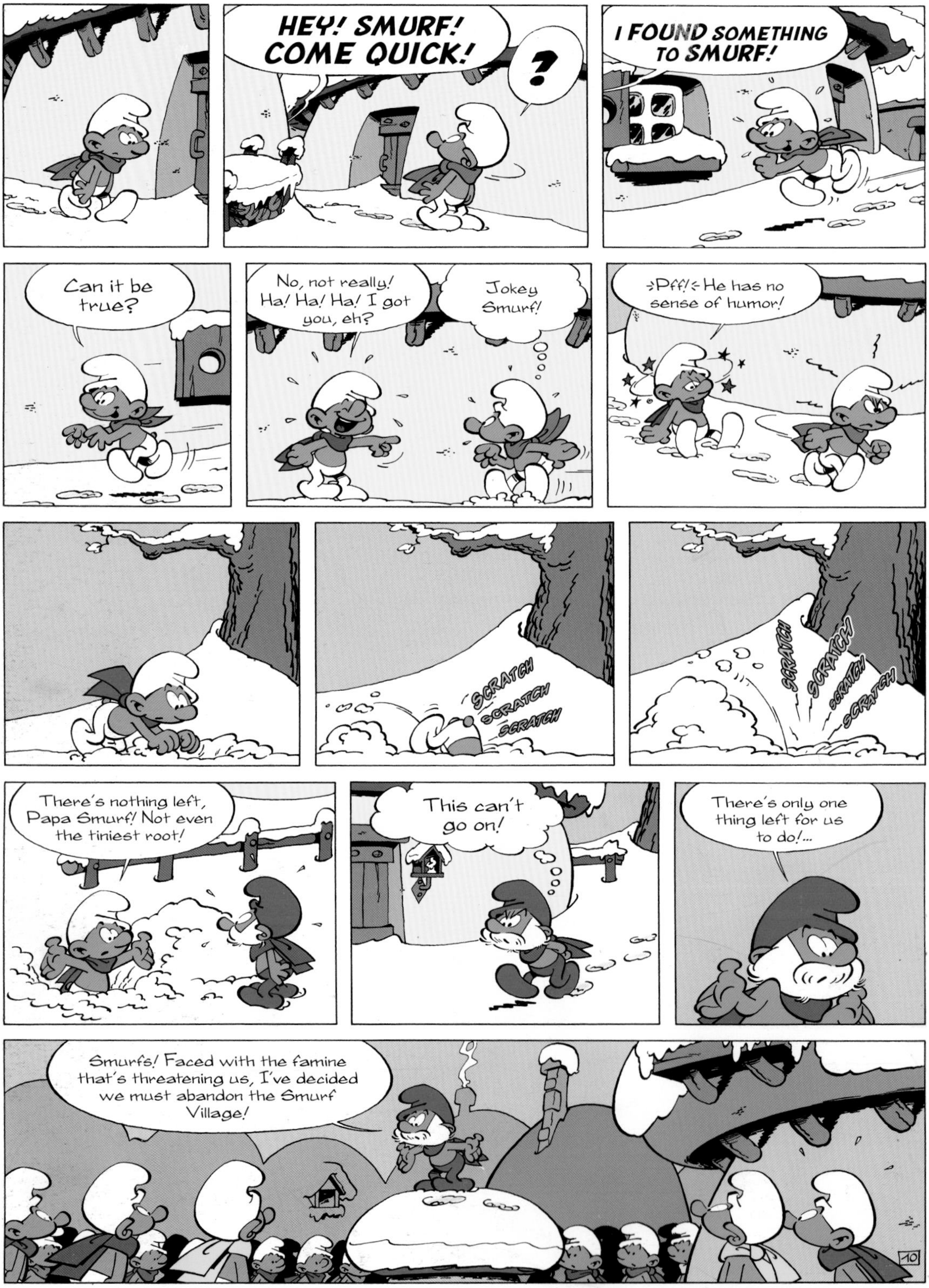
HEY! SMURF! COME QUICK!
?
I FOUND SOMETHING TO SMURF!
Can it be true?
No, not really! Ha! Ha! Ha! I got you, eh?
Jokey Smurf!
Pff! He has no sense of humor!
SCRATCH
SCRATCH
SCRATCH
SCRATCH
SCRATCH
SCRATCH
SCRATCH
There's nothing left, Papa Smurf! Not even the tiniest root!
This can't go on!
There's only one thing left for us to do!...
Smurfs! Faced with the famine that's threatening us, I've decided we must abandon the Smurf Village!
10

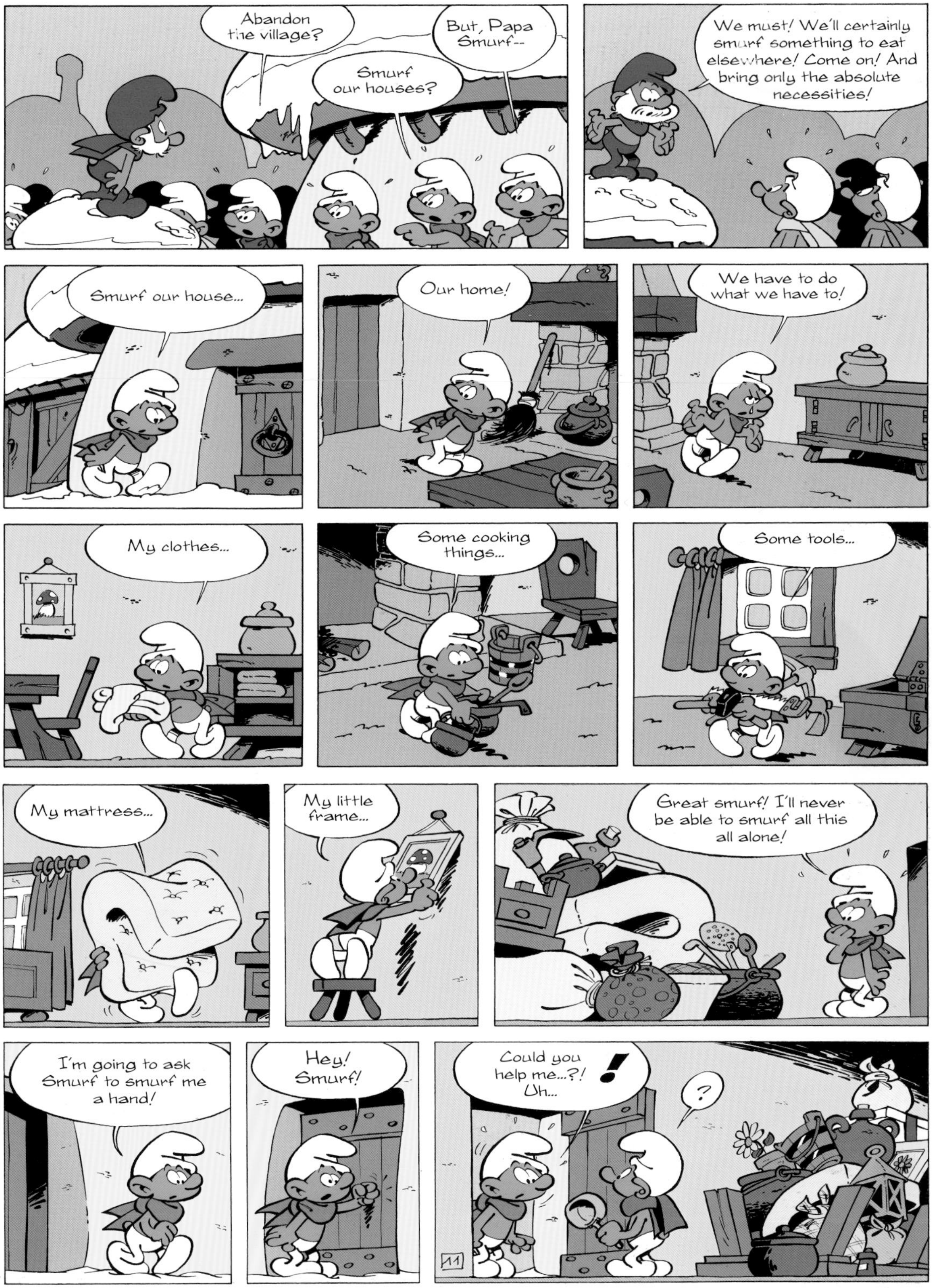
Abandon the village?
Smurf our houses?
But, Papa Smurf--
We must! We'll certainly smurf something to eat elsewhere! Come on! And bring only the absolute necessities!
Smurf our house...
Our home!
We have to do what we have to!
My clothes...
Some cooking things...
Some tools...
My mattress...
My little frame...
Great smurf! I'll never be able to smurf all this all alone!
I'm going to ask Smurf to smurf me a hand!
Hey! Smurf!
Could you help me...?! Uh...
!
?
11

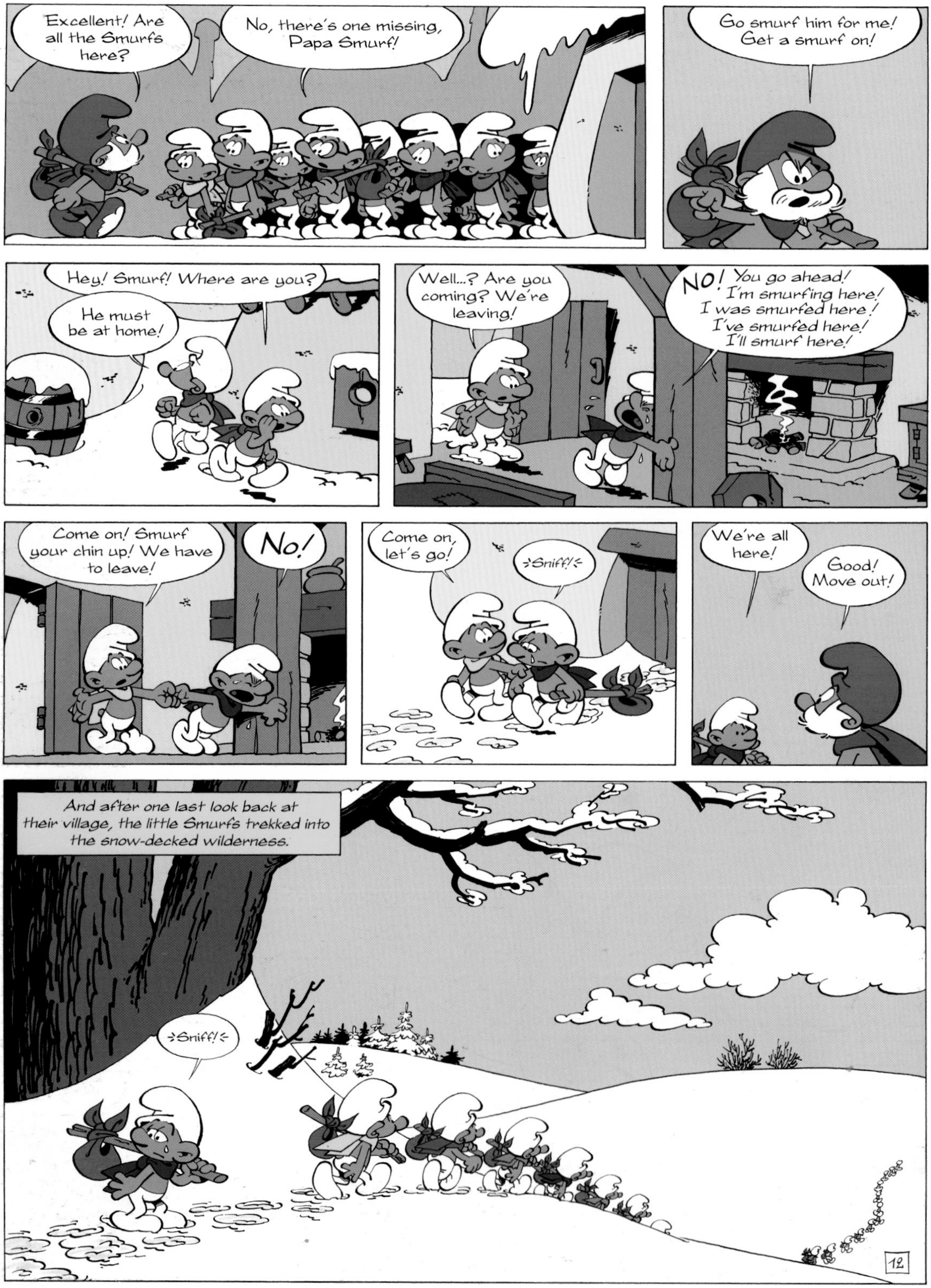
Excellent! Are all the Smurfs here?
No, there's one missing, Papa Smurf!
Go smurf him for me! Get a smurf on!
Hey! Smurf! Where are you?
He must be at home!
Well...? Are you coming? We're leaving!
NO! You go ahead! I'm smurfing here! I was smurfed here! I've smurfed here! I'll smurf here!
Come on! Smurf your chin up! We have to leave!
No!
Come on, let's go!
Sniff!
We're all here!
Good! Move out!
And after one last look back at their village, the little Smurfs trekked into the snow-decked wilderness.
Sniff!
12

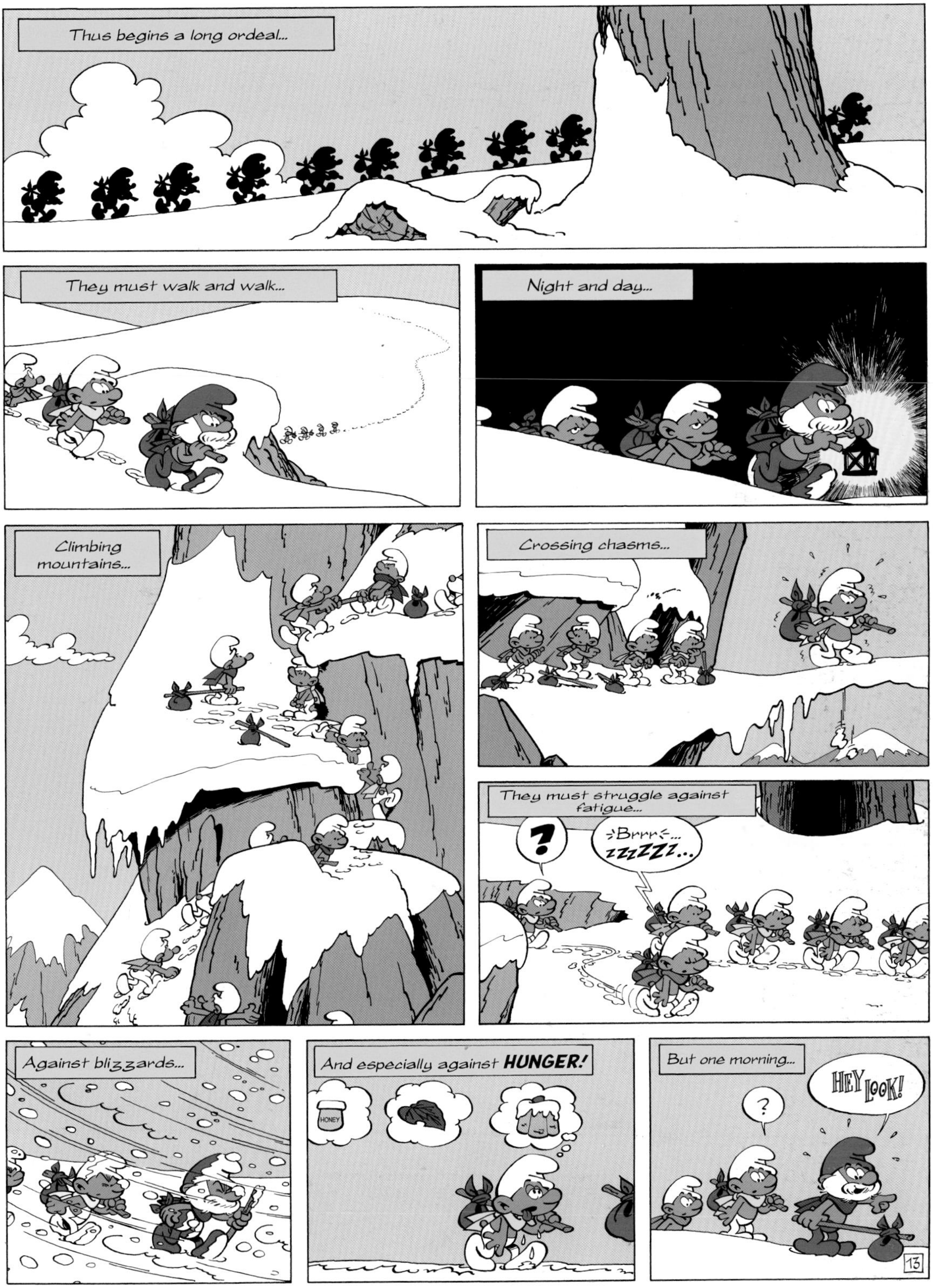

Thus begins a long ordeal...
They must walk and walk...
Night and day...
Climbing mountains...
Crossing chasms...
They must struggle against fatigue...
?
Brrr...
ZZZZZZ...
Against blizzards...
And especially against HUNGER!
HONEY
But one morning...
?
HEY LOOK!
13

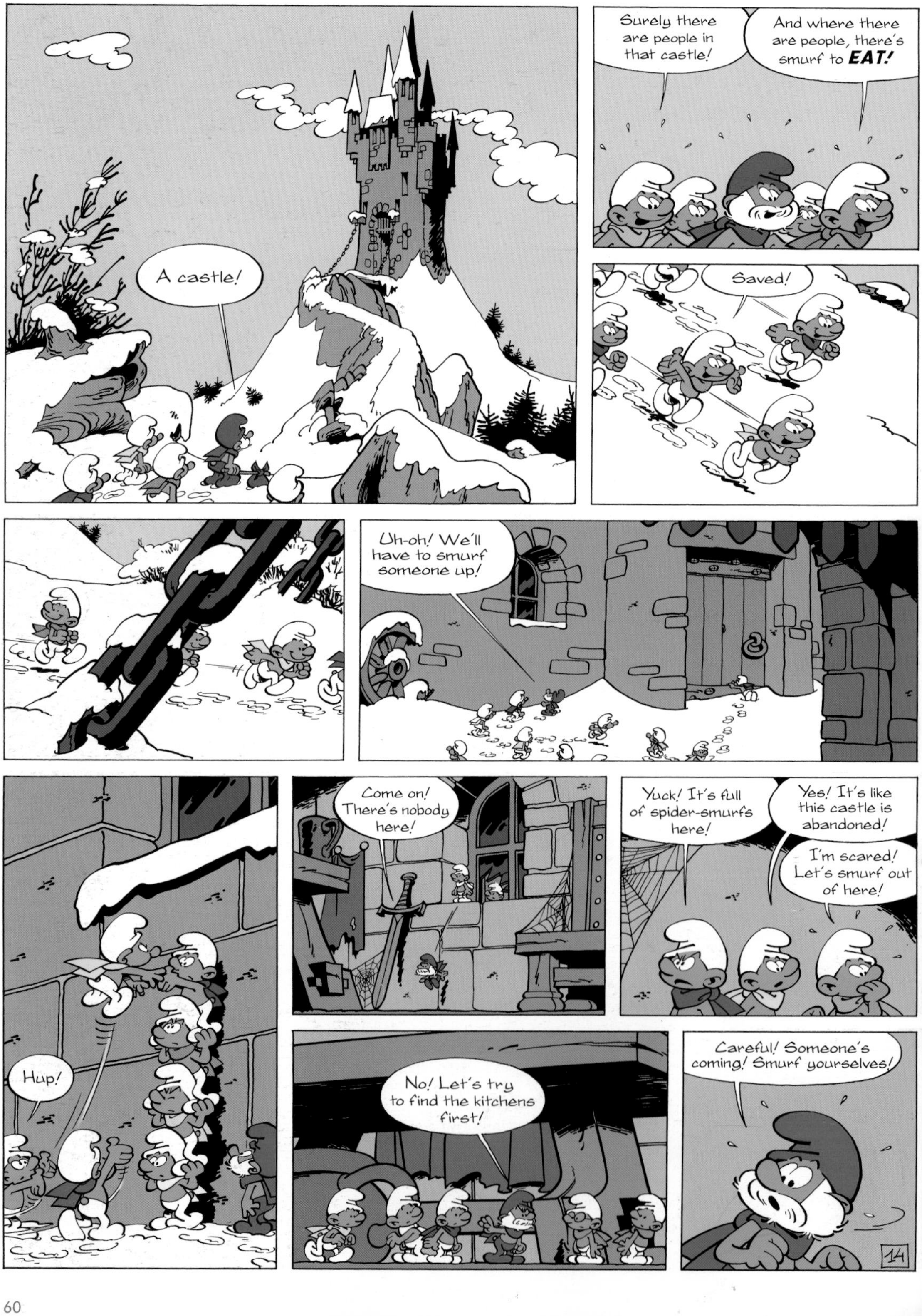
A castle!
Surely there are people in that castle!
And where there are people, there's smurf to EAT!
Saved!
Uh-oh! We'll have to smurf someone up!
Hup!
Come on! There's nobody here!
Yuck! It's full of spider-smurfs here!
Yes! It's like this castle is abandoned!
I'm scared! Let's smurf out of here!
No! Let's try to find the kitchens first!
Careful! Someone's coming! Smurf yourselves!
14

Whew! It was just a mouse. Someone's coming! Smurf yourselves!

I was a-smurf!

Indeed, maybe his hole leads to the kitchen?

Come on! Follow me!

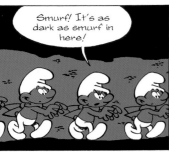
Smurf! It's as dark as smurf in here!

Hello? It's like we're in an armoire!

Nobody to the left...

Nobody to the right...

Okay! Let's go!

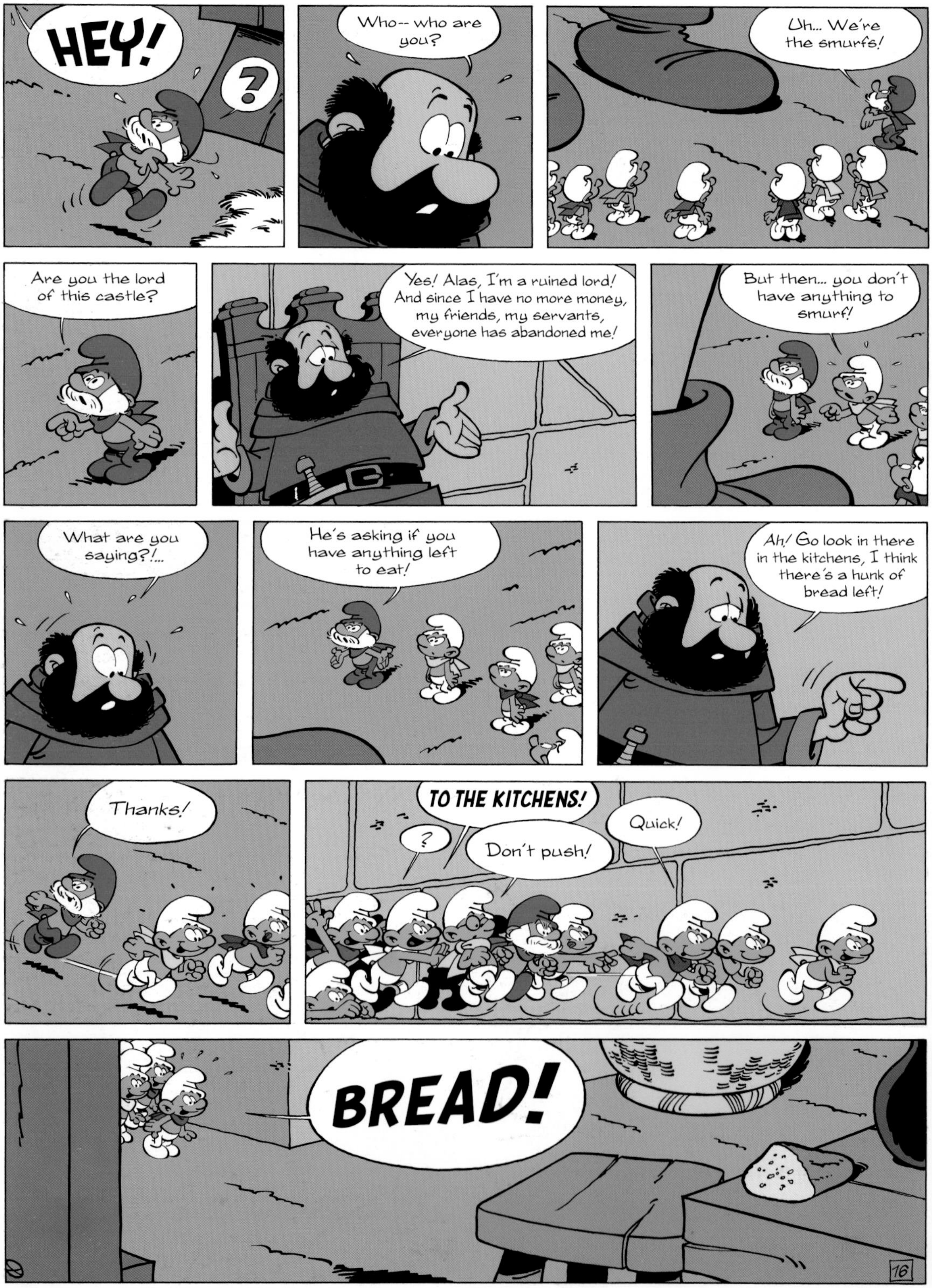
HEY!
?
Who-- who are you?
Uh... We're the smurfs!
Are you the lord of this castle?
Yes! Alas, I'm a ruined lord! And since I have no more money, my friends, my servants, everyone has abandoned me!
But then... you don't have anything to smurf!
What are you saying?!...
He's asking if you have anything left to eat!
Ah! Go look in there in the kitchens, I think there's a hunk of bread left!
Thanks!
TO THE KITCHENS!
?
Don't push!
Quick!
BREAD!
16

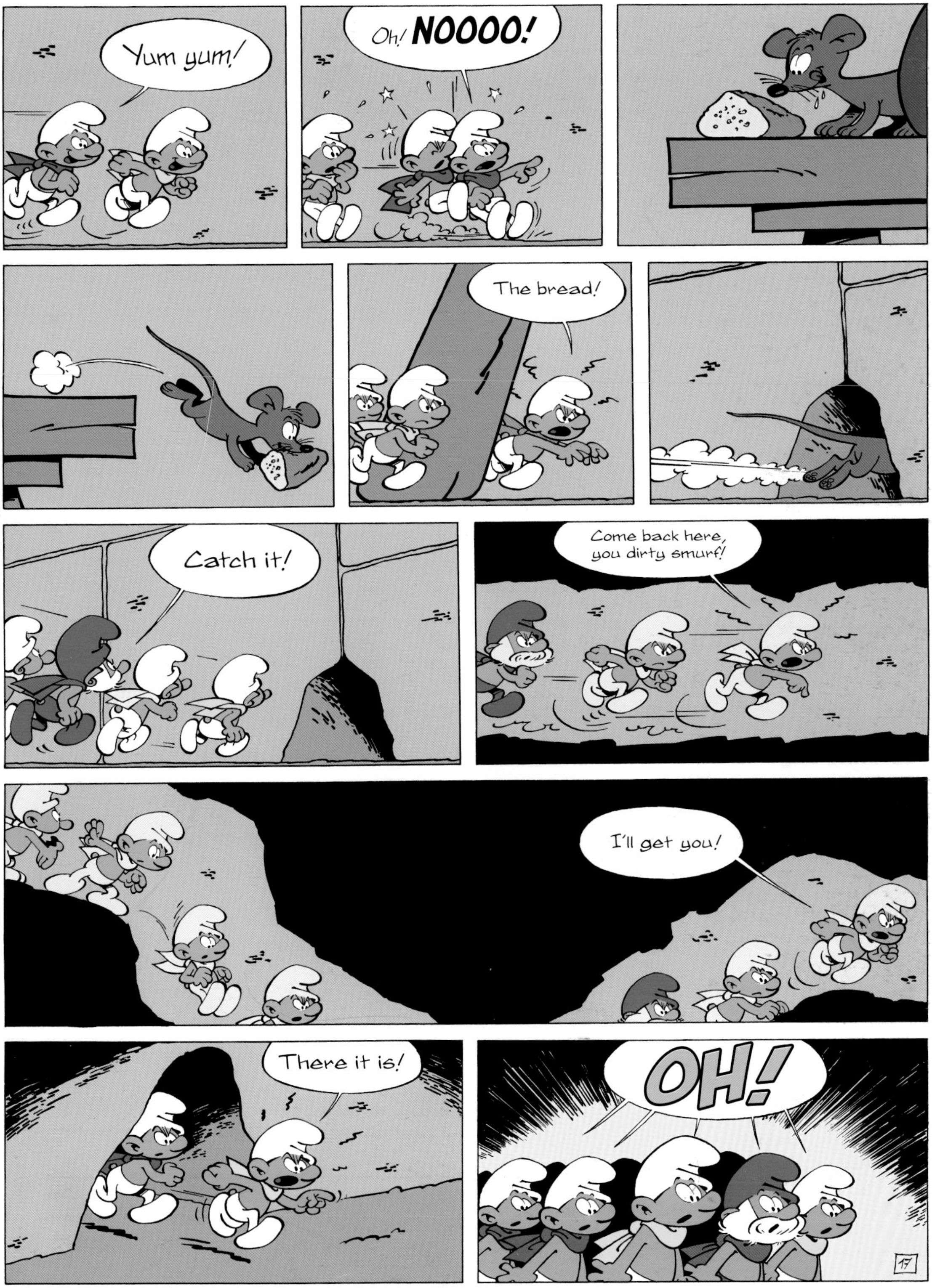
Yum yum!
Oh! NOOOO!
The bread!
Catch it!
Come back here, you dirty smurf!
I'll get you!
There it is!
OH!
17

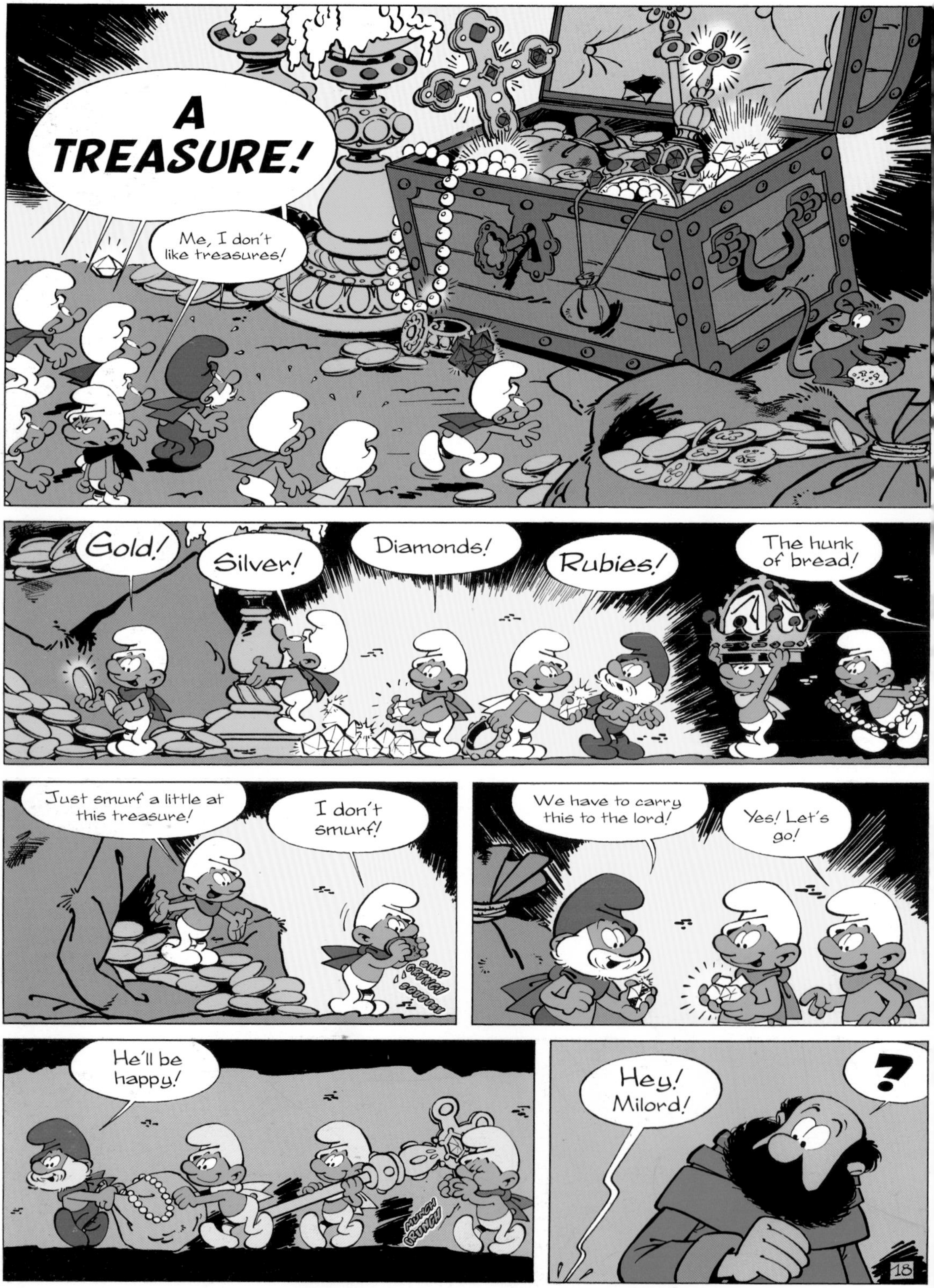
A TREASURE!
Me, I don't like treasures!
Gold!
Silver!
Diamonds!
Rubies!
The hunk of bread!
Just smurf a little at this treasure!
I don't smurf!
SNAP
CRUNCH
SQUOOSH
We have to carry this to the lord!
Yes! Let's go!
He'll be happy!
MUNCH
CRUNCH
Hey! Milord!
?
18

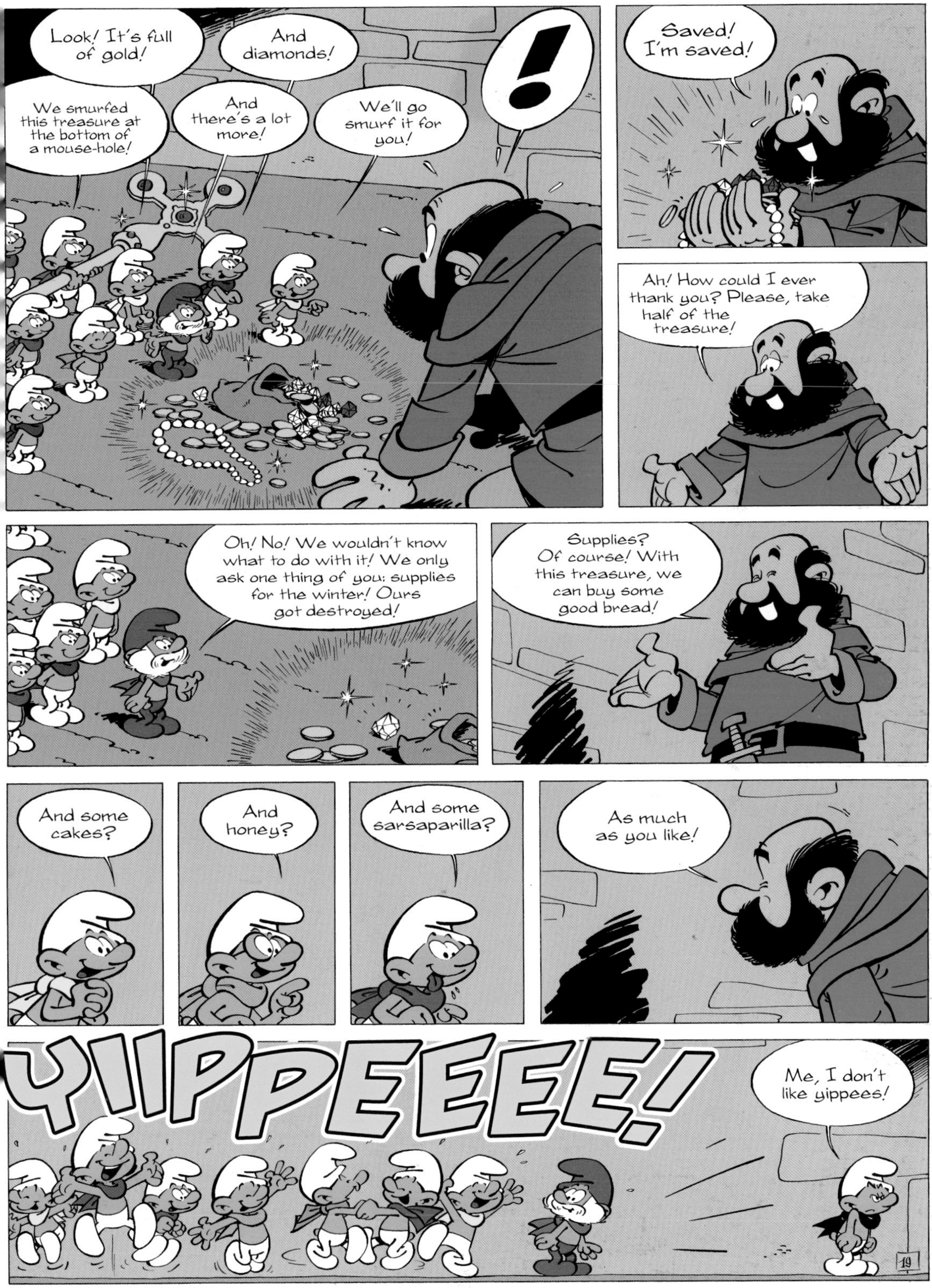
Look! It's full of gold!
And diamonds!
We smurfed this treasure at the bottom of a mouse-hole!
And there's a lot more!
We'll go smurf it for you!
!
Saved! I'm saved!
Ah! How could I ever thank you? Please, take half of the treasure!
Oh! No! We wouldn't know what to do with it! We only ask one thing of you: supplies for the winter! Ours got destroyed!
Supplies? Of course! With this treasure, we can buy some good bread!
And some cakes?
And honey?
And some sarsaparilla?
As much as you like!
YIIPPEEEE!
Me, I don't like yippees!
19

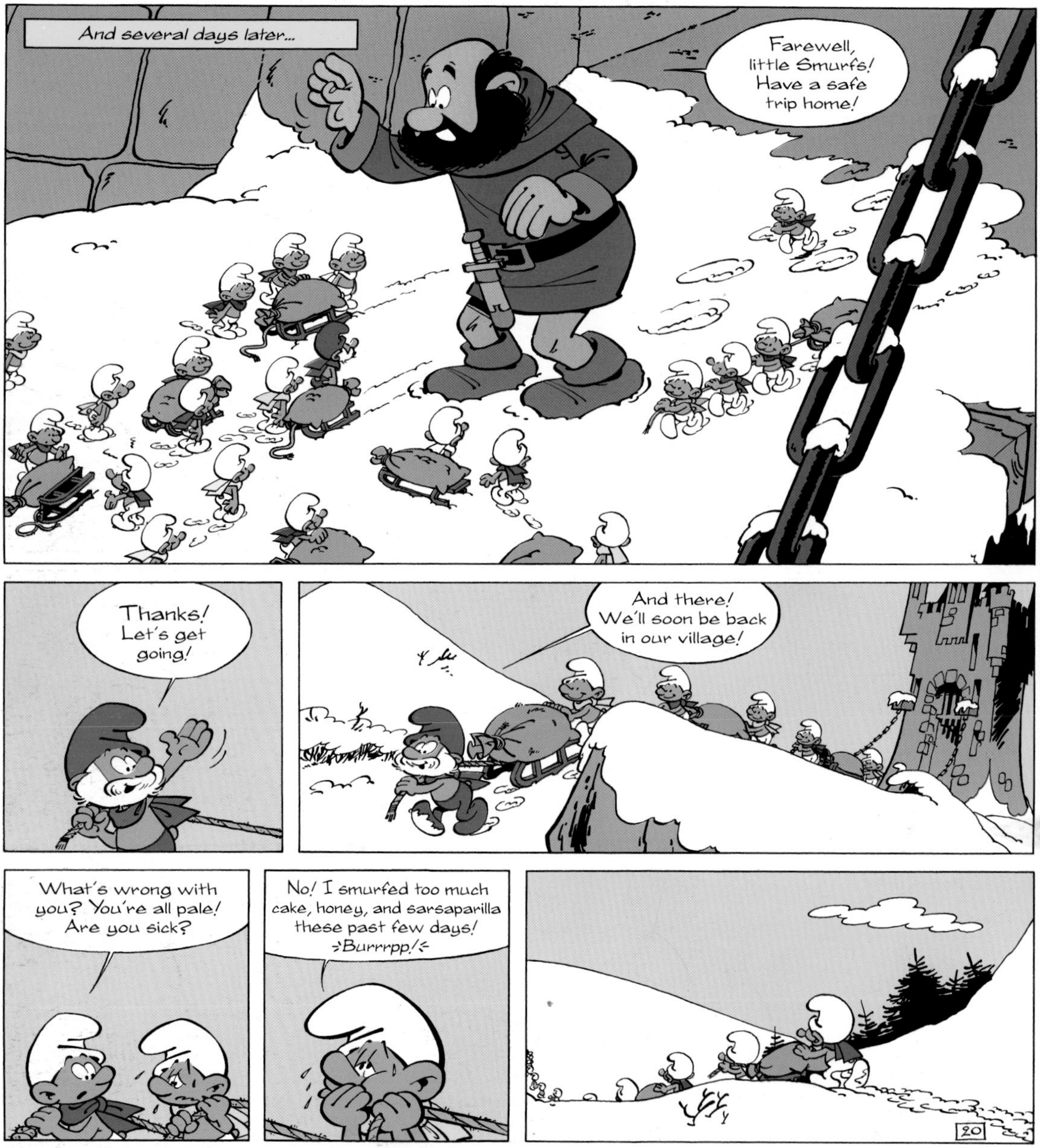
And several days later...
Farewell, little Smurfs! Have a safe trip home!
Thanks! Let's get going!
And there! We'll soon be back in our village!
What's wrong with you? You're all pale! Are you sick?
No! I smurfed too much cake, honey, and sarsaparilla these past few days! ≫Burrrpp!≪
20

And that was the **END** of the Hungry Smurfs.

THE SMURFS AND THE EGG

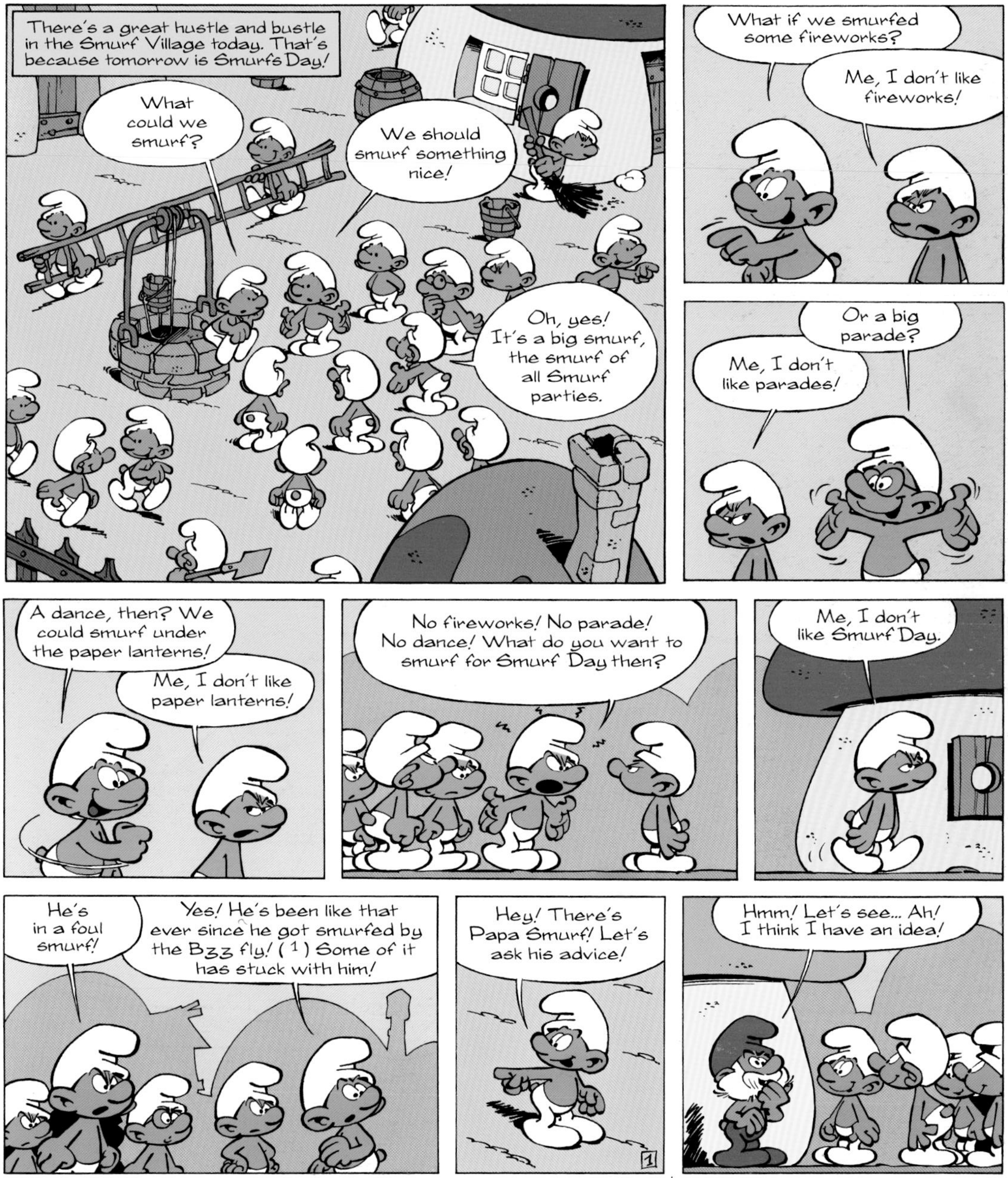

There's a great hustle and bustle in the Smurf Village today. That's because tomorrow is Smurfs Day!
What could we smurf?
We should smurf something nice!
Oh, yes! It's a big smurf, the smurf of all Smurf parties.
What if we smurfed some fireworks?
Me, I don't like fireworks!
Or a big parade?
Me, I don't like parades!
A dance, then? We could smurf under the paper lanterns!
Me, I don't like paper lanterns!
No fireworks! No parade! No dance! What do you want to smurf for Smurf Day then?
Me, I don't like Smurf Day.
He's in a foul smurf!
Yes! He's been like that ever since he got smurfed by the Bzz fly! (1) Some of it has stuck with him!
Hey! There's Papa Smurf! Let's ask his advice!
Hmm! Let's see... Ah! I think I have an idea!
1

(1) See THE SMURFS 3 IN 1 #1 "The Purple Smurfs" or THE SMURFS ANTHOLOGY Vol. 1.

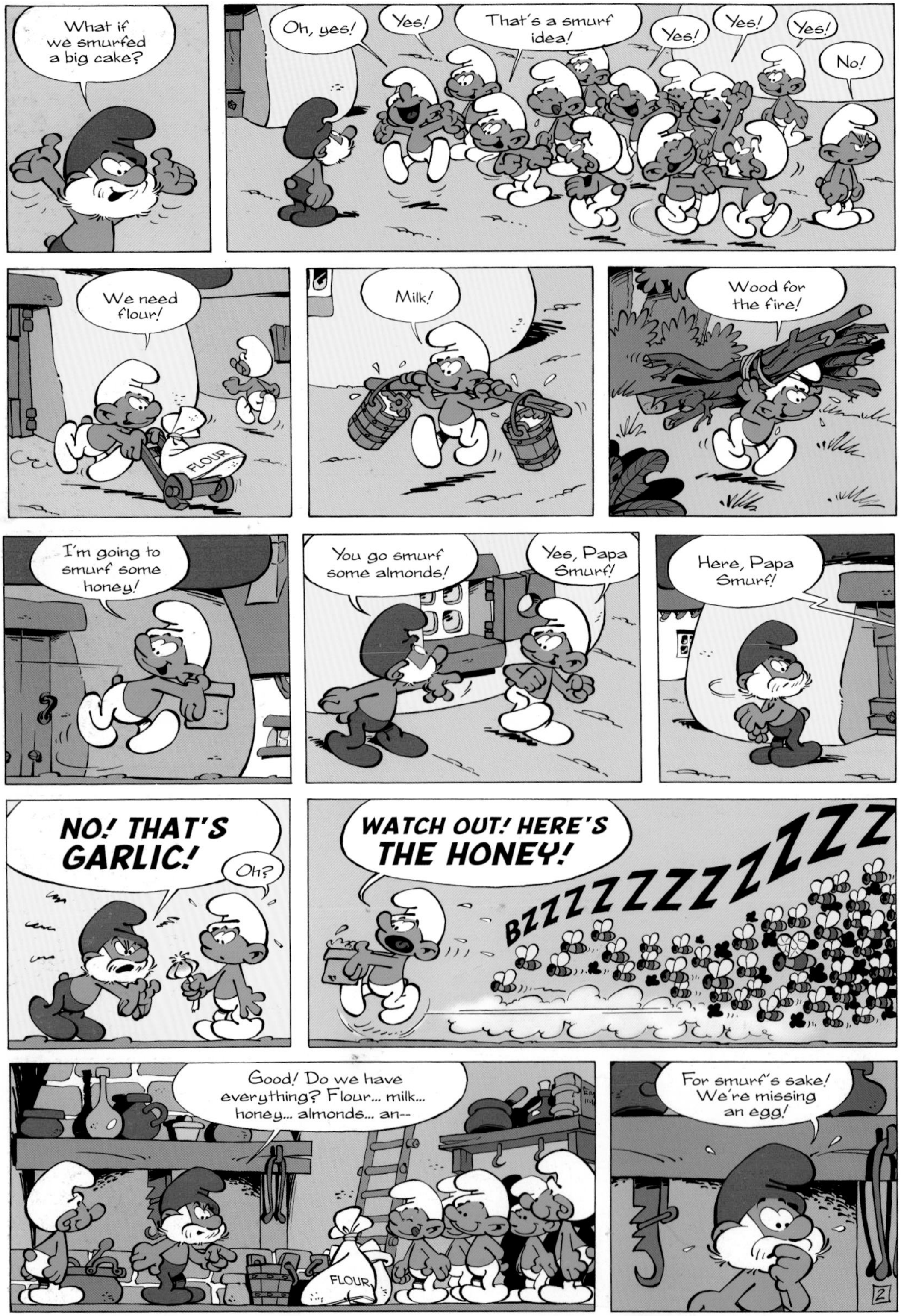
What if we smurfed a big cake?
Oh, yes!
Yes!
That's a smurf idea!
Yes!
Yes!
Yes!
No!
We need flour!
FLOUR
Milk!
Wood for the fire!
I'm going to smurf some honey!
You go smurf some almonds!
Yes, Papa Smurf!
Here, Papa Smurf!
NO! THAT'S GARLIC!
Oh?
WATCH OUT! HERE'S THE HONEY!
BZZZZZZZZZZZZ
Good! Do we have everything? Flour... milk... honey... almonds... an--
FLOUR
For smurf's sake! We're missing an egg!
2

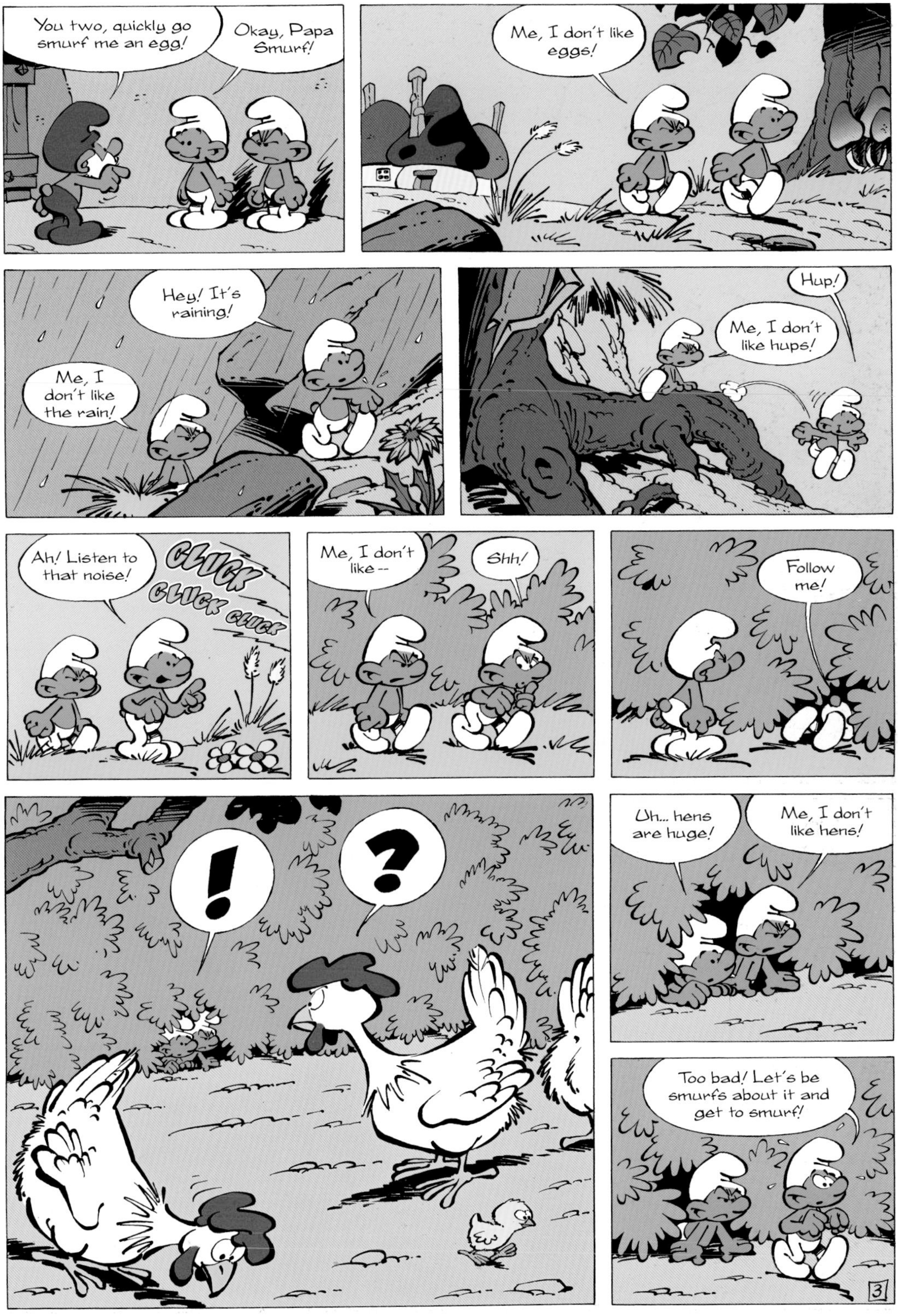
You two, quickly go smurf me an egg!
Okay, Papa Smurf!
Me, I don't like eggs!
Hey! It's raining!
Me, I don't like the rain!
Hup!
Me, I don't like hups!
Ah! Listen to that noise!
CLUCK
CLUCK
CLUCK
Me, I don't like --
Shh!
Follow me!
!
?
Uh... hens are huge!
Me, I don't like hens!
Too bad! Let's be smurfs about it and get to smurf!
3

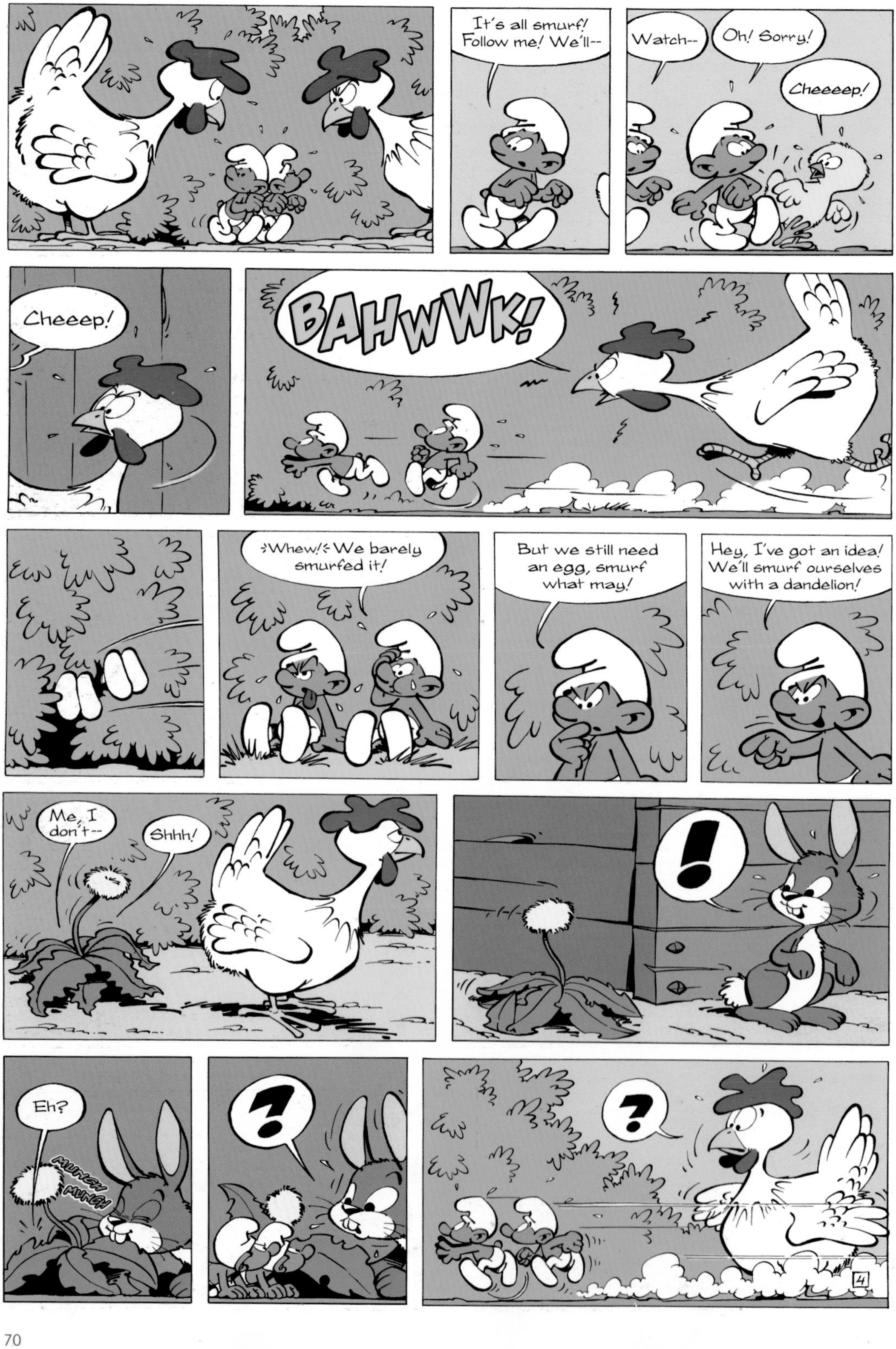
It's all smurf! Follow me! We'll--
Watch--
Oh! Sorry!
Cheeeep!
Cheeep!
BAHWWK!
Whew! We barely smurfed it!
But we still need an egg, smurf what may!
Hey, I've got an idea! We'll smurf ourselves with a dandelion!
Me, I don't--
Shhh!
!
Eh?
MUNCH MUNCH
?
?
4

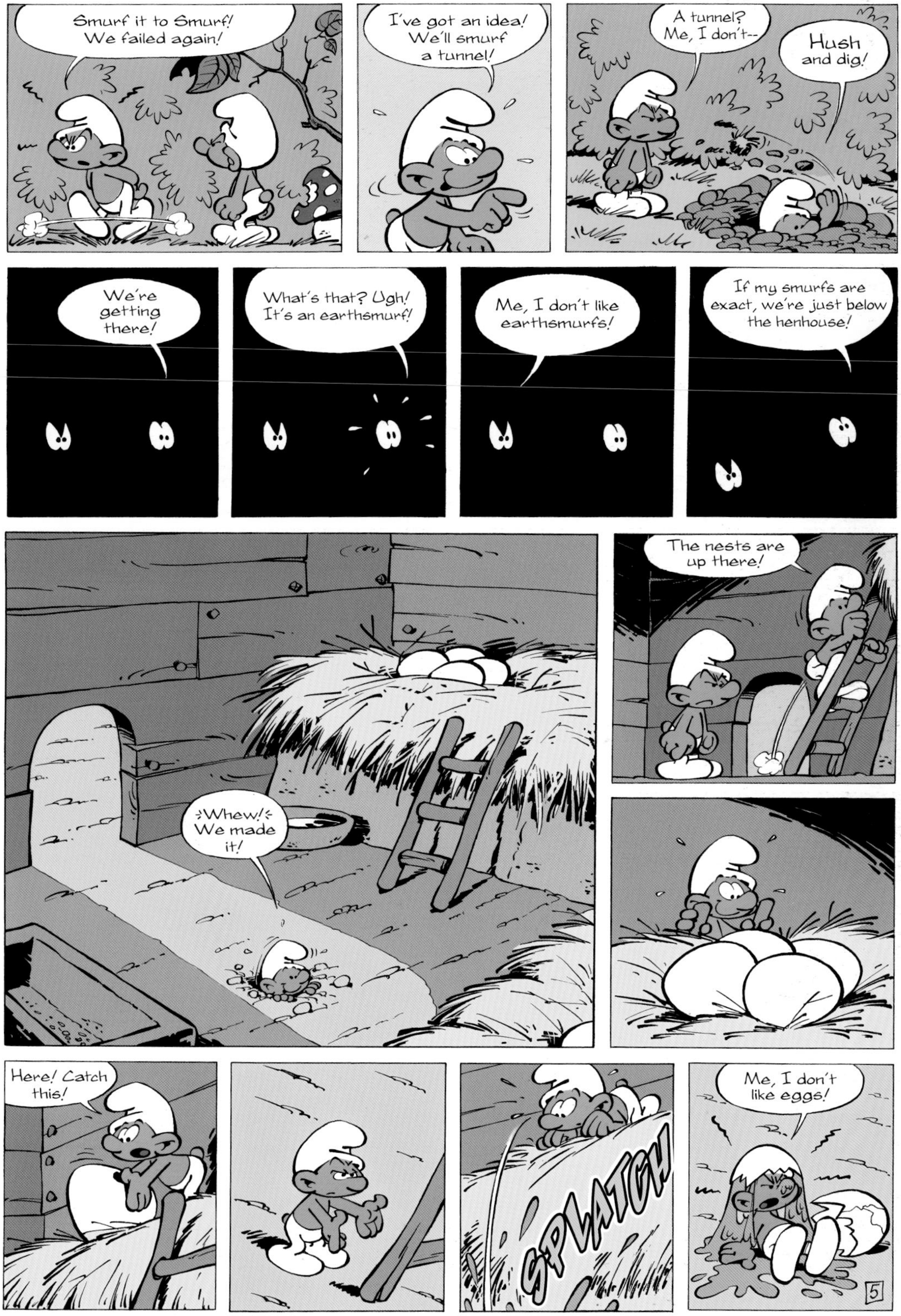
Smurf it to Smurf! We failed again!
I've got an idea! We'll smurf a tunnel!
A tunnel? Me, I don't--
Hush and dig!
We're getting there!
What's that? Ugh! It's an earthsmurf!
Me, I don't like earthsmurfs!
If my smurfs are exact, we're just below the henhouse!
Whew! We made it!
The nests are up there!
Here! Catch this!
SPLATCH
Me, I don't like eggs!
5

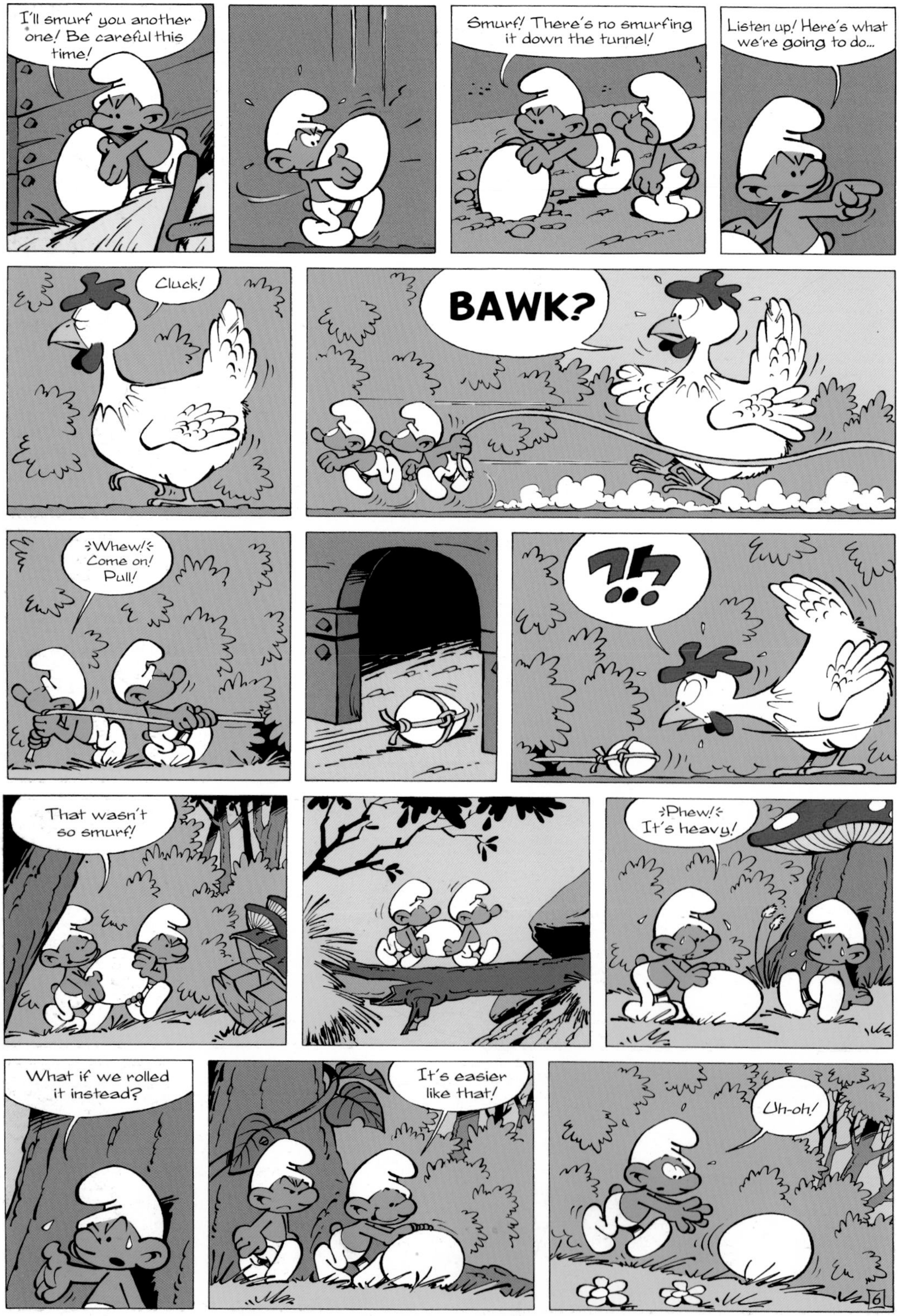

I'll smurf you another one! Be careful this time!
Smurf! There's no smurfing it down the tunnel!
Listen up! Here's what we're going to do...
Cluck!
BAWK?
Whew! Come on! Pull!
?!?...
That wasn't so smurf!
Phew! It's heavy!
What if we rolled it instead?
It's easier like that!
Uh-oh!
6

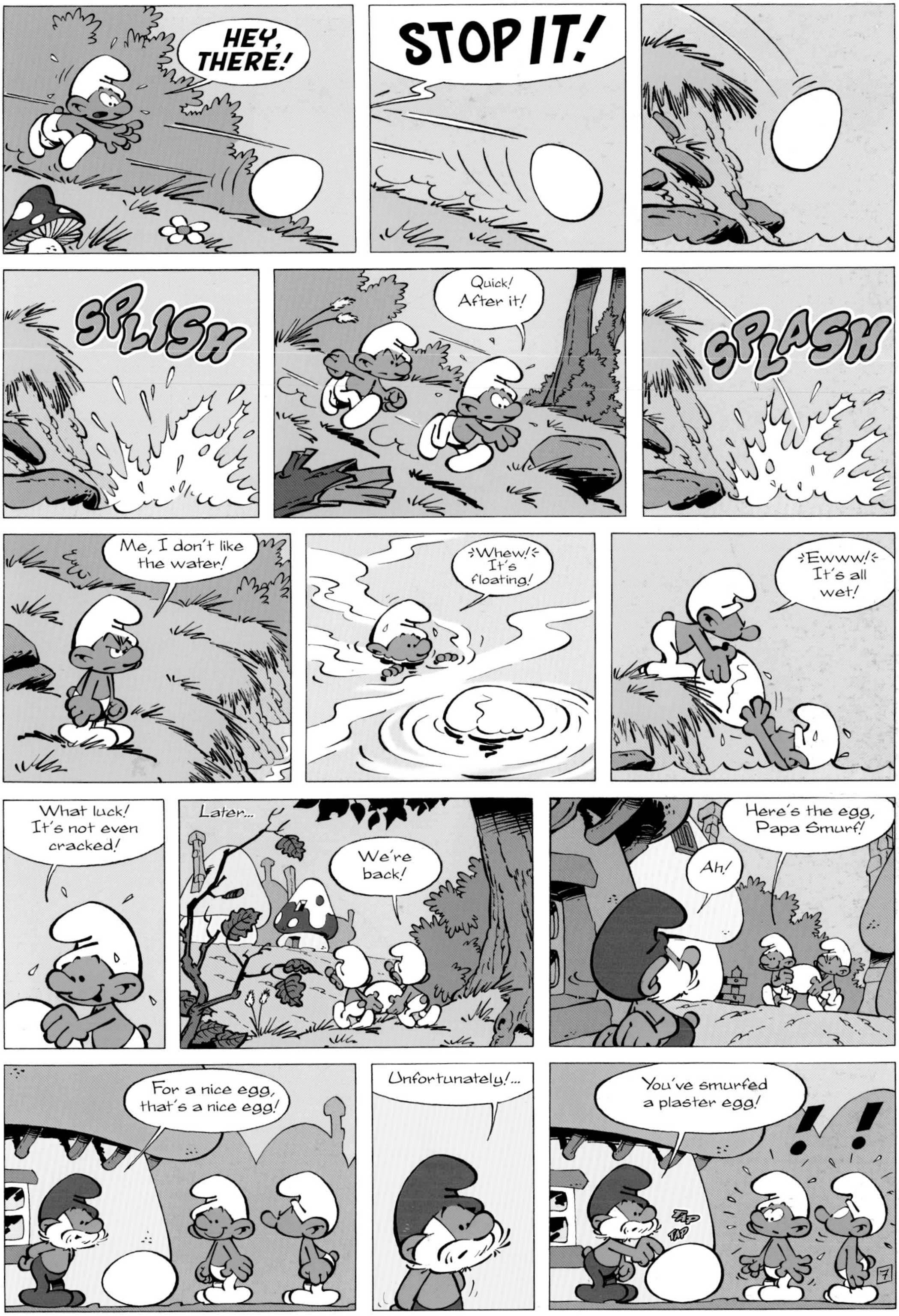
HEY, THERE!
STOP IT!
SPLISH
Quick! After it!
SPLASH
Me, I don't like the water!
Whew! It's floating!
Ewww! It's all wet!
What luck! It's not even cracked!
Later...
We're back!
Here's the egg, Papa Smurf!
Ah!
For a nice egg, that's a nice egg!
Unfortunately!...
You've smurfed a plaster egg!
TAP TAP
! !
7

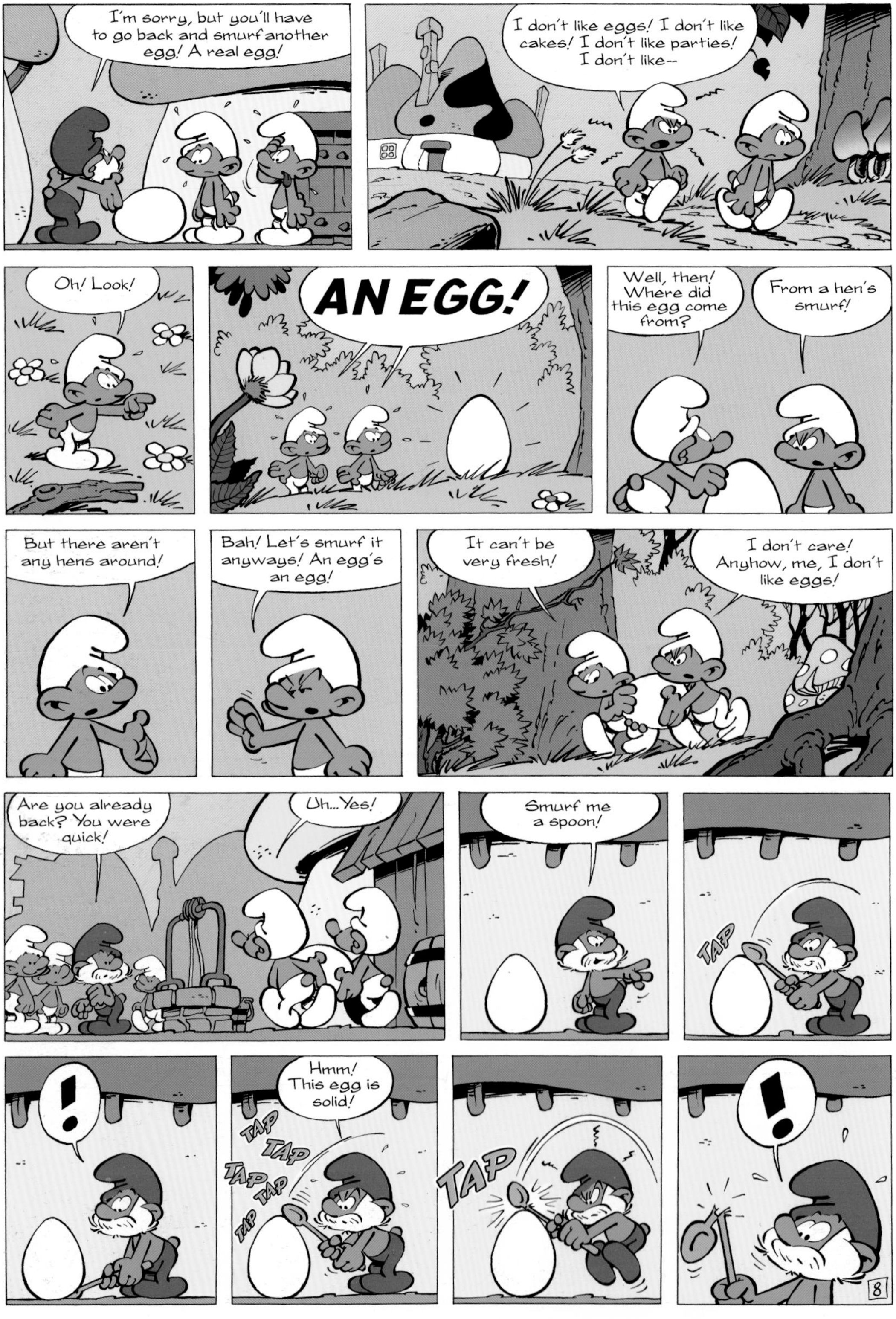
I'm sorry, but you'll have to go back and smurf another egg! A real egg!
I don't like eggs! I don't like cakes! I don't like parties! I don't like--
Oh! Look!
AN EGG!
Well, then! Where did this egg come from?
From a hen's smurf!
But there aren't any hens around!
Bah! Let's smurf it anyways! An egg's an egg!
It can't be very fresh!
I don't care! Anyhow, me, I don't like eggs!
Are you already back? You were quick!
Uh... Yes!
Smurf me a spoon!
TAP
!
Hmm! This egg is solid!
TAP TAP TAP TAP TAP
TAP
!
8

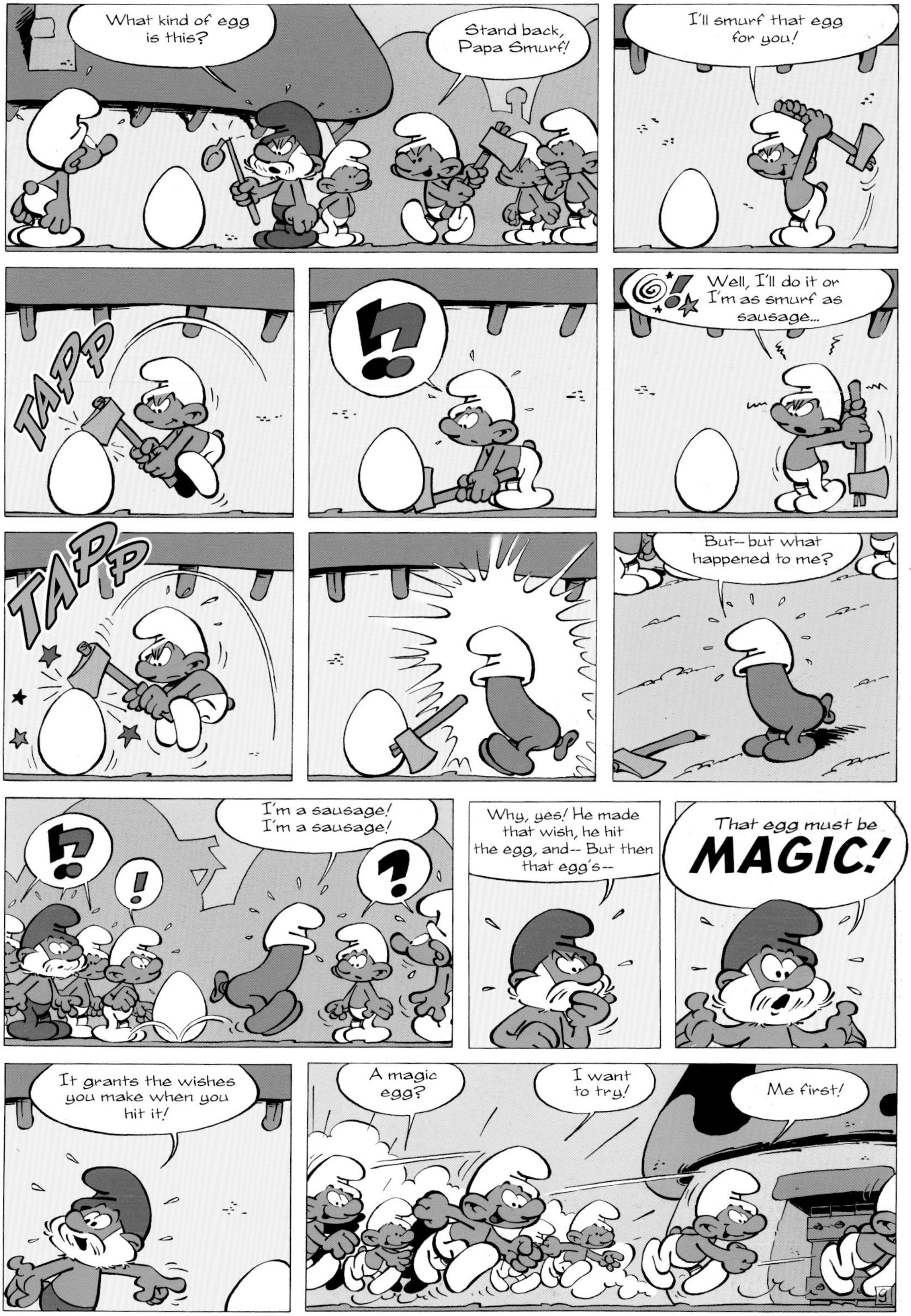
What kind of egg is this?
Stand back, Papa Smurf!
I'll smurf that egg for you!
TAPP
Well, I'll do it or I'm as smurf as sausage...
TAPP
But-- but what happened to me?
I'm a sausage! I'm a sausage!
Why, yes! He made that wish, he hit the egg, and-- But then that egg's--
That egg must be MAGIC!
It grants the wishes you make when you hit it!
A magic egg?
I want to try!
Me first!
9

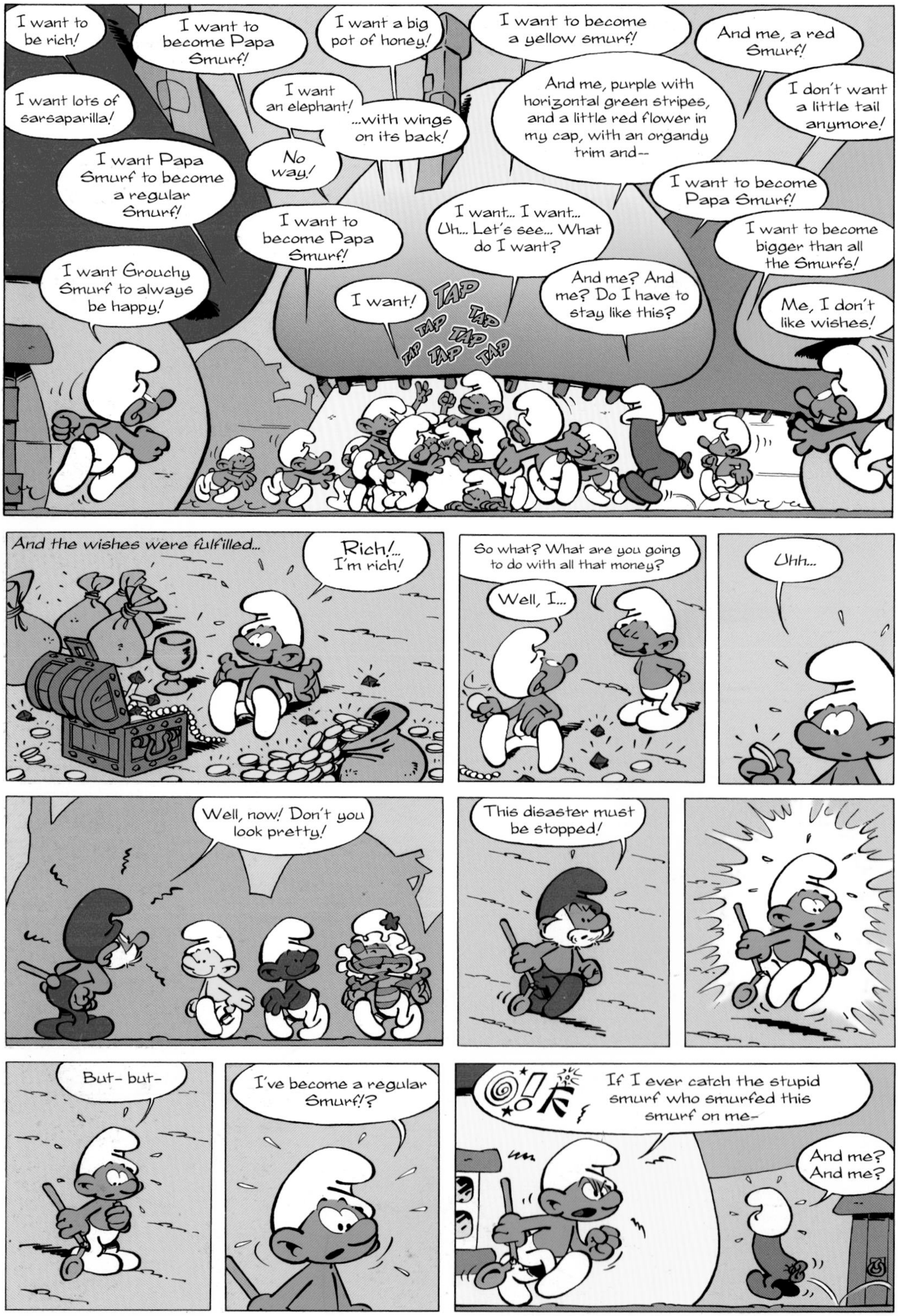
I want to be rich!
I want to become Papa Smurf!
I want a big pot of honey!
I want to become a yellow smurf!
And me, a red Smurf!
I want lots of sarsaparilla!
I want an elephant!
...with wings on its back!
No way!
And me, purple with horizontal green stripes, and a little red flower in my cap, with an organdy trim and--
I don't want a little tail anymore!
I want Papa Smurf to become a regular Smurf!
I want to become Papa Smurf!
I want... I want... Uh... Let's see... What do I want?
I want to become Papa Smurf!
I want to become bigger than all the Smurfs!
I want Grouchy Smurf to always be happy!
I want!
TAP TAP TAP TAP TAP TAP TAP TAP
And me? And me? Do I have to stay like this?
Me, I don't like wishes!
And the wishes were fulfilled...
Rich!... I'm rich!
So what? What are you going to do with all that money?
Well, I...
Uhh...
Well, now! Don't you look pretty!
This disaster must be stopped!
But- but-
I've become a regular Smurf!?
If I ever catch the stupid smurf who smurfed this smurf on me-
And me? And me?

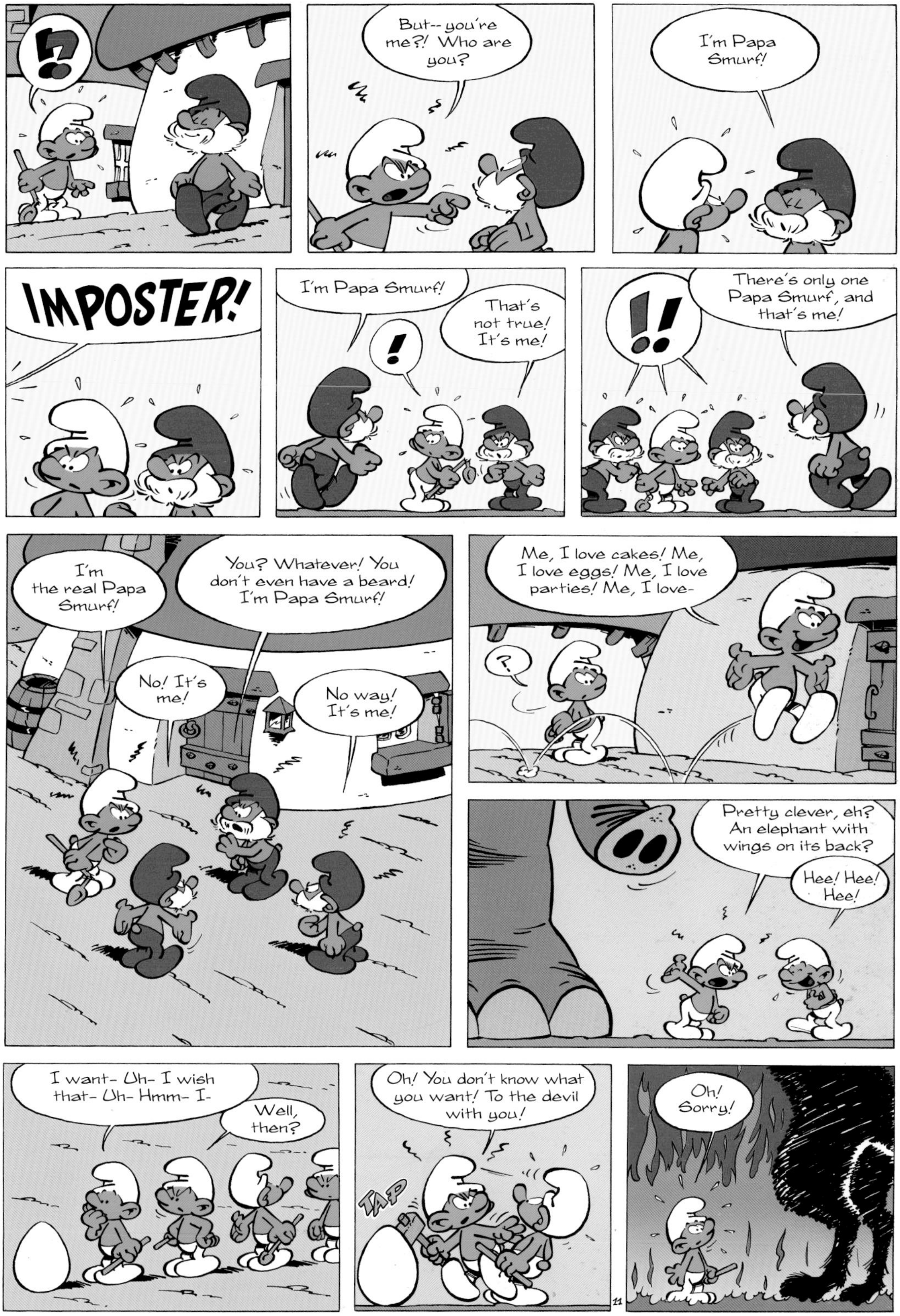
!?
But-- you're me?! Who are you?
I'm Papa Smurf!
IMPOSTER!
I'm Papa Smurf!
!
That's not true! It's me!
!!
There's only one Papa Smurf, and that's me!
I'm the real Papa Smurf!
You? Whatever! You don't even have a beard! I'm Papa Smurf!
No! It's me!
No way! It's me!
Me, I love cakes! Me, I love eggs! Me, I love parties! Me, I love-
?
Pretty clever, eh? An elephant with wings on its back?
Hee! Hee! Hee!
I want- Uh- I wish that- Uh- Hmm- I-
Well, then?
Oh! You don't know what you want! To the devil with you!
TAP
Oh! Sorry!

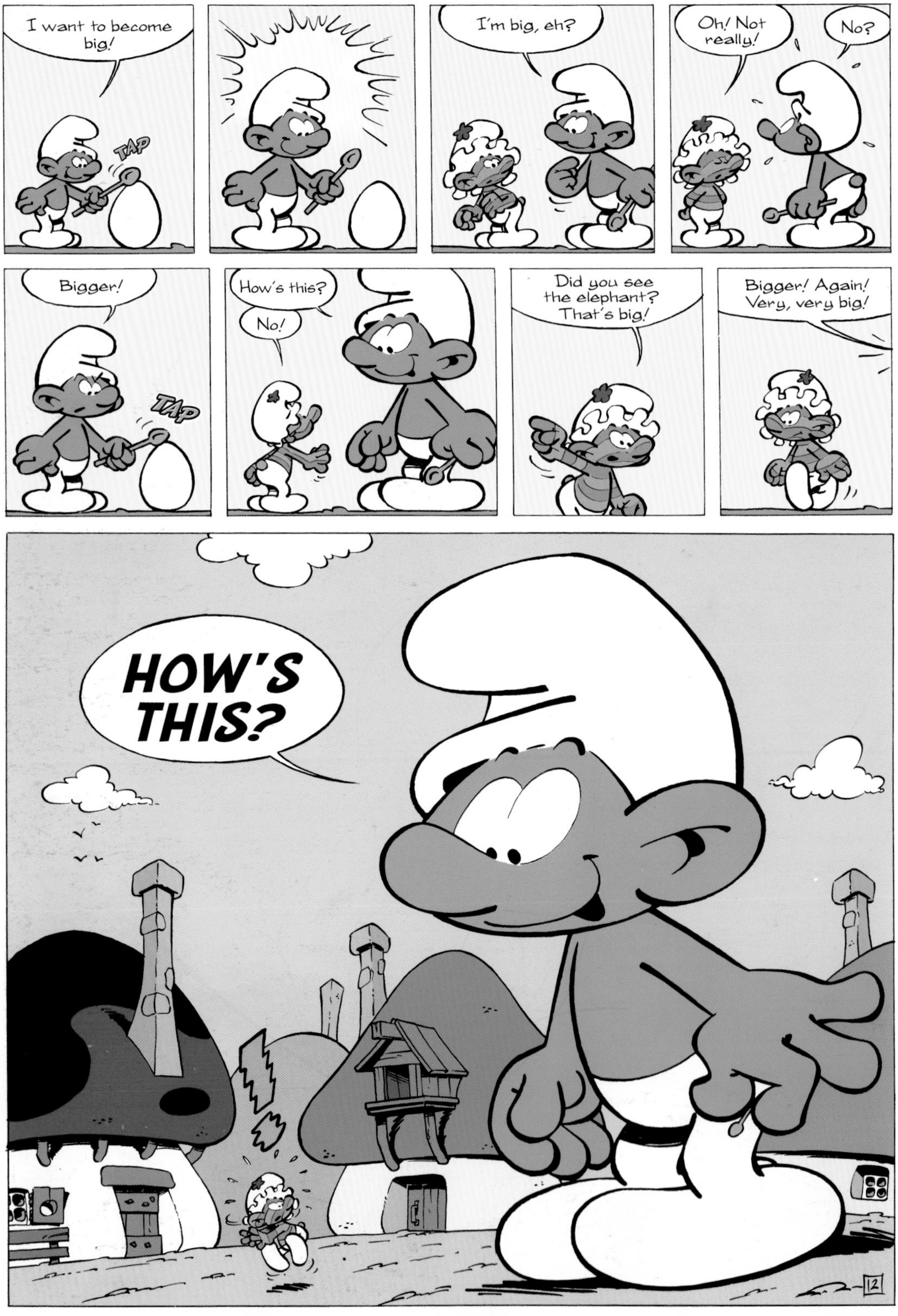
I want to become big!
TAP
I'm big, eh?
Oh! Not really!
No?
Bigger!
TAP
How's this?
No!
Did you see the elephant? That's big!
Bigger! Again! Very, very big!
HOW'S THIS?
12

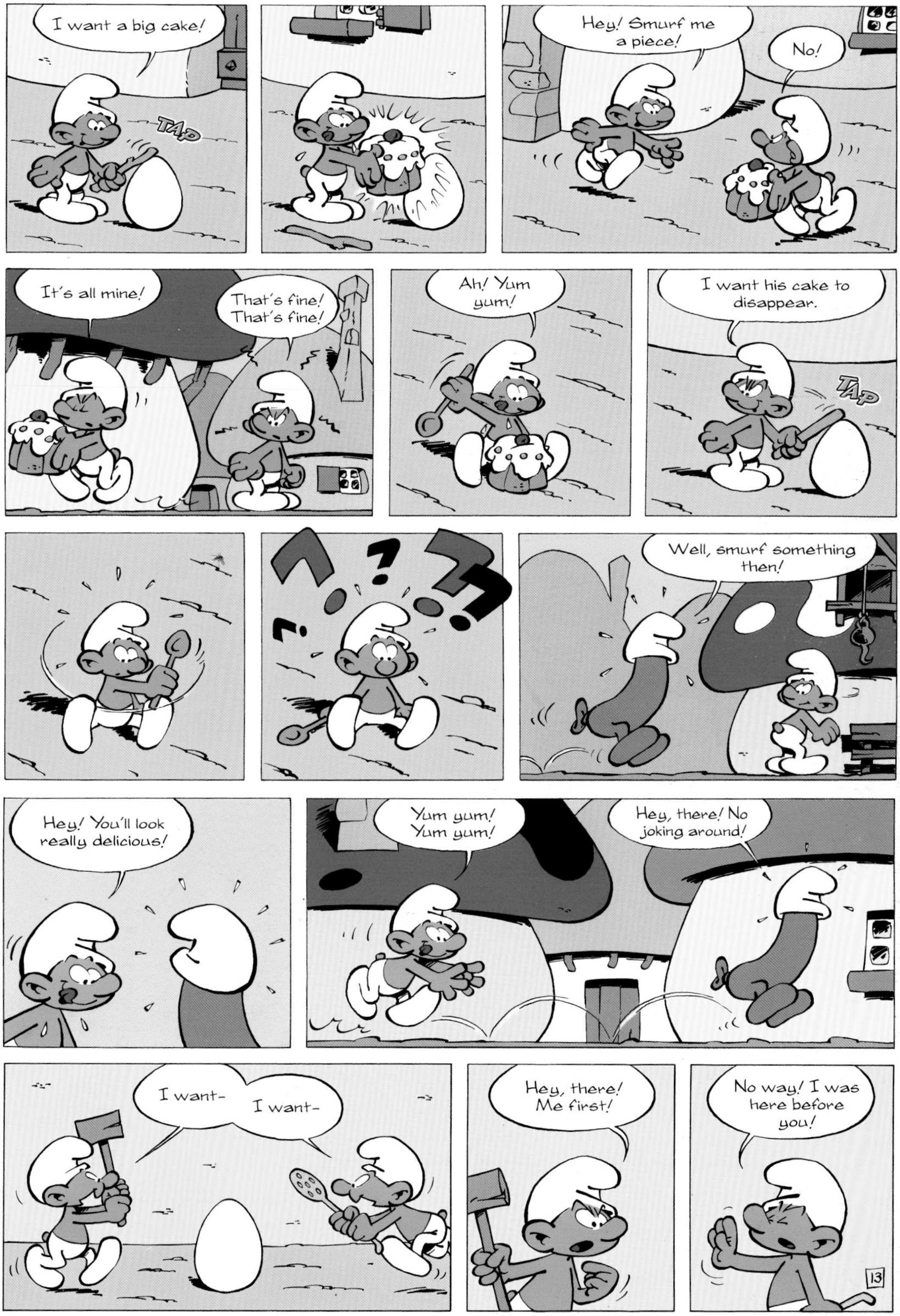
I want a big cake!
TAP
Hey! Smurf me a piece!
No!
It's all mine!
That's fine! That's fine!
Ah! Yum yum!
I want his cake to disappear.
TAP
Well, smurf something then!
Hey! You'll look really delicious!
Yum yum! Yum yum!
Hey, there! No joking around!
I want-
I want-
Hey, there! Me first!
No way! I was here before you!
13

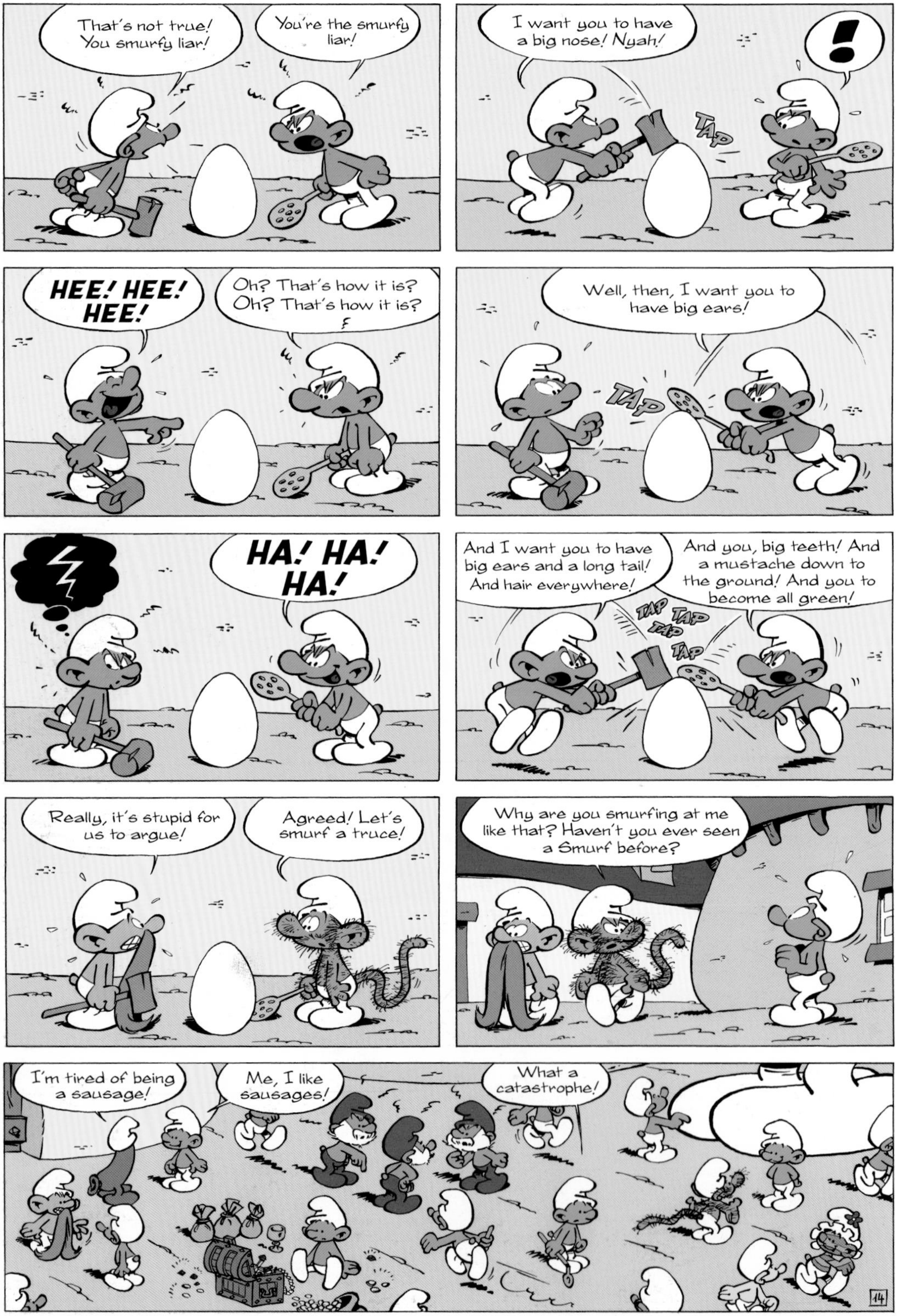
That's not true! You smurfy liar!
You're the smurfy liar!
I want you to have a big nose! Nyah!
TAP
!
HEE! HEE! HEE!
Oh? That's how it is? Oh? That's how it is?
Well, then, I want you to have big ears!
TAP
HA! HA! HA!
And I want you to have big ears and a long tail! And hair everywhere!
And you, big teeth! And a mustache down to the ground! And you to become all green!
TAP TAP TAP TAP
Really, it's stupid for us to argue!
Agreed! Let's smurf a truce!
Why are you smurfing at me like that? Haven't you ever seen a Smurf before?
I'm tired of being a sausage!
Me, I like sausages!
What a catastrophe!
14

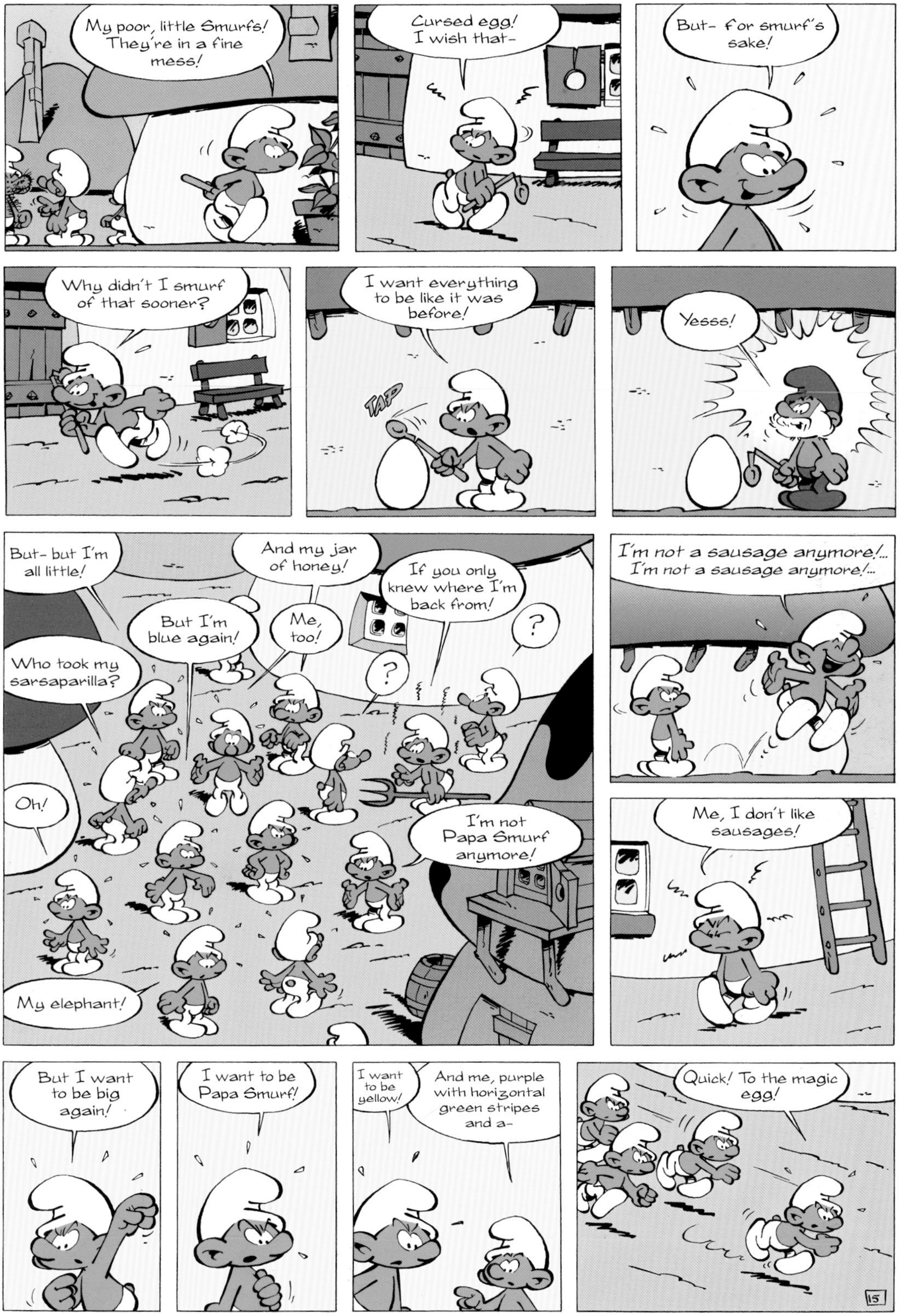
My poor, little Smurfs! They're in a fine mess!
Cursed egg! I wish that-
But- for smurf's sake!
Why didn't I smurf of that sooner?
I want everything to be like it was before!
TAP
Yesss!
But- but I'm all little!
And my jar of honey!
If you only knew where I'm back from!
But I'm blue again!
Me, too!
?
?
Who took my sarsaparilla?
Oh!
I'm not Papa Smurf anymore!
My elephant!
I'm not a sausage anymore!... I'm not a sausage anymore!...
Me, I don't like sausages!
But I want to be big again!
I want to be Papa Smurf!
I want to be yellow!
And me, purple with horizontal green stripes and a-
Quick! To the magic egg!
15

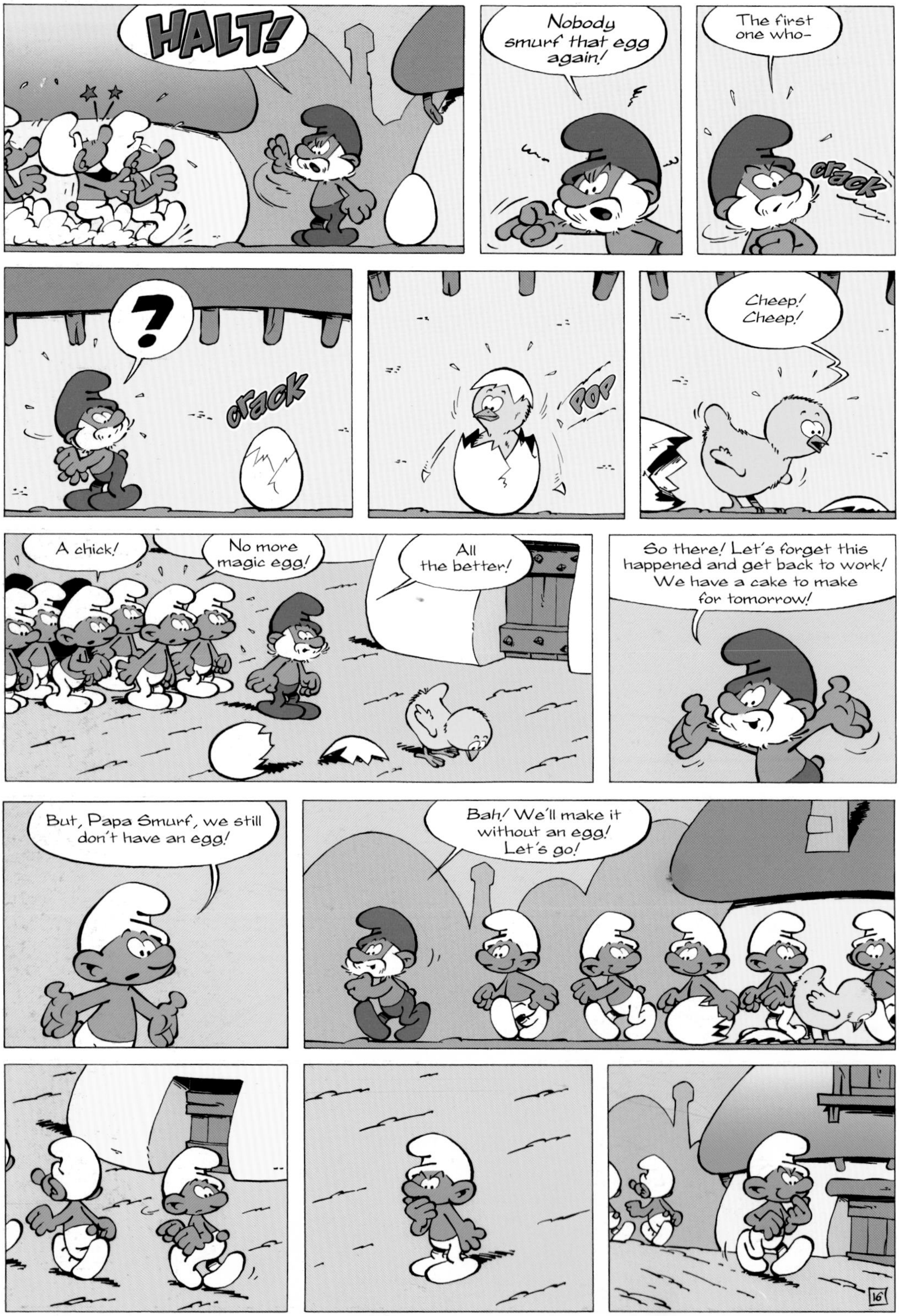

HALT!
Nobody smurf that egg again!
The first one who-
crack
?
crack
POP
Cheep! Cheep!
A chick!
No more magic egg!
All the better!
So there! Let's forget this happened and get back to work! We have a cake to make for tomorrow!
But, Papa Smurf, we still don't have an egg!
Bah! We'll make it without an egg! Let's go!
16

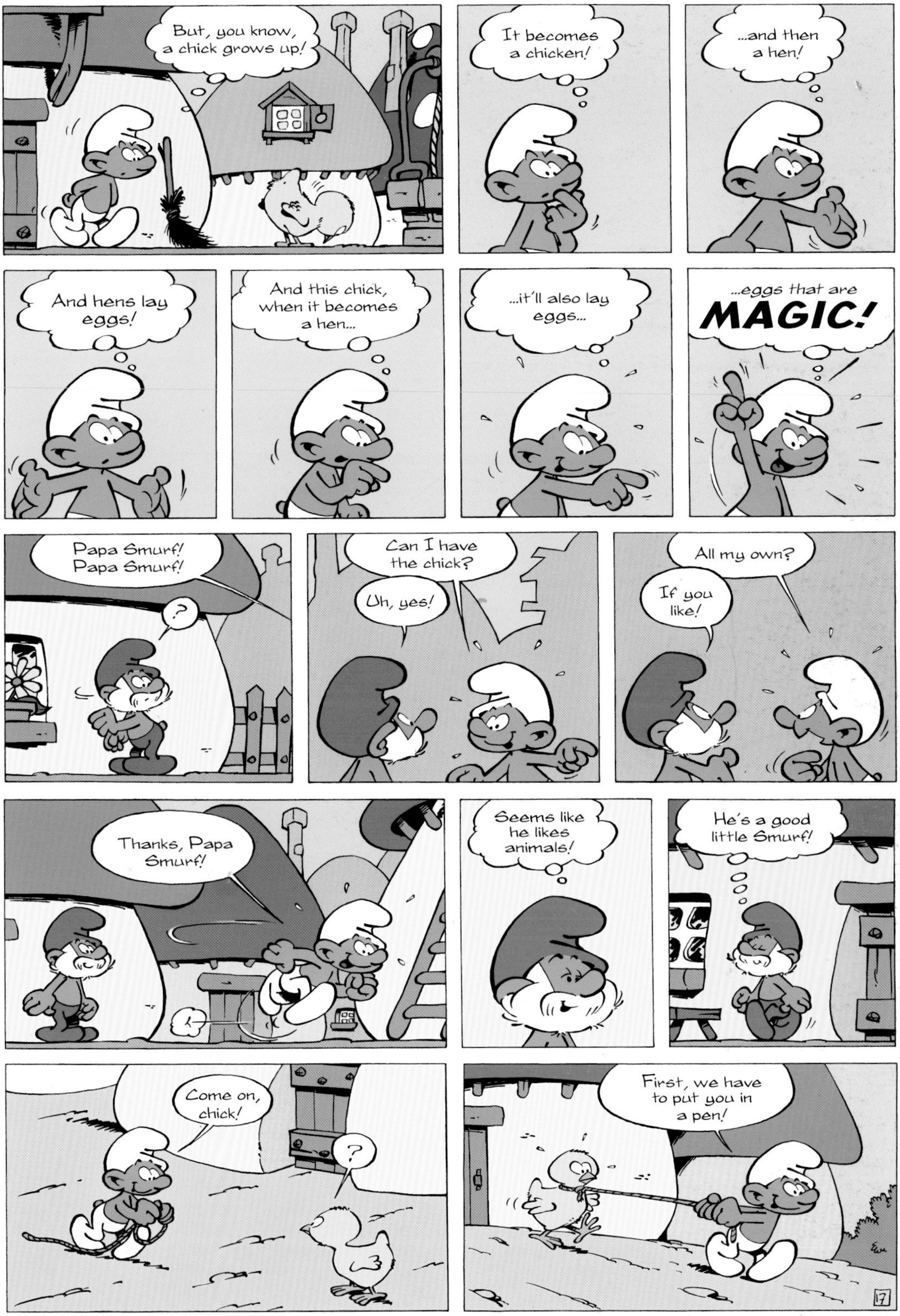

But, you know, a chick grows up!
It becomes a chicken!
...and then a hen!
And hens lay eggs!
And this chick, when it becomes a hen...
...it'll also lay eggs...
...eggs that are MAGIC!
Papa Smurf! Papa Smurf!
?
Can I have the chick?
Uh, yes!
All my own?
If you like!
Thanks, Papa Smurf!
Seems like he likes animals!
He's a good little Smurf!
Come on, chick!
?
First, we have to put you in a pen!
17

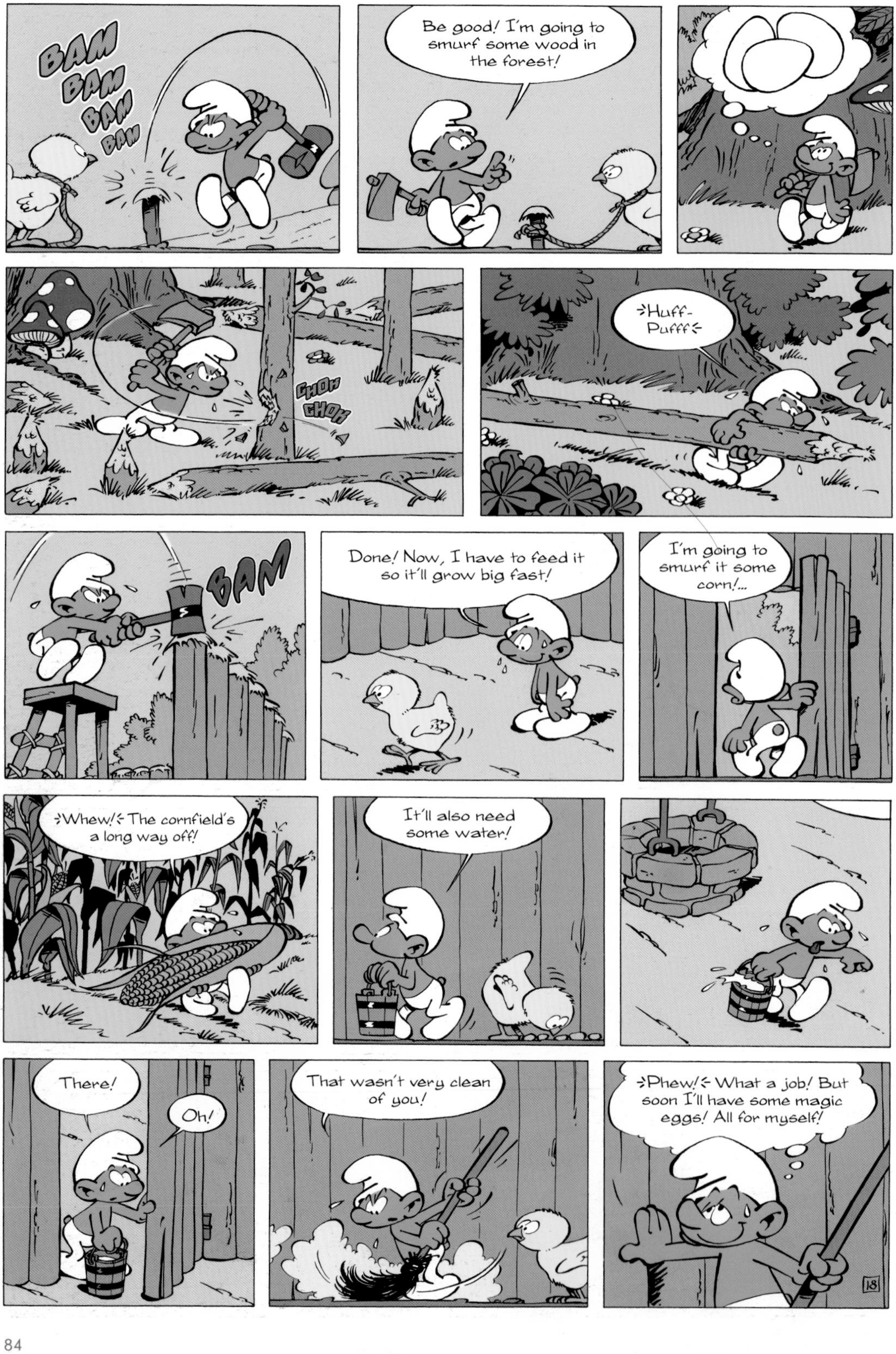
BAM BAM BAM BAM
Be good! I'm going to smurf some wood in the forest!
CHOK CHOK
>Huff- Pufff<
BAM
Done! Now, I have to feed it so it'll grow big fast!
I'm going to smurf it some corn!...
>Whew!< The cornfield's a long way off!
It'll also need some water!
There!
Oh!
That wasn't very clean of you!
>Phew!< What a job! But soon I'll have some magic eggs! All for myself!
18

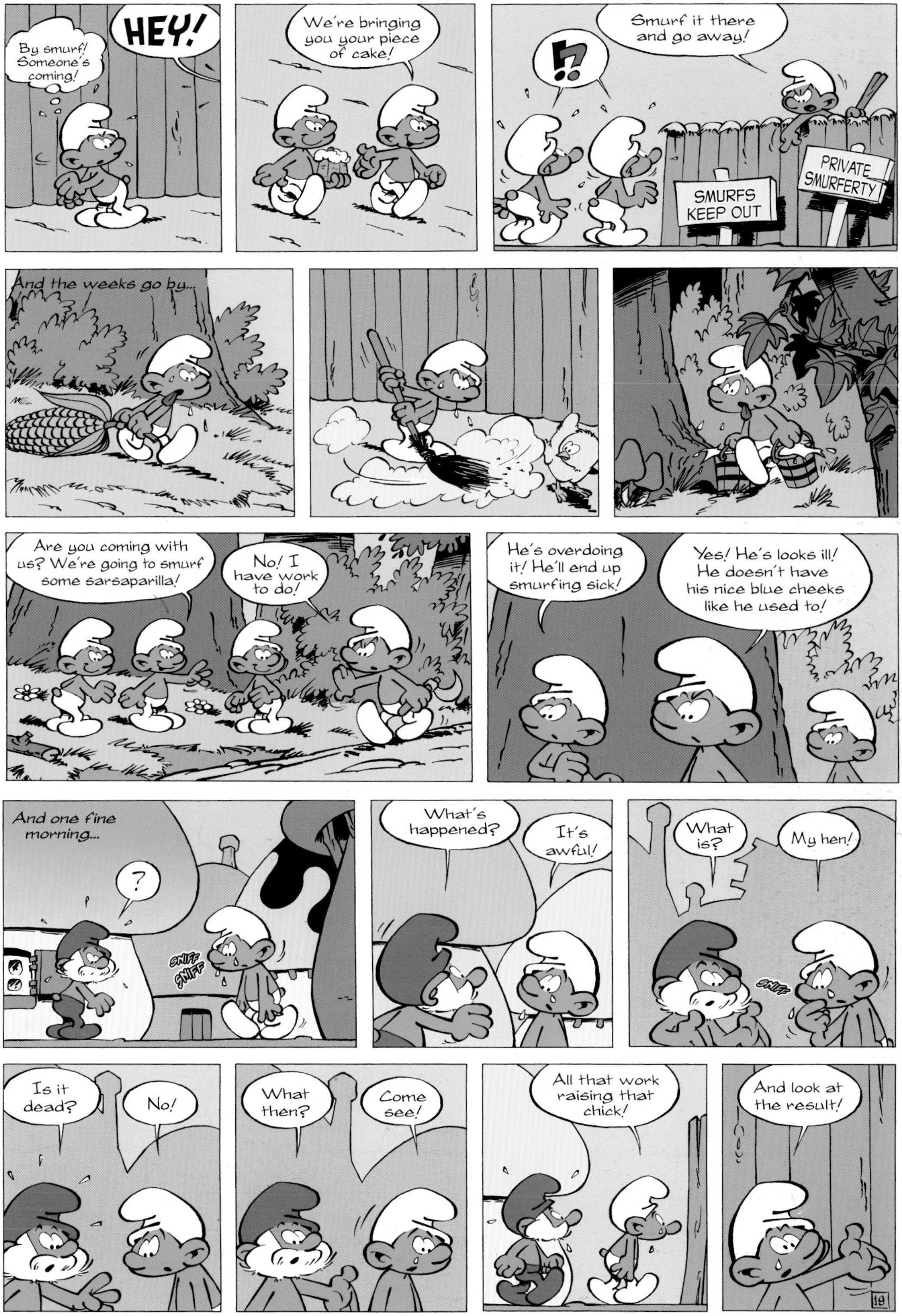
By smurf! Someone's coming!
HEY!
We're bringing you your piece of cake!
?!
Smurf it there and go away!
SMURFS KEEP OUT
PRIVATE SMURFERTY
And the weeks go by...
Are you coming with us? We're going to smurf some sarsaparilla!
No! I have work to do!
He's overdoing it! He'll end up smurfing sick!
Yes! He's looks ill! He doesn't have his nice blue cheeks like he used to!
And one fine morning...
?
SNIFF SNIFF
What's happened?
It's awful!
What is?
My hen!
SNIFF
Is it dead?
No!
What then?
Come see!
All that work raising that chick!
And look at the result!
19

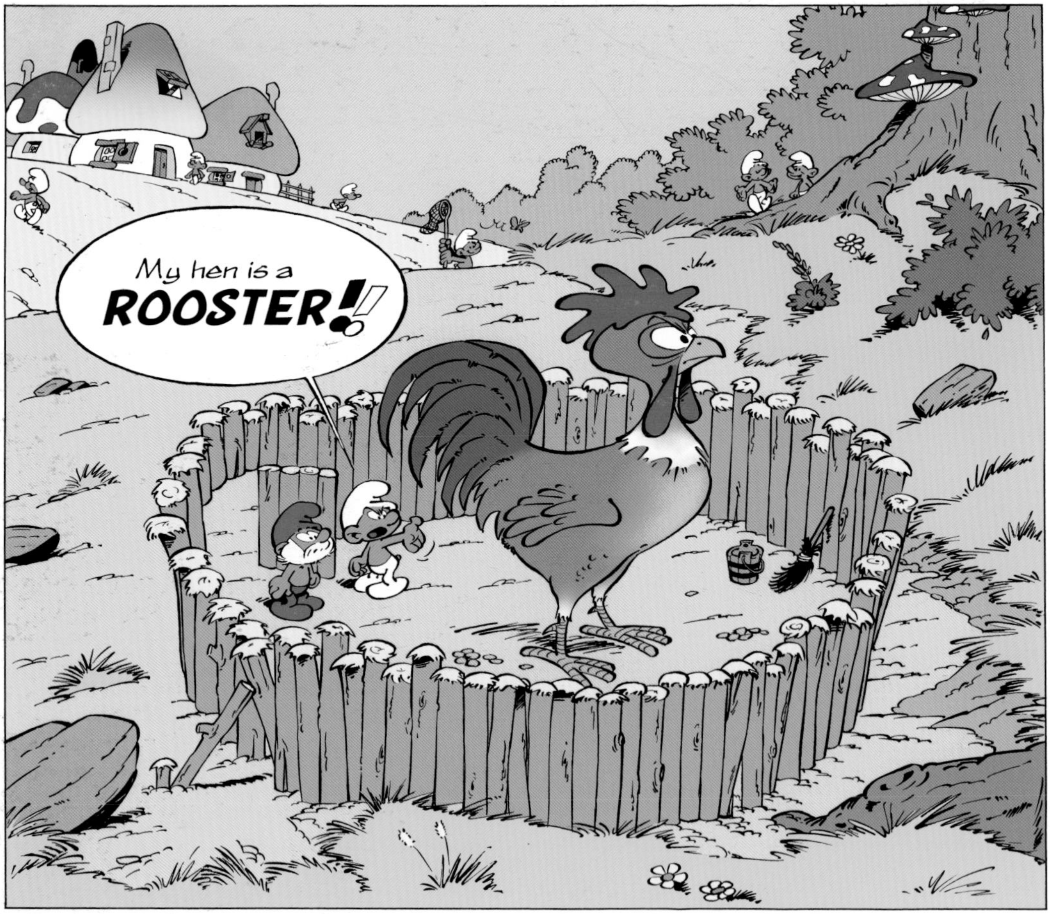
My hen is a ROOSTER!!

THE END

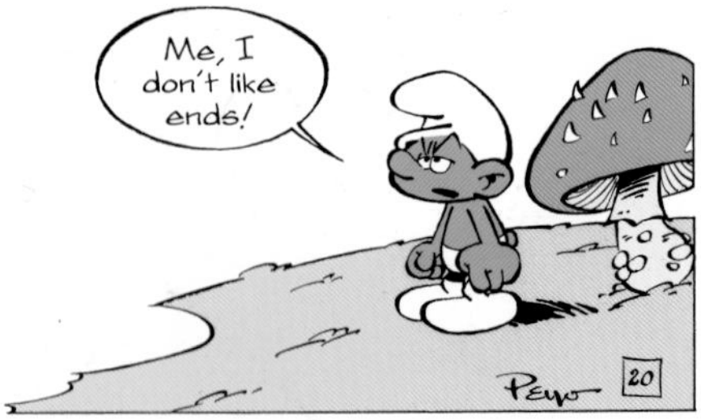
Me, I don't like ends!

THE FAKE SMURF

by Peyo

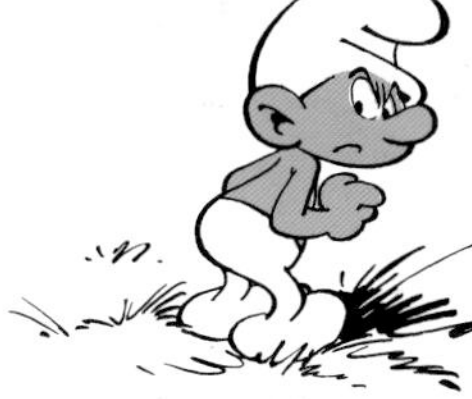

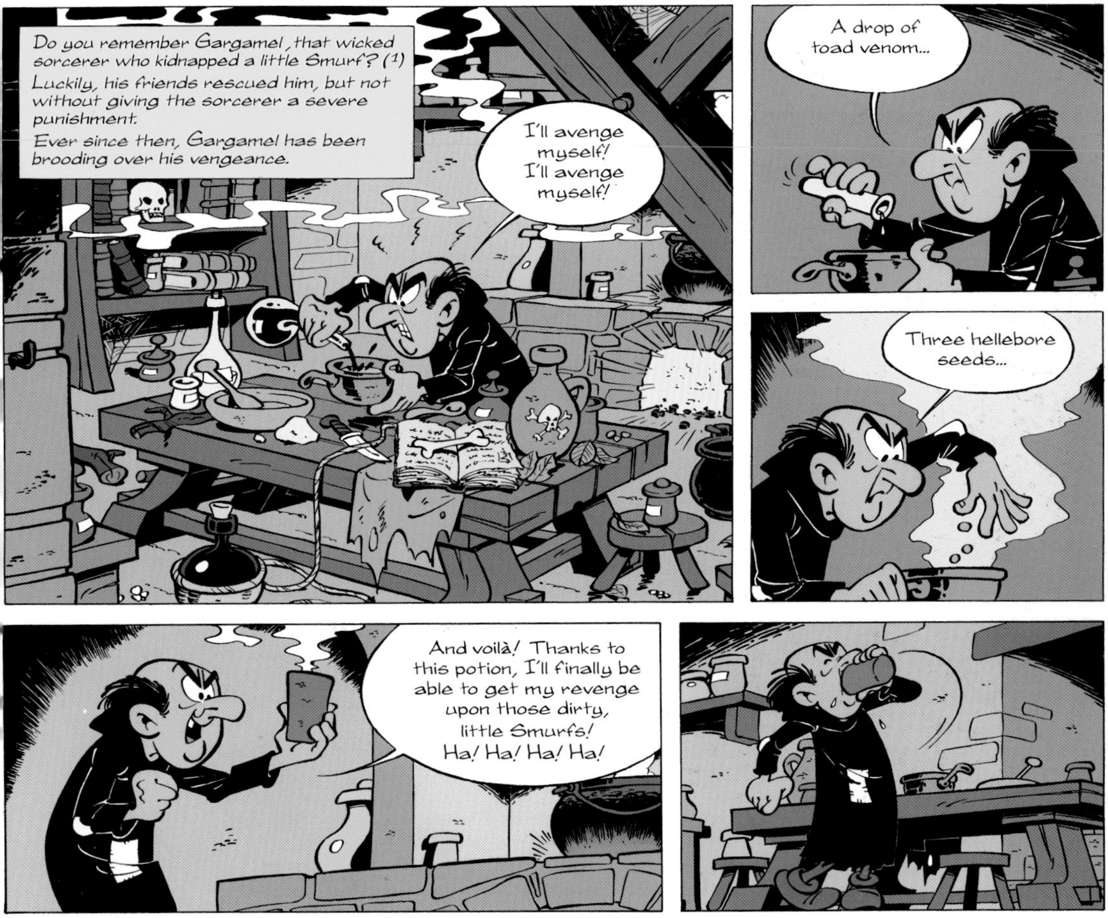

Do you remember Gargamel, that wicked sorcerer who kidnapped a little Smurf? (1)
Luckily, his friends rescued him, but not without giving the sorcerer a severe punishment.
Ever since then, Gargamel has been brooding over his vengeance.
I'll avenge myself! I'll avenge myself!
A drop of toad venom...
Three hellebore seeds...
And voilà! Thanks to this potion, I'll finally be able to get my revenge upon those dirty, little Smurfs! Ha! Ha! Ha! Ha!
POOF
HA! HA! HA!
1

(1) See THE SMURFS #9 "Gargamel and the Smurfs" or THE SMURFS ANTHOLOGY Vol. 1.

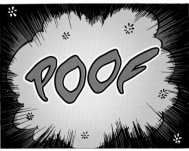

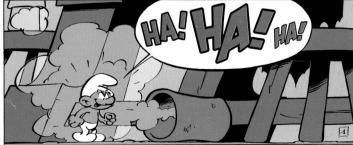

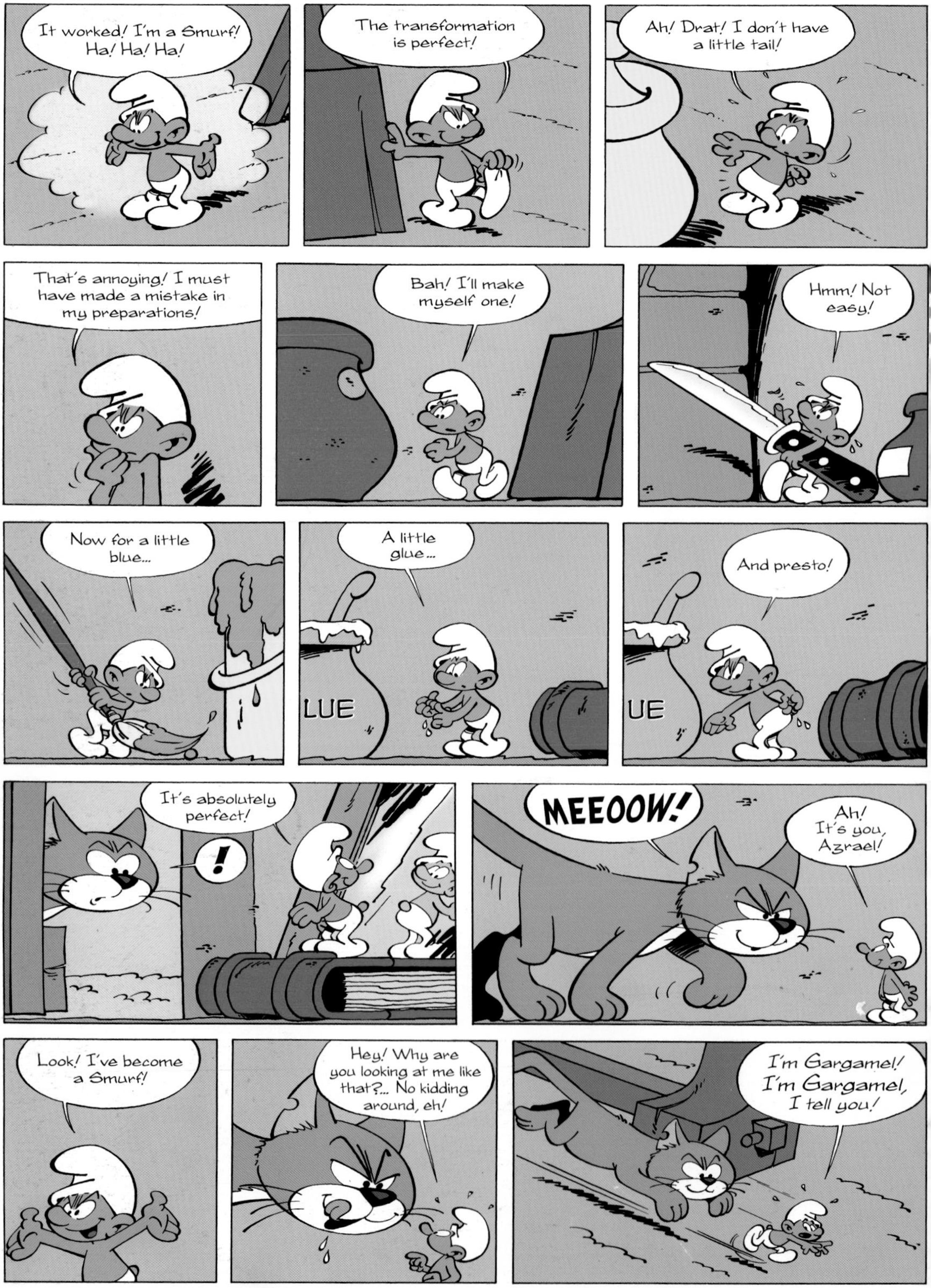
It worked! I'm a Smurf! Ha! Ha! Ha!
The transformation is perfect!
Ah! Drat! I don't have a little tail!
That's annoying! I must have made a mistake in my preparations!
Bah! I'll make myself one!
Hmm! Not easy!
Now for a little blue...
A little glue...
LUE
And presto!
UE
It's absolutely perfect!
!
MEEOOW!
Ah! It's you, Azrael!
Look! I've become a Smurf!
Hey! Why are you looking at me like that?... No kidding around, eh!
I'm Gargamel! I'm Gargamel, I tell you!

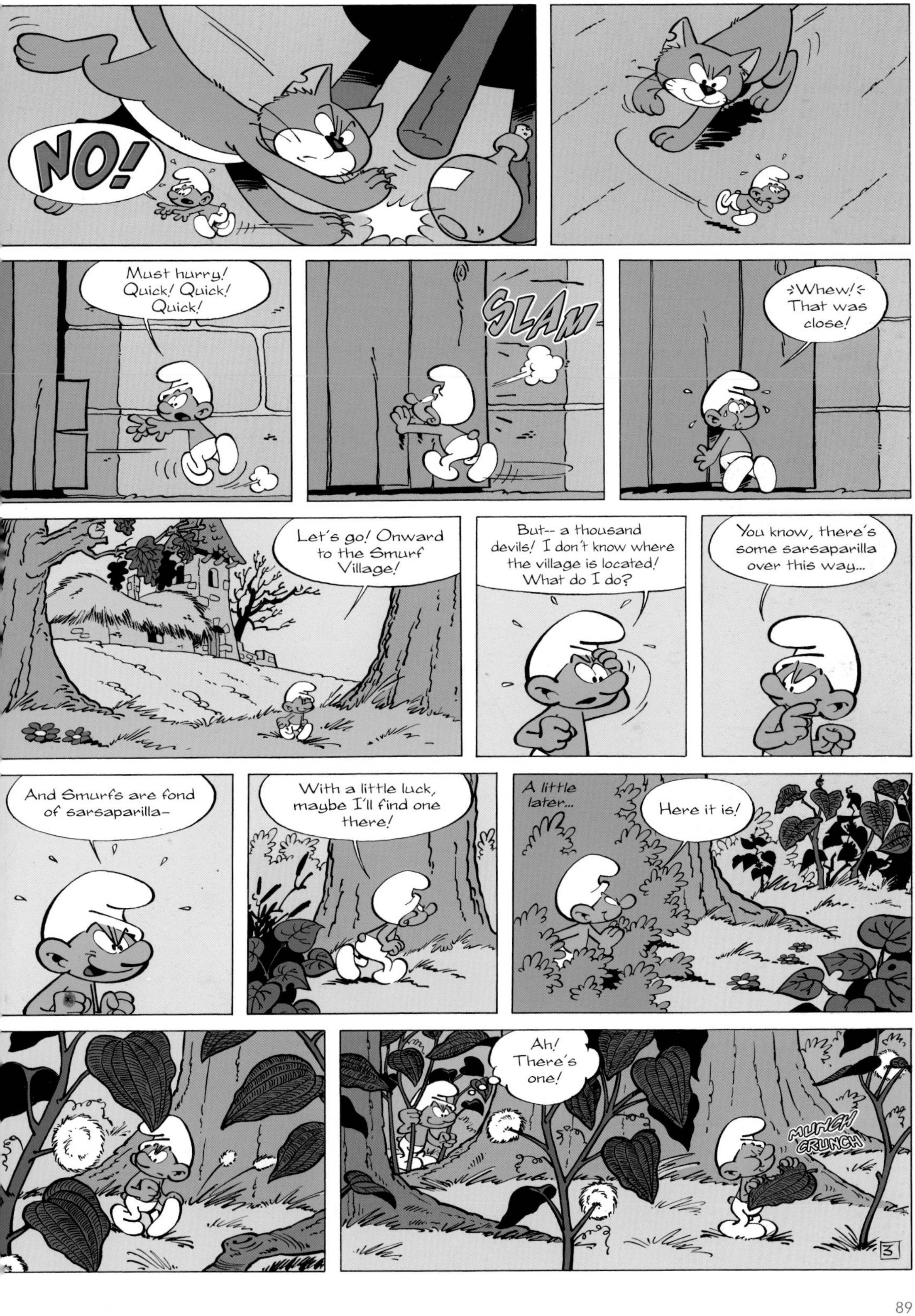
NO!
Must hurry! Quick! Quick! Quick!
SLAM
Whew! That was close!
Let's go! Onward to the Smurf Village!
But-- a thousand devils! I don't know where the village is located! What do I do?
You know, there's some sarsaparilla over this way...
And Smurfs are fond of sarsaparilla-
With a little luck, maybe I'll find one there!
A little later...
Here it is!
Ah! There's one!
MUNCH CRUNCH
3

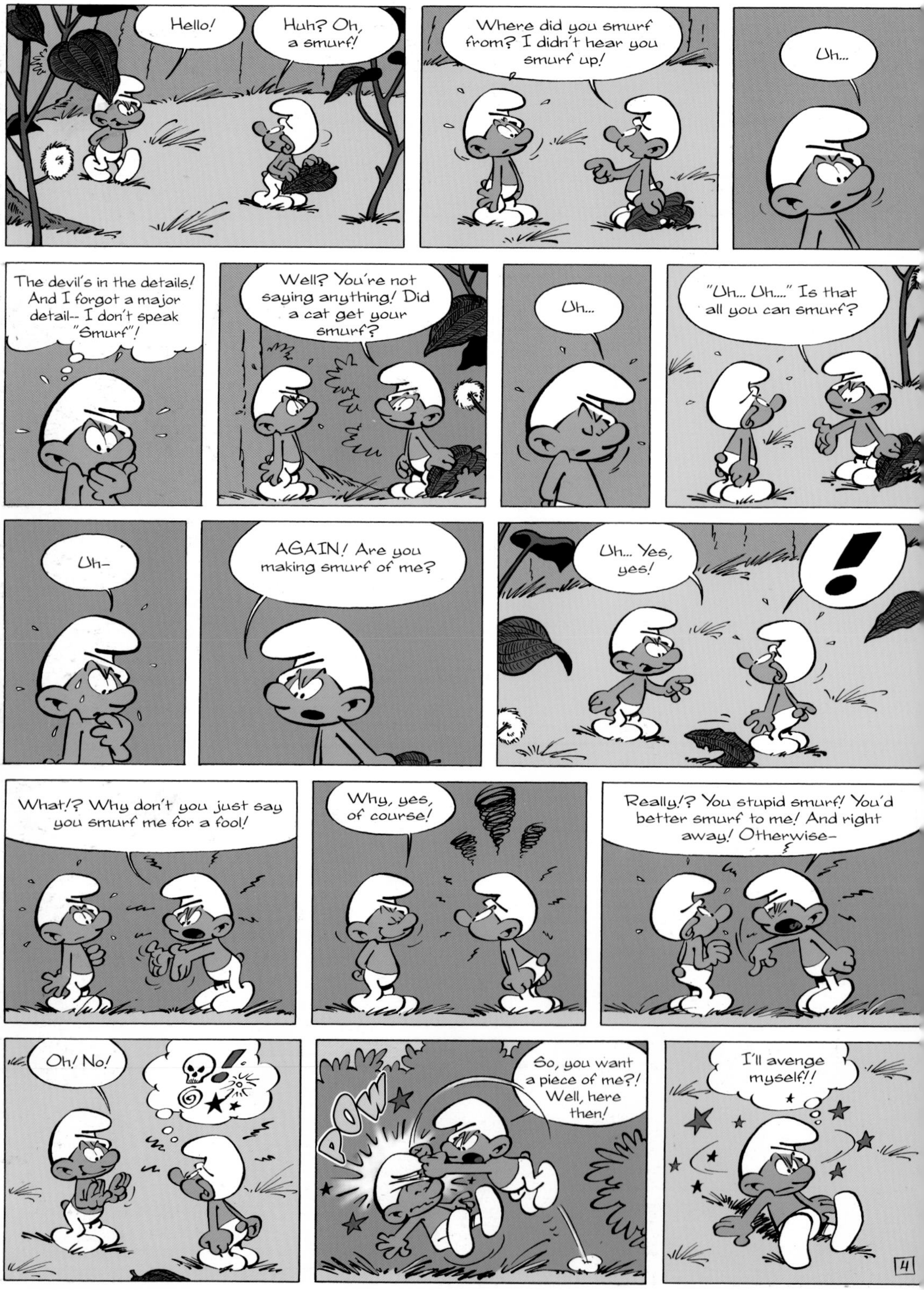
Hello!
Huh? Oh, a smurf!
Where did you smurf from? I didn't hear you smurf up!
Uh...
The devil's in the details! And I forgot a major detail-- I don't speak "Smurf"!
Well? You're not saying anything! Did a cat get your smurf?
Uh...
"Uh... Uh...." Is that all you can smurf?
Uh-
AGAIN! Are you making smurf of me?
Uh... Yes, yes!
!
What!? Why don't you just say you smurf me for a fool!
Why, yes, of course!
Really!? You stupid smurf! You'd better smurf to me! And right away! Otherwise-
Oh! No!
POW
So, you want a piece of me?! Well, here then!
I'll avenge myself!!
4

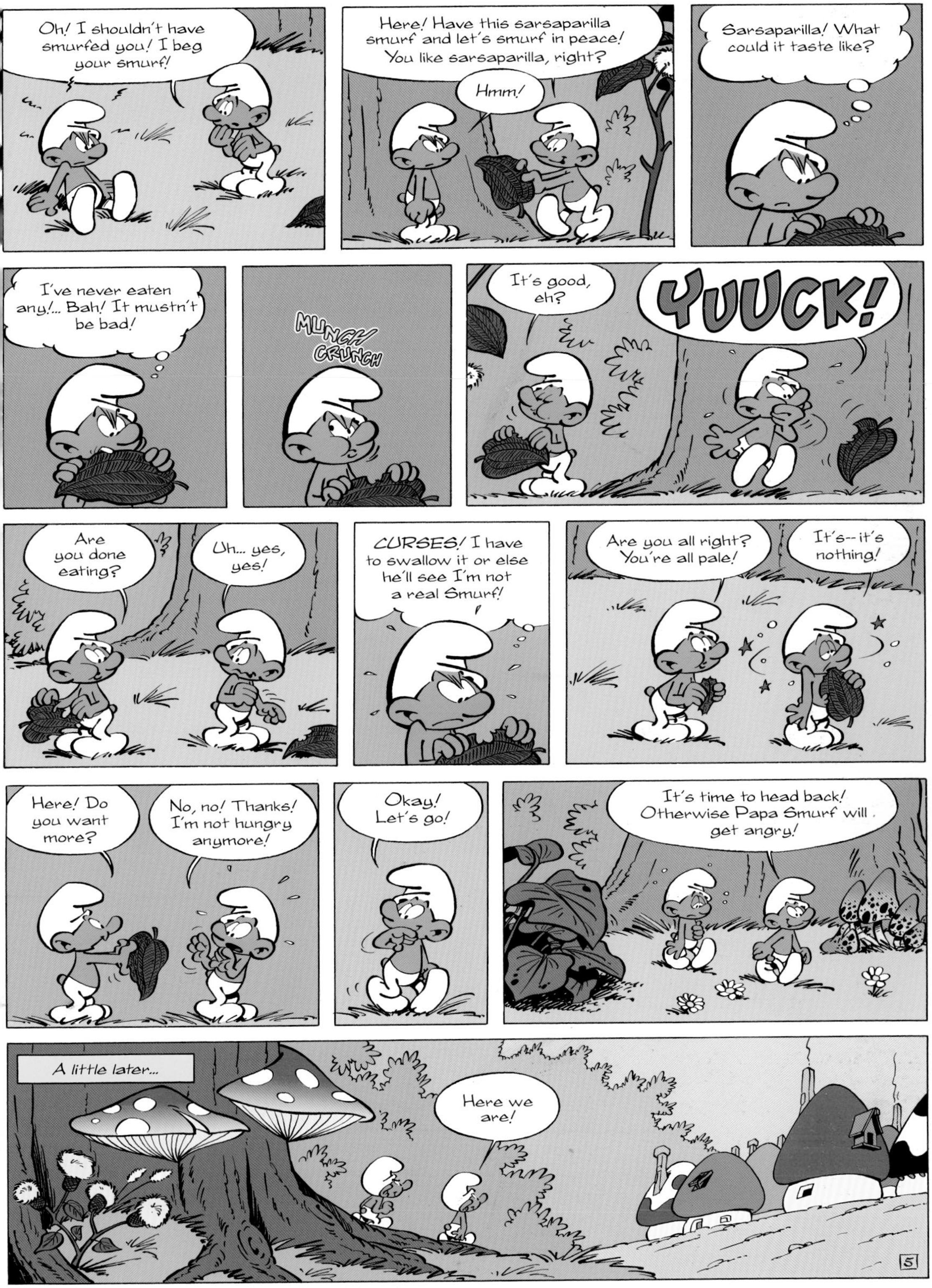

Oh! I shouldn't have smurfed you! I beg your smurf!
Here! Have this sarsaparilla smurf and let's smurf in peace! You like sarsaparilla, right?
Hmm!
Sarsaparilla! What could it taste like?
I've never eaten any!... Bah! It mustn't be bad!
MUNCH CRUNCH
It's good, eh?
YUUCK!
Are you done eating?
Uh... yes, yes!
CURSES! I have to swallow it or else he'll see I'm not a real Smurf!
Are you all right? You're all pale!
It's-- it's nothing!
Here! Do you want more?
No, no! Thanks! I'm not hungry anymore!
Okay! Let's go!
It's time to head back! Otherwise Papa Smurf will get angry!
A little later...
Here we are!
5

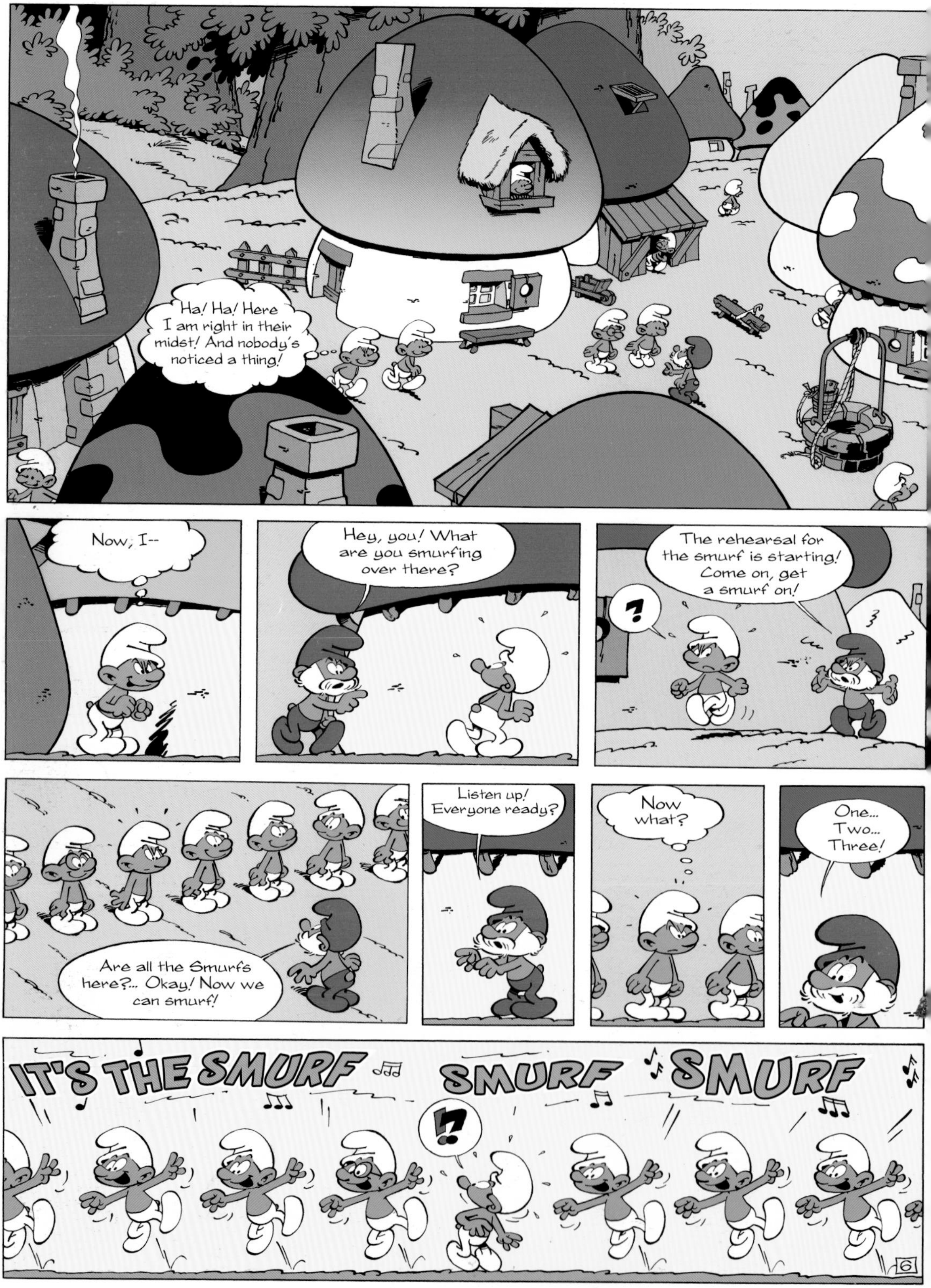
Ha! Ha! Here I am right in their midst! And nobody's noticed a thing!
Now, I--
Hey, you! What are you smurfing over there?
?
The rehearsal for the smurf is starting! Come on, get a smurf on!
Are all the Smurfs here?... Okay! Now we can smurf!
Listen up! Everyone ready?
Now what?
One... Two... Three!
IT'S THE SMURF SMURF SMURF
!?
6

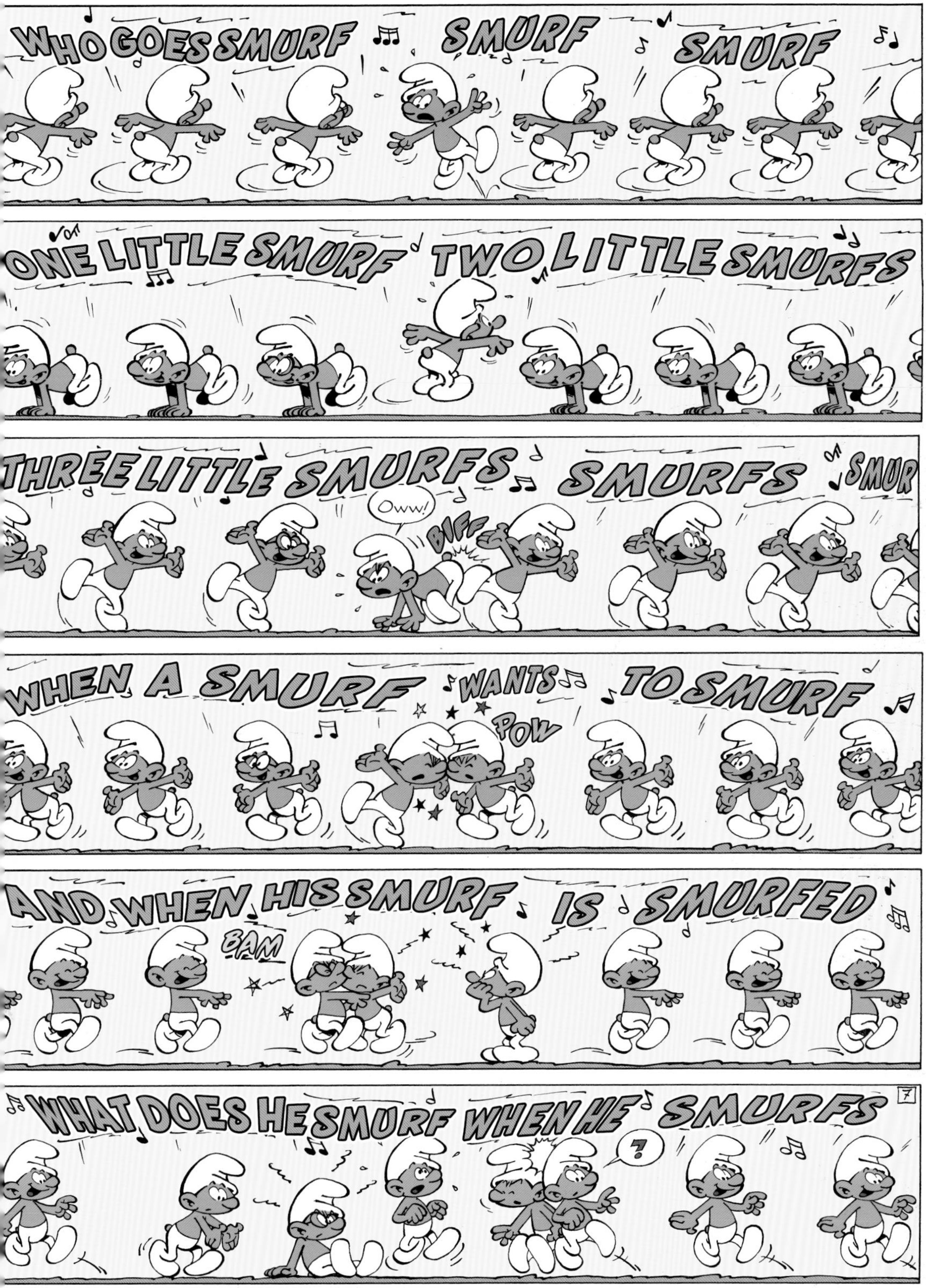
WHO GOES SMURF
SMURF
SMURF
ONE LITTLE SMURF
TWO LITTLE SMURFS
THREE LITTLE SMURFS
SMURFS
SMUR
OWW!
BIFF
WHEN A SMURF
WANTS
TO SMURF
POW
AND WHEN HIS SMURF
IS
SMURFED
BAM
WHAT DOES HE SMURF WHEN HE
SMURFS
?
7

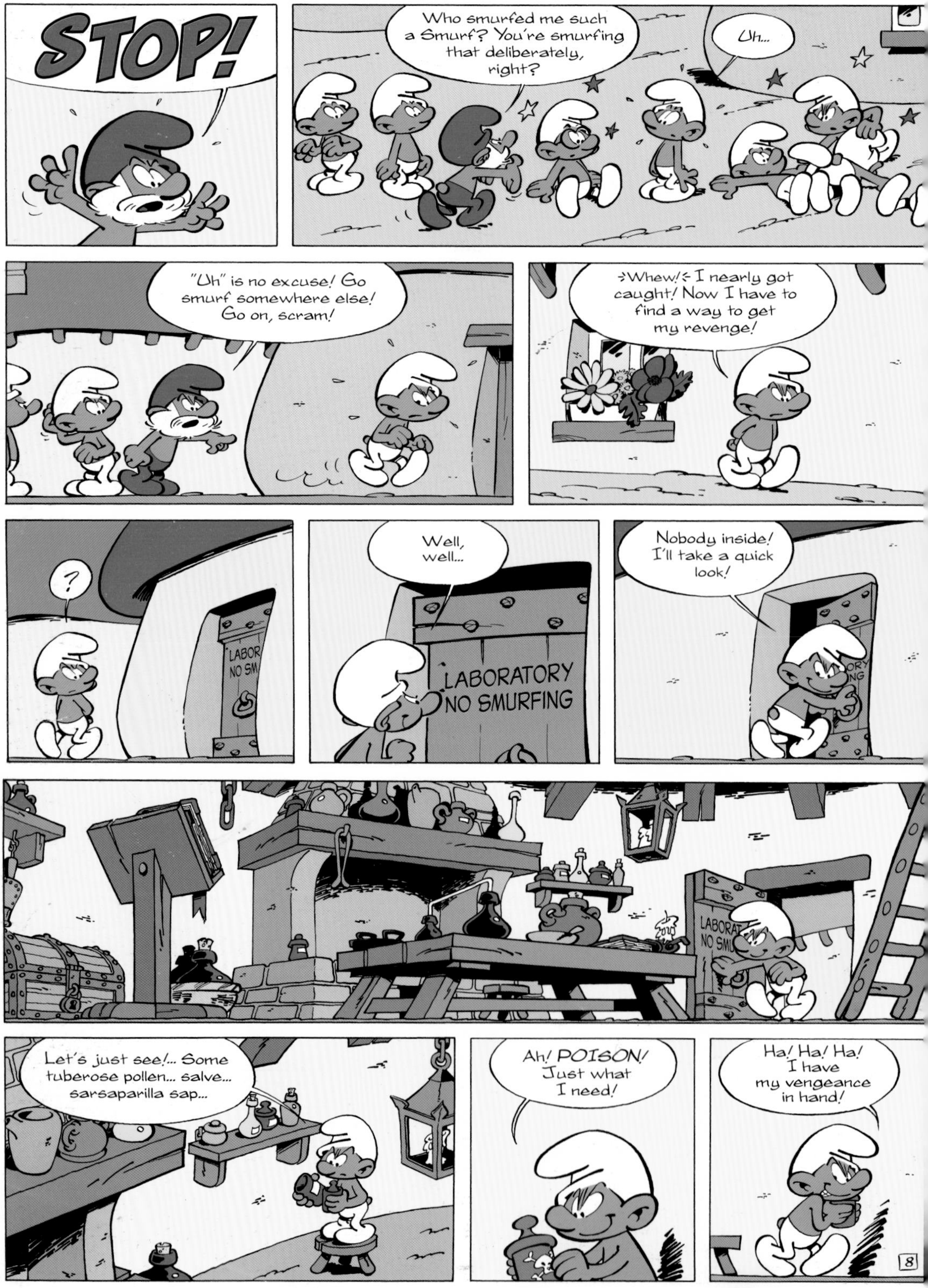
STOP!
Who smurfed me such a Smurf? You're smurfing that deliberately, right?
Uh...
"Uh" is no excuse! Go smurf somewhere else! Go on, scram!
Whew! I nearly got caught! Now I have to find a way to get my revenge!
?
Well, well...
LABORATORY NO SMURFING
Nobody inside! I'll take a quick look!
Let's just see!... Some tuberose pollen... salve... sarsaparilla sap...
Ah! POISON! Just what I need!
Ha! Ha! Ha! I have my vengeance in hand!
8

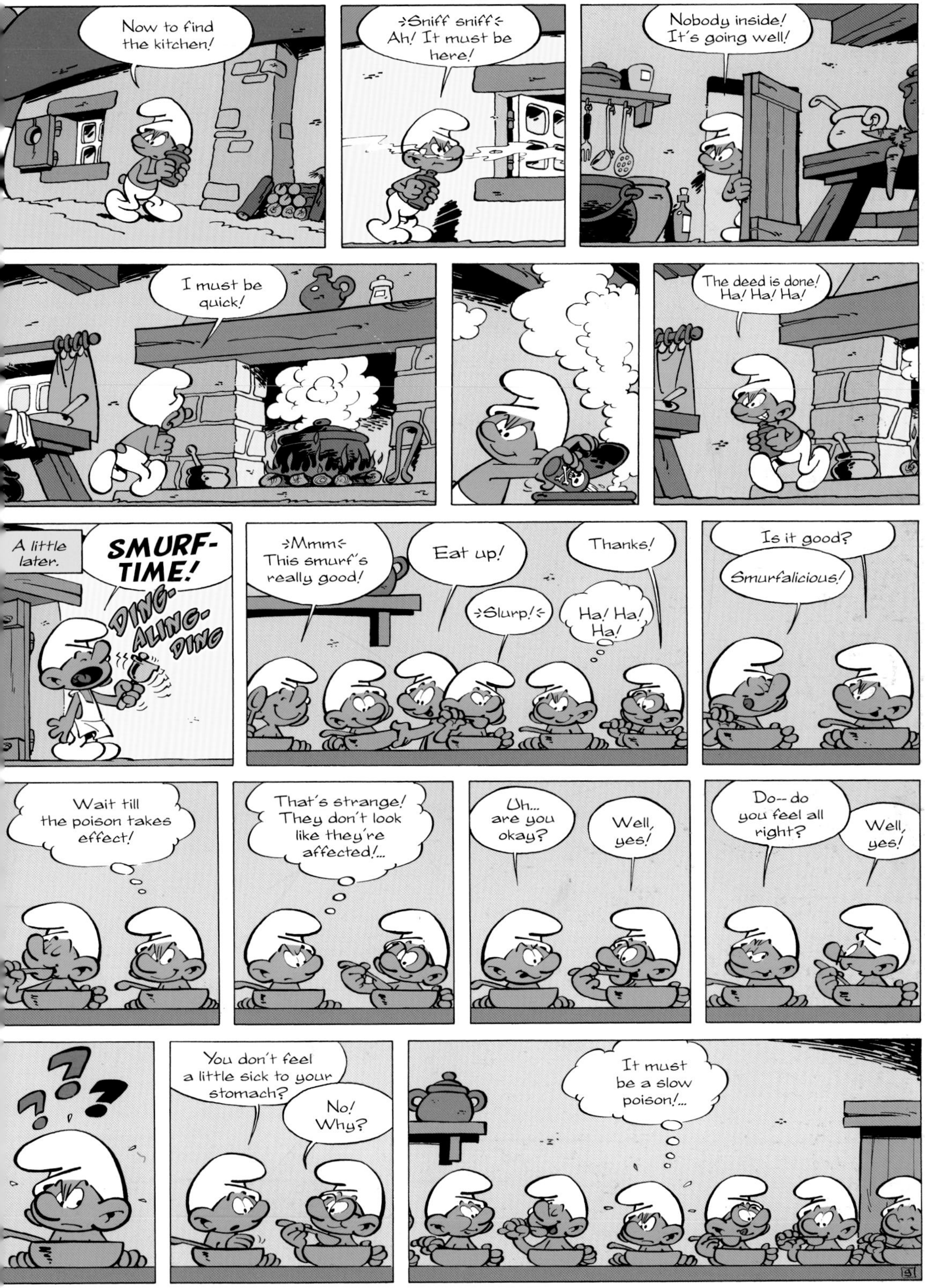
Now to find the kitchen!
-Sniff sniff- Ah! It must be here!
Nobody inside! It's going well!
I must be quick!
The deed is done! Ha! Ha! Ha!
A little later.
SMURF-TIME!
DING-ALING-DING
-Mmm- This smurf's really good!
Eat up!
Thanks!
-Slurp!-
Ha! Ha! Ha!
Is it good?
Smurfalicious!
Wait till the poison takes effect!
That's strange! They don't look like they're affected!...
Uh... are you okay?
Well, yes!
Do-- do you feel all right?
Well, yes!
You don't feel a little sick to your stomach?
No! Why?
It must be a slow poison!...

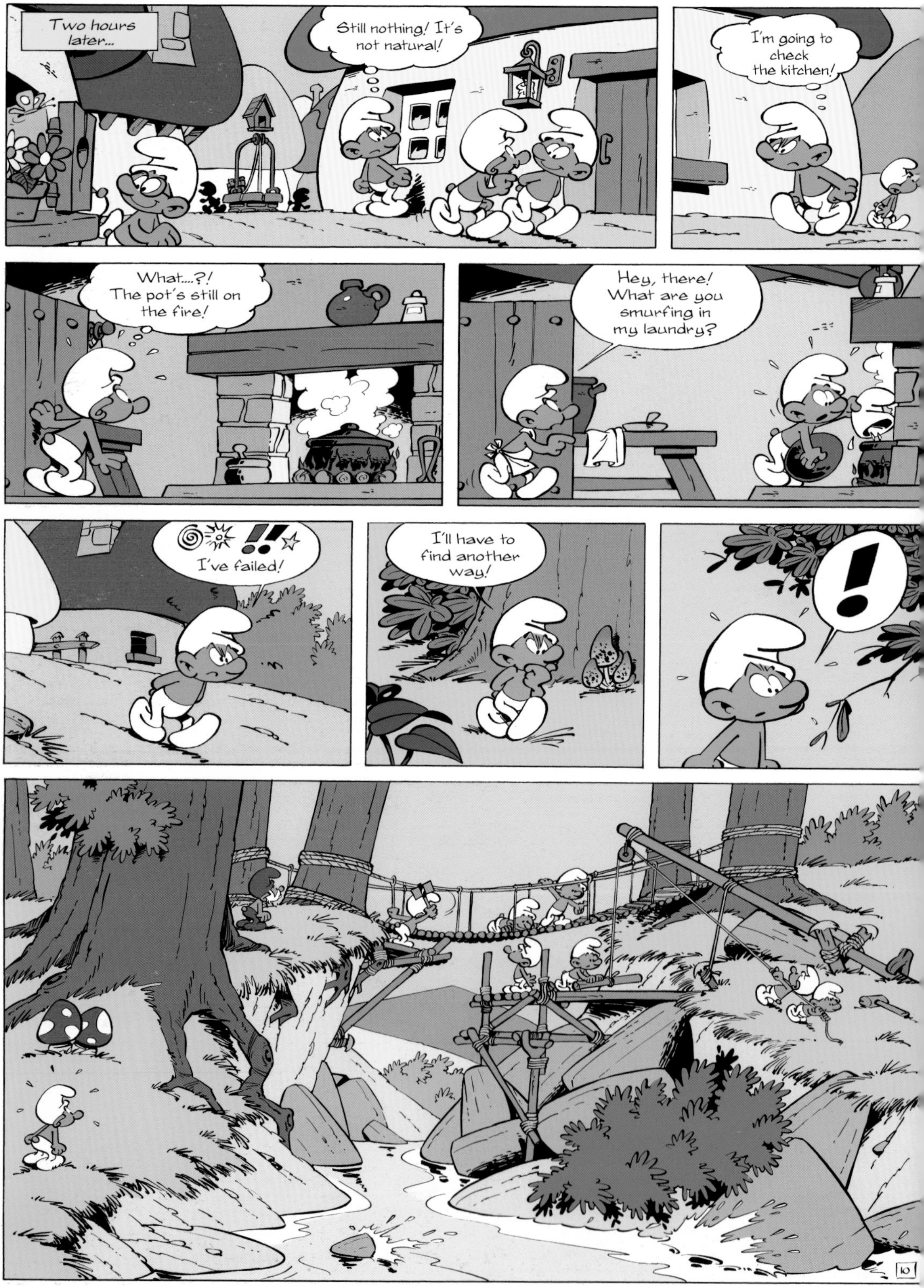

Two hours later...
Still nothing! It's not natural!
I'm going to check the kitchen!
What...?! The pot's still on the fire!
Hey, there! What are you smurfing in my laundry?
!! I've failed!
I'll have to find another way!
!
10

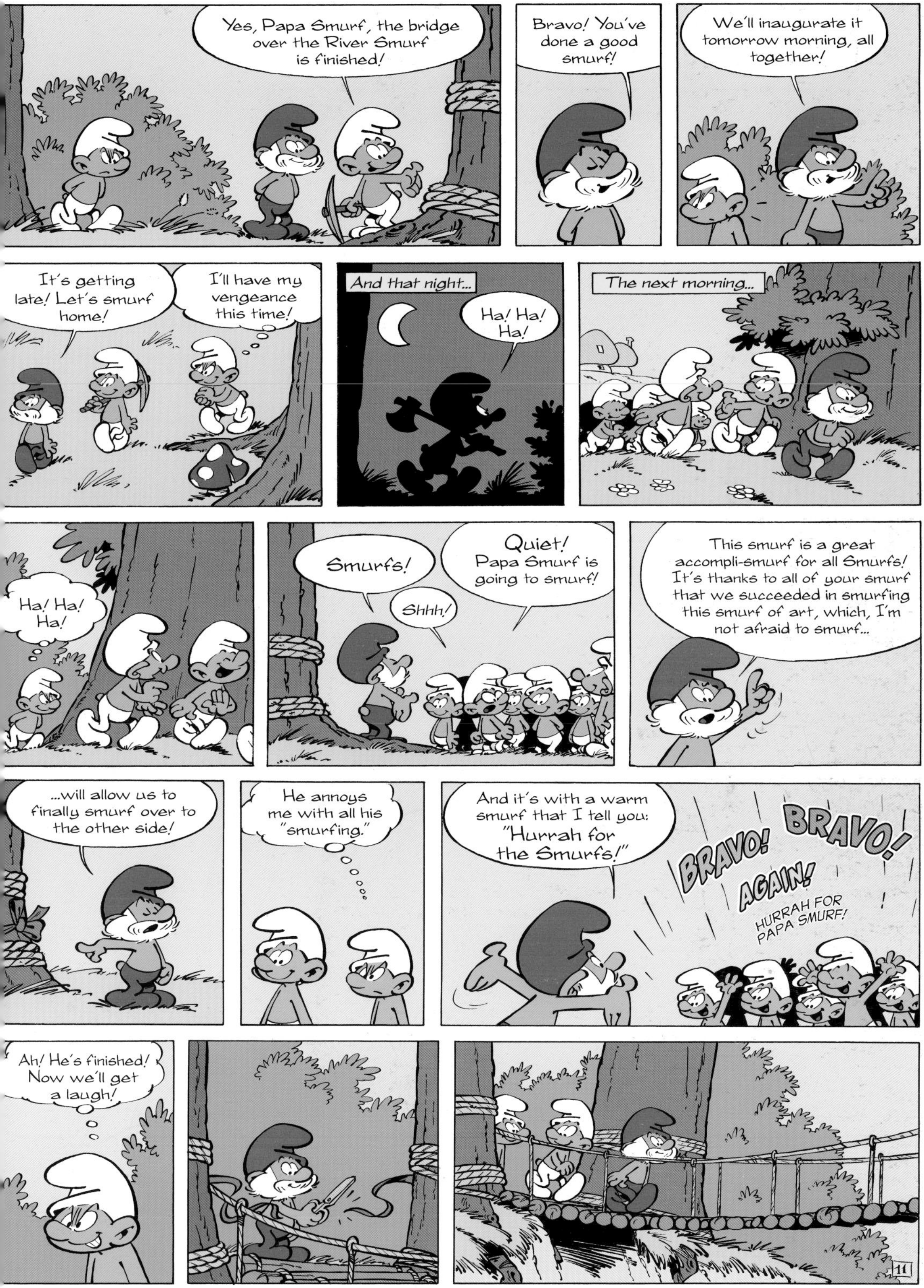
Yes, Papa Smurf, the bridge over the River Smurf is finished!
Bravo! You've done a good smurf!
We'll inaugurate it tomorrow morning, all together!
It's getting late! Let's smurf home!
I'll have my vengeance this time!
And that night...
Ha! Ha! Ha!
The next morning...
Ha! Ha! Ha!
Smurfs!
Shhh!
Quiet! Papa Smurf is going to smurf!
This smurf is a great accompli-smurf for all Smurfs! It's thanks to all of your smurf that we succeeded in smurfing this smurf of art, which, I'm not afraid to smurf...
...will allow us to finally smurf over to the other side!
He annoys me with all his "smurfing."
And it's with a warm smurf that I tell you: "Hurrah for the Smurfs!"
BRAVO!
BRAVO!
AGAIN!
HURRAH FOR PAPA SMURF!
Ah! He's finished! Now we'll get a laugh!
11

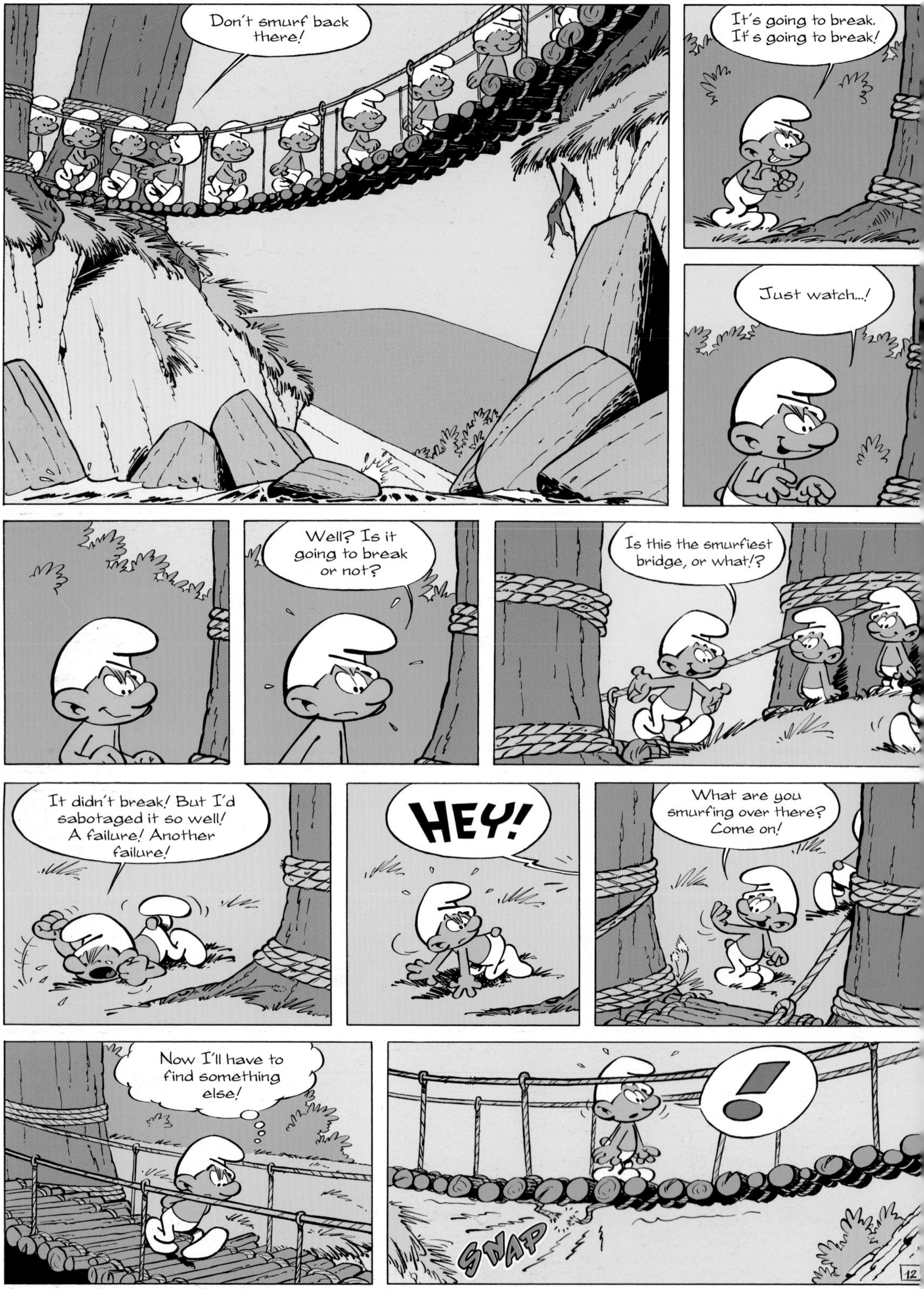
Don't smurf back there!
It's going to break. It's going to break!
Just watch...!
Well? Is it going to break or not?
Is this the smurfiest bridge, or what!?
It didn't break! But I'd sabotaged it so well! A failure! Another failure!
HEY!
What are you smurfing over there? Come on!
Now I'll have to find something else!
!
SNAP
12

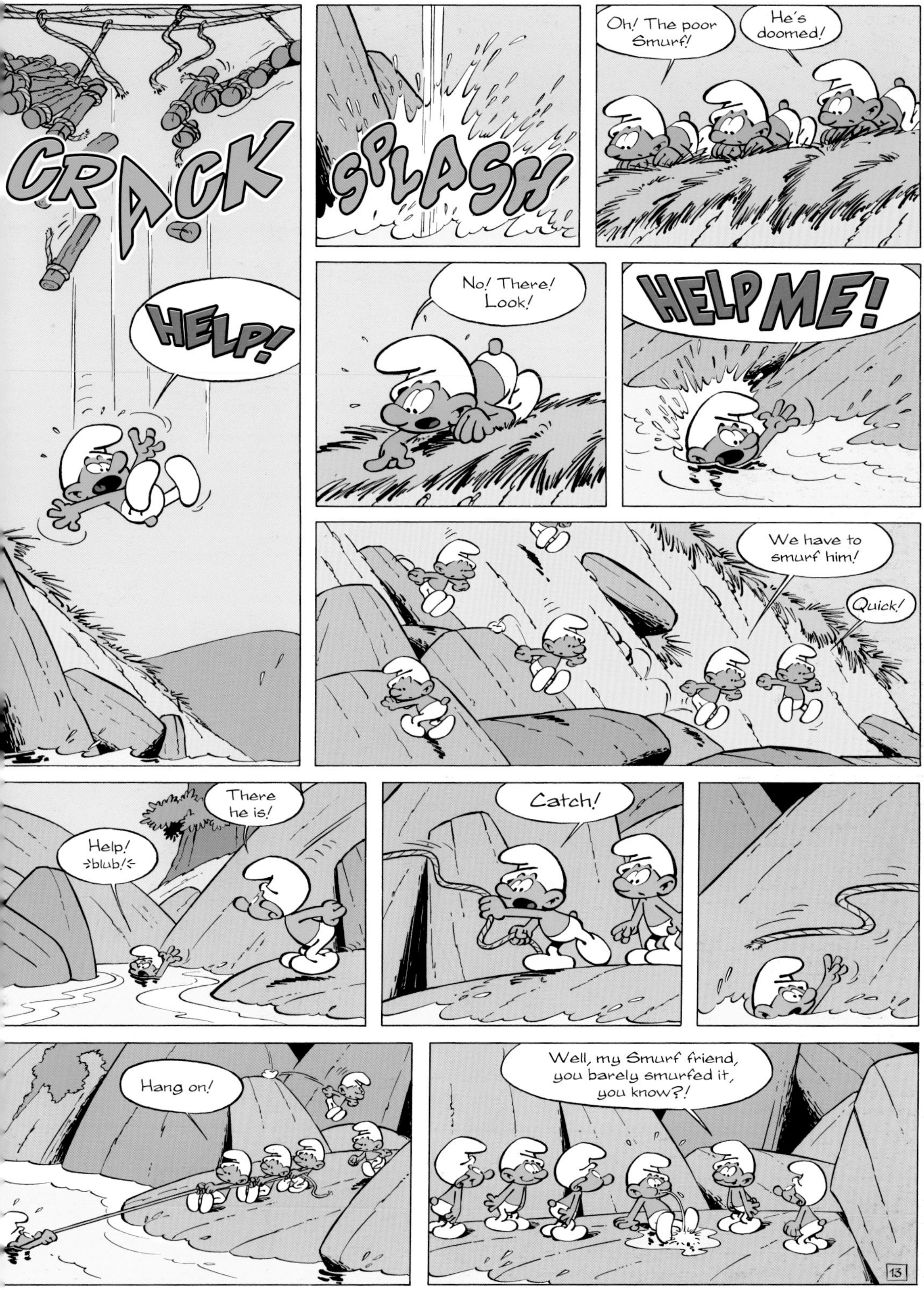

CRACK
HELP!
SPLASH
Oh! The poor Smurf!
He's doomed!
No! There! Look!
HELP ME!
We have to smurf him!
Quick!
There he is!
Help! ⊰blub!⊱
Catch!
Hang on!
Well, my Smurf friend, you barely smurfed it, you know?!
13

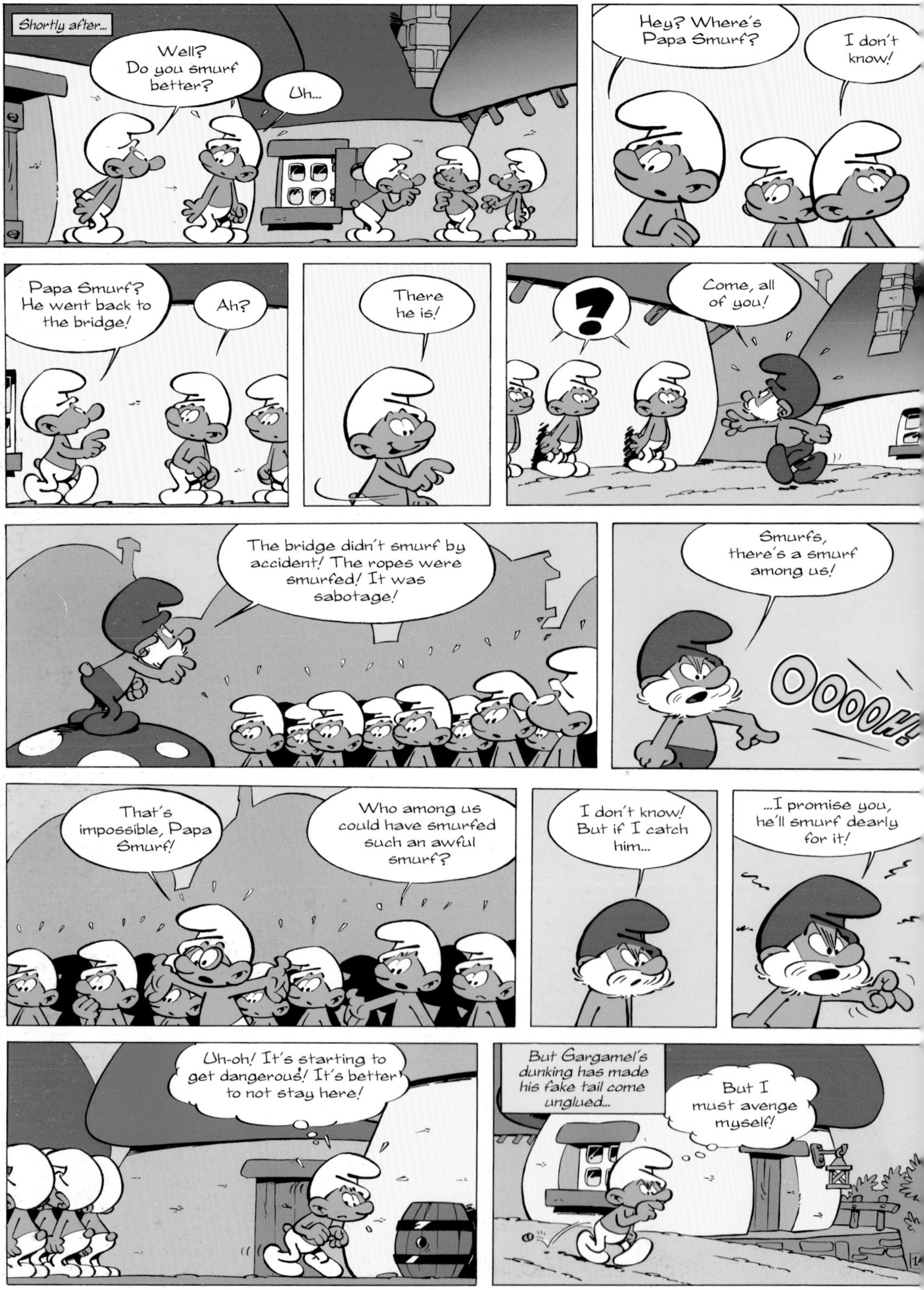

Shortly after...
Well? Do you smurf better?
Uh...
Hey? Where's Papa Smurf?
I don't know!
Papa Smurf? He went back to the bridge!
Ah?
There he is!
?
Come, all of you!
The bridge didn't smurf by accident! The ropes were smurfed! It was sabotage!
Smurfs, there's a smurf among us!
OOOOH!
That's impossible, Papa Smurf!
Who among us could have smurfed such an awful smurf?
I don't know! But if I catch him...
...I promise you, he'll smurf dearly for it!
Uh-oh! It's starting to get dangerous! It's better to not stay here!
But Gargamel's dunking has made his fake tail come unglued...
But I must avenge myself!

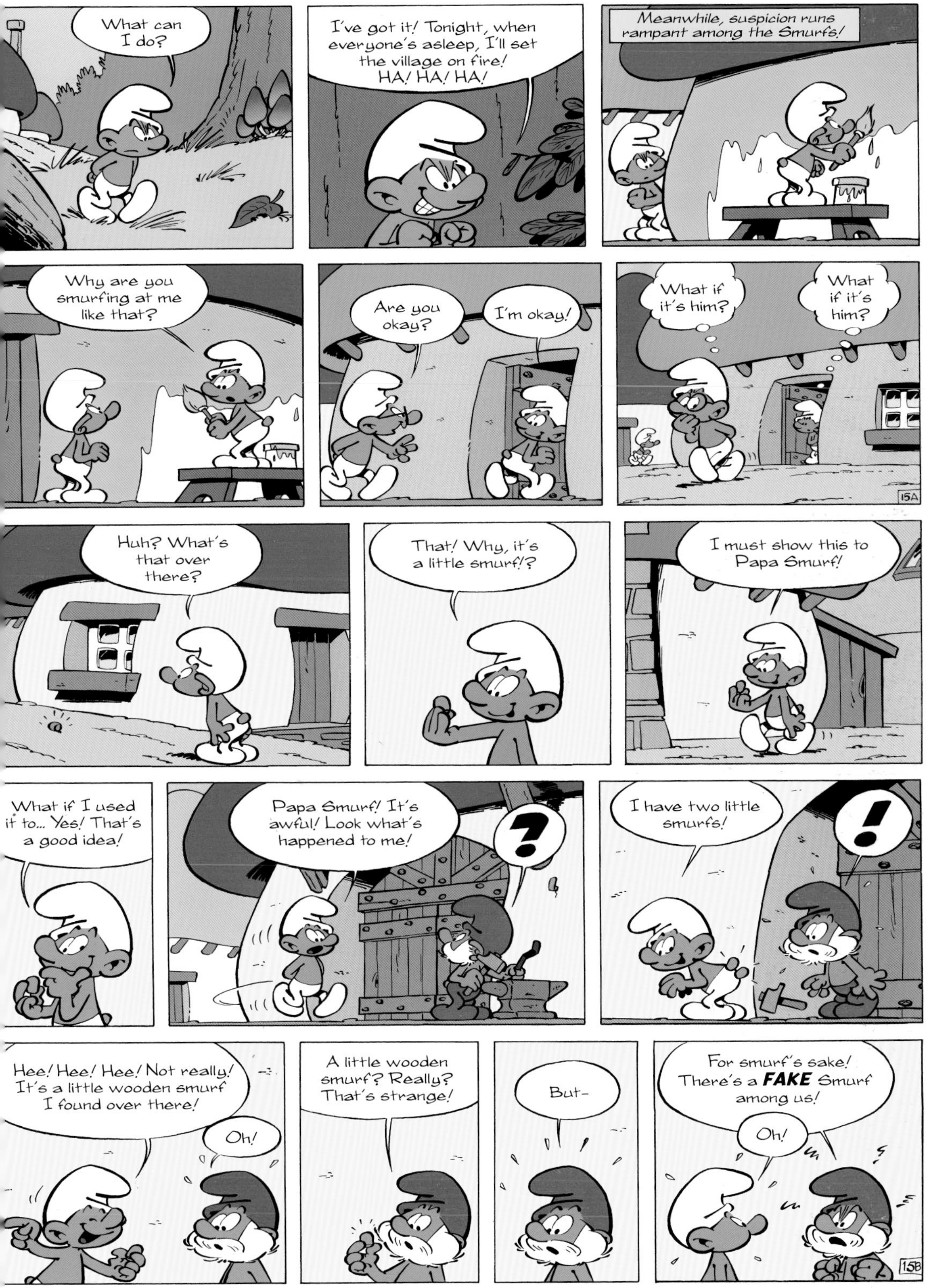

What can I do?
I've got it! Tonight, when everyone's asleep, I'll set the village on fire! HA! HA! HA!
Meanwhile, suspicion runs rampant among the Smurfs!
Why are you smurfing at me like that?
Are you okay?
I'm okay!
What if it's him?
What if it's him?
15A
Huh? What's that over there?
That! Why, it's a little smurf!?
I must show this to Papa Smurf!
What if I used it to... Yes! That's a good idea!
Papa Smurf! It's awful! Look what's happened to me!
?
I have two little smurfs!
!
Hee! Hee! Hee! Not really! It's a little wooden smurf I found over there!
Oh!
A little wooden smurf? Really? That's strange!
But-
For smurf's sake! There's a **FAKE** Smurf among us!
Oh!
15B

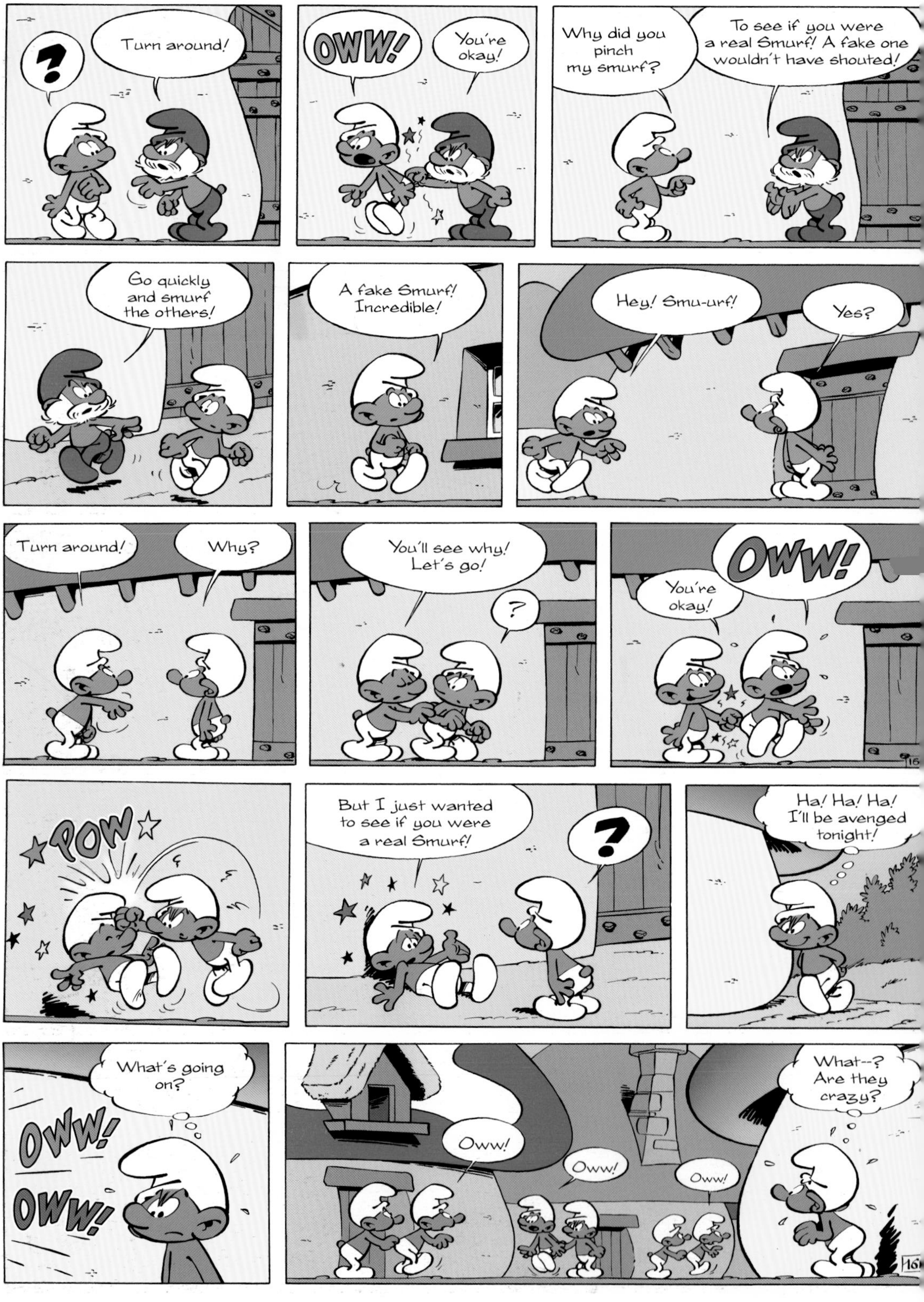
?
Turn around!
OWW!
You're okay!
Why did you pinch my smurf?
To see if you were a real Smurf! A fake one wouldn't have shouted!
Go quickly and smurf the others!
A fake Smurf! Incredible!
Hey! Smu-urf!
Yes?
Turn around!
Why?
You'll see why! Let's go!
?
OWW!
You're okay!
POW
But I just wanted to see if you were a real Smurf!
?
Ha! Ha! Ha! I'll be avenged tonight!
What's going on?
OWW!
OWW!
What--? Are they crazy?
Oww!
Oww!
Oww!

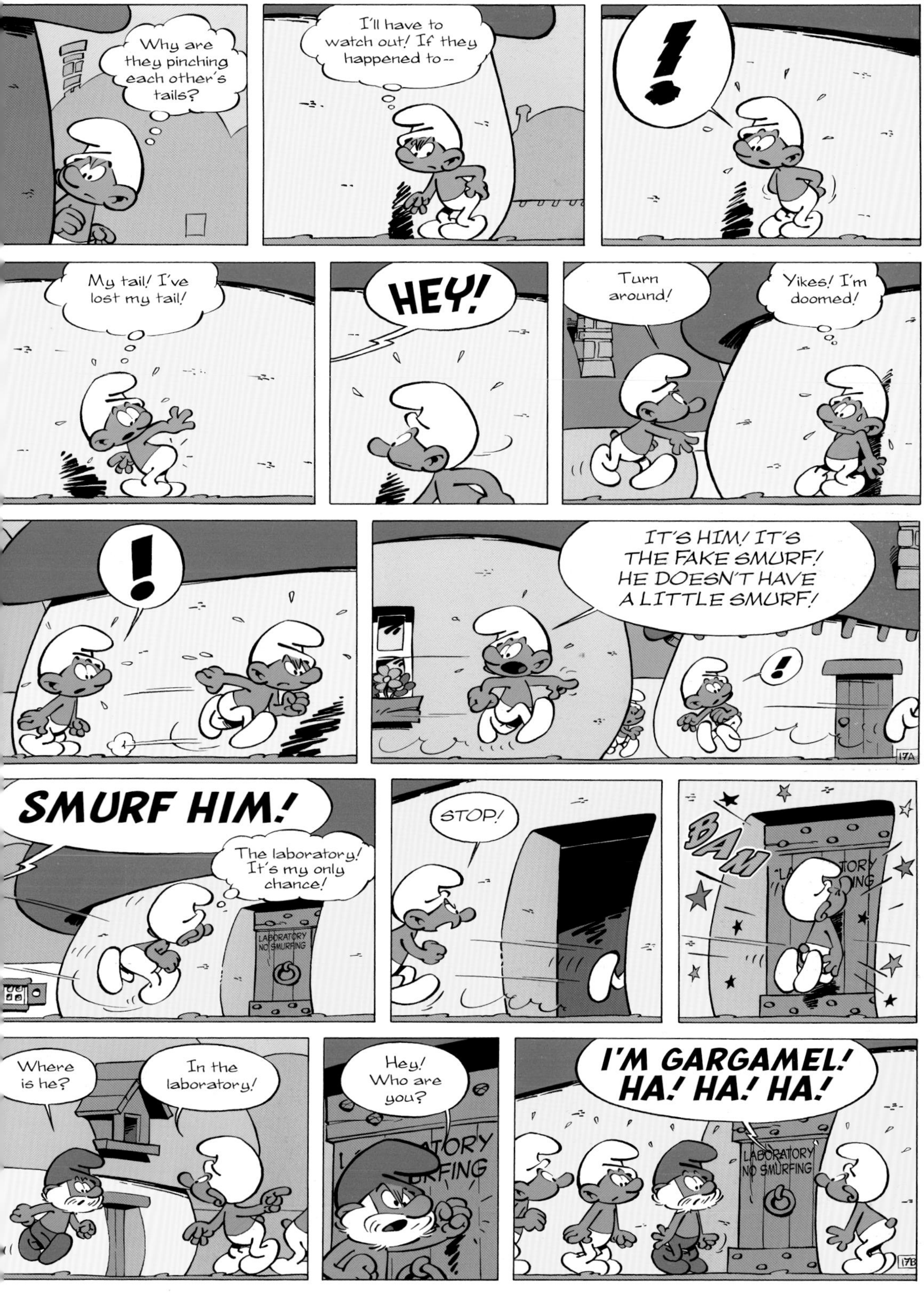
Why are they pinching each other's tails?
I'll have to watch out! If they happened to --
!
My tail! I've lost my tail!
HEY!
Turn around!
Yikes! I'm doomed!
!
IT'S HIM! IT'S THE FAKE SMURF! HE DOESN'T HAVE A LITTLE SMURF!
!
17A
SMURF HIM!
The laboratory! It's my only chance!
LABORATORY NO SMURFING
STOP!
BAM
Where is he?
In the laboratory!
Hey! Who are you?
I'M GARGAMEL! HA! HA! HA!
LABORATORY NO SMURFING
17B

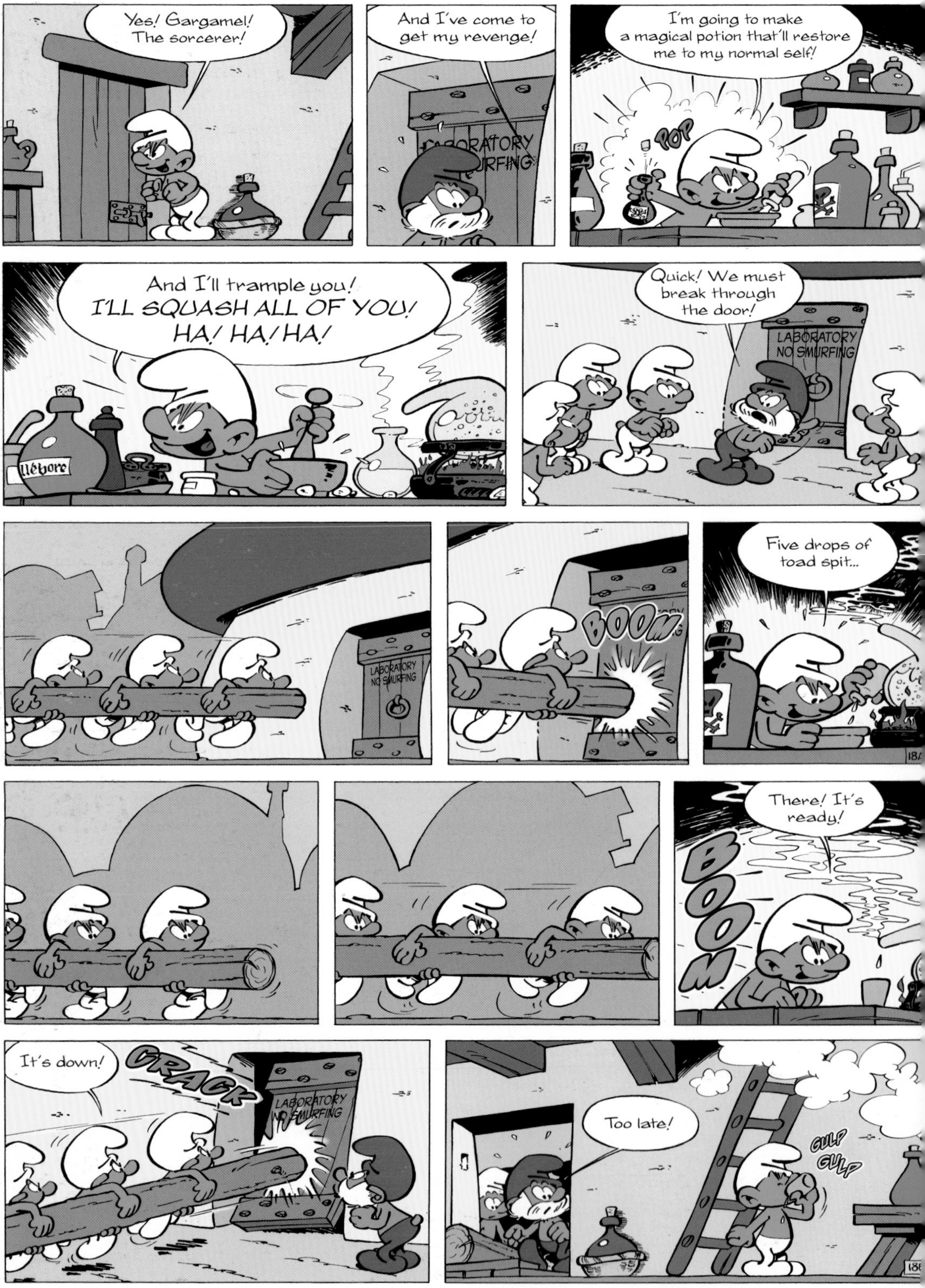
Yes! Gargamel! The sorcerer!
And I've come to get my revenge!
LABORATORY
I'm going to make a magical potion that'll restore me to my normal self!
POP
And I'll trample you! I'LL SQUASH ALL OF YOU! HA! HA! HA!
Quick! We must break through the door!
LABORATORY NO SMURFING
LABORATORY NO SMURFING
BOOM
Five drops of toad spit...
There! It's ready!
BOOM
It's down!
CRACK
LABORATORY NO SMURFING
Too late!
GULP
GULP

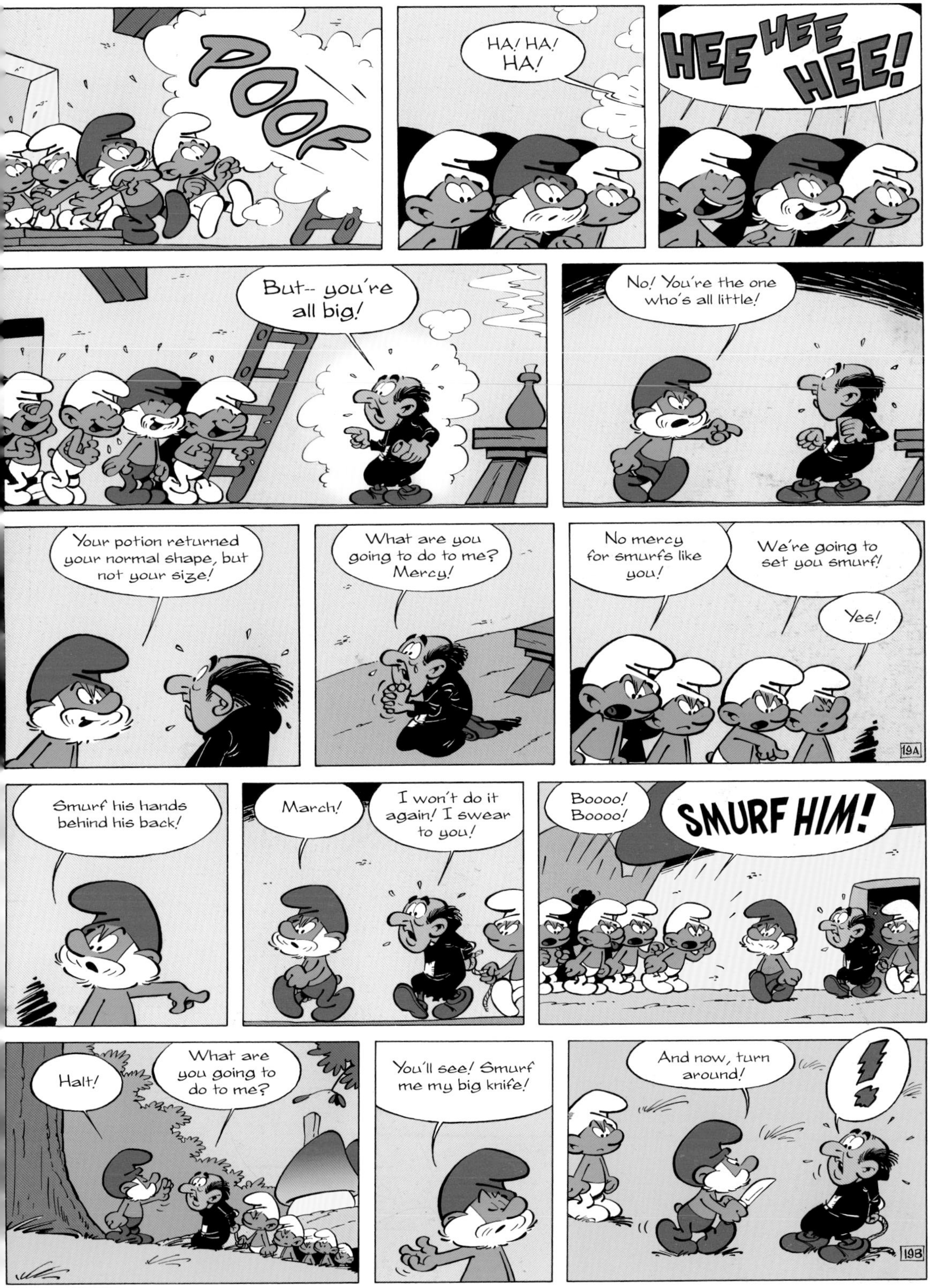
POOF
HA! HA! HA!
HEE HEE HEE!
But-- you're all big!
No! You're the one who's all little!
Your potion returned your normal shape, but not your size!
What are you going to do to me? Mercy!
No mercy for smurfs like you!
We're going to set you smurf!
Yes!
19A
Smurf his hands behind his back!
March!
I won't do it again! I swear to you!
Boooo! Boooo!
SMURF HIM!
Halt!
What are you going to do to me?
You'll see! Smurf me my big knife!
And now, turn around!
19B

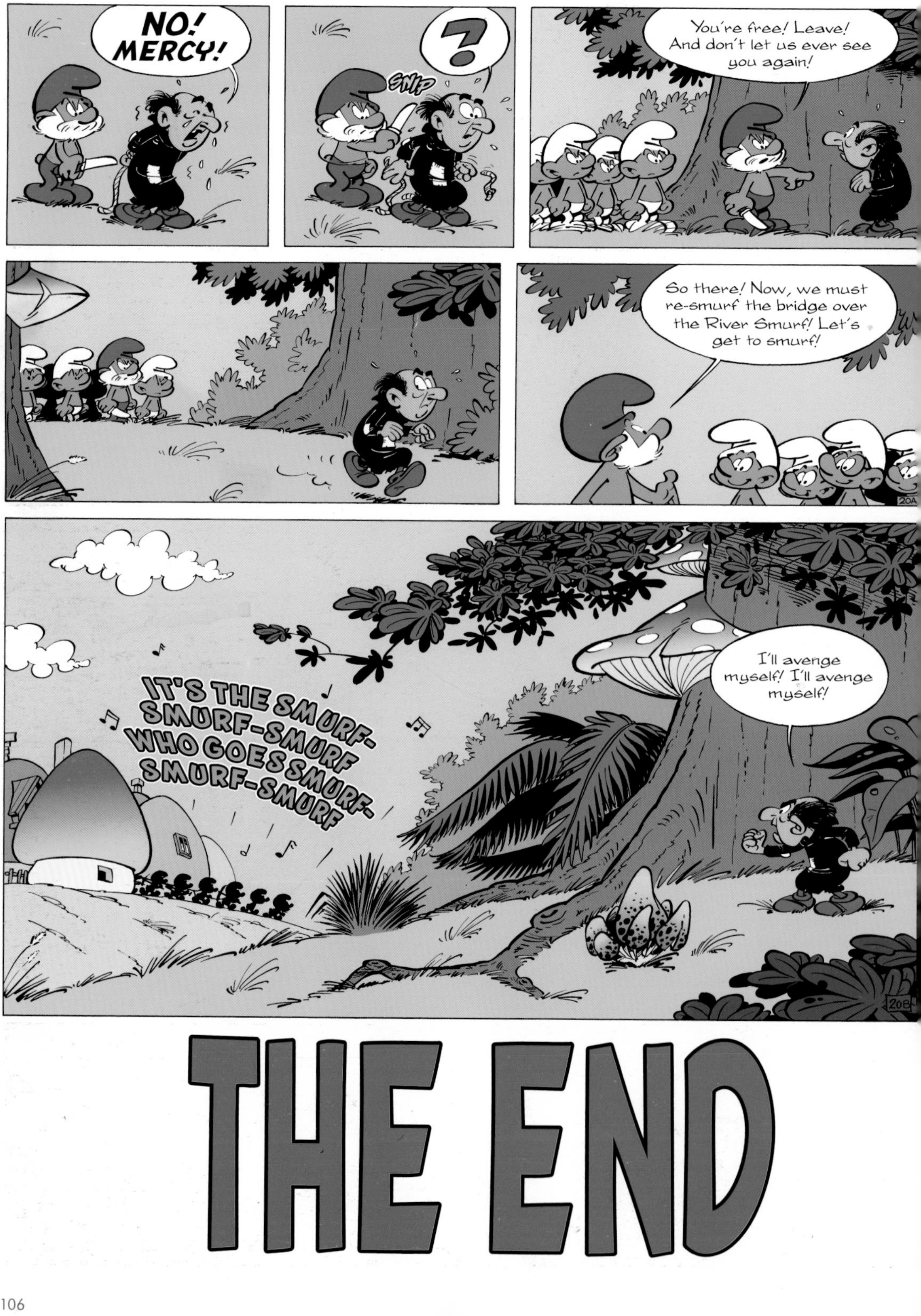
NO! MERCY!
SNIP
?
You're free! Leave! And don't let us ever see you again!
So there! Now, we must re-smurf the bridge over the River Smurf! Let's get to smurf!
20A
IT'S THE SMURF-SMURF-SMURF WHO GOES SMURF-SMURF-SMURF
I'll avenge myself! I'll avenge myself!
20B

THE END

THE HUNDREDTH SMURF

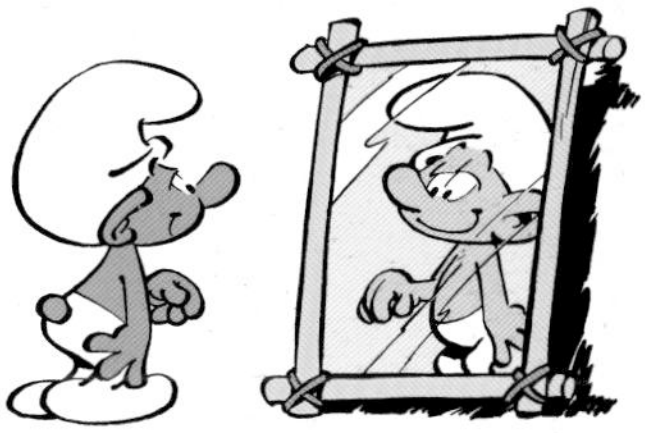

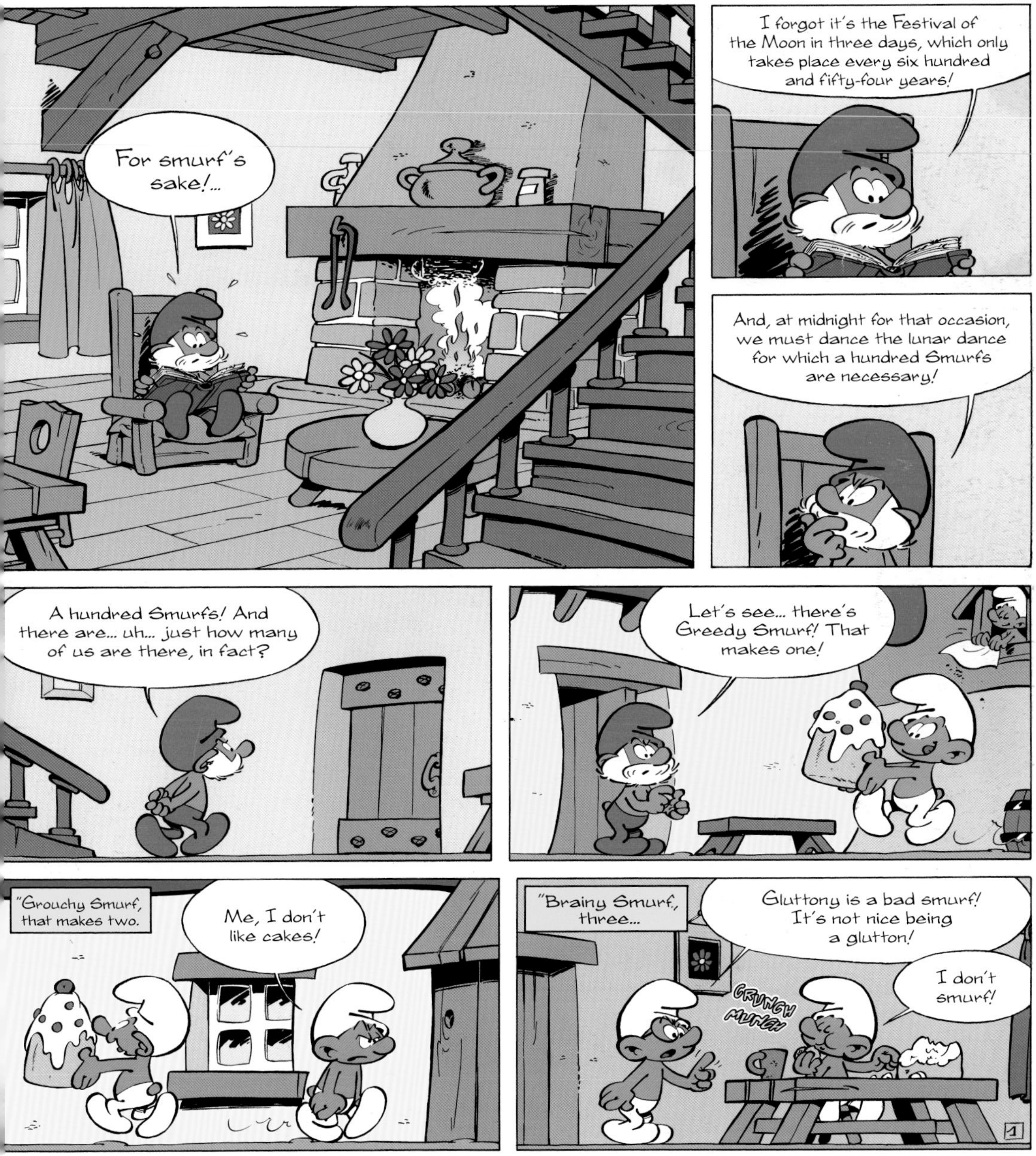

For smurf's sake!...
I forgot it's the Festival of the Moon in three days, which only takes place every six hundred and fifty-four years!
And, at midnight for that occasion, we must dance the lunar dance for which a hundred Smurfs are necessary!
A hundred Smurfs! And there are... uh... just how many of us are there, in fact?
Let's see... there's Greedy Smurf! That makes one!
"Grouchy Smurf, that makes two.
Me, I don't like cakes!
"Brainy Smurf, three...
Gluttony is a bad smurf! It's not nice being a glutton!
GRUNCH MUNCH
I don't smurf!
1

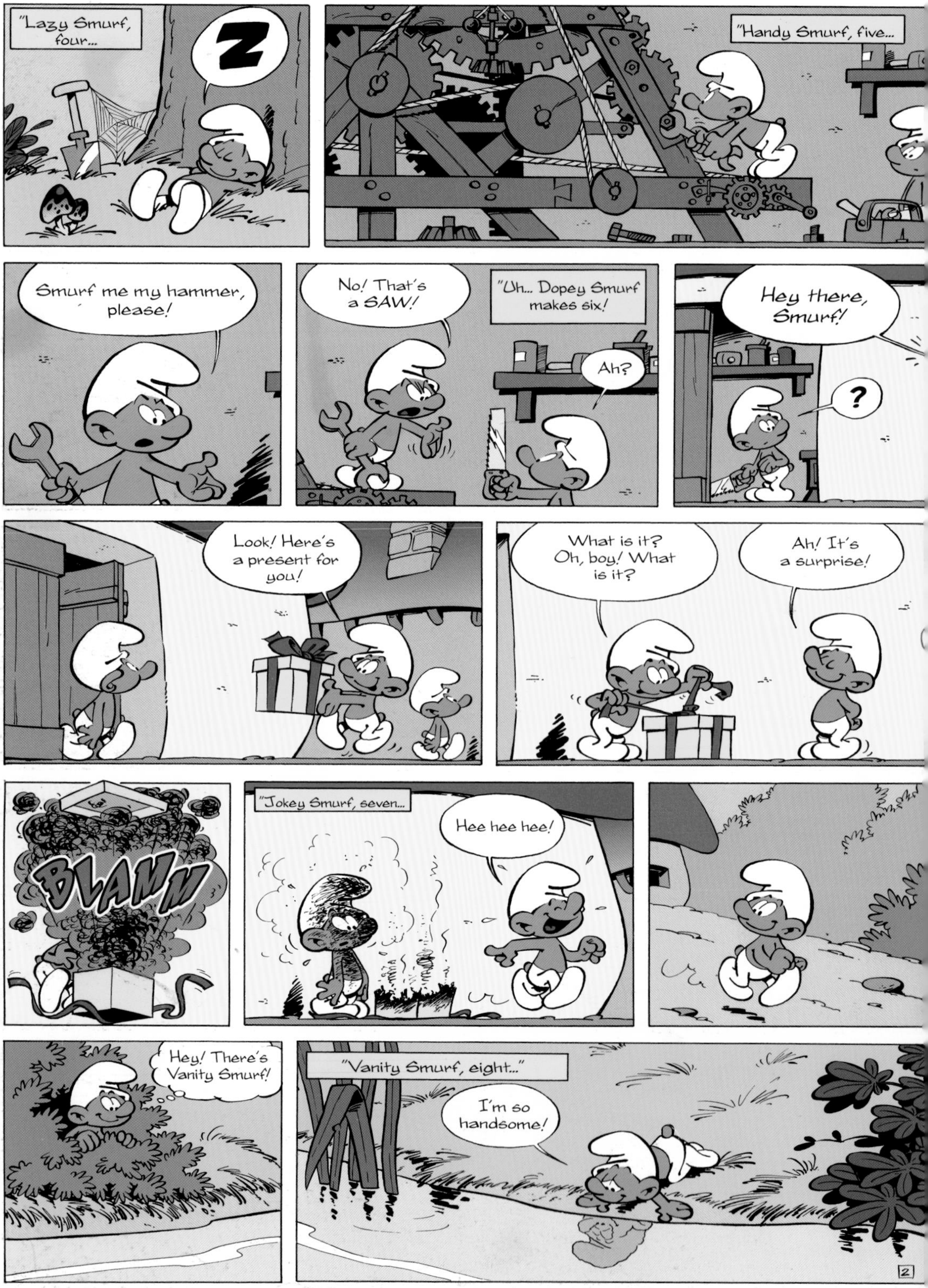
"Lazy Smurf, four...
Z
"Handy Smurf, five...
Smurf me my hammer, please!
No! That's a SAW!
"Uh... Dopey Smurf makes six!
Ah?
Hey there, Smurf!
?
Look! Here's a present for you!
What is it? Oh, boy! What is it?
Ah! It's a surprise!
BLAMM
"Jokey Smurf, seven...
Hee hee hee!
Hey! There's Vanity Smurf!
"Vanity Smurf, eight..."
I'm so handsome!
2

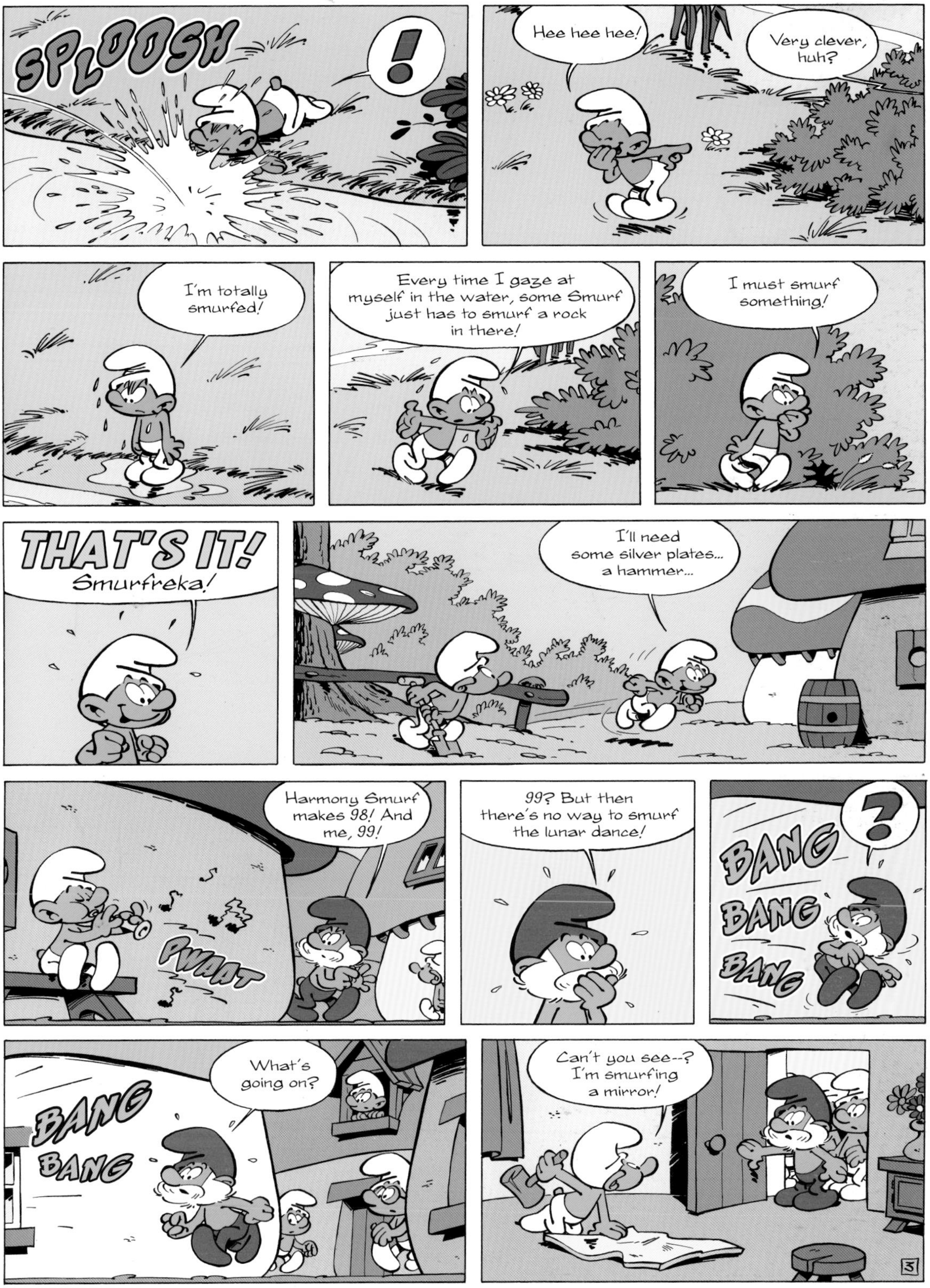

SPLOOSH
!
Hee hee hee!
Very clever, huh?
I'm totally smurfed!
Every time I gaze at myself in the water, some Smurf just has to smurf a rock in there!
I must smurf something!
THAT'S IT! Smurfreka!
I'll need some silver plates... a hammer...
Harmony Smurf makes 98! And me, 99!
PWAAT
99? But then there's no way to smurf the lunar dance!
BANG BANG BANG
?
BANG BANG
What's going on?
Can't you see--? I'm smurfing a mirror!
3

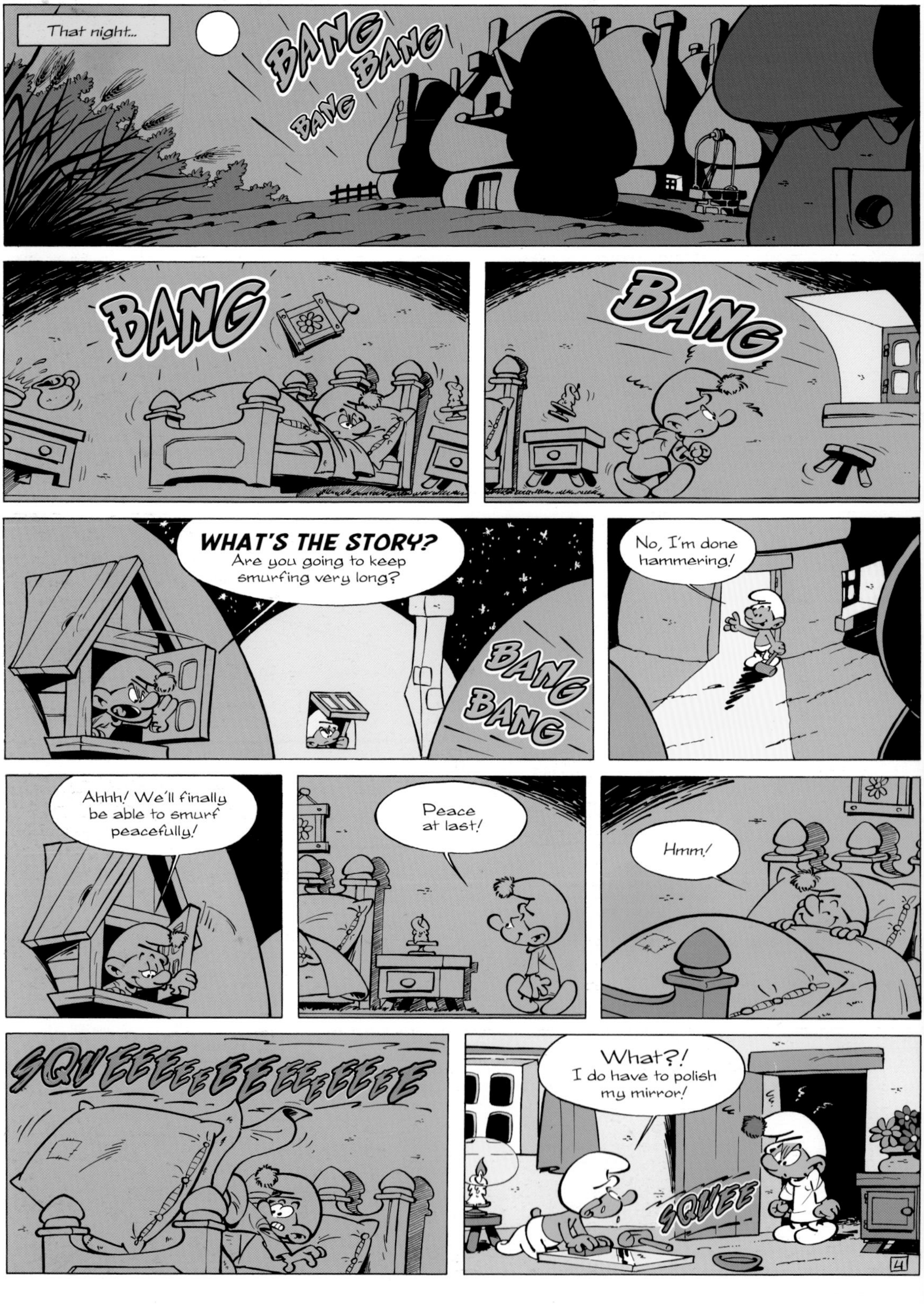

That night...
BANG
BANG
BANG
BANG
BANG
WHAT'S THE STORY? Are you going to keep smurfing very long?
BANG
BANG
No, I'm done hammering!
Ahhh! We'll finally be able to smurf peacefully!
Peace at last!
Hmm!
SQUEEEEEEEEEEEEEEEEE
What?! I do have to polish my mirror!
SQUEE
4

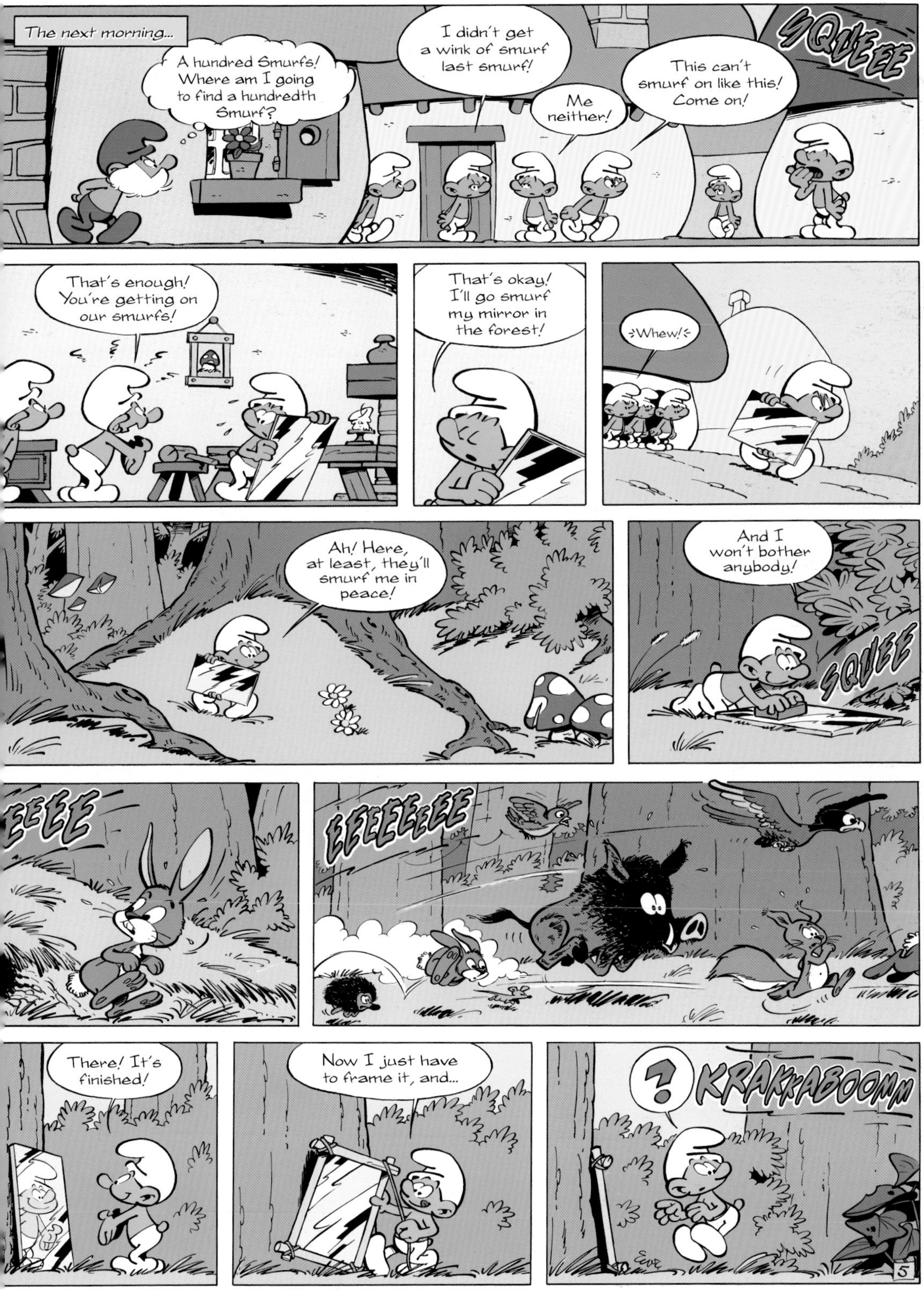
The next morning...
A hundred Smurfs! Where am I going to find a hundredth Smurf?
I didn't get a wink of smurf last smurf!
Me neither!
This can't smurf on like this! Come on!
SQUEEE
That's enough! You're getting on our smurfs!
That's okay! I'll go smurf my mirror in the forest!
Whew!
Ah! Here, at least, they'll smurf me in peace!
And I won't bother anybody!
SQUEE
EEEE
EEEEEEEE
There! It's finished!
Now I just have to frame it, and...
?
KRAKKABOOMM

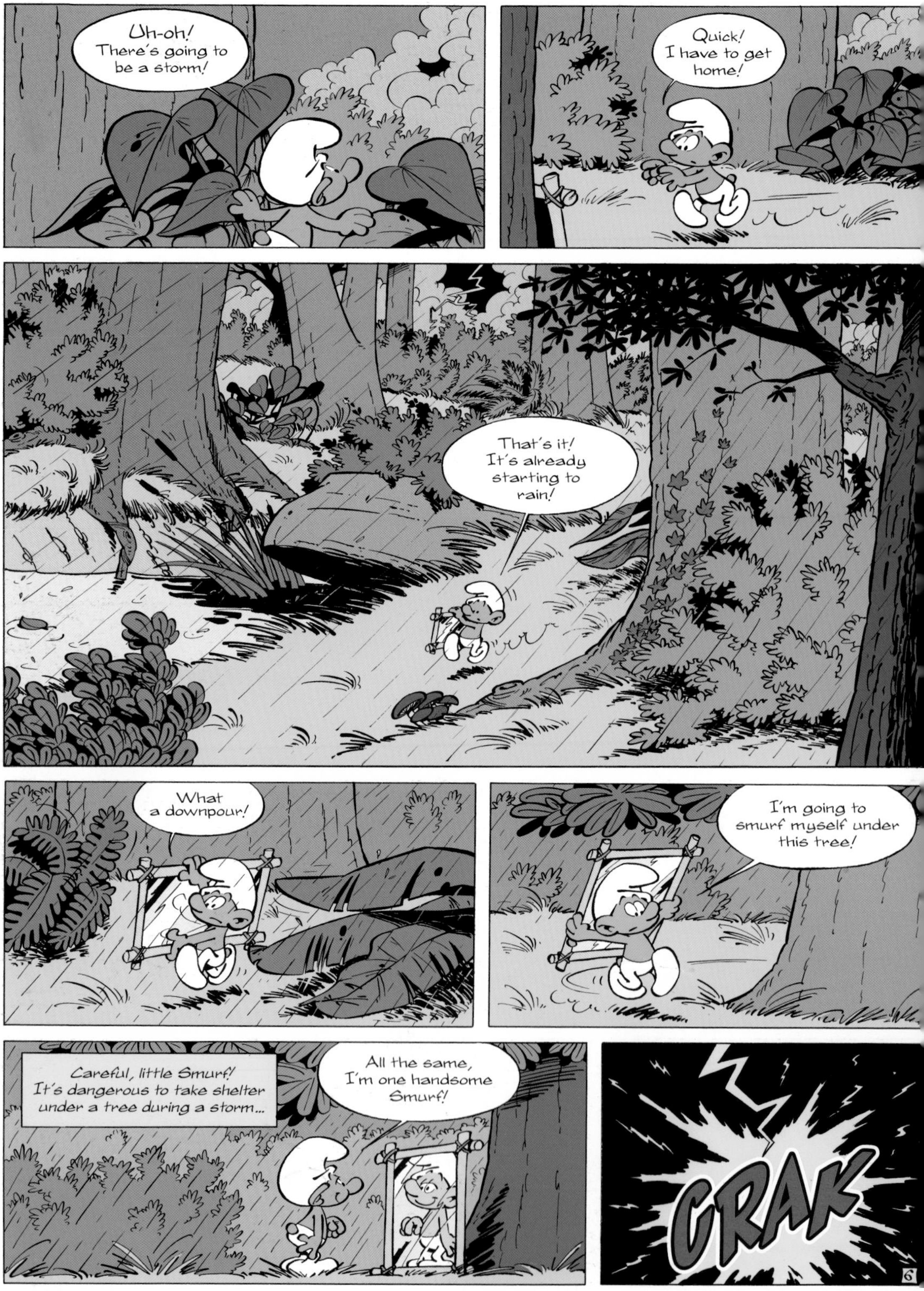
Uh-oh! There's going to be a storm!
Quick! I have to get home!
That's it! It's already starting to rain!
What a downpour!
I'm going to smurf myself under this tree!
Careful, little Smurf! It's dangerous to take shelter under a tree during a storm...
All the same, I'm one handsome Smurf!
CRAK
6

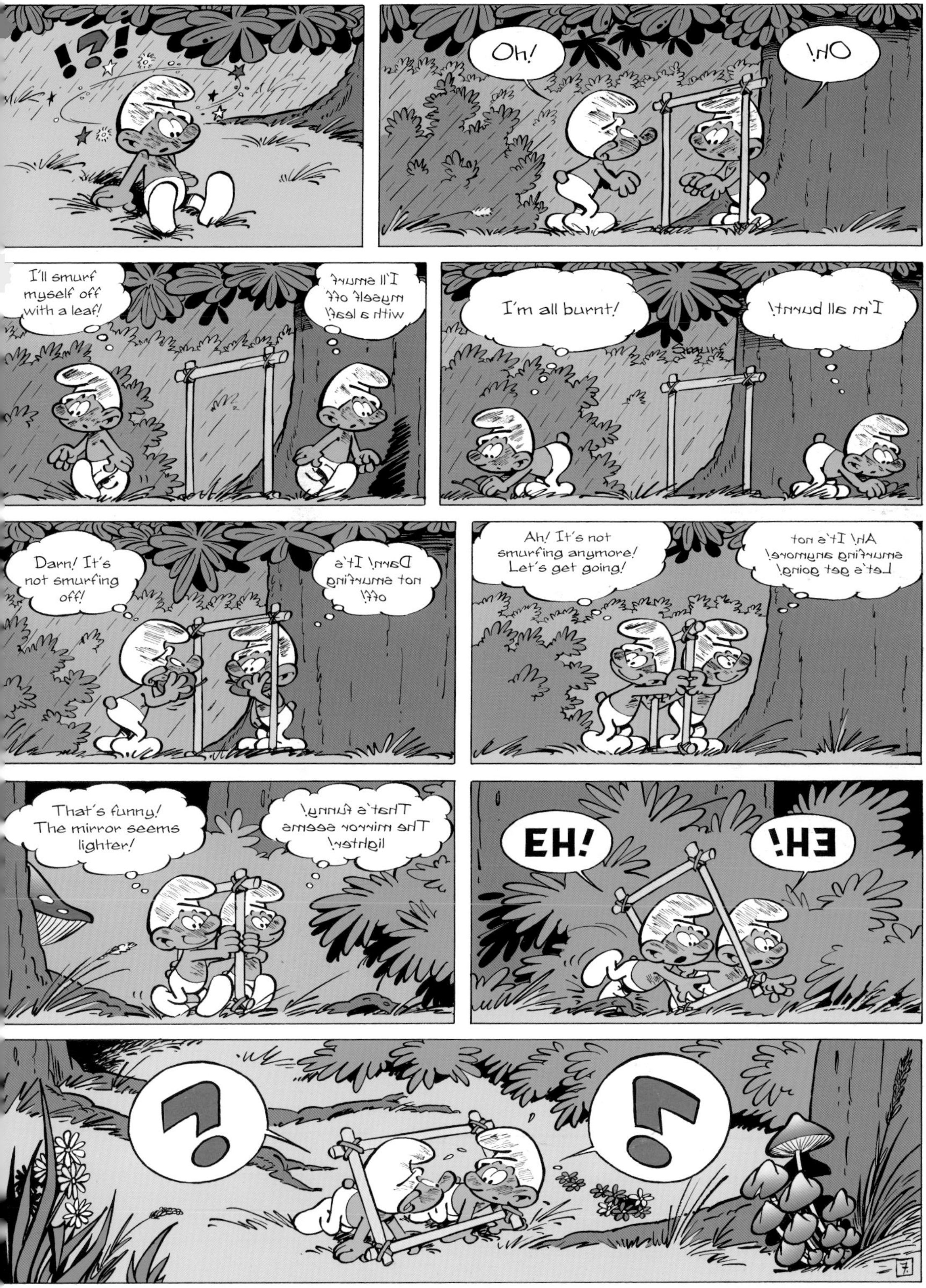
!?!
Oh!
Oh!
I'll smurf myself off with a leaf!
I'll smurf myself off with a leaf!
I'm all burnt!
I'm all burnt!
Darn! It's not smurfing off!
Darn! It's not smurfing off!
Ah! It's not smurfing anymore! Let's get going!
Ah! It's not smurfing anymore! Let's get going!
That's funny! The mirror seems lighter!
That's funny! The mirror seems lighter!
EH!
EH!

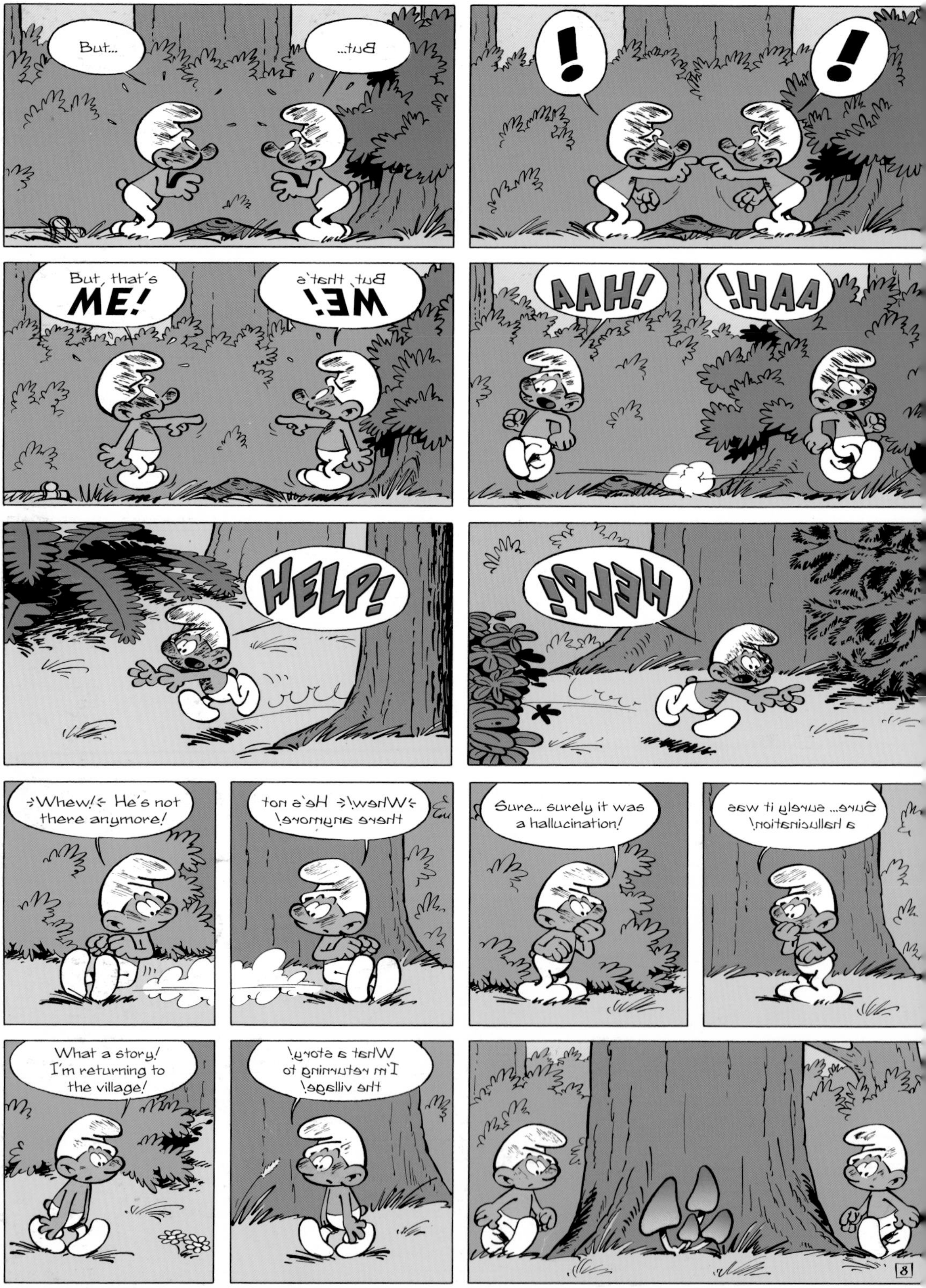
But...
But...
!
!
But, that's ME!
But, that's ME!
AAH!
AAH!
HELP!
HELP!
Whew! He's not there anymore!
Whew! He's not there anymore!
Sure... surely it was a hallucination!
Sure... surely it was a hallucination!
What a story! I'm returning to the village!
What a story! I'm returning to the village!
8

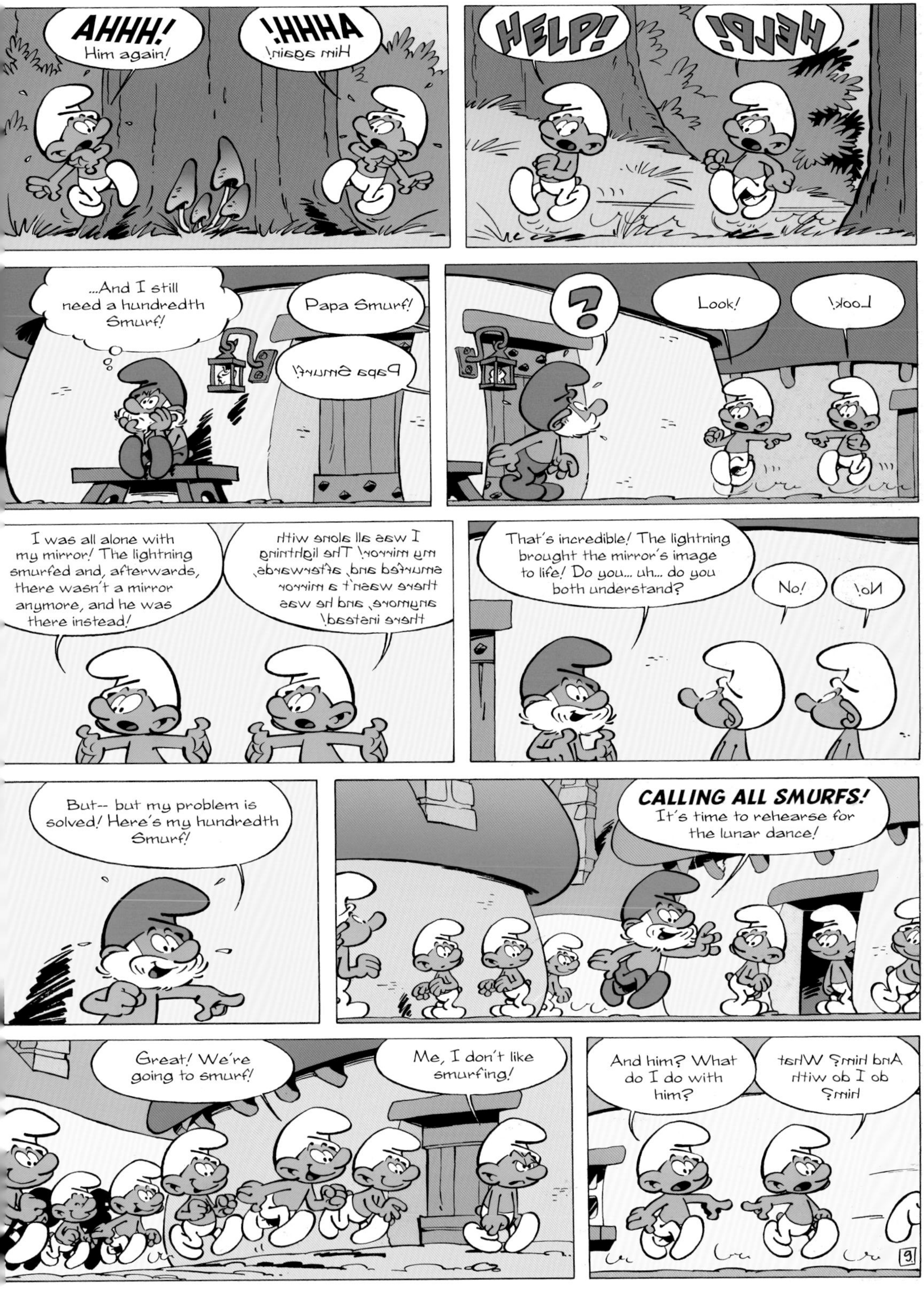
AHHH! Him again!
AHHH! Him again!
HELP!
HELP!
...And I still need a hundredth Smurf!
Papa Smurf!
Papa Smurf!
?
Look!
Look!
I was all alone with my mirror! The lightning smurfed and, afterwards, there wasn't a mirror anymore, and he was there instead!
I was all alone with my mirror! The lightning smurfed and, afterwards, there wasn't a mirror anymore, and he was there instead!
That's incredible! The lightning brought the mirror's image to life! Do you... uh... do you both understand?
No!
No!
But-- but my problem is solved! Here's my hundredth Smurf!
CALLING ALL SMURFS! It's time to rehearse for the lunar dance!
Great! We're going to smurf!
Me, I don't like smurfing!
And him? What do I do with him?
And him? What do I do with him?
9

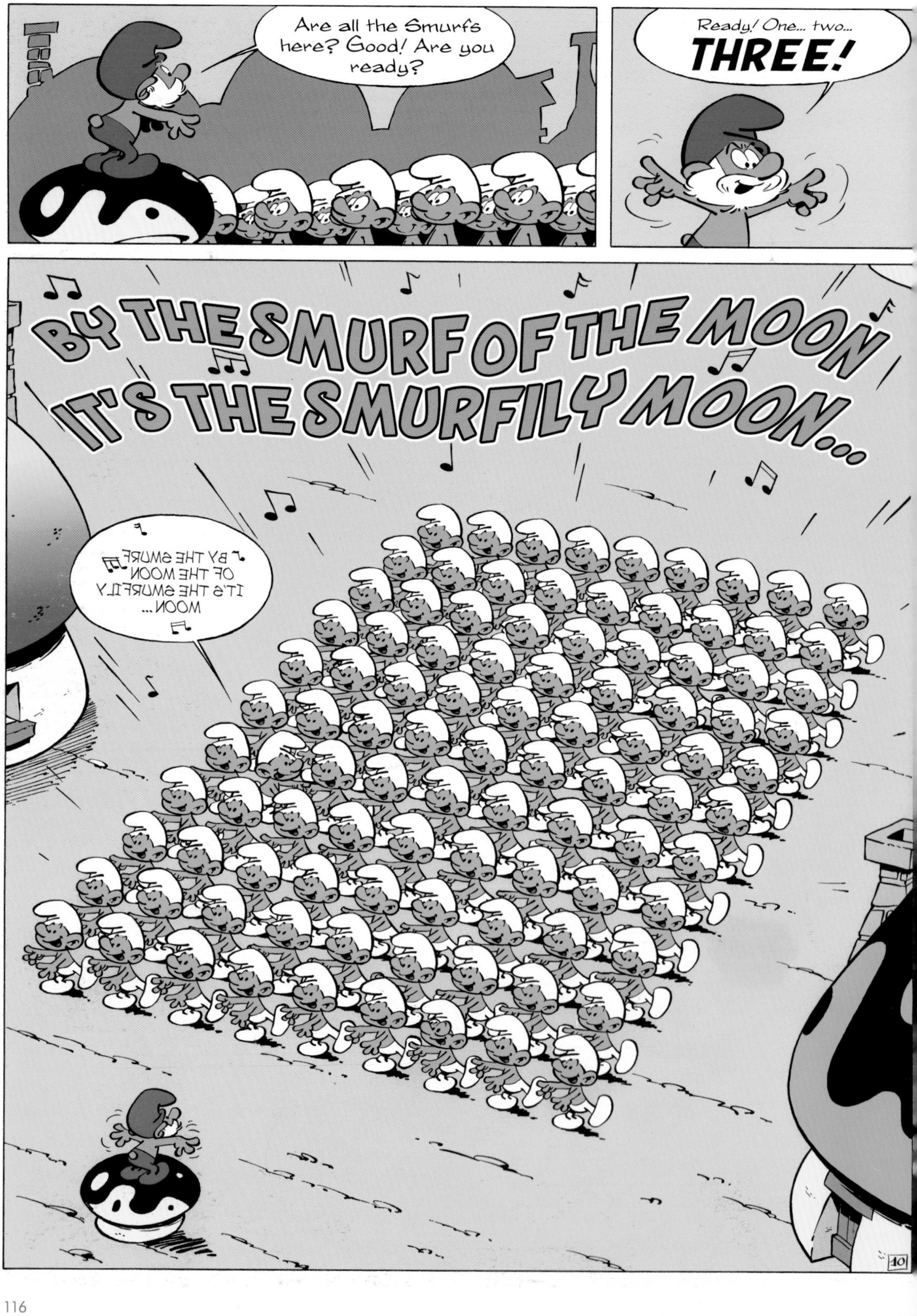
Are all the Smurfs here? Good! Are you ready?
Ready! One... two... THREE!
BY THE SMURF OF THE MOON IT'S THE SMURFILY MOON...
BY THE SMURF OF THE MOON IT'S THE SMURFILY MOON...
10

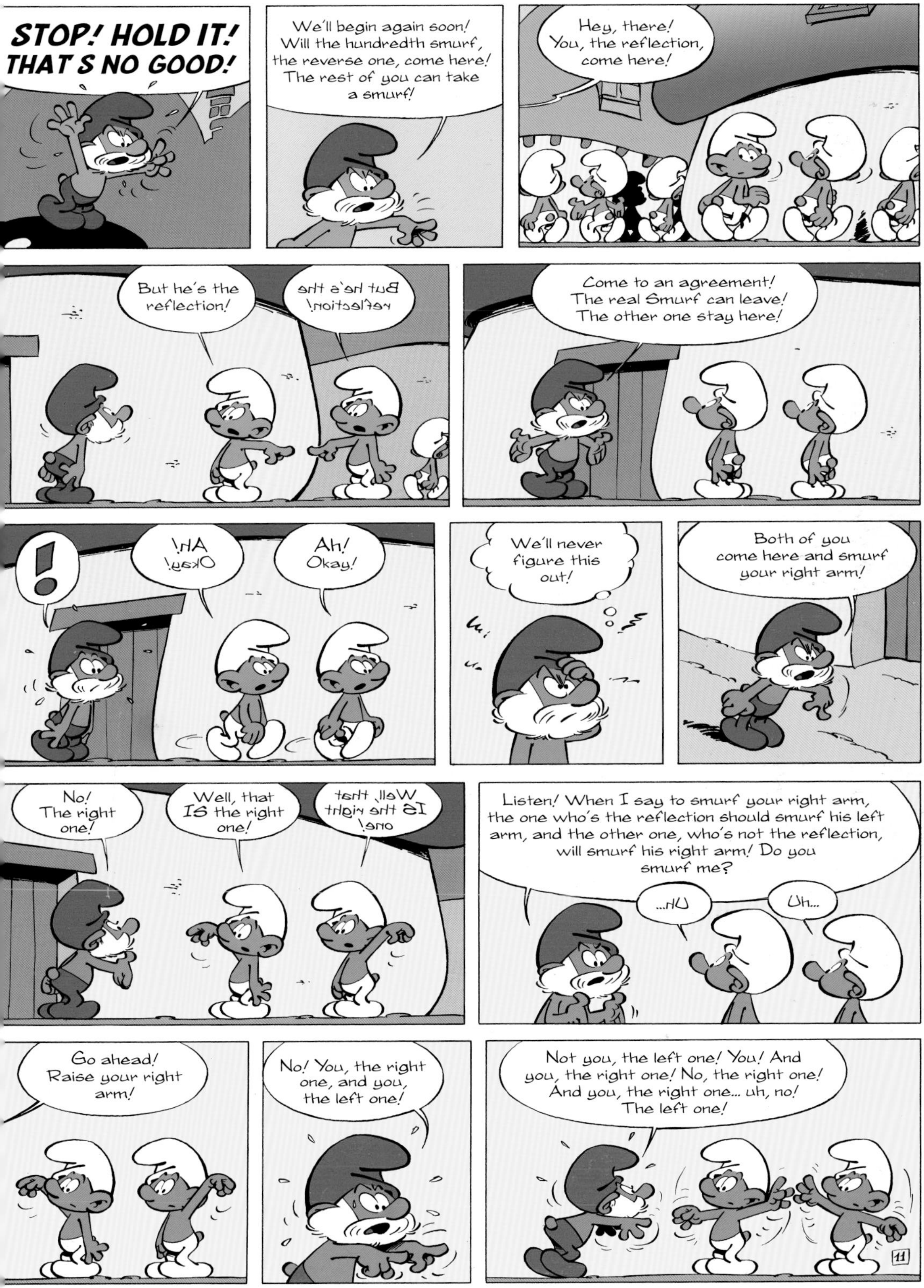
STOP! HOLD IT! THAT'S NO GOOD!
We'll begin again soon! Will the hundredth smurf, the reverse one, come here! The rest of you can take a smurf!
Hey, there! You, the reflection, come here!
But he's the reflection!
But he's the reflection!
Come to an agreement! The real Smurf can leave! The other one stay here!
!
Ah! Okay!
Ah! Okay!
We'll never figure this out!
Both of you come here and smurf your right arm!
No! The right one!
Well, that IS the right one!
Well, that IS the right one!
Listen! When I say to smurf your right arm, the one who's the reflection should smurf his left arm, and the other one, who's not the reflection, will smurf his right arm! Do you smurf me?
Uh...
Uh...
Go ahead! Raise your right arm!
No! You, the right one, and you, the left one!
Not you, the left one! You! And you, the right one! No, the right one! And you, the right one... uh, no! The left one!
11

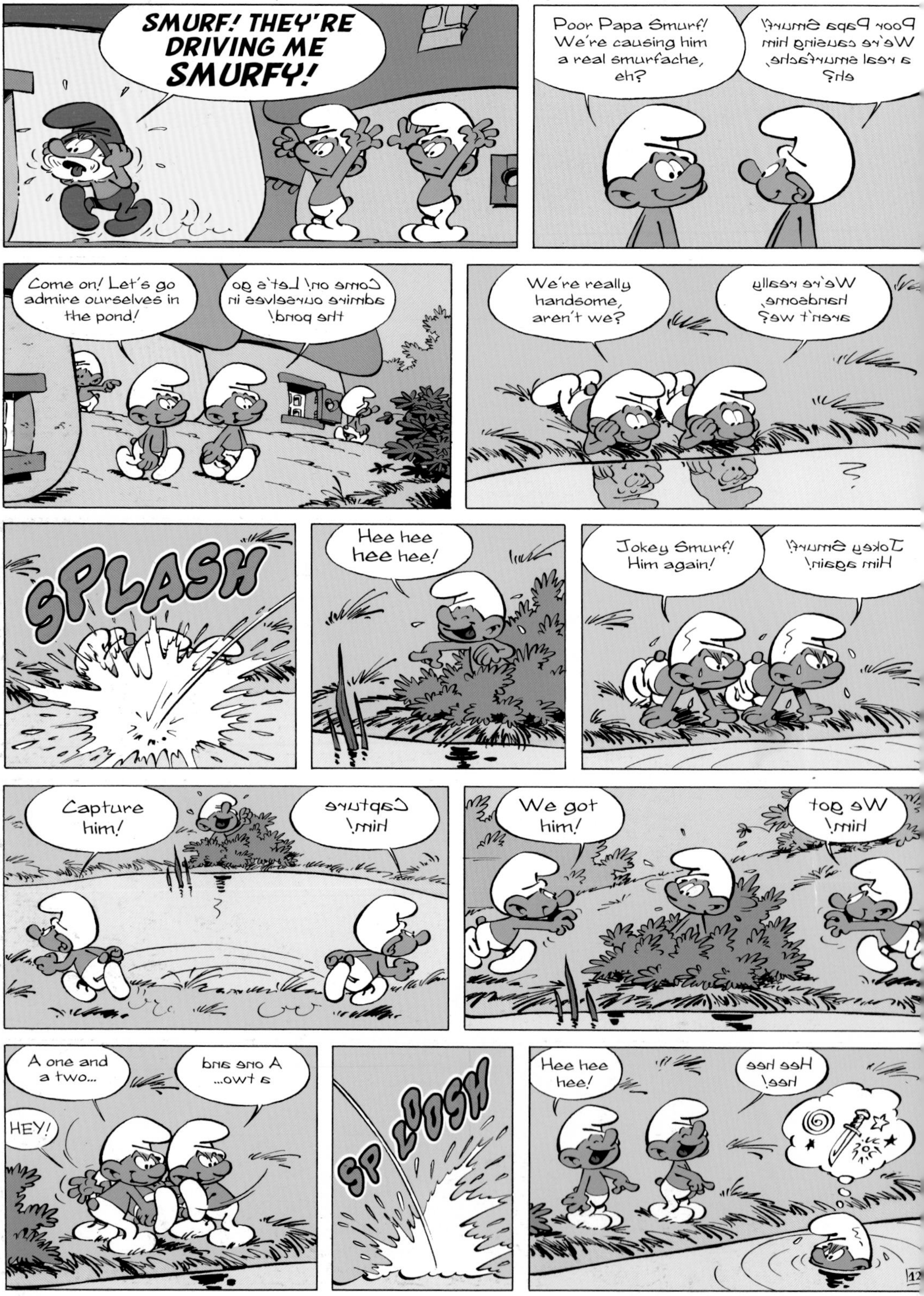

SMURF! THEY'RE DRIVING ME SMURFY!
Poor Papa Smurf! We're causing him a real smurfache, eh?
Poor Papa Smurf! We're causing him a real smurfache, eh?
Come on! Let's go admire ourselves in the pond!
Come on! Let's go admire ourselves in the pond!
We're really handsome, aren't we?
We're really handsome, aren't we?
SPLASH
Hee hee hee hee!
Jokey Smurf! Him again!
Jokey Smurf! Him again!
Capture him!
Capture him!
We got him!
We got him!
A one and a two...
A one and a two...
HEY!
SPLOOSH
Hee hee hee!
Hee hee hee!
12

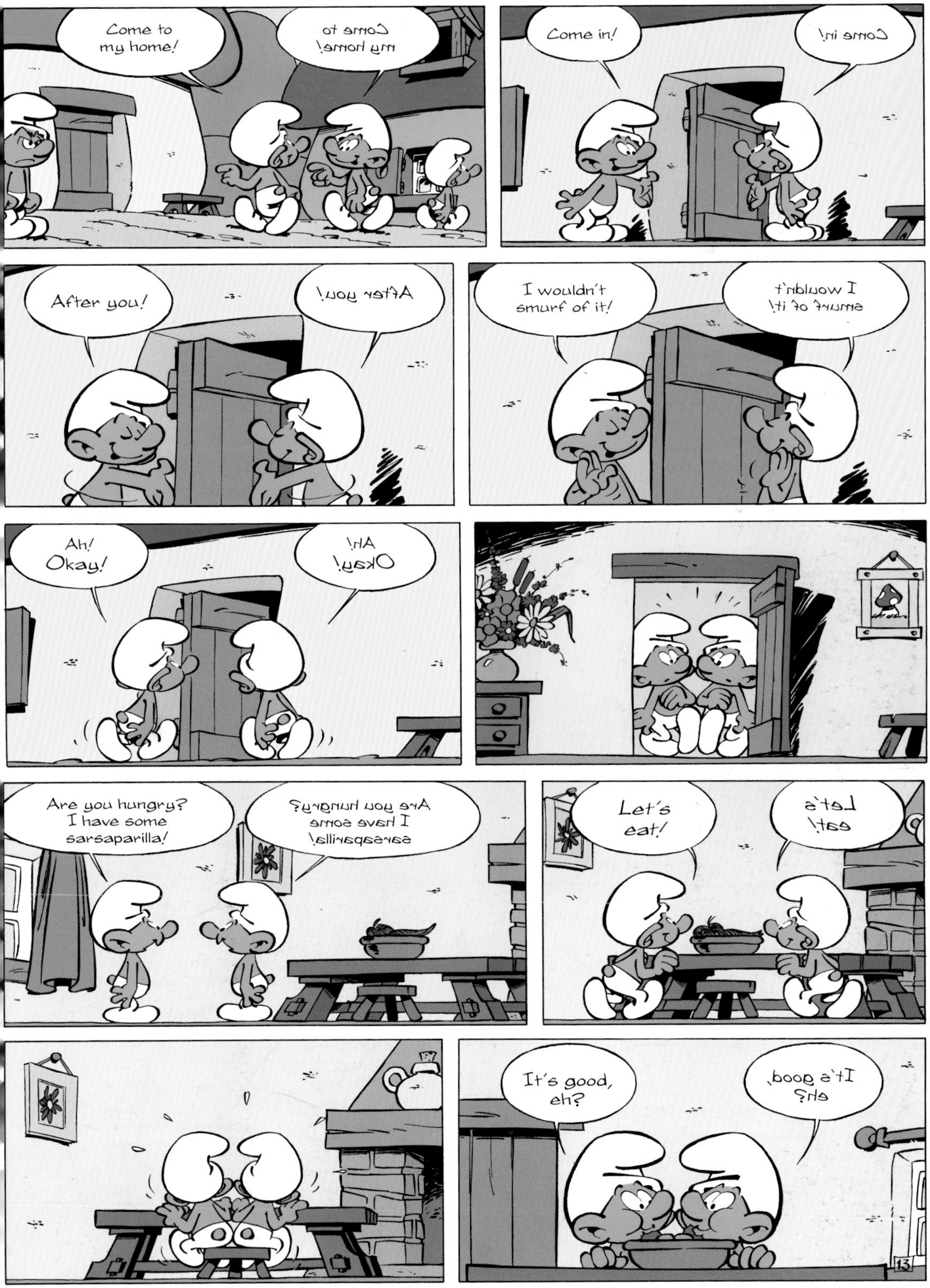
Come to my home!
Come to my home!
Come in!
Come in!
After you!
After you!
I wouldn't smurf of it!
I wouldn't smurf of it!
Ah! Okay!
Ah! Okay!
Are you hungry? I have some sarsaparilla!
Are you hungry? I have some sarsaparilla!
Let's eat!
Let's eat!
It's good, eh?
It's good, eh?
13

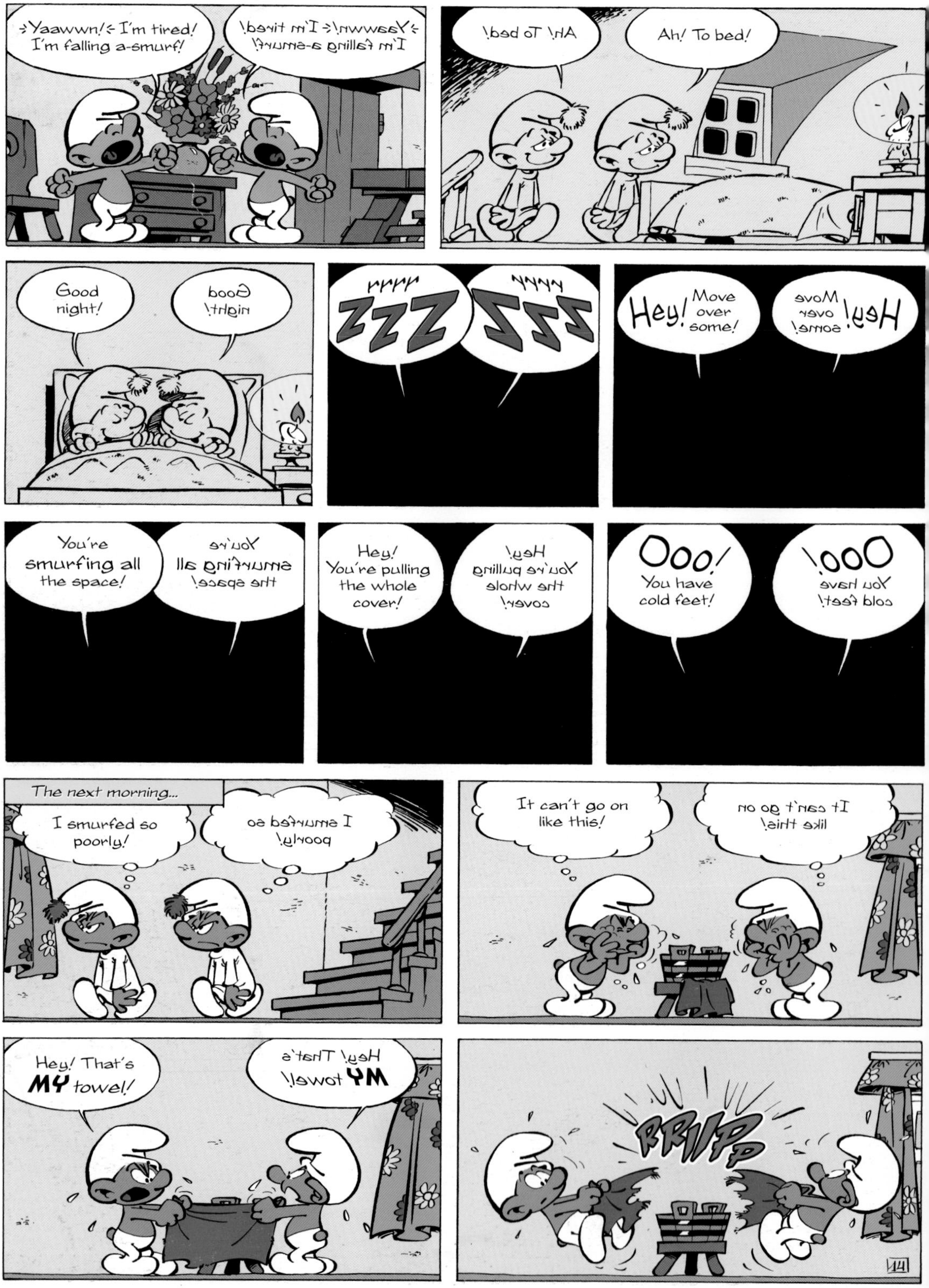

Yaawwn! I'm tired! I'm falling a-smurf!
Yaawwn! I'm tired! I'm falling a-smurf!
Ah! To bed!
Ah! To bed!
Good night!
Good night!
rrrr ZZZ
rrrr ZZZ
Hey! Move over some!
Hey! Move over some!
You're smurfing all the space!
You're smurfing all the space!
Hey! You're pulling the whole cover!
Hey! You're pulling the whole cover!
Ooo! You have cold feet!
Ooo! You have cold feet!
The next morning...
I smurfed so poorly!
I smurfed so poorly!
It can't go on like this!
It can't go on like this!
Hey! That's MY towel!
Hey! That's MY towel!
RRIPP
14

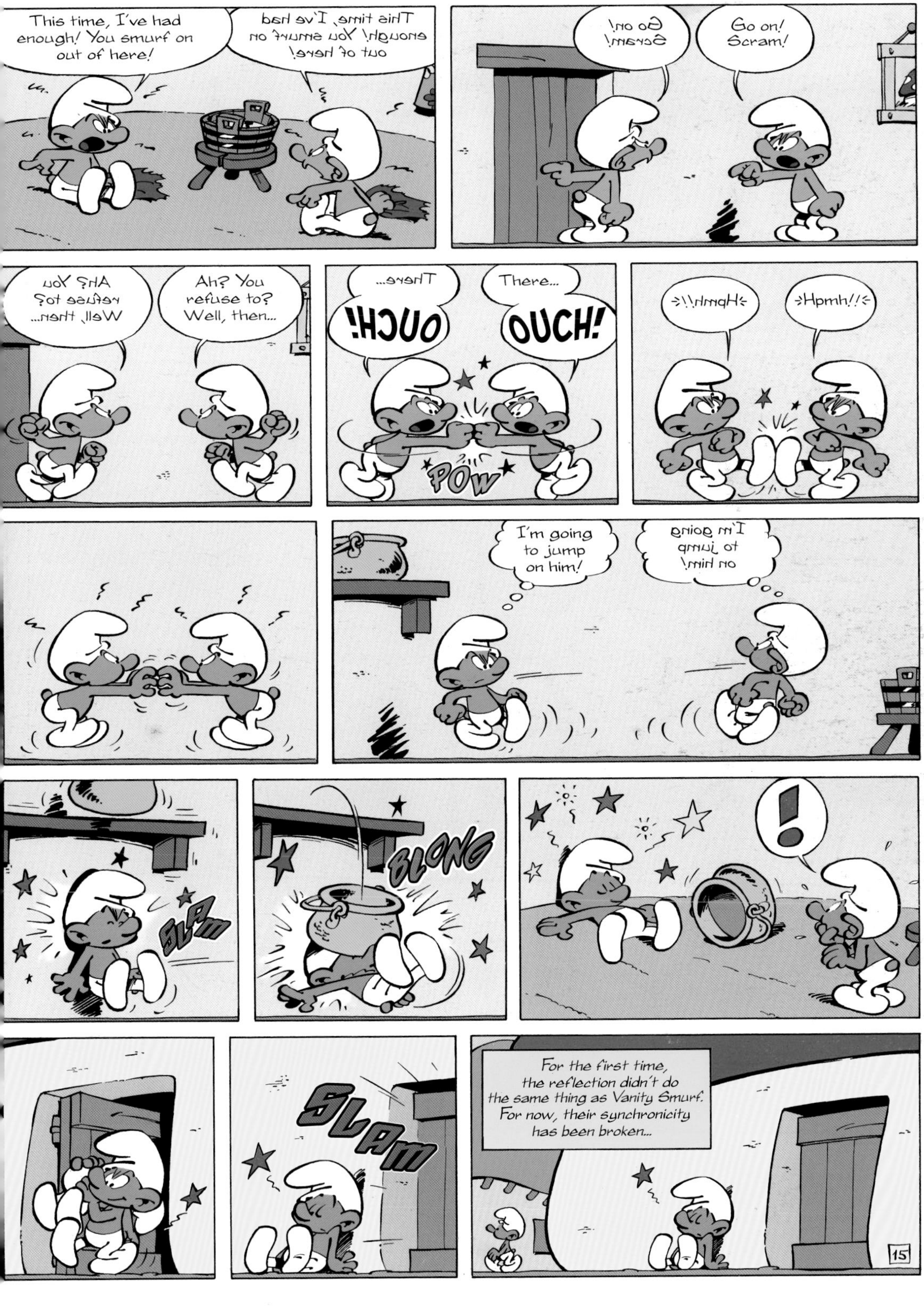

This time, I've had enough! You smurf on out of here!
This time, I've had enough! You smurf on out of here!
Go on! Scram!
Go on! Scram!
Ah? You refuse to? Well, then...
Ah? You refuse to? Well, then...
There...
There...
OUCH!
OUCH!
POW
Hpmh!!
Hpmh!!
I'm going to jump on him!
I'm going to jump on him!
SLAM
BLONG
!
SLAM
For the first time, the reflection didn't do the same thing as Vanity Smurf. For now, their synchronicity has been broken...
15

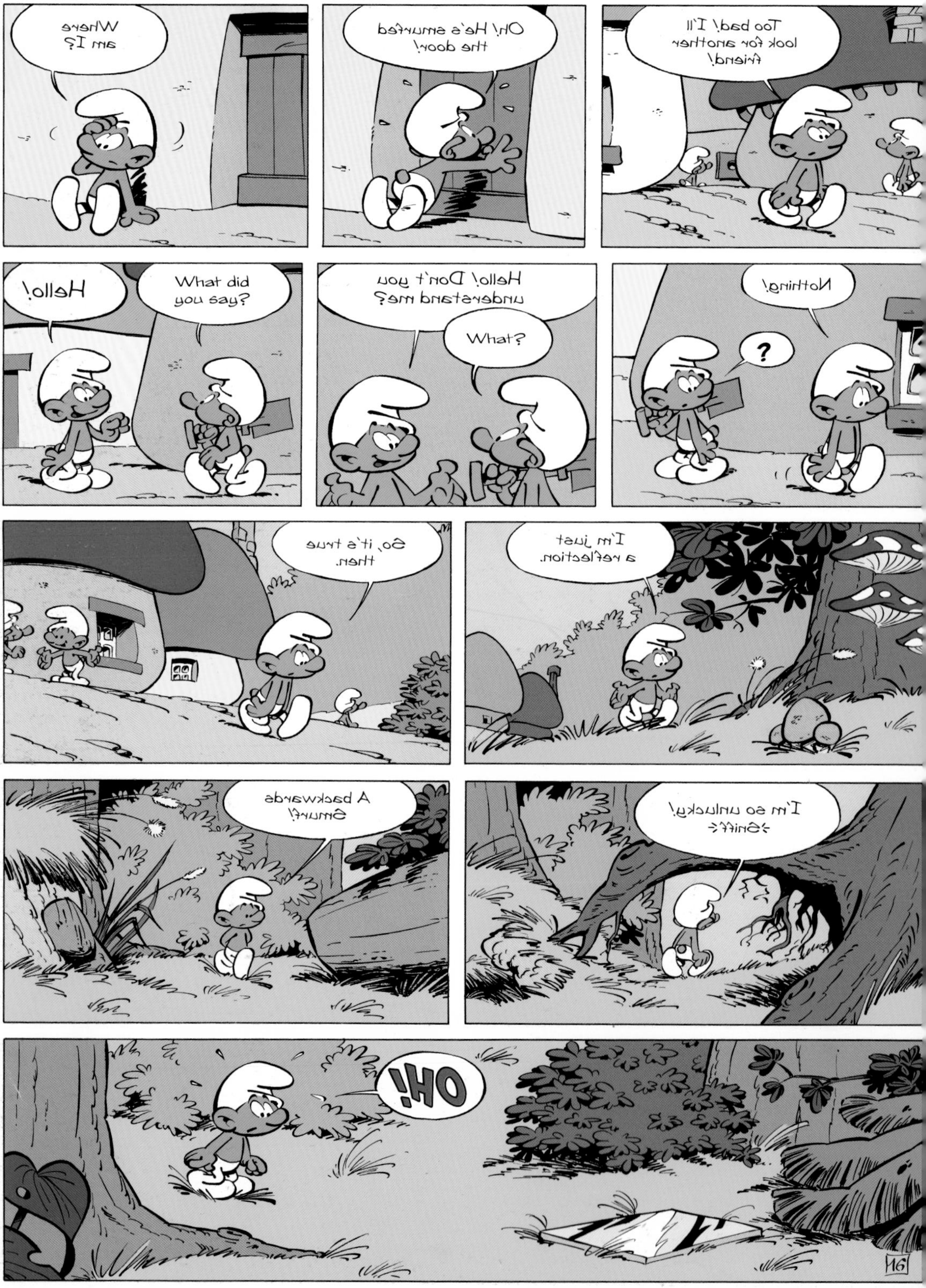

Where am I?
Oh! He's smurfed the door!
Too bad! I'll look for another friend!
Hello!
What did you say?
Hello! Don't you understand me?
What?
?
Nothing!
So, it's true then.
I'm just a reflection.
A backwards Smurf!
I'm so unlucky! *Sniff*
OH!
16

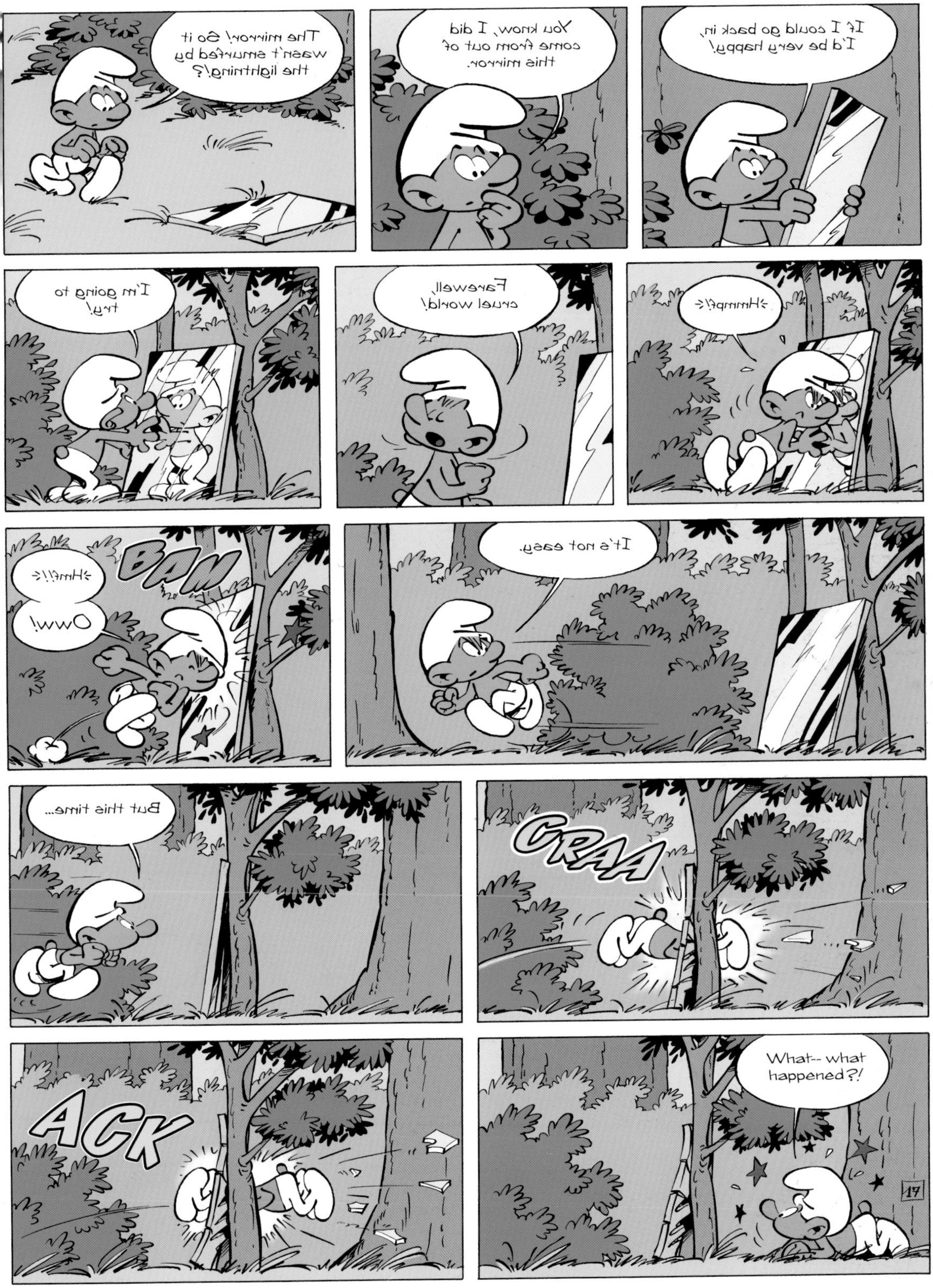
The mirror! So it wasn't smurfed by the lightning?!
You know, I did come from out of this mirror.
If I could go back in, I'd be very happy!
I'm going to try!
Farewell, cruel world!
Hmmpf!
BAM
Hmf!!
Oww!
It's not easy.
But this time...
CRAA
ACK
What-- what happened?!
17

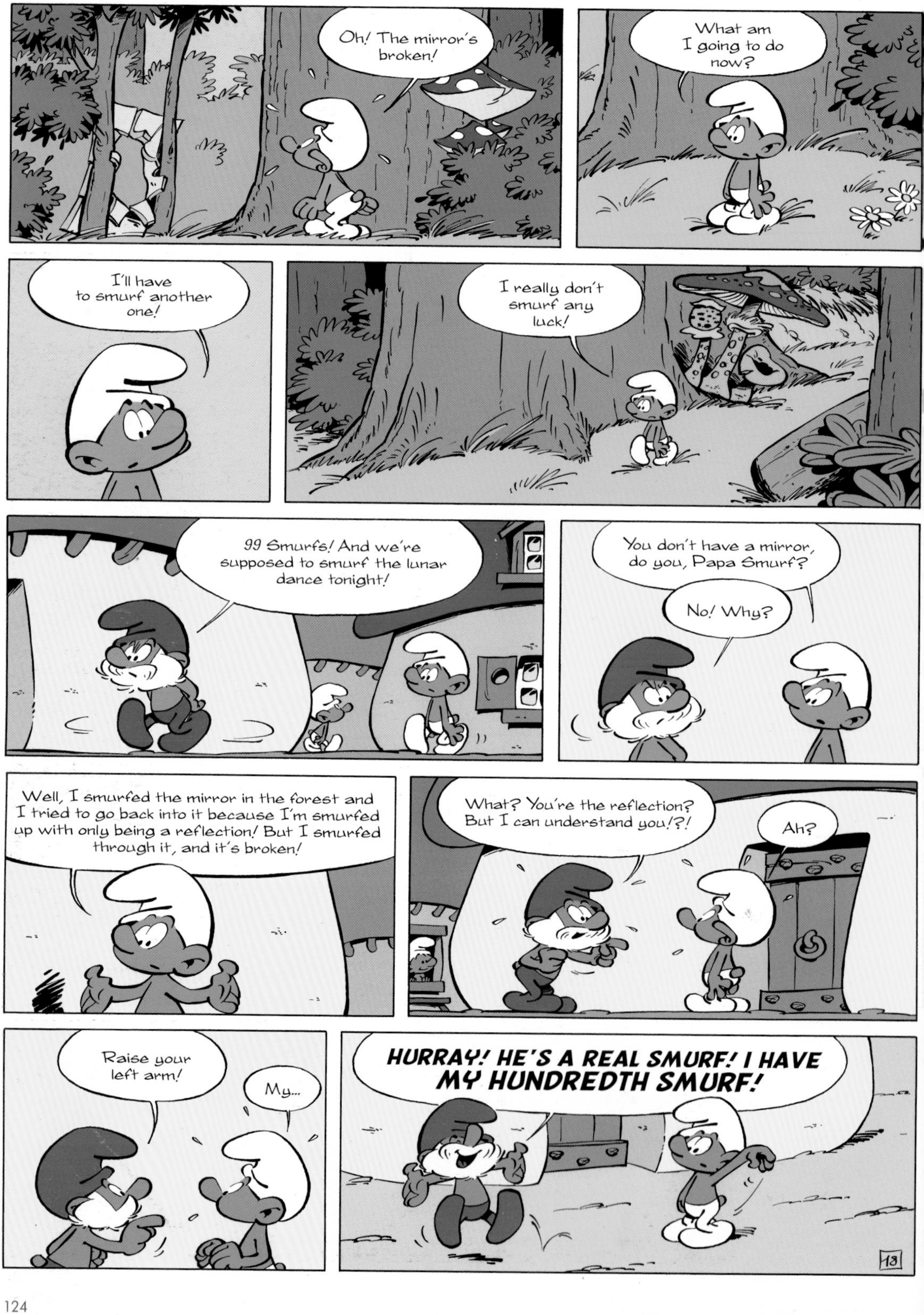
Oh! The mirror's broken!
What am I going to do now?
I'll have to smurf another one!
I really don't smurf any luck!
99 Smurfs! And we're supposed to smurf the lunar dance tonight!
You don't have a mirror, do you, Papa Smurf?
No! Why?
Well, I smurfed the mirror in the forest and I tried to go back into it because I'm smurfed up with only being a reflection! But I smurfed through it, and it's broken!
What? You're the reflection? But I can understand you!?!
Ah?
Raise your left arm!
My...
HURRAY! HE'S A REAL SMURF! I HAVE MY HUNDREDTH SMURF!
18

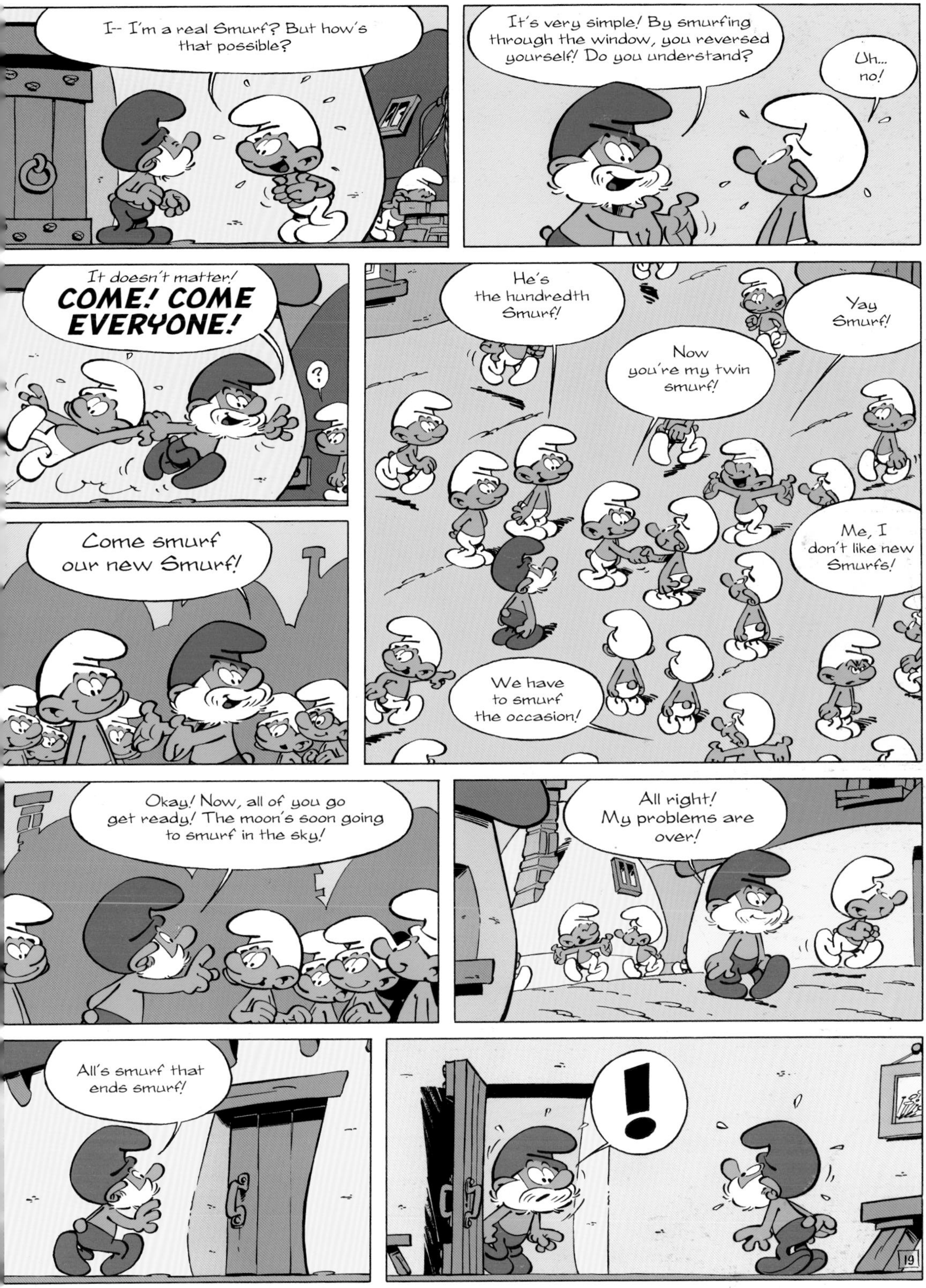
I-- I'm a real Smurf? But how's that possible?
It's very simple! By smurfing through the window, you reversed yourself! Do you understand?
Uh... no!
It doesn't matter! COME! COME EVERYONE!
?
Come smurf our new Smurf!
He's the hundredth Smurf!
Yay Smurf!
Now you're my twin smurf!
Me, I don't like new Smurfs!
We have to smurf the occasion!
Okay! Now, all of you go get ready! The moon's soon going to smurf in the sky!
All right! My problems are over!
All's smurf that ends smurf!
!
19

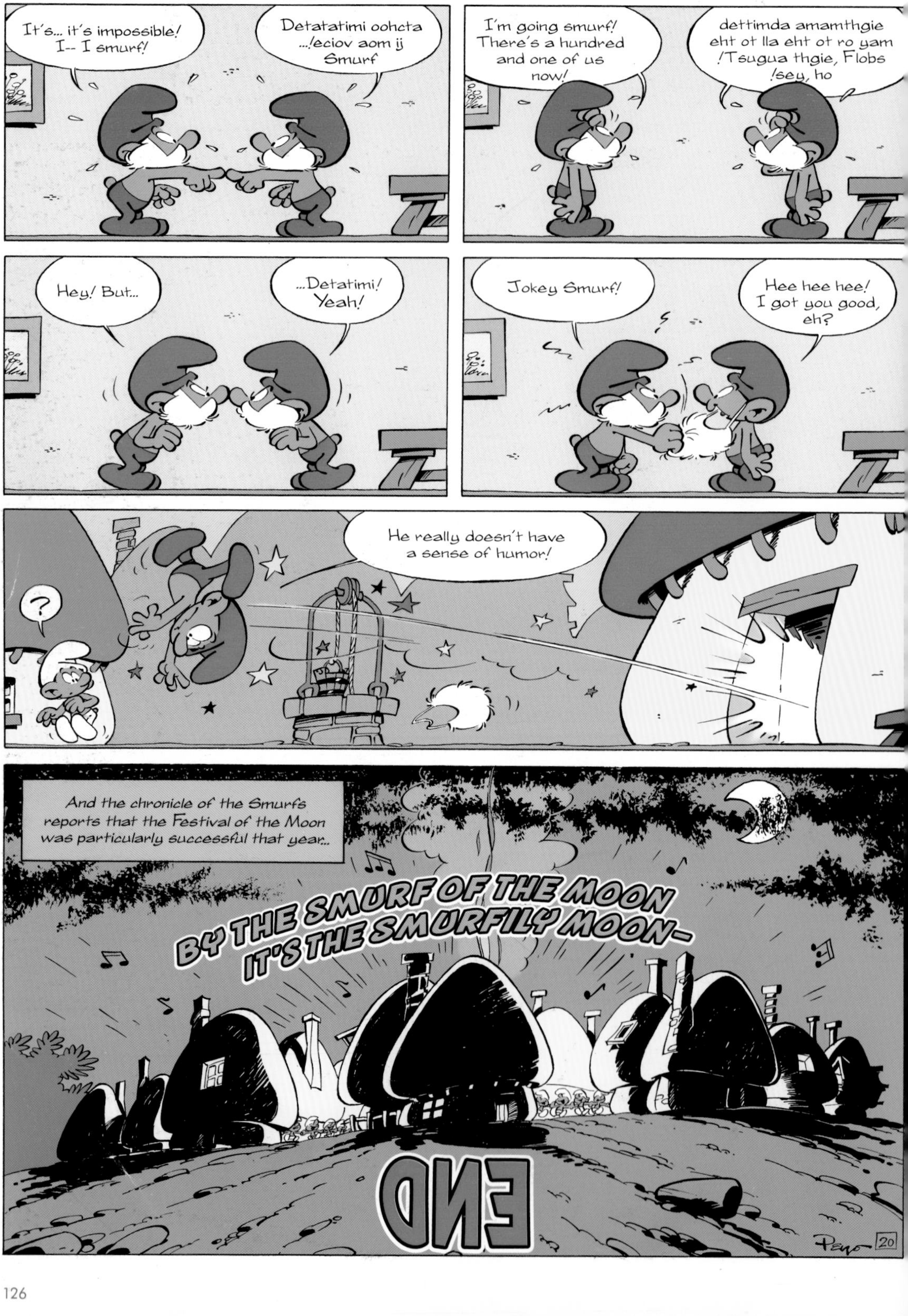
It's... it's impossible! I-- I smurf!
Detatatimi oohcta ...!eciov aom ij Smurf
I'm going smurf! There's a hundred and one of us now!
dettimda amamthgie eht ot lla eht ot ro yam !Tsugua thgie, Flobs !sey, ho
Hey! But...
...Detatimi! Yeah!
Jokey Smurf!
Hee hee hee! I got you good, eh?
?
He really doesn't have a sense of humor!
And the chronicle of the Smurfs reports that the Festival of the Moon was particularly successful that year...
BY THE SMURF OF THE MOON IT'S THE SMURFILY MOON-
END
Peyo
20

THE SMURFS AND THE HOWLIBIRD

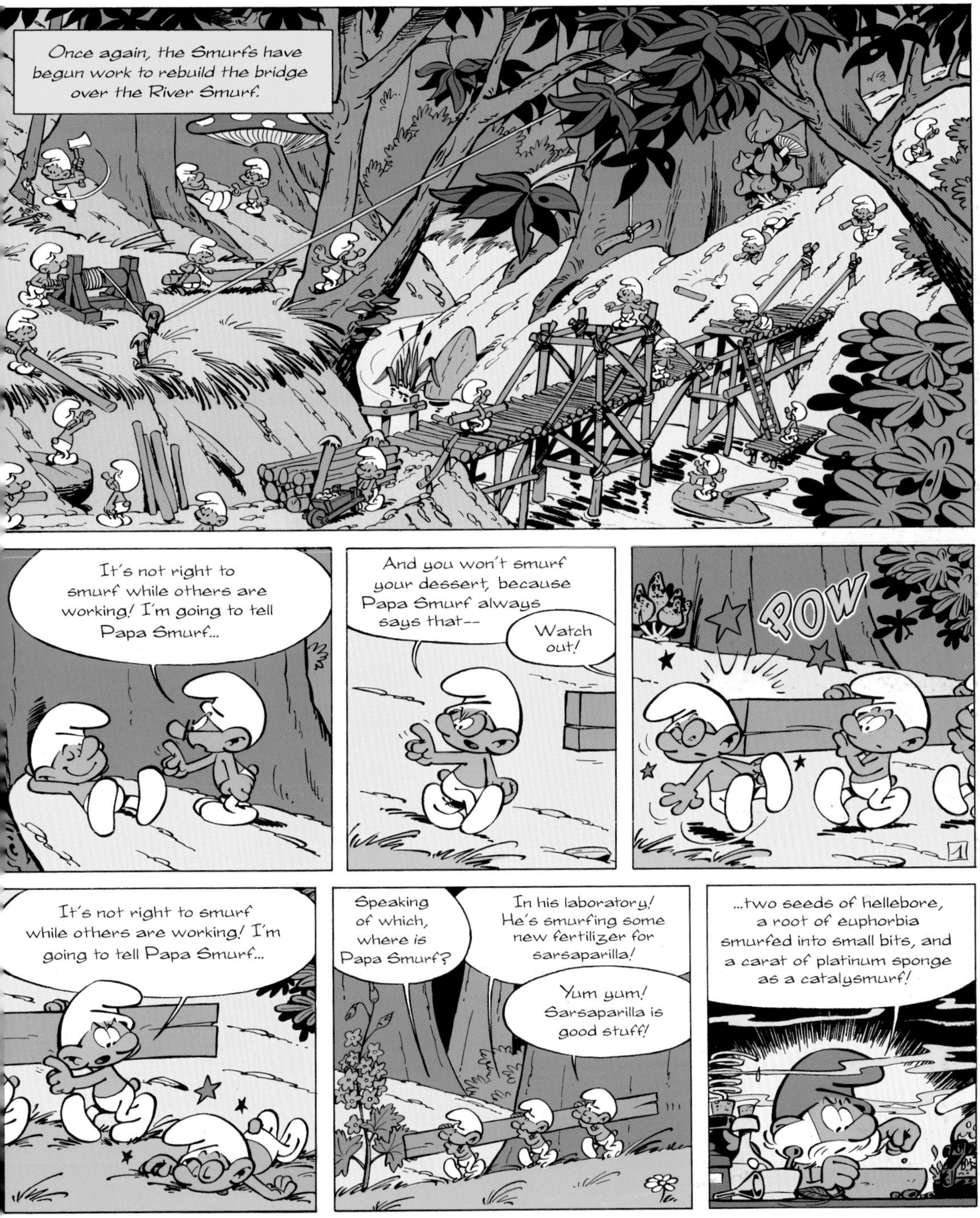

Once again, the Smurfs have begun work to rebuild the bridge over the River Smurf.
It's not right to smurf while others are working! I'm going to tell Papa Smurf...
And you won't smurf your dessert, because Papa Smurf always says that--
Watch out!
POW
1
It's not right to smurf while others are working! I'm going to tell Papa Smurf...
Speaking of which, where is Papa Smurf?
In his laboratory! He's smurfing some new fertilizer for sarsaparilla!
Yum yum! Sarsaparilla is good stuff!
...two seeds of hellebore, a root of euphorbia smurfed into small bits, and a carat of platinum sponge as a catalysmurf!

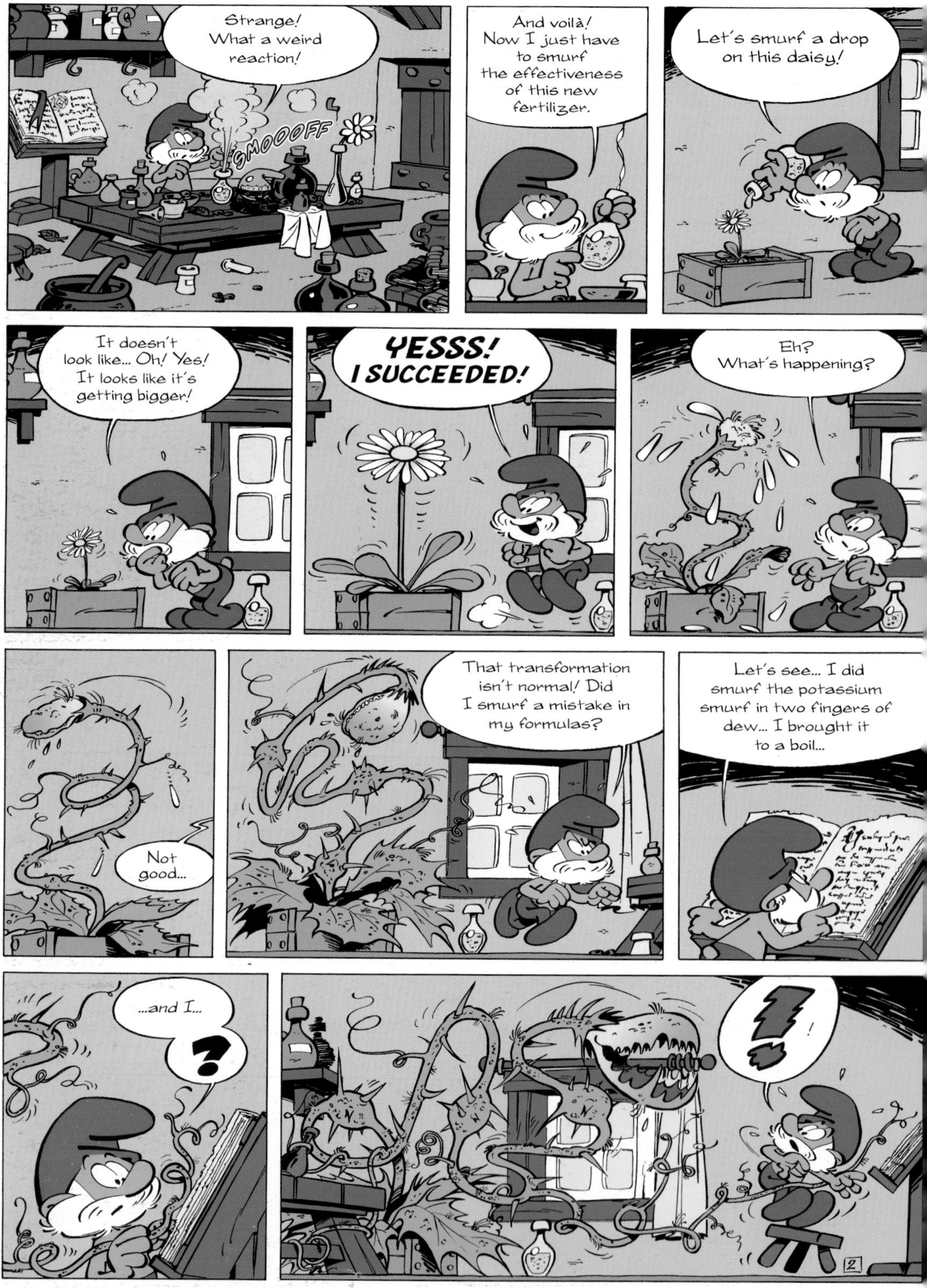

Strange! What a weird reaction!
SMOOOFF
And voilà! Now I just have to smurf the effectiveness of this new fertilizer.
Let's smurf a drop on this daisy!
It doesn't look like... Oh! Yes! It looks like it's getting bigger!
YESSS! I SUCCEEDED!
Eh? What's happening?
Not good...
That transformation isn't normal! Did I smurf a mistake in my formulas?
Let's see... I did smurf the potassium smurf in two fingers of dew... I brought it to a boil...
...and I...
?
!
!

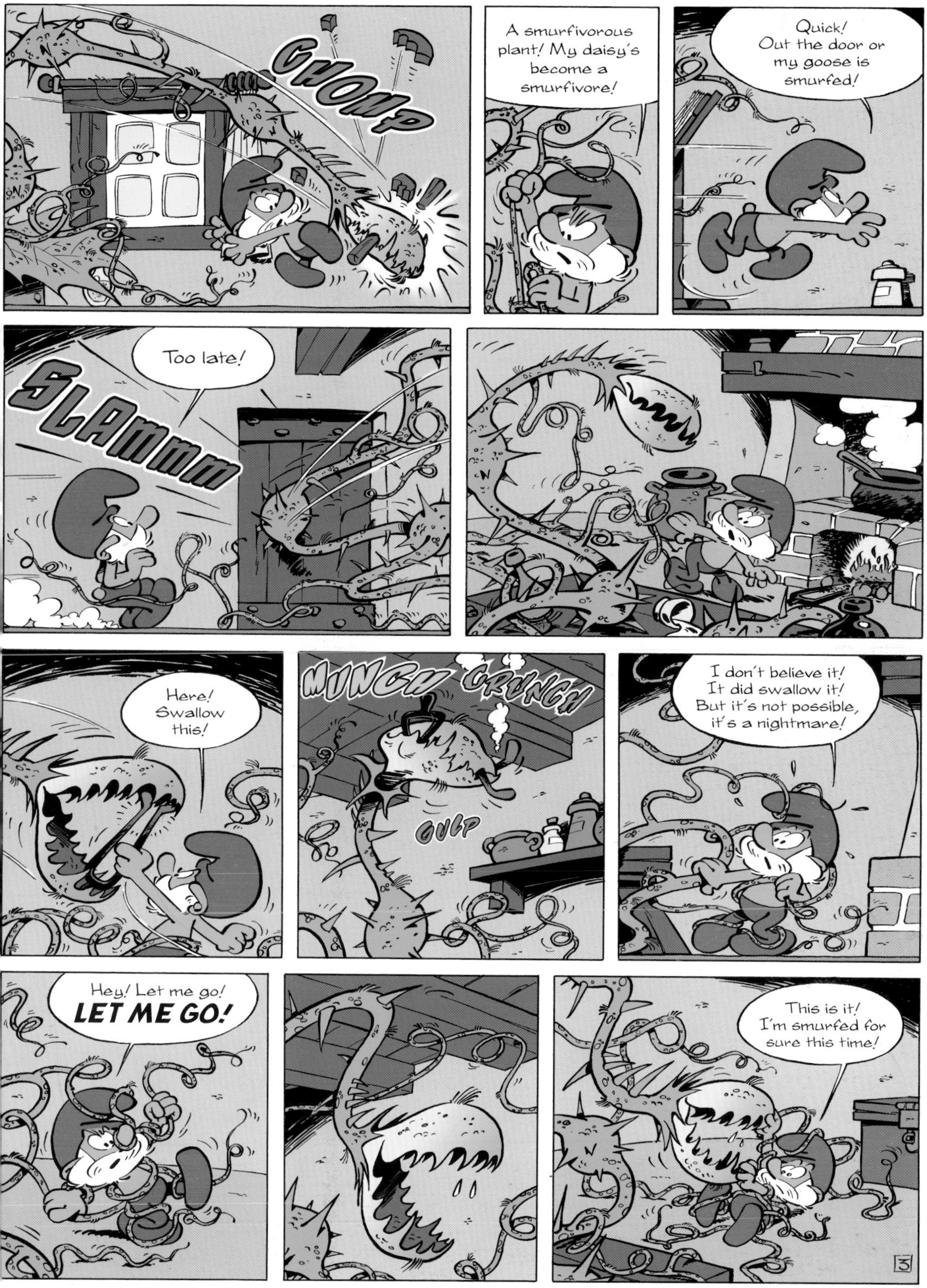
GCHOMP
A smurfivorous plant! My daisy's become a smurfivore!
Quick! Out the door or my goose is smurfed!
Too late!
SLAMMM
Here! Swallow this!
MUNCH CRUNCH
GULP
I don't believe it! It did swallow it! But it's not possible, it's a nightmare!
Hey! Let me go! LET ME GO!
This is it! I'm smurfed for sure this time!
3

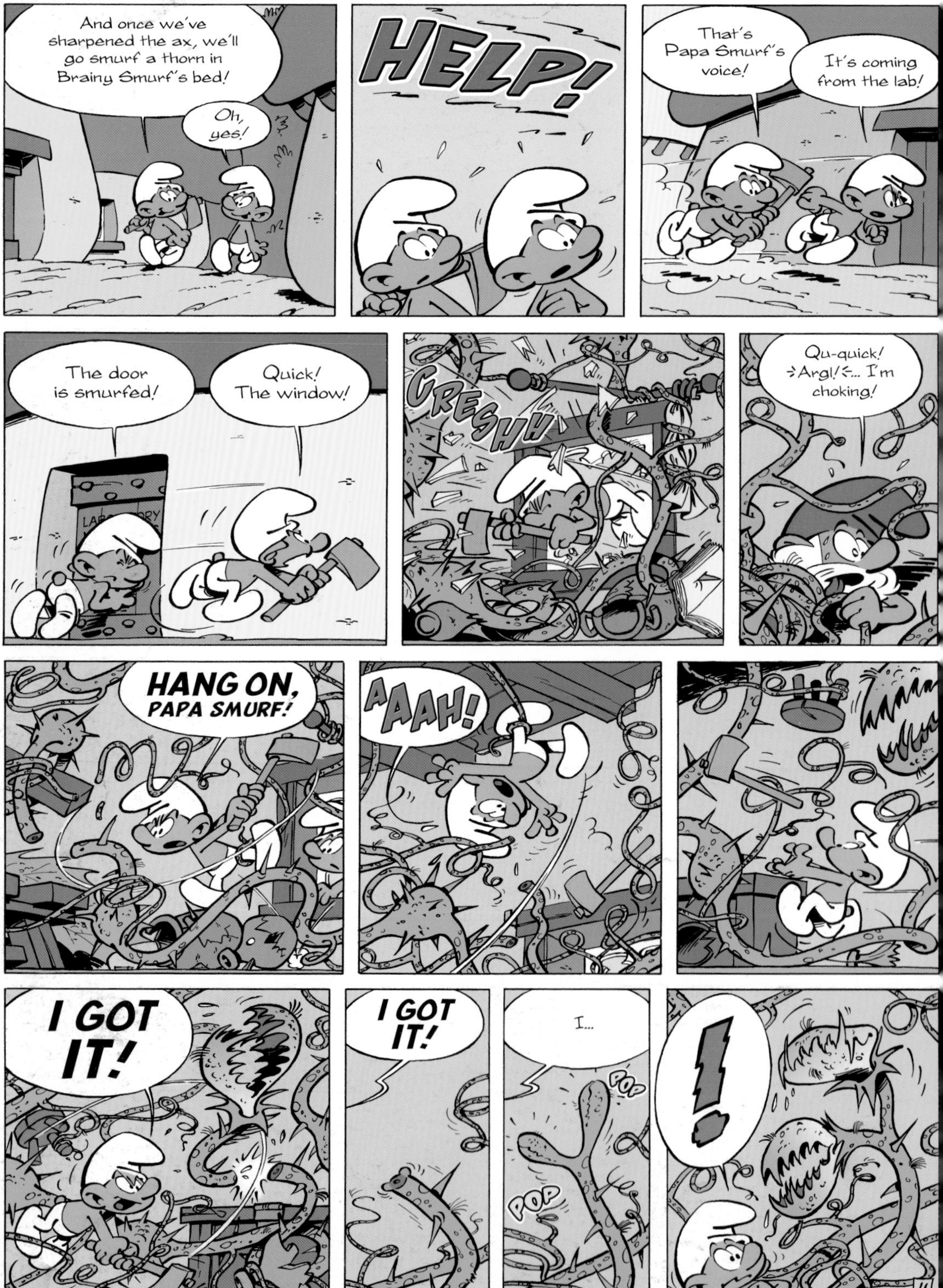

And once we've sharpened the ax, we'll go smurf a thorn in Brainy Smurf's bed!
Oh, yes!
HELP!
That's Papa Smurf's voice!
It's coming from the lab!
The door is smurfed!
Quick! The window!
CRESHH
Qu-quick! Argl! ... I'm choking!
HANG ON, PAPA SMURF!
AAAH!
I GOT IT!
I GOT IT!
I...
POP
POP
!
4

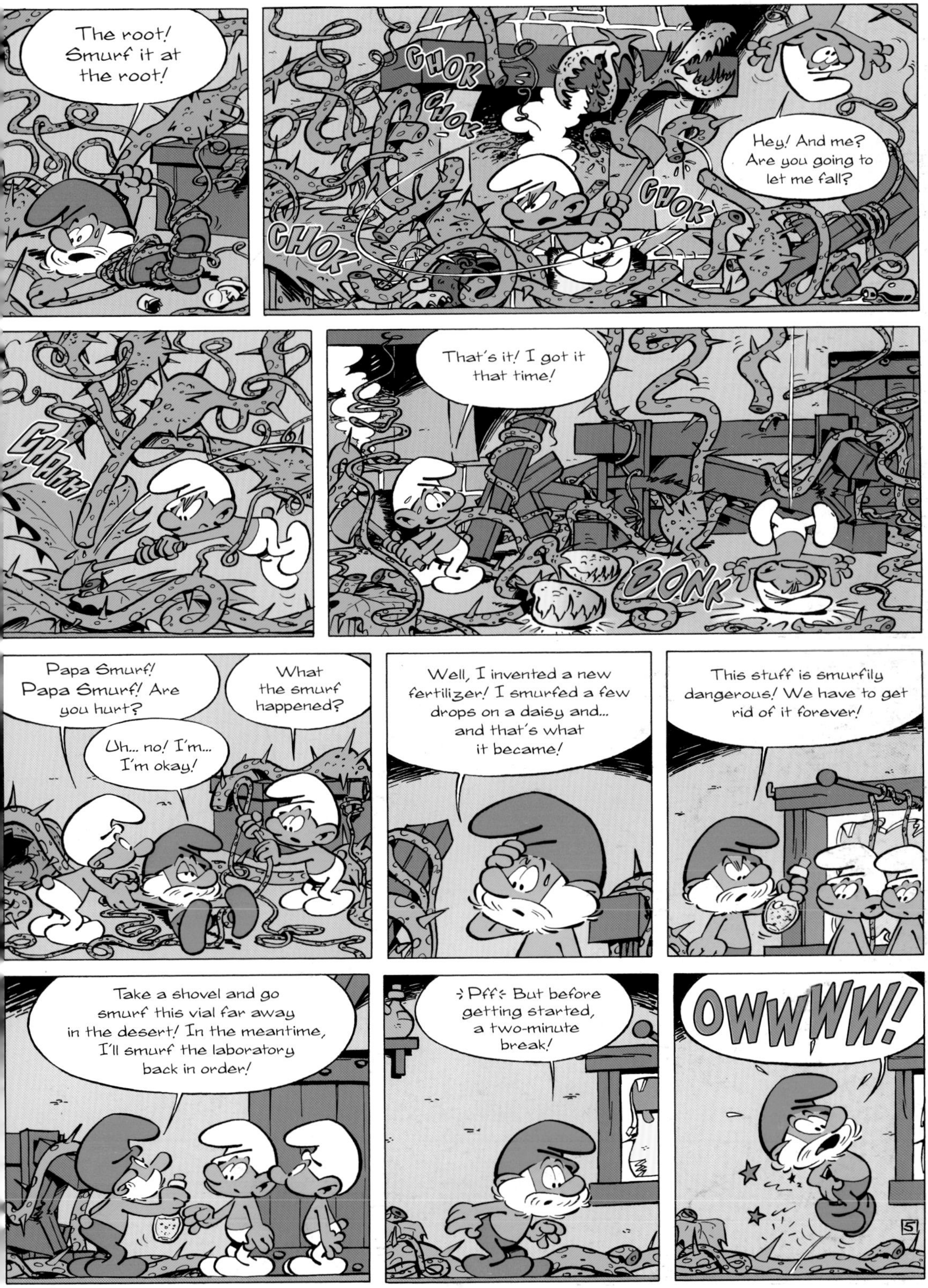
The root! Smurf it at the root!
CHOK
CHOK
GHOK
CHOK
Hey! And me? Are you going to let me fall?
CHHKK
That's it! I got it that time!
BONK
Papa Smurf! Papa Smurf! Are you hurt?
Uh... no! I'm... I'm okay!
What the smurf happened?
Well, I invented a new fertilizer! I smurfed a few drops on a daisy and... and that's what it became!
This stuff is smurfily dangerous! We have to get rid of it forever!
Take a shovel and go smurf this vial far away in the desert! In the meantime, I'll smurf the laboratory back in order!
Pff But before getting started, a two-minute break!
OWWWW!
5

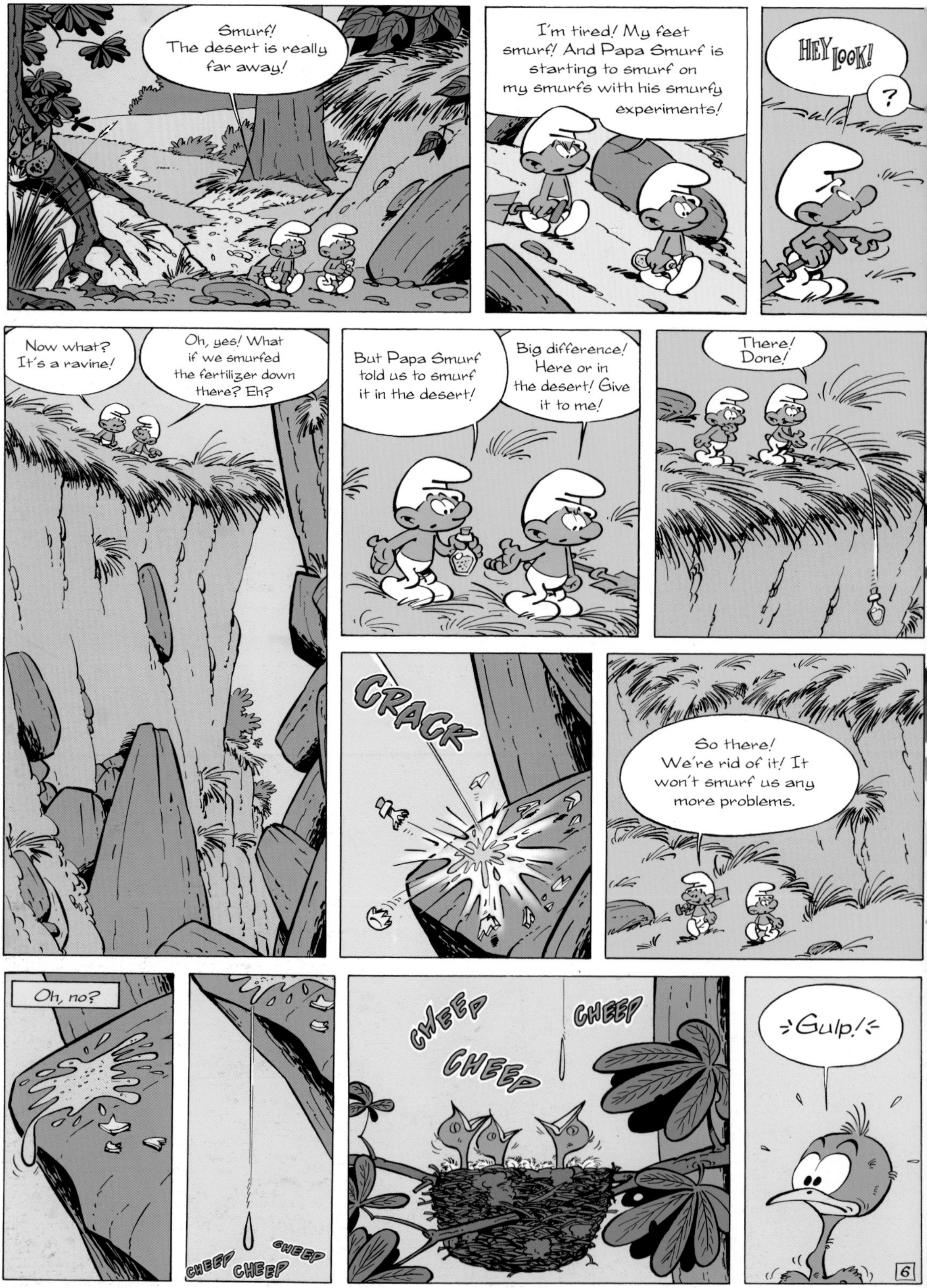
Smurf! The desert is really far away!
I'm tired! My feet smurf! And Papa Smurf is starting to smurf on my smurfs with his smurfy experiments!
HEY LOOK!
?
Now what? It's a ravine!
Oh, yes! What if we smurfed the fertilizer down there? Eh?
But Papa Smurf told us to smurf it in the desert!
Big difference! Here or in the desert! Give it to me!
There! Done!
CRACK
So there! We're rid of it! It won't smurf us any more problems.
Oh, no?
CHEEP CHEEP CHEEP
CHEEP CHEEP CHEEP
Gulp!
6

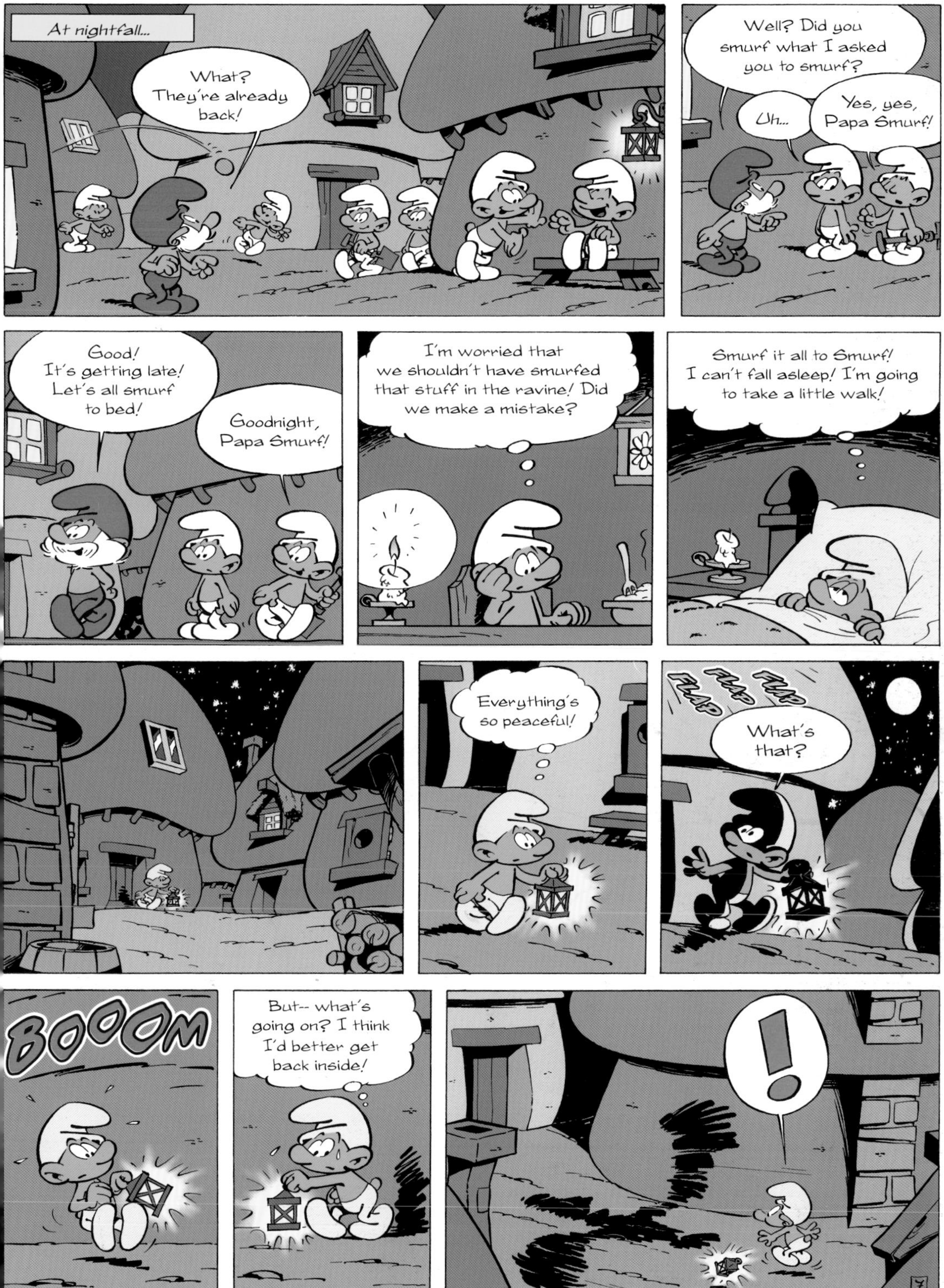
At nightfall...
What? They're already back!
Well? Did you smurf what I asked you to smurf?
Uh...
Yes, yes, Papa Smurf!
Good! It's getting late! Let's all smurf to bed!
Goodnight, Papa Smurf!
I'm worried that we shouldn't have smurfed that stuff in the ravine! Did we make a mistake?
Smurf it all to Smurf! I can't fall asleep! I'm going to take a little walk!
Everything's so peaceful!
FLAP FLAP FLAP
What's that?
BOOOM
But-- what's going on? I think I'd better get back inside!
!
7

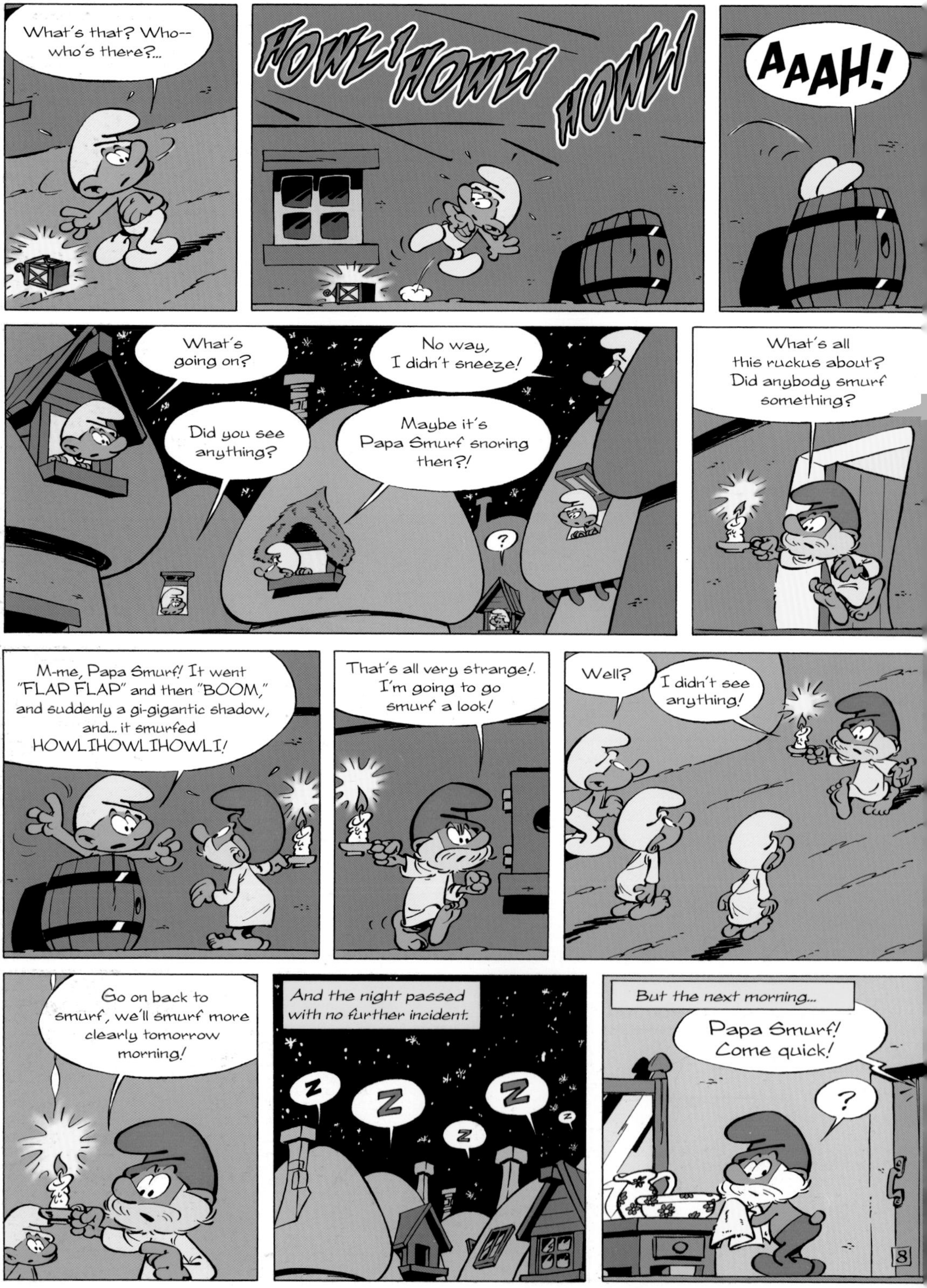

What's that? Who--
who's there?...
HOWLI HOWLI HOWLI
AAAH!
What's going on?
No way, I didn't sneeze!
Did you see anything?
Maybe it's Papa Smurf snoring then?!
?
What's all this ruckus about? Did anybody smurf something?
M-me, Papa Smurf! It went "FLAP FLAP" and then "BOOM," and suddenly a gi-gigantic shadow, and... it smurfed HOWLIHOWLIHOWLI!
That's all very strange!. I'm going to go smurf a look!
Well?
I didn't see anything!
Go on back to smurf, we'll smurf more clearly tomorrow morning!
And the night passed with no further incident.
Z
Z
Z
Z
Z
But the next morning...
Papa Smurf! Come quick!
?
8

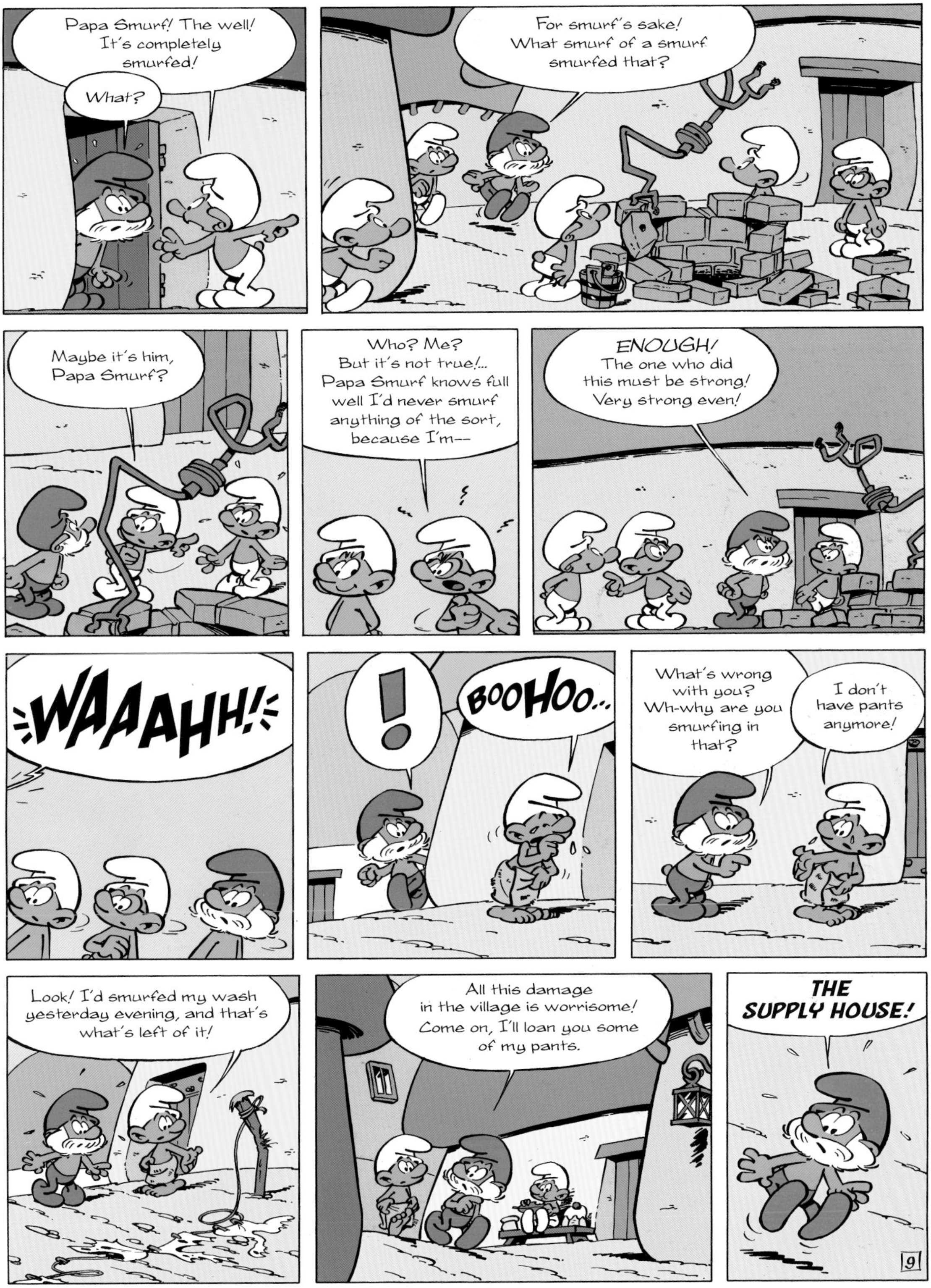
Papa Smurf! The well! It's completely smurfed!
What?
For smurf's sake! What smurf of a smurf smurfed that?
Maybe it's him, Papa Smurf?
Who? Me? But it's not true!... Papa Smurf knows full well I'd never smurf anything of the sort, because I'm--
ENOUGH! The one who did this must be strong! Very strong even!
WAAAHH!
!
BOOHOO...
What's wrong with you? Wh-why are you smurfing in that?
I don't have pants anymore!
Look! I'd smurfed my wash yesterday evening, and that's what's left of it!
All this damage in the village is worrisome! Come on, I'll loan you some of my pants.
THE SUPPLY HOUSE!
9

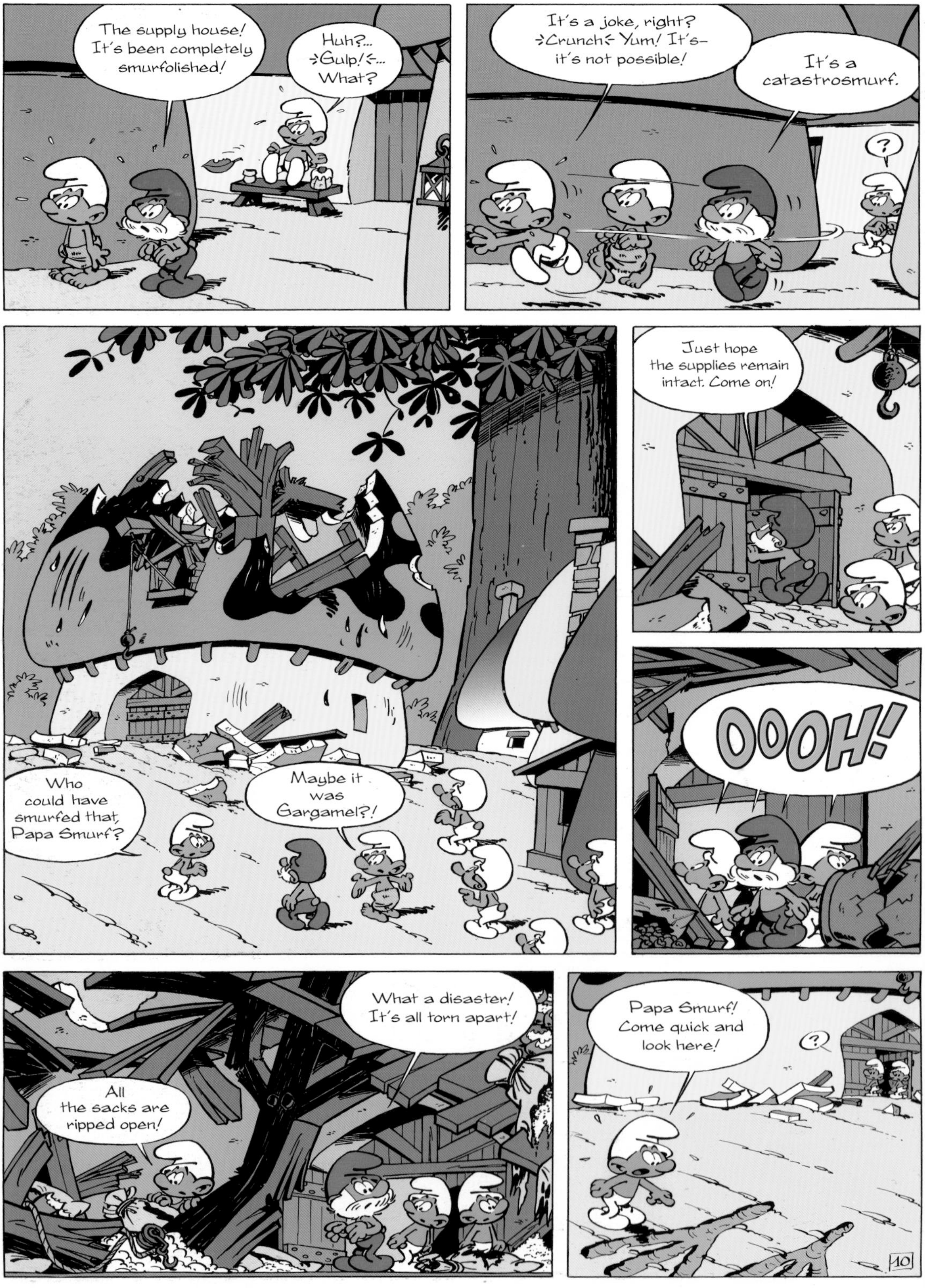
The supply house! It's been completely smurfolished!
Huh?... >Gulp!<... What?
It's a joke, right? >Crunch< Yum! It's- it's not possible!
It's a catastrosmurf.
?
Just hope the supplies remain intact. Come on!
Who could have smurfed that, Papa Smurf?
Maybe it was Gargamel?!
OOOH!
What a disaster! It's all torn apart!
All the sacks are ripped open!
Papa Smurf! Come quick and look here!
?
10

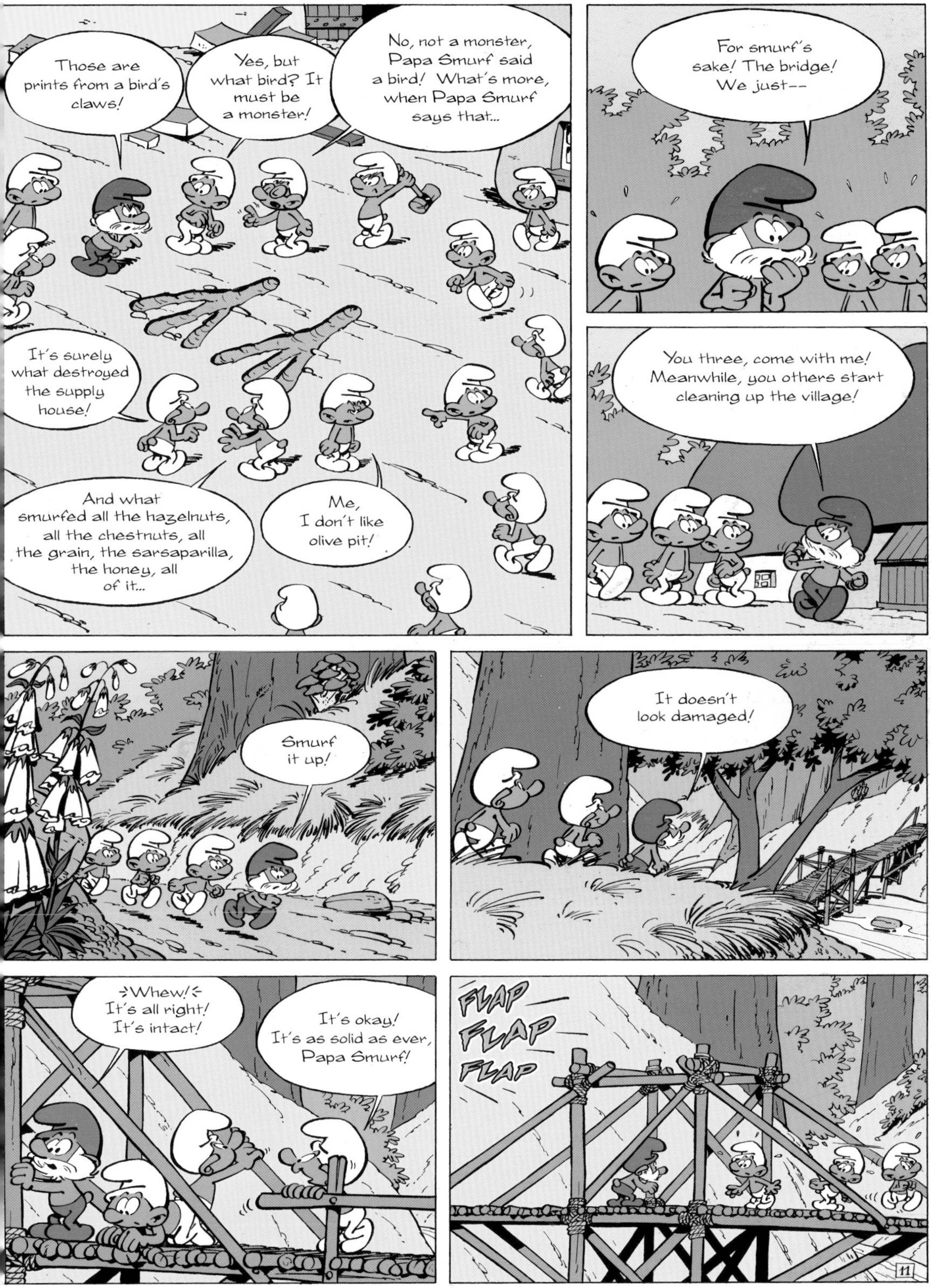
Those are prints from a bird's claws!
Yes, but what bird? It must be a monster!
No, not a monster, Papa Smurf said a bird! What's more, when Papa Smurf says that...
It's surely what destroyed the supply house!
And what smurfed all the hazelnuts, all the chestnuts, all the grain, the sarsaparilla, the honey, all of it...
Me, I don't like olive pit!
For smurf's sake! The bridge! We just--
You three, come with me! Meanwhile, you others start cleaning up the village!
Smurf it up!
It doesn't look damaged!
Whew! It's all right! It's intact!
It's okay! It's as solid as ever, Papa Smurf!
FLAP
FLAP
FLAP
11

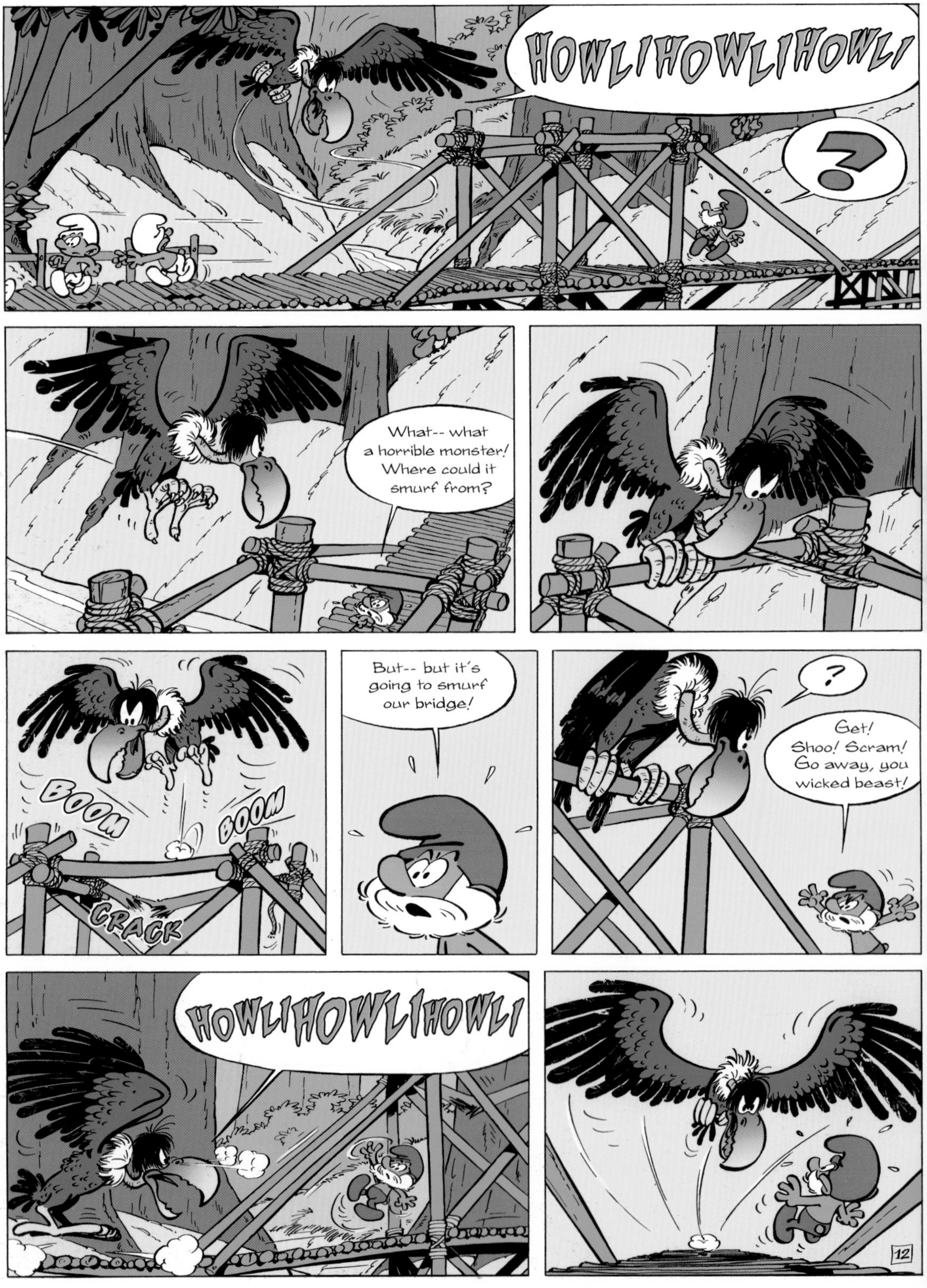
HOWLIHOWLIHOWLI
?
What-- what a horrible monster! Where could it smurf from?
BOOM
BOOM
CRACK
But-- but it's going to smurf our bridge!
?
Get! Shoo! Scram! Go away, you wicked beast!
HOWLIHOWLIHOWLI
12

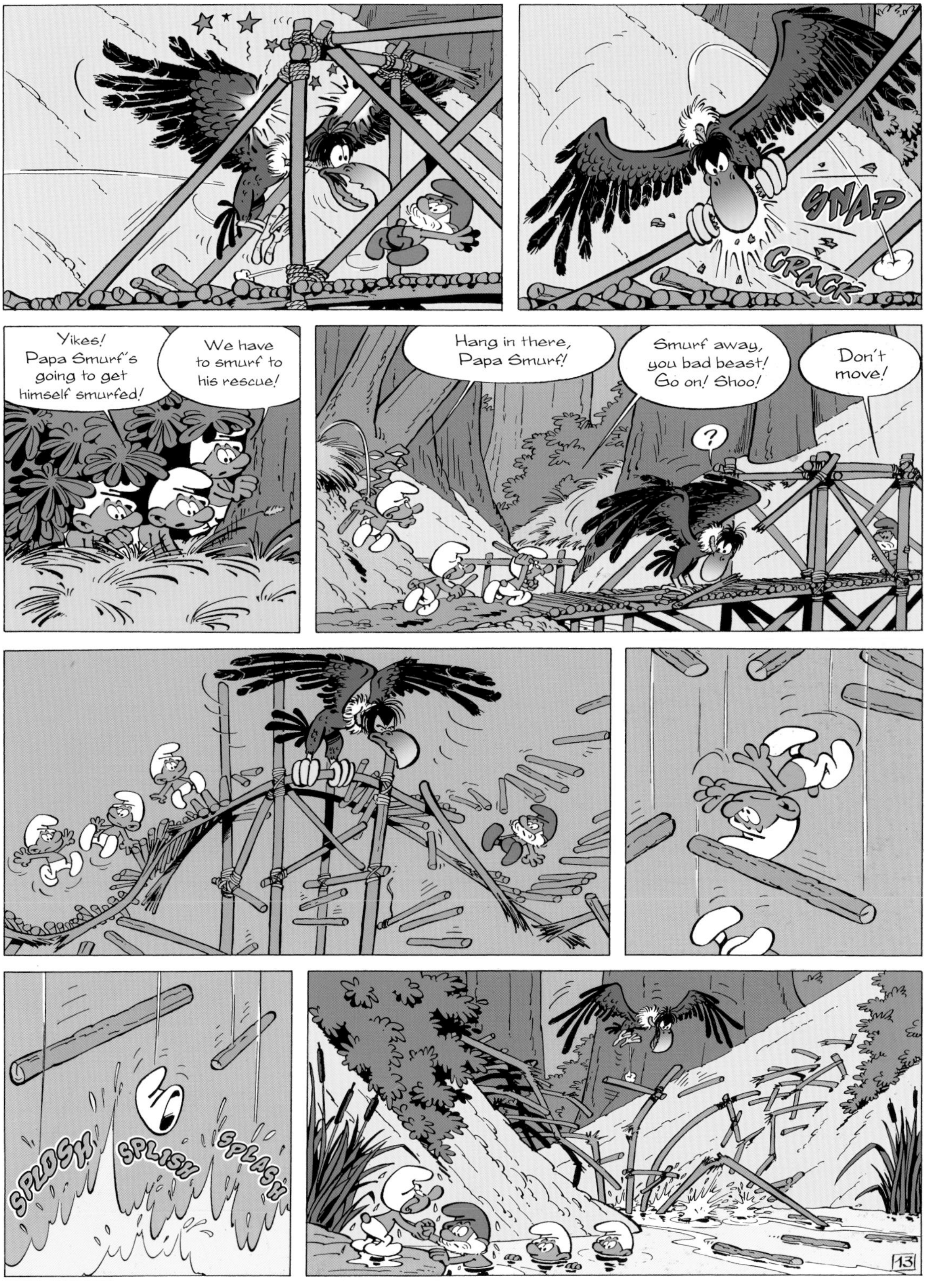
SNAP
CRACK
Yikes! Papa Smurf's going to get himself smurfed!
We have to smurf to his rescue!
Hang in there, Papa Smurf!
Smurf away, you bad beast! Go on! Shoo!
Don't move!
?
SPLOSH
SPLISH
SPLASH
13

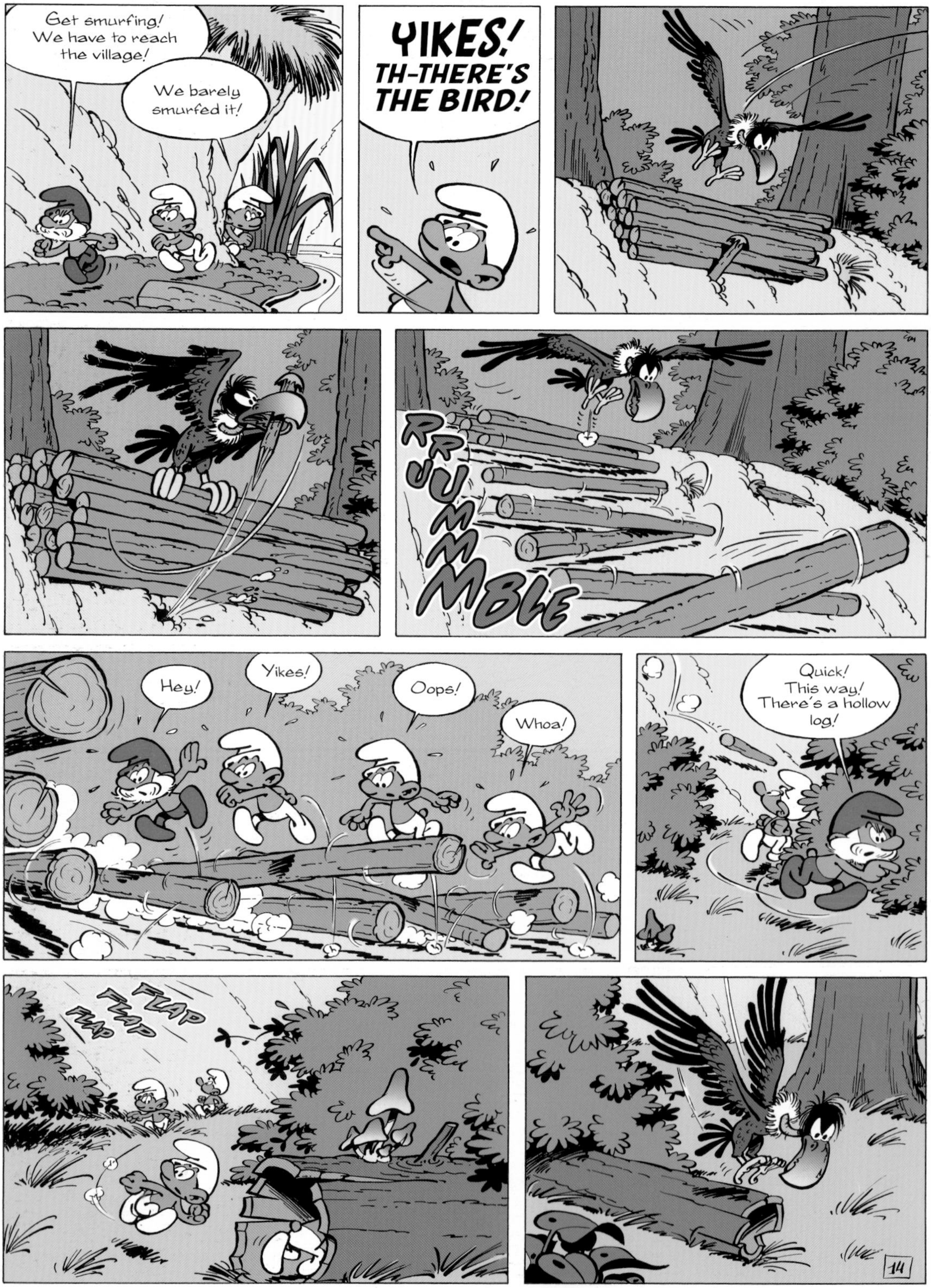

Get smurfing! We have to reach the village!
We barely smurfed it!
YIKES! TH-THERE'S THE BIRD!
RRUUMMMBLE
Hey!
Yikes!
Oops!
Whoa!
Quick! This way! There's a hollow log!
FLAP FLAP FLAP
14

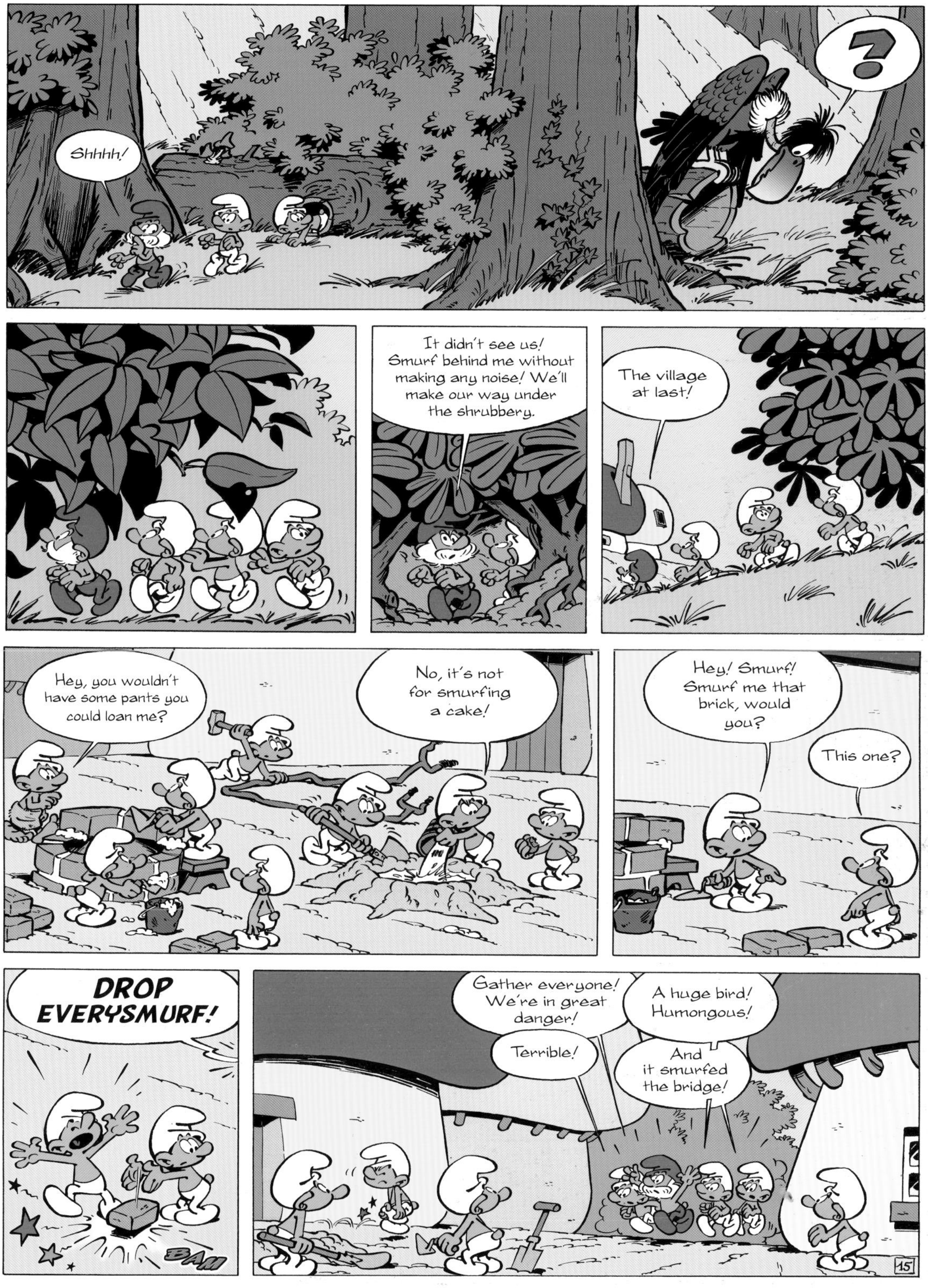
?
Shhhh!
It didn't see us! Smurf behind me without making any noise! We'll make our way under the shrubbery.
The village at last!
Hey, you wouldn't have some pants you could loan me?
No, it's not for smurfing a cake!
Hey! Smurf! Smurf me that brick, would you?
This one?
DROP EVERYSMURF!
BAM
Gather everyone! We're in great danger!
A huge bird! Humongous!
Terrible!
And it smurfed the bridge!
15

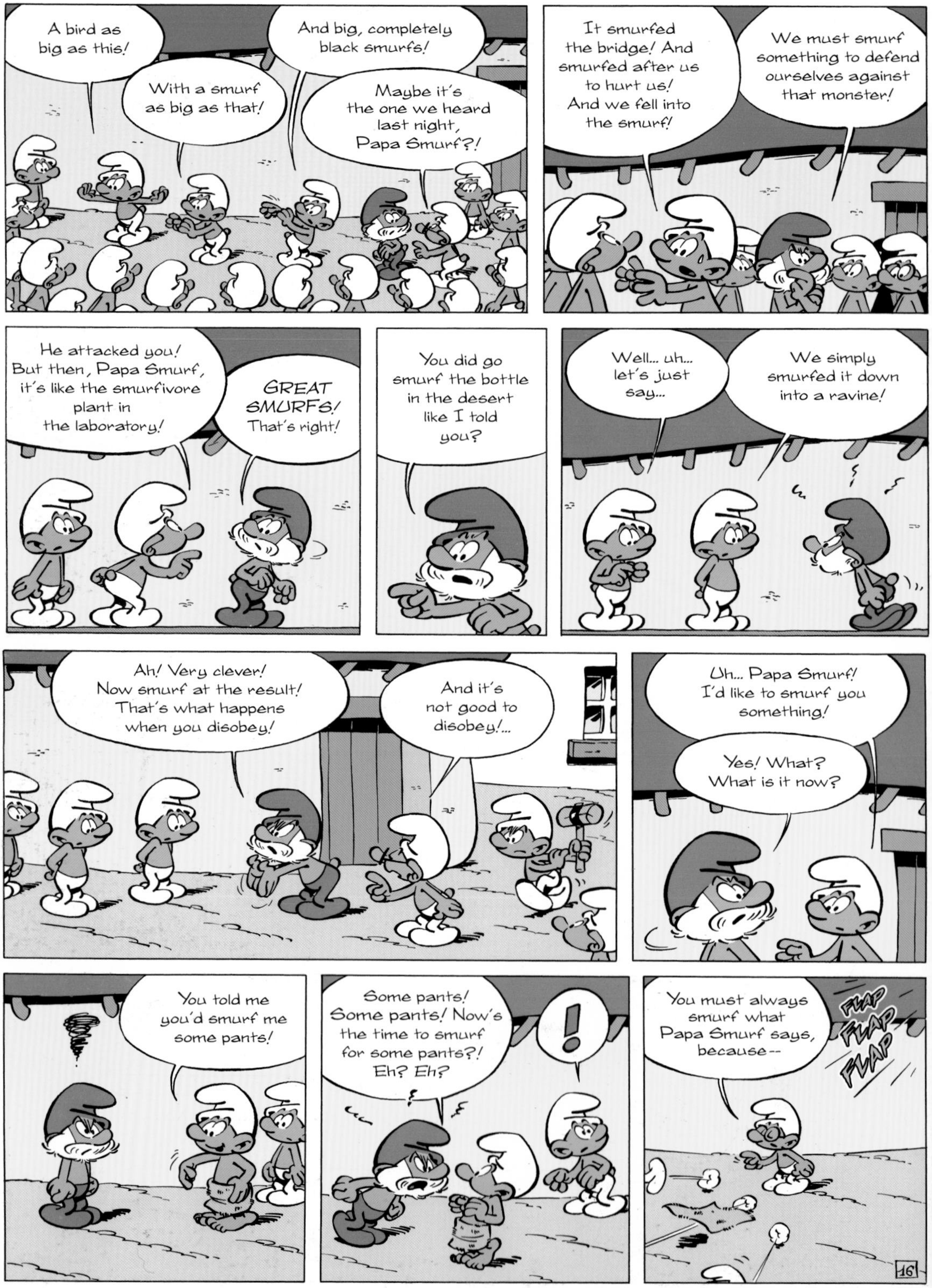
A bird as big as this!
With a smurf as big as that!
And big, completely black smurfs!
Maybe it's the one we heard last night, Papa Smurf?!
It smurfed the bridge! And smurfed after us to hurt us! And we fell into the smurf!
We must smurf something to defend ourselves against that monster!
He attacked you! But then, Papa Smurf, it's like the smurfivore plant in the laboratory!
GREAT SMURFS! That's right!
You did go smurf the bottle in the desert like I told you?
Well... uh... let's just say...
We simply smurfed it down into a ravine!
Ah! Very clever! Now smurf at the result! That's what happens when you disobey!
And it's not good to disobey!...
Uh... Papa Smurf! I'd like to smurf you something!
Yes! What? What is it now?
You told me you'd smurf me some pants!
Some pants! Some pants! Now's the time to smurf for some pants?! Eh? Eh?
!
You must always smurf what Papa Smurf says, because--
FLAP FLAP FLAP
16

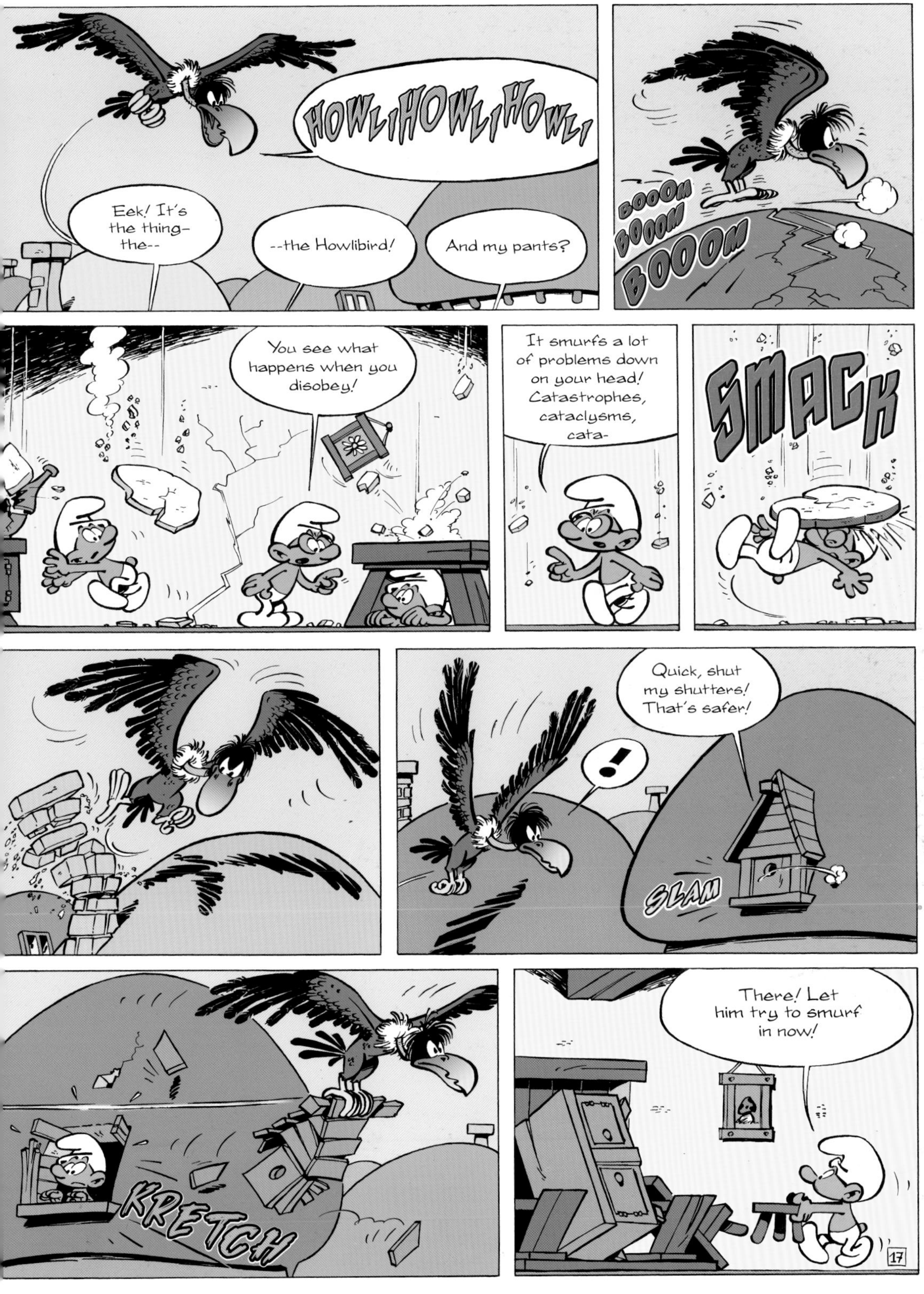
HOWLIHOWLIHOWLI
Eek! It's the thing-the--
--the Howlibird!
And my pants?
BOOOM BOOOM BOOOM
You see what happens when you disobey!
It smurfs a lot of problems down on your head! Catastrophes, cataclysms, cata-
SMACK
!
Quick, shut my shutters! That's safer!
SLAM
KRETCH
There! Let him try to smurf in now!
17

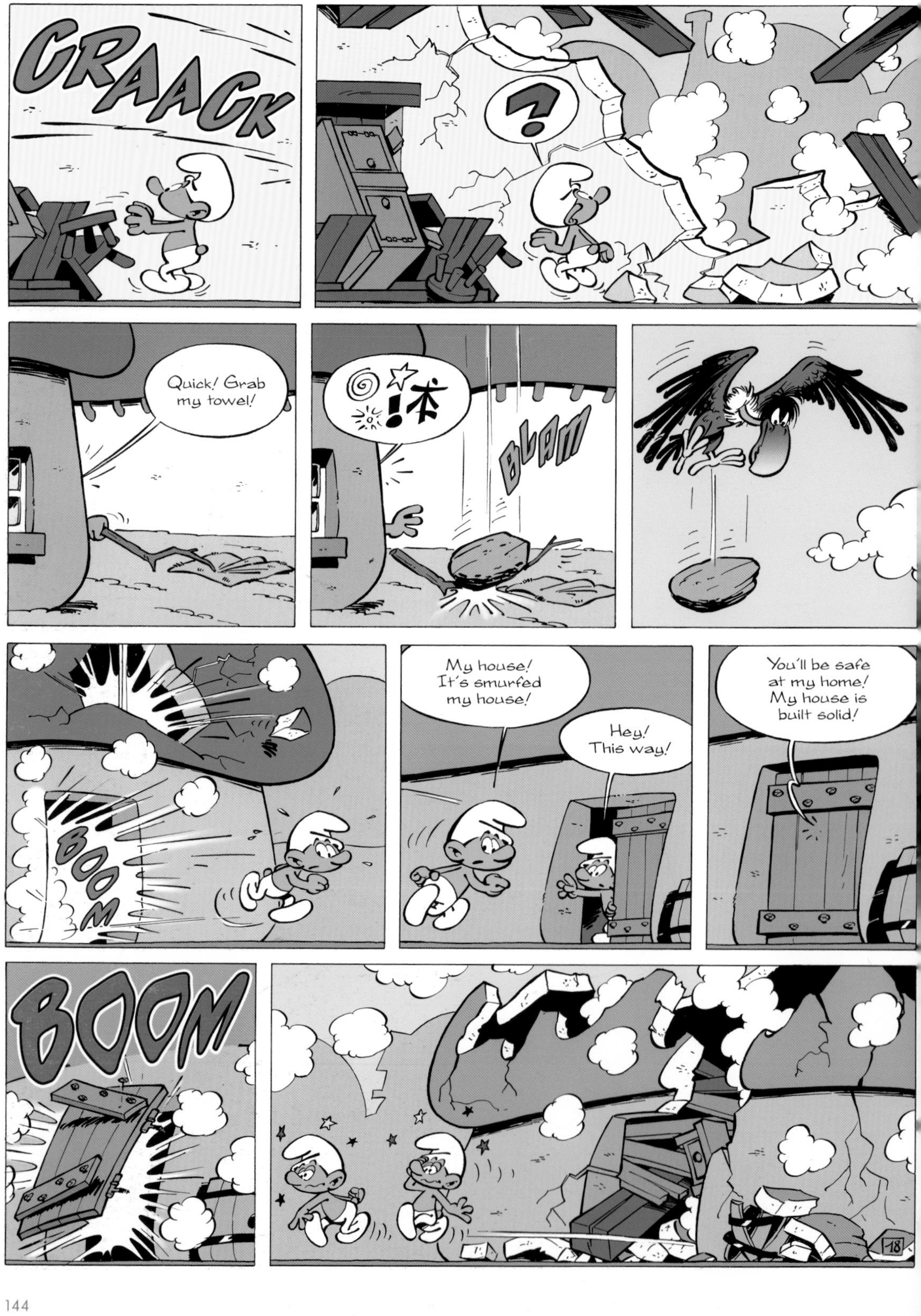
CRAACK
?
Quick! Grab my towel!
BLAM
My house! It's smurfed my house!
Hey! This way!
You'll be safe at my home! My house is built solid!
BOOM
18

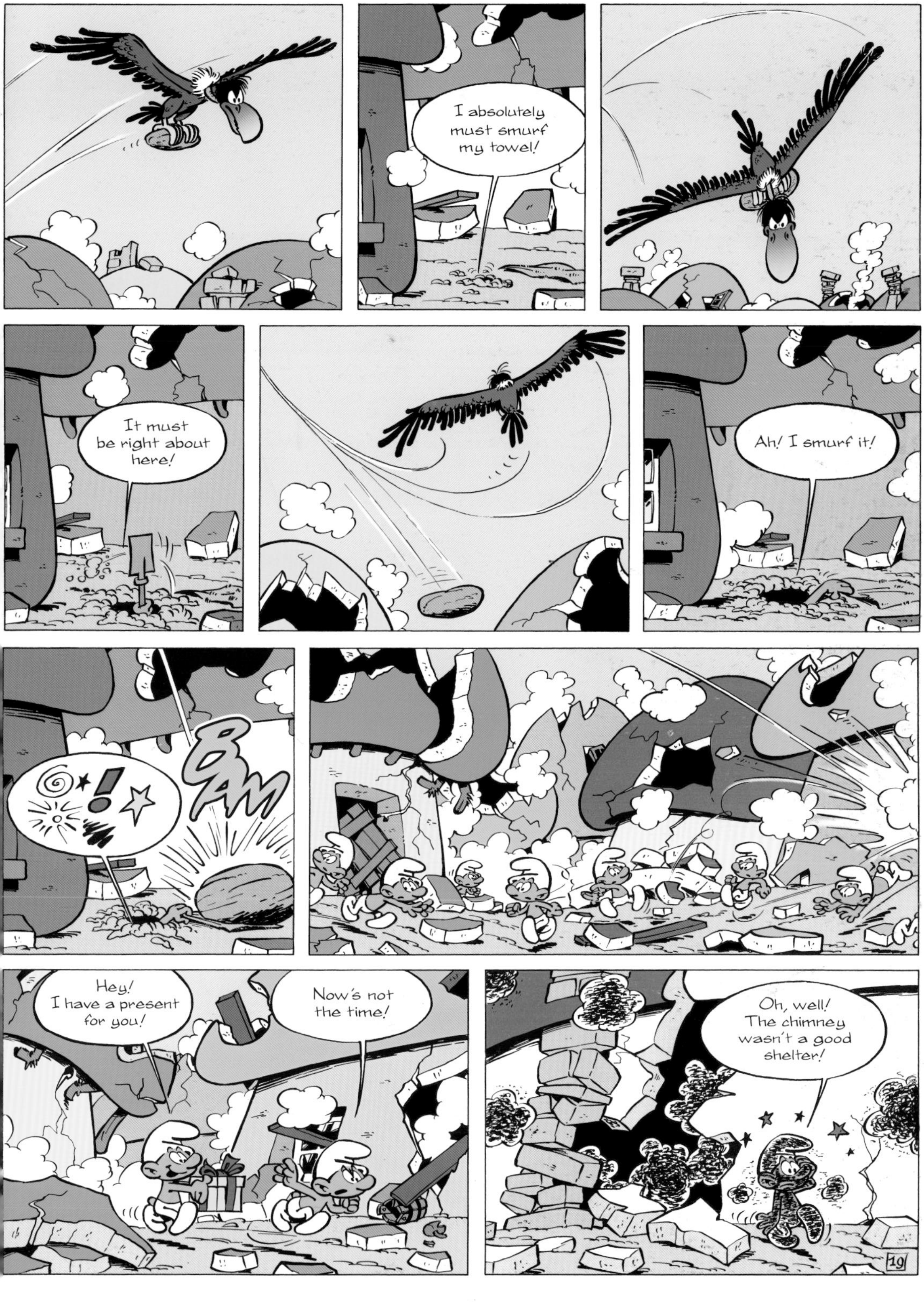
I absolutely must smurf my towel!
It must be right about here!
Ah! I smurf it!
BAM
Hey! I have a present for you!
Now's not the time!
Oh, well! The chimney wasn't a good shelter!
19

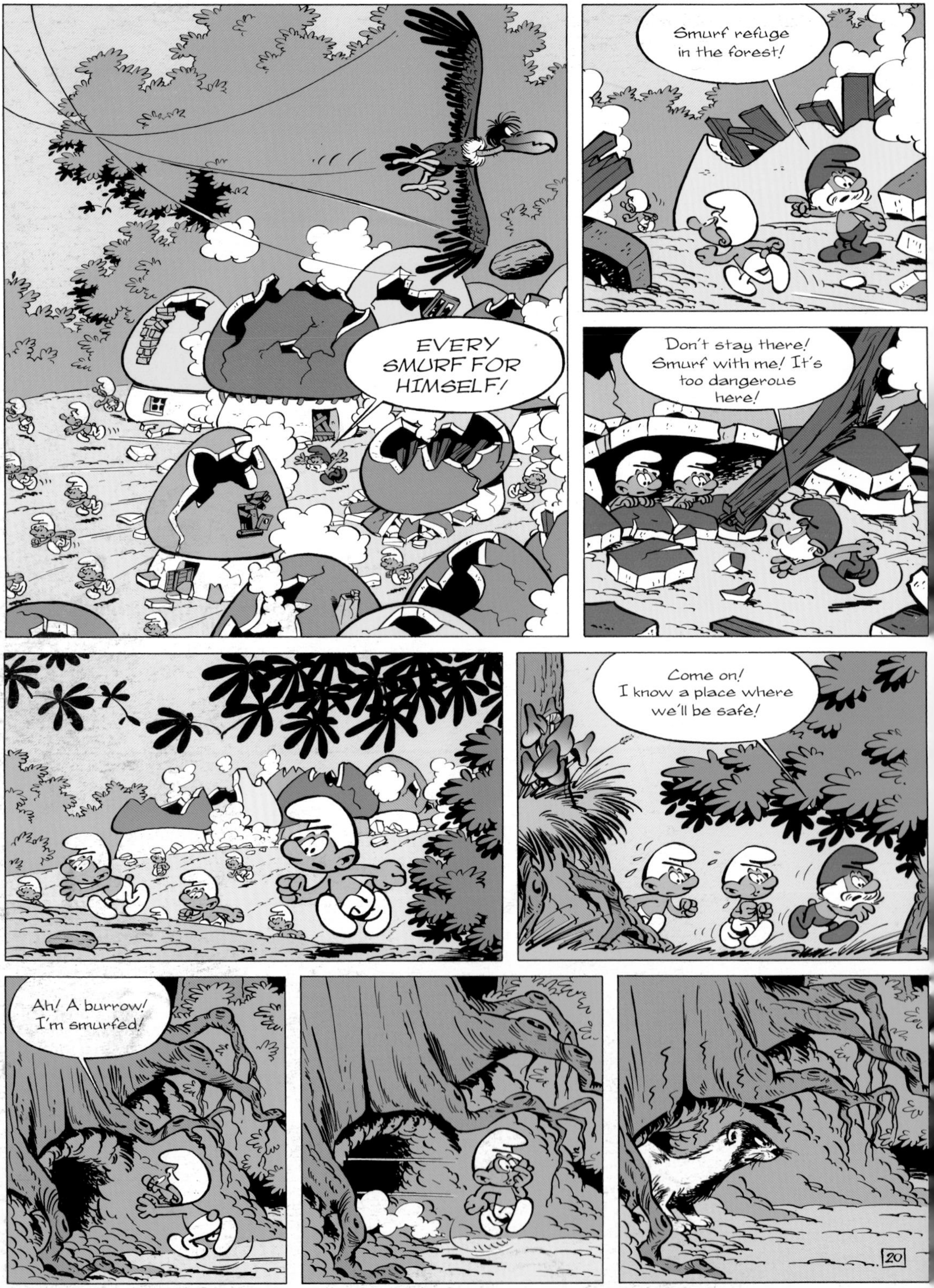
EVERY SMURF FOR HIMSELF!
Smurf refuge in the forest!
Don't stay there! Smurf with me! It's too dangerous here!
Come on! I know a place where we'll be safe!
Ah! A burrow! I'm smurfed!
20

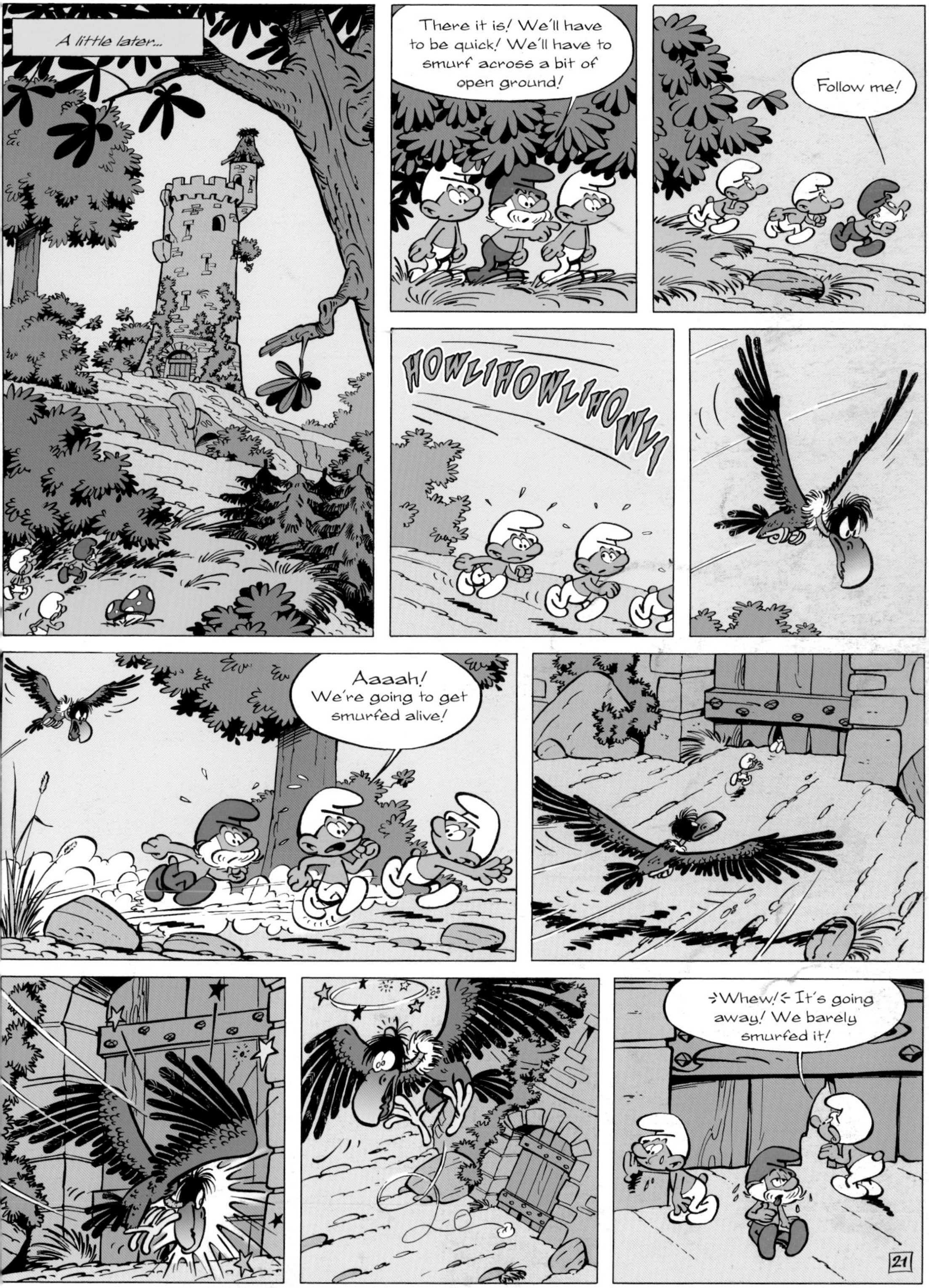

A little later...
There it is! We'll have to be quick! We'll have to smurf across a bit of open ground!
Follow me!
HOWLIHOWLIHOWL!
Aaaah! We're going to get smurfed alive!
Whew! It's going away! We barely smurfed it!
21

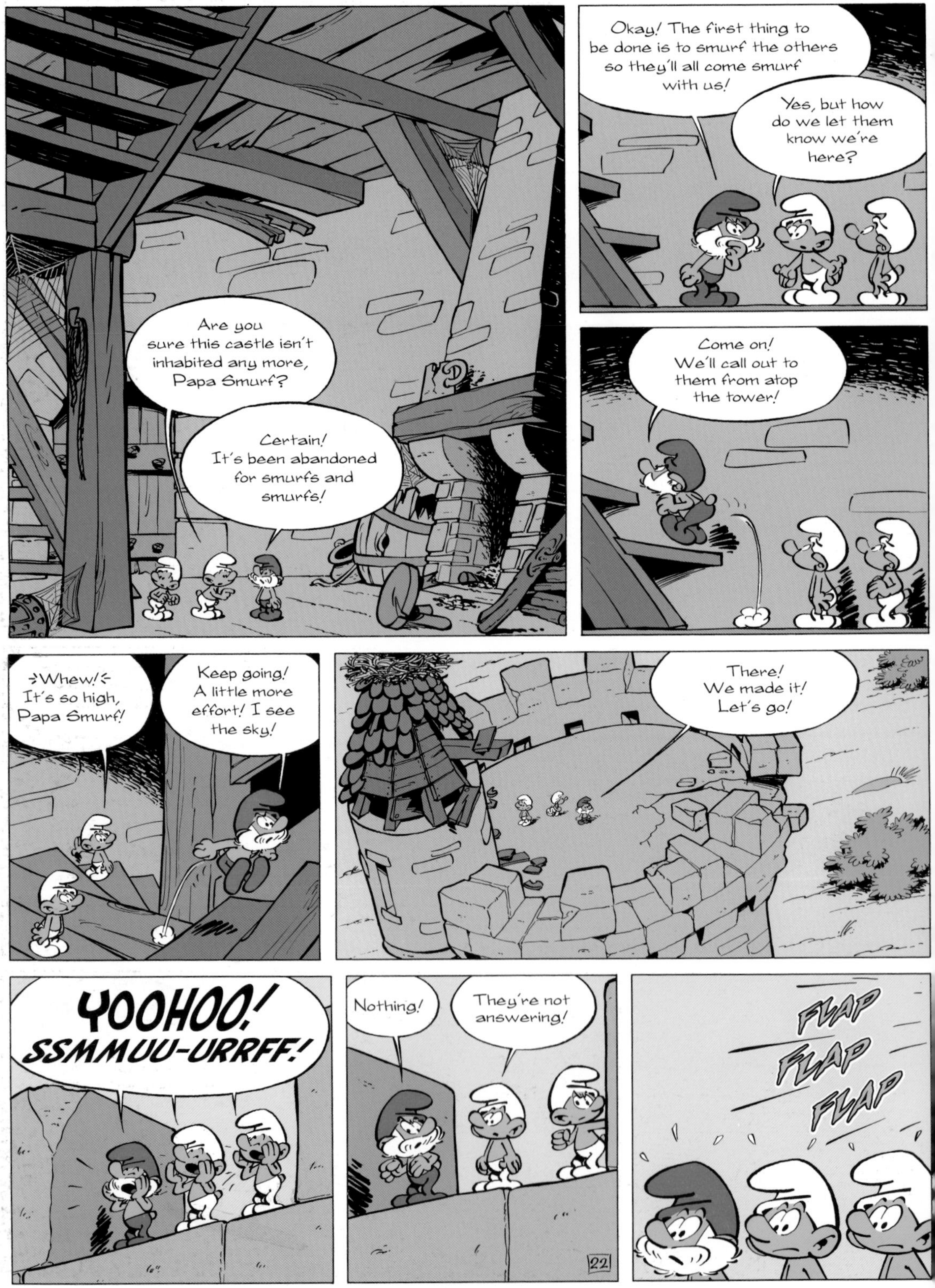

Are you sure this castle isn't inhabited any more, Papa Smurf?
Certain! It's been abandoned for smurfs and smurfs!
Okay! The first thing to be done is to smurf the others so they'll all come smurf with us!
Yes, but how do we let them know we're here?
Come on! We'll call out to them from atop the tower!
⇒Whew!⇐ It's so high, Papa Smurf!
Keep going! A little more effort! I see the sky!
There! We made it! Let's go!
YOOHOO! SSMMUU-URRFF!
Nothing!
They're not answering!
22
FLAP
FLAP
FLAP

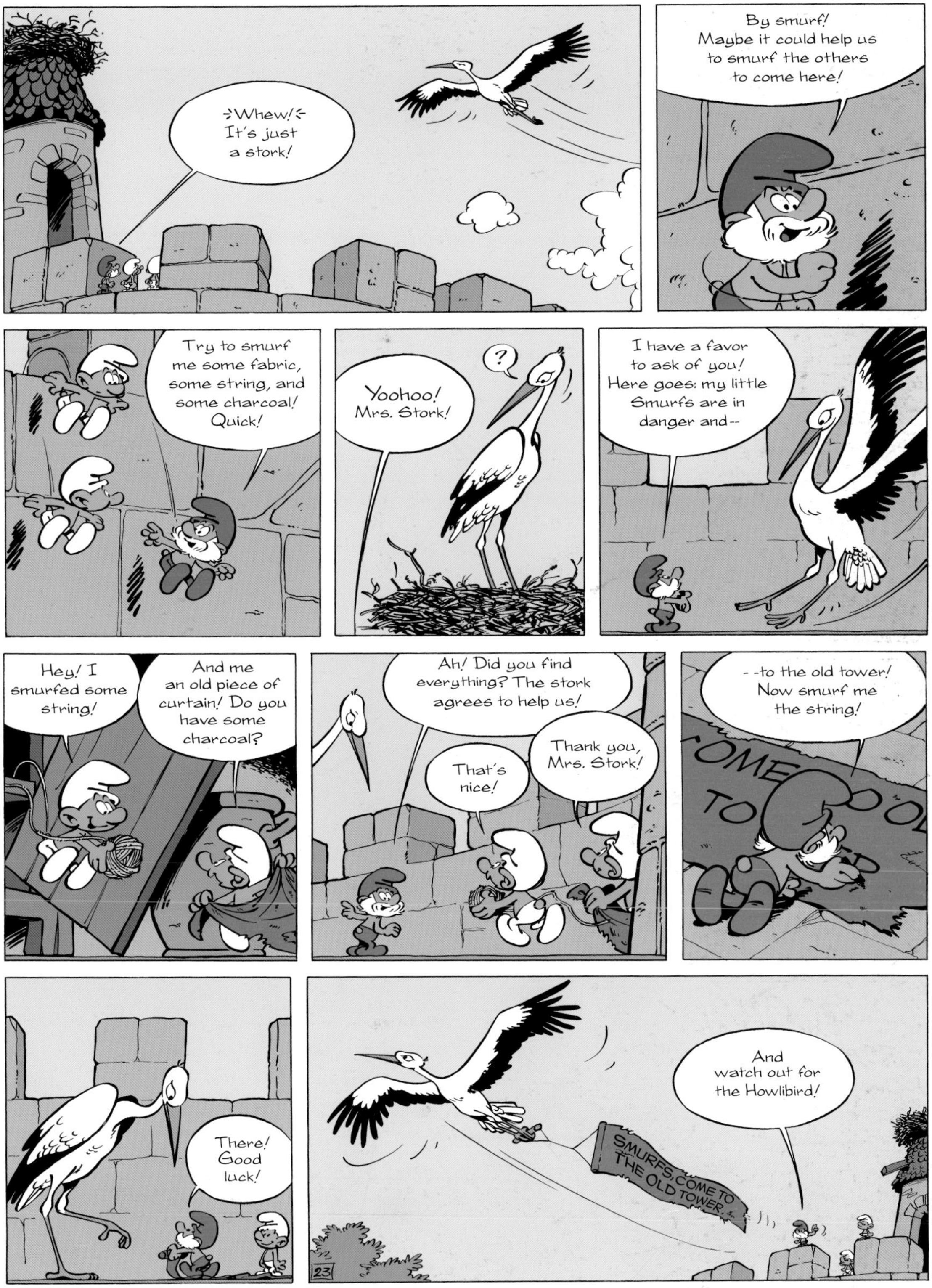

Whew! It's just a stork!
By smurf! Maybe it could help us to smurf the others to come here!
Try to smurf me some fabric, some string, and some charcoal! Quick!
?
Yoohoo! Mrs. Stork!
I have a favor to ask of you! Here goes: my little Smurfs are in danger and--
Hey! I smurfed some string!
And me an old piece of curtain! Do you have some charcoal?
Ah! Did you find everything? The stork agrees to help us!
That's nice!
Thank you, Mrs. Stork!
--to the old tower! Now smurf me the string!
There! Good luck!
And watch out for the Howlibird!
SMURFS, COME TO THE OLD TOWER
23

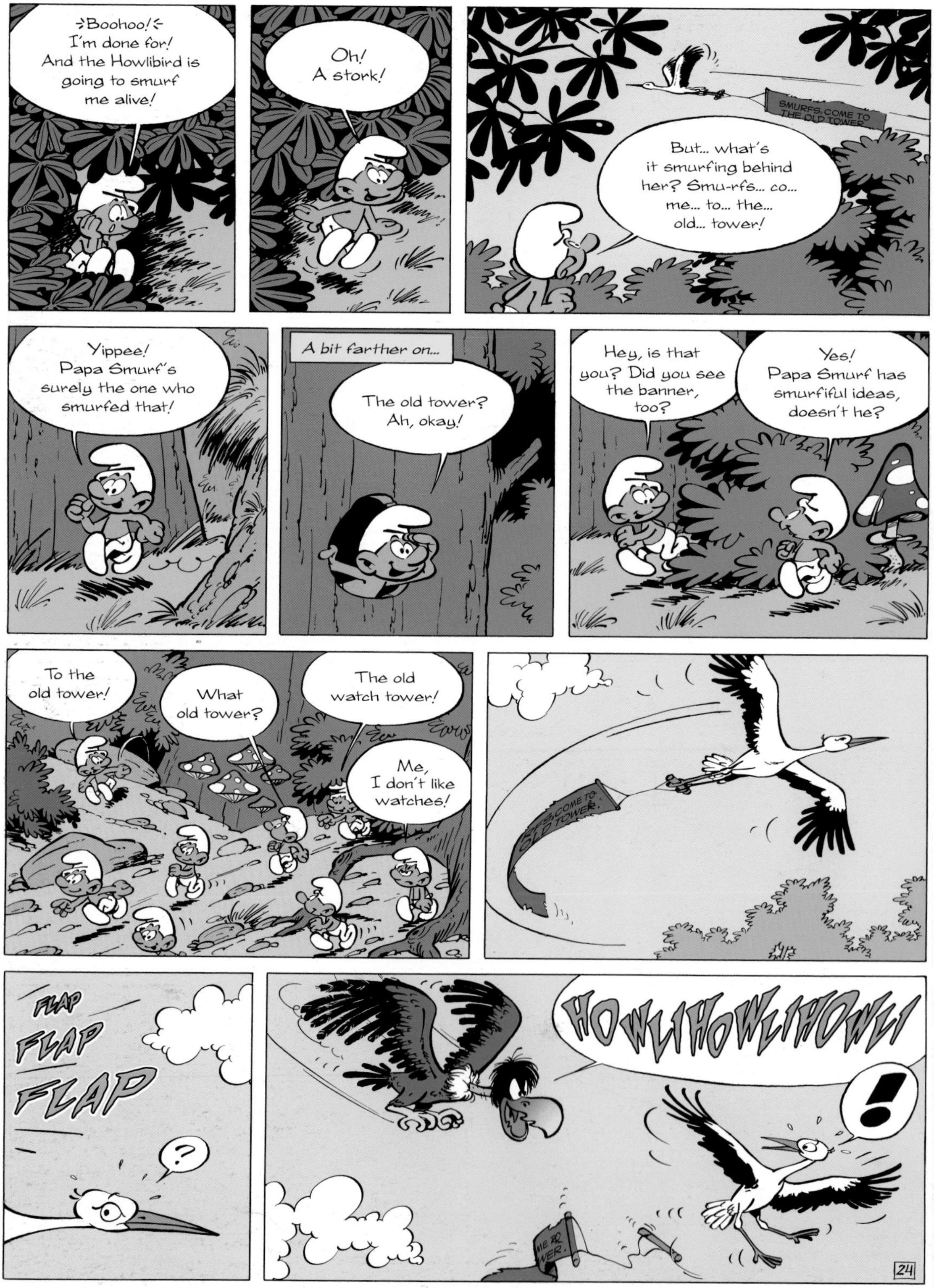

Boohoo! I'm done for! And the Howlibird is going to smurf me alive!
Oh! A stork!
SMURFS, COME TO THE OLD TOWER
But... what's it smurfing behind her? Smu-rfs... co... me... to... the... old... tower!
Yippee! Papa Smurf's surely the one who smurfed that!
A bit farther on...
The old tower? Ah, okay!
Hey, is that you? Did you see the banner, too?
Yes! Papa Smurf has smurfiful ideas, doesn't he?
To the old tower!
What old tower?
The old watch tower!
Me, I don't like watches!
FLAP
FLAP
FLAP
?
HOWLIHOWLIHOWLI
!
24

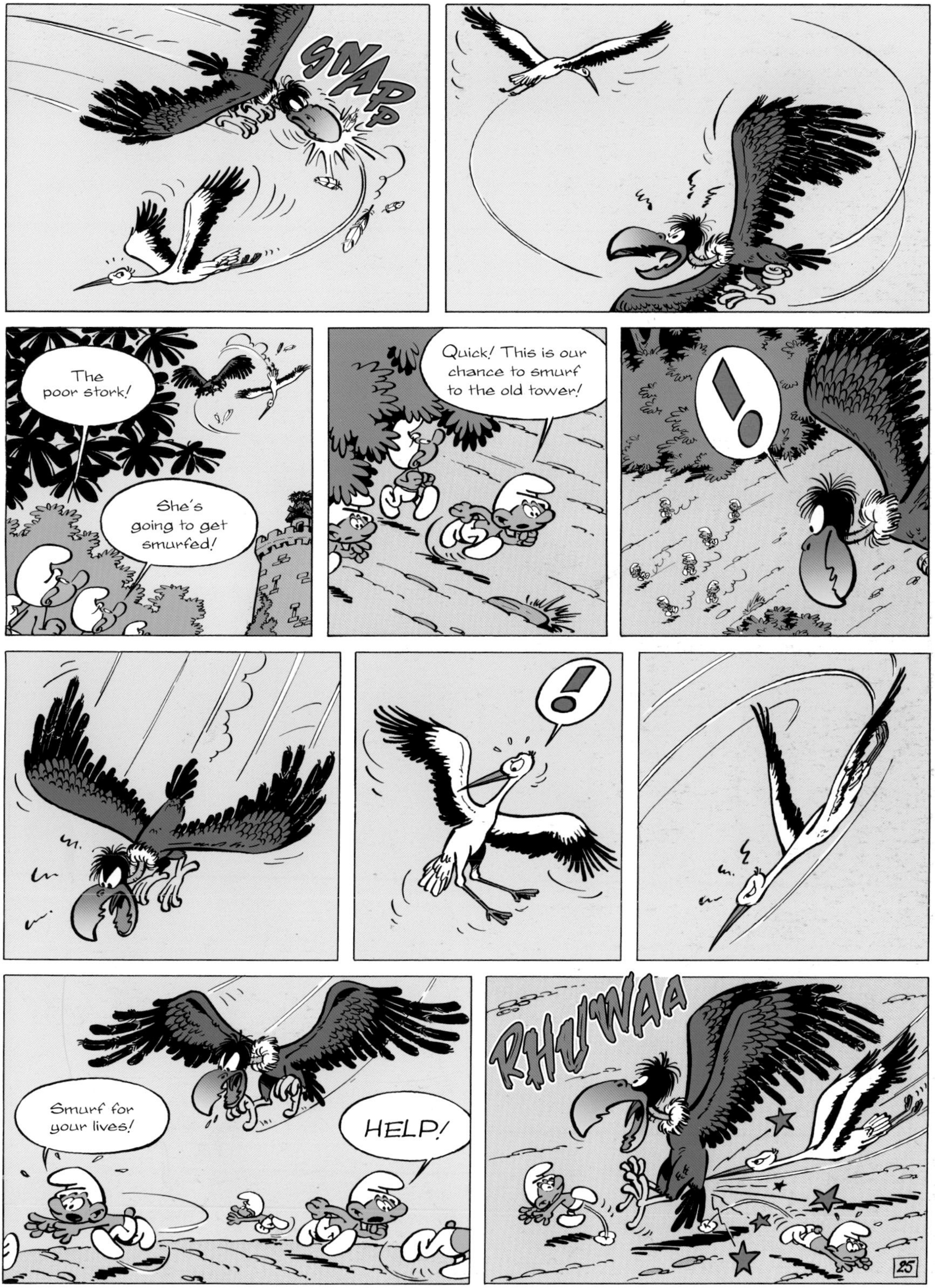
SNAPP
The poor stork!
She's going to get smurfed!
Quick! This is our chance to smurf to the old tower!
!
!
Smurf for your lives!
HELP!
RHUWAA
25

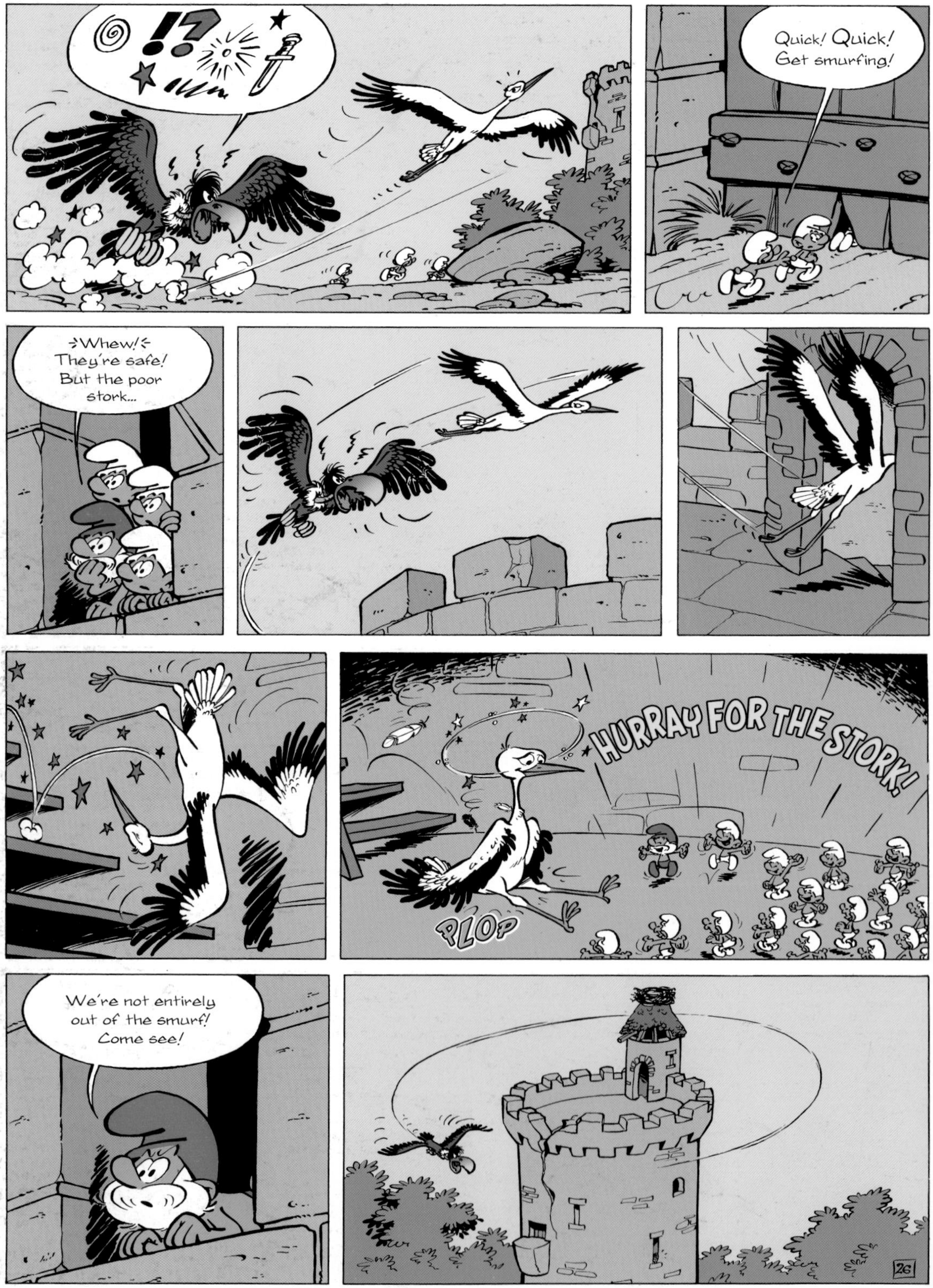

Quick! Quick!
Get smurfing!
Whew! They're safe! But the poor stork...
HURRAY FOR THE STORK!
PLOP
We're not entirely out of the smurf! Come see!
26

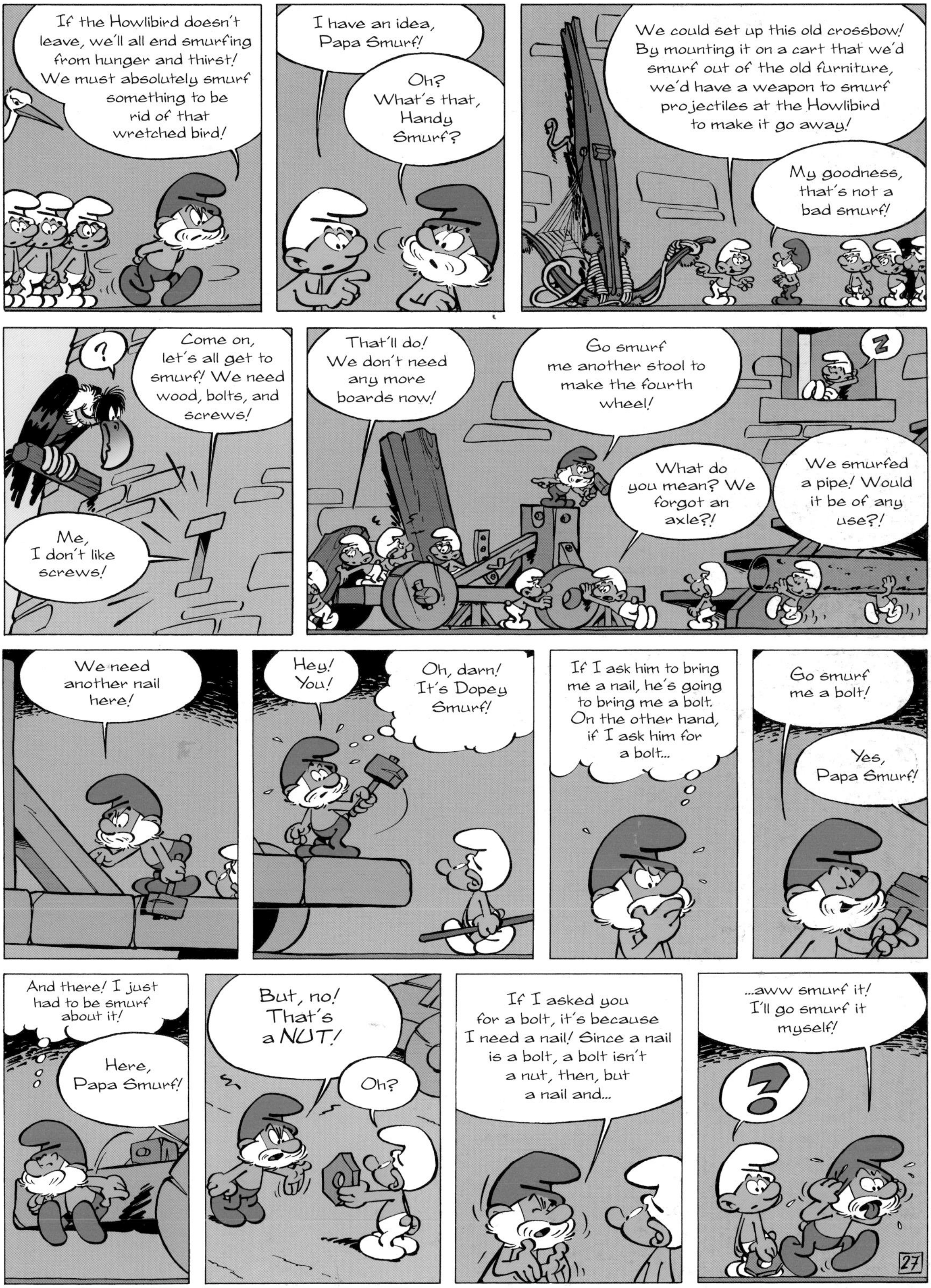
If the Howlibird doesn't leave, we'll all end smurfing from hunger and thirst! We must absolutely smurf something to be rid of that wretched bird!
I have an idea, Papa Smurf!
Oh? What's that, Handy Smurf?
We could set up this old crossbow! By mounting it on a cart that we'd smurf out of the old furniture, we'd have a weapon to smurf projectiles at the Howlibird to make it go away!
My goodness, that's not a bad smurf!
?
Come on, let's all get to smurf! We need wood, bolts, and screws!
Me, I don't like screws!
That'll do! We don't need any more boards now!
Go smurf me another stool to make the fourth wheel!
Z
What do you mean? We forgot an axle?!
We smurfed a pipe! Would it be of any use?!
We need another nail here!
Hey! You!
Oh, darn! It's Dopey Smurf!
If I ask him to bring me a nail, he's going to bring me a bolt. On the other hand, if I ask him for a bolt...
Go smurf me a bolt!
Yes, Papa Smurf!
And there! I just had to be smurf about it!
Here, Papa Smurf!
But, no! That's a NUT!
Oh?
If I asked you for a bolt, it's because I need a nail! Since a nail is a bolt, a bolt isn't a nut, then, but a nail and...
...aww smurf it! I'll go smurf it myself!
?
27

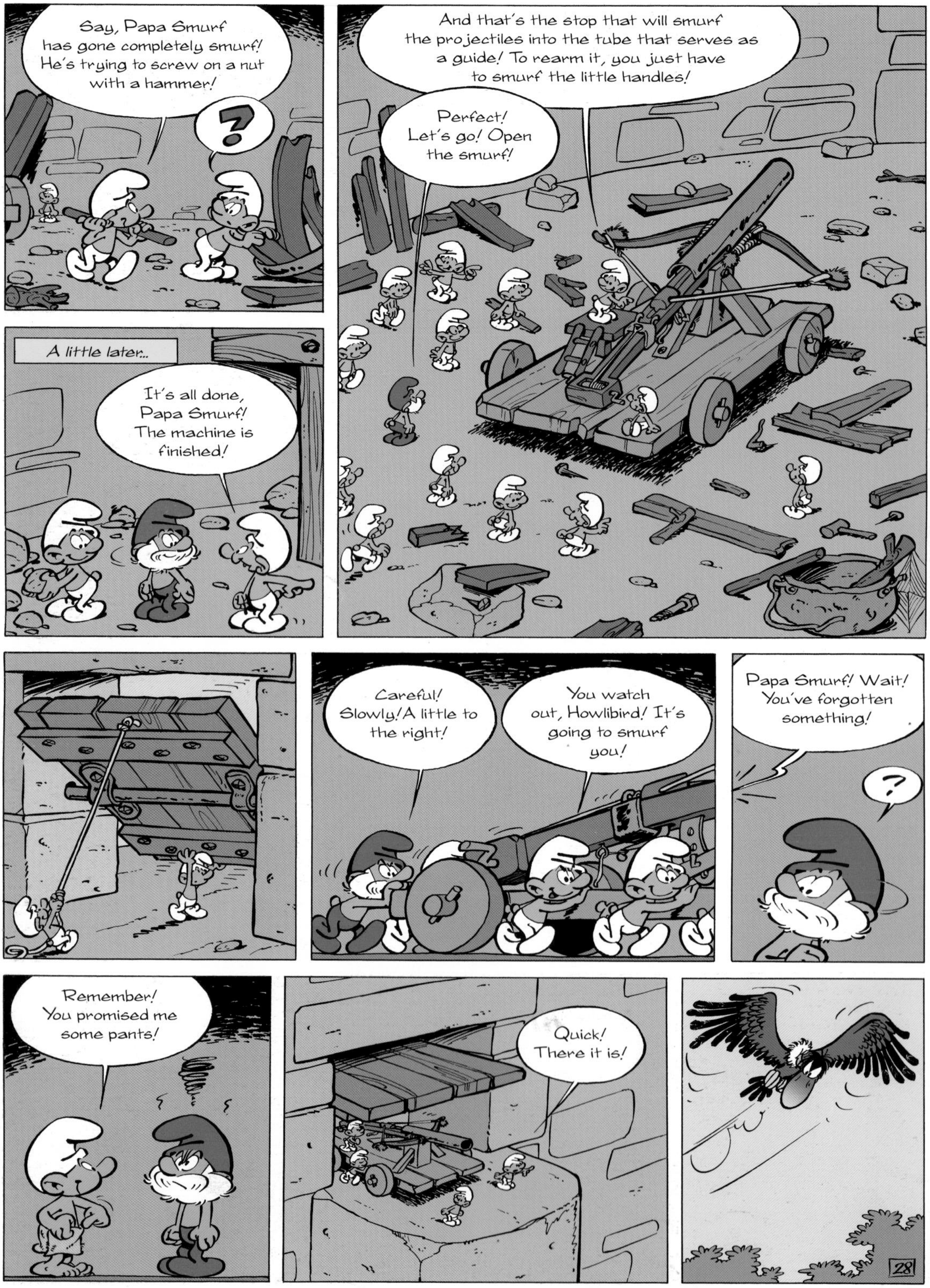
Say, Papa Smurf has gone completely smurf! He's trying to screw on a nut with a hammer!
?
And that's the stop that will smurf the projectiles into the tube that serves as a guide! To rearm it, you just have to smurf the little handles!
Perfect! Let's go! Open the smurf!
A little later...
It's all done, Papa Smurf! The machine is finished!
Careful! Slowly! A little to the right!
You watch out, Howlibird! It's going to smurf you!
Papa Smurf! Wait! You've forgotten something!
?
Remember! You promised me some pants!
Quick! There it is!
28

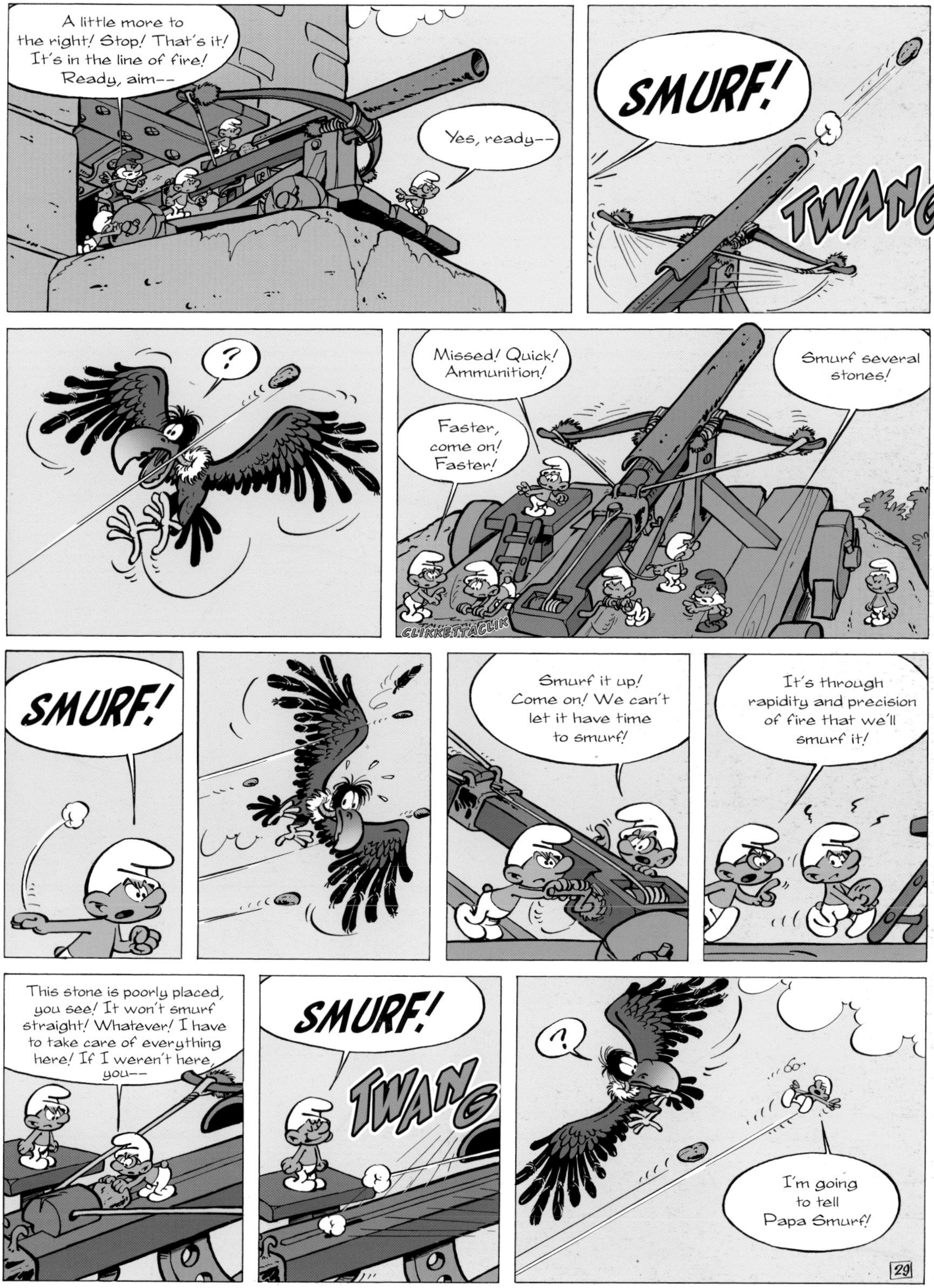
A little more to the right! Stop! That's it! It's in the line of fire! Ready, aim--
Yes, ready--
SMURF!
TWANG
?
Missed! Quick! Ammunition!
Faster, come on! Faster!
Smurf several stones!
CLIKKETTTACLIK
SMURF!
Smurf it up! Come on! We can't let it have time to smurf!
It's through rapidity and precision of fire that we'll smurf it!
This stone is poorly placed, you see! It won't smurf straight! Whatever! I have to take care of everything here! If I weren't here, you--
SMURF!
TWANG
?
I'm going to tell Papa Smurf!
29

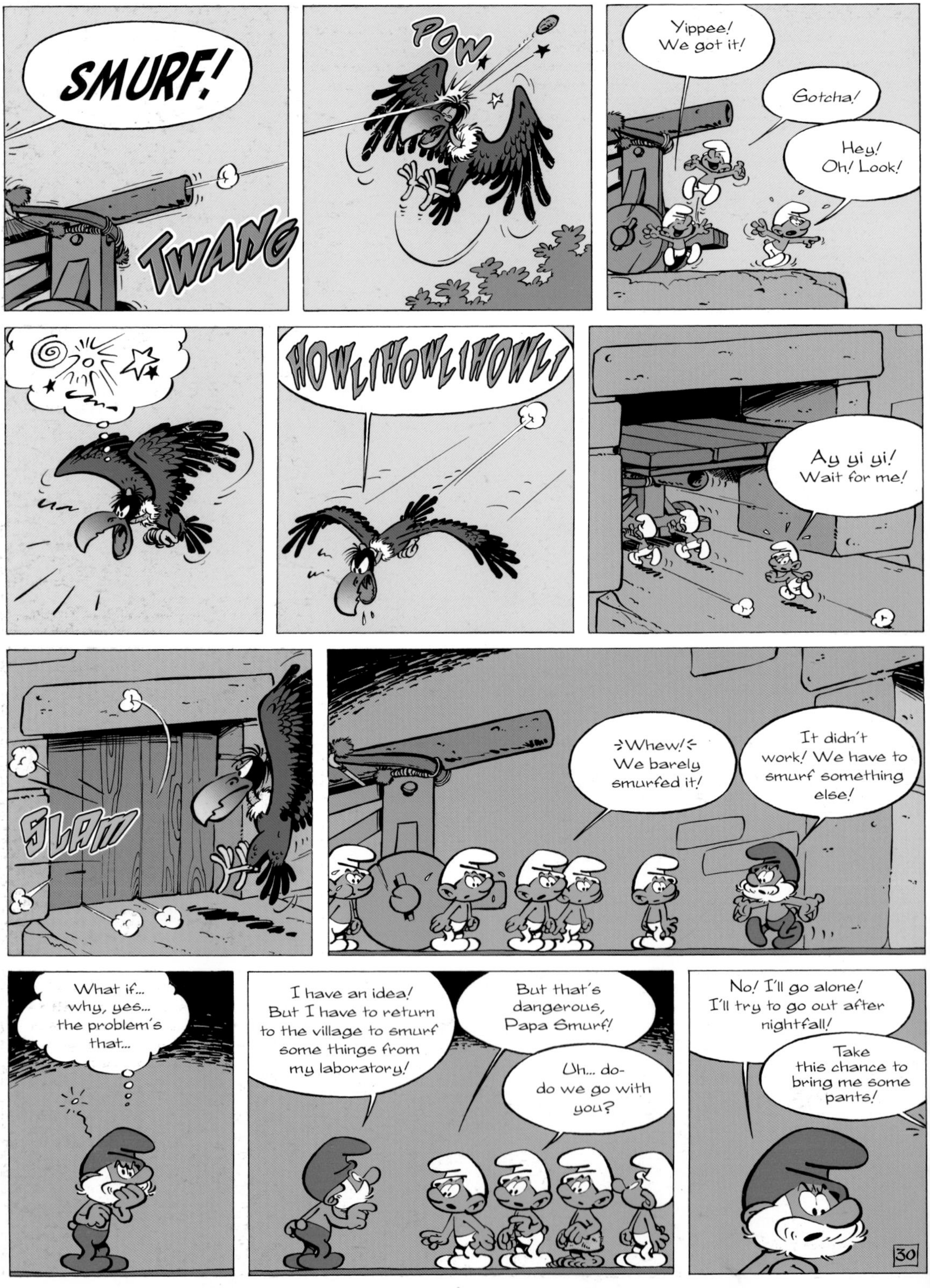
SMURF!
TWANG
POW
Yippee! We got it!
Gotcha!
Hey! Oh! Look!
HOWL! HOWL! HOWL!
Ay yi yi! Wait for me!
SLAM
Whew! We barely smurfed it!
It didn't work! We have to smurf something else!
What if... why, yes... the problem's that...
I have an idea! But I have to return to the village to smurf some things from my laboratory!
But that's dangerous, Papa Smurf!
Uh... do- do we go with you?
No! I'll go alone! I'll try to go out after nightfall!
Take this chance to bring me some pants!
30

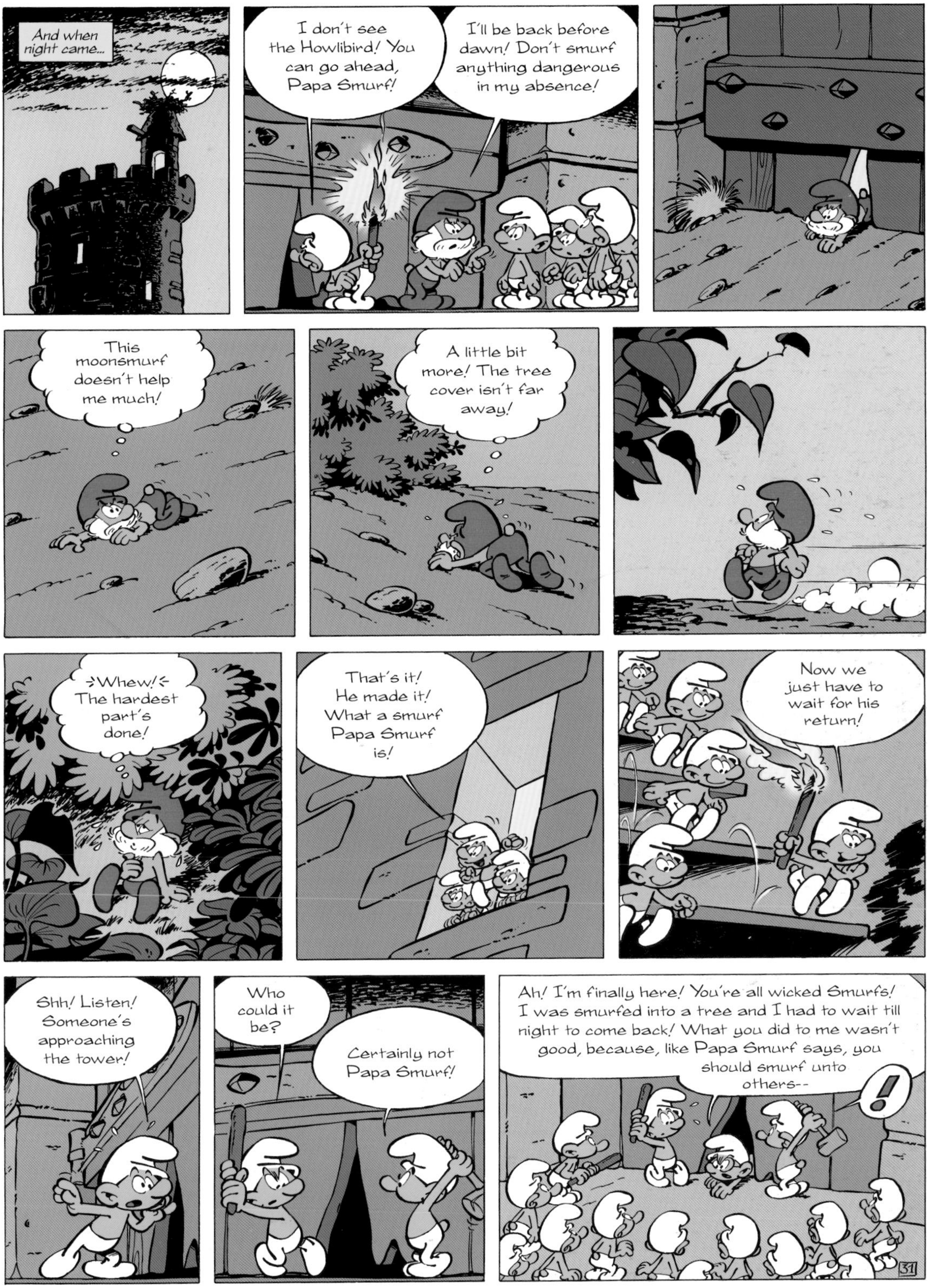

And when night came...
I don't see the Howlibird! You can go ahead, Papa Smurf!
I'll be back before dawn! Don't smurf anything dangerous in my absence!
This moonsmurf doesn't help me much!
A little bit more! The tree cover isn't far away!
Whew! The hardest part's done!
That's it! He made it! What a smurf Papa Smurf is!
Now we just have to wait for his return!
Shh! Listen! Someone's approaching the tower!
Who could it be?
Certainly not Papa Smurf!
Ah! I'm finally here! You're all wicked Smurfs! I was smurfed into a tree and I had to wait till night to come back! What you did to me wasn't good, because, like Papa Smurf says, you should smurf unto others--
!
31

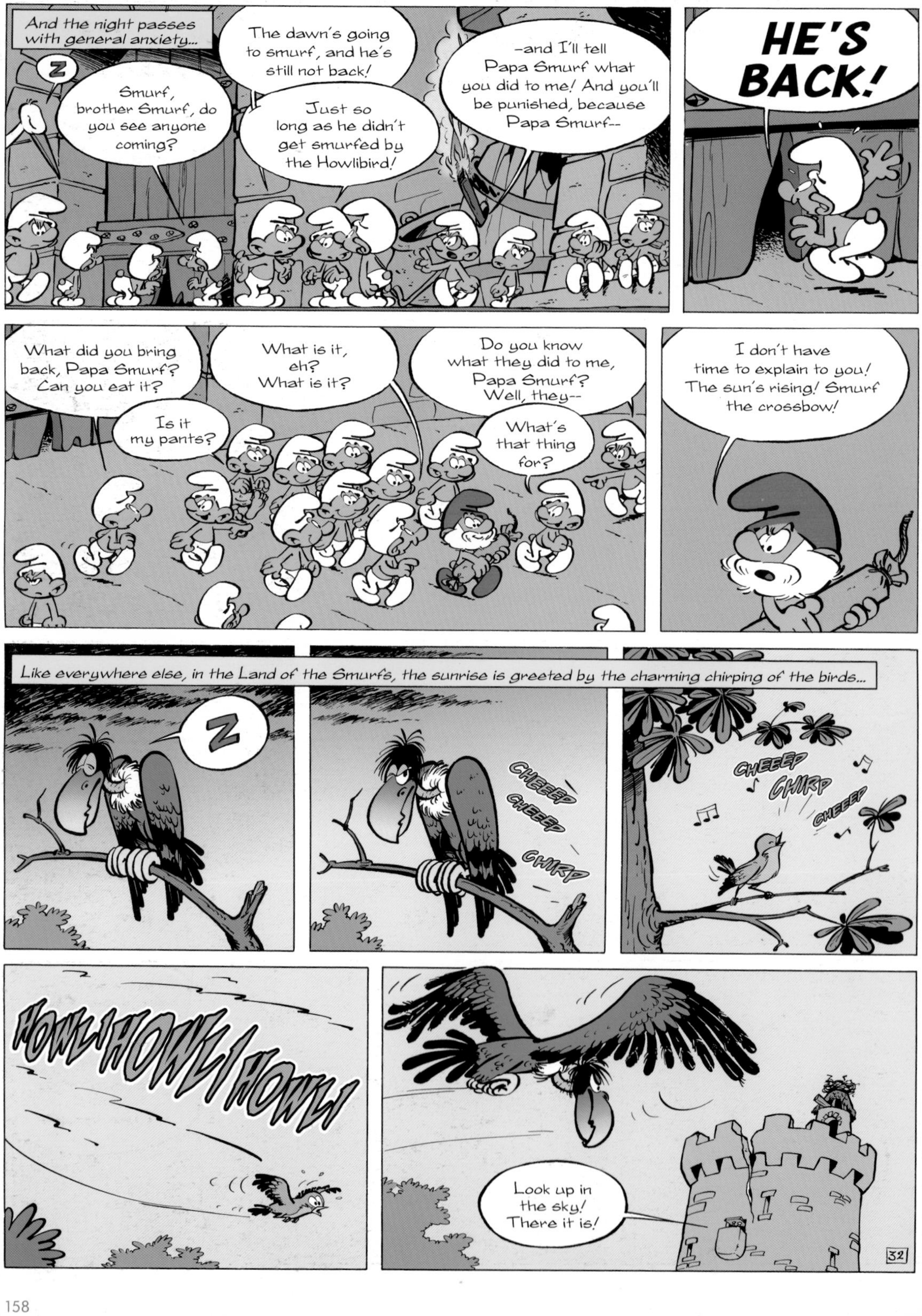
And the night passes with general anxiety...
Z
Smurf, brother Smurf, do you see anyone coming?
The dawn's going to smurf, and he's still not back!
Just so long as he didn't get smurfed by the Howlibird!
-and I'll tell Papa Smurf what you did to me! And you'll be punished, because Papa Smurf--
HE'S BACK!
What did you bring back, Papa Smurf? Can you eat it?
Is it my pants?
What is it, eh? What is it?
Do you know what they did to me, Papa Smurf? Well, they--
What's that thing for?
I don't have time to explain to you! The sun's rising! Smurf the crossbow!
Like everywhere else, in the Land of the Smurfs, the sunrise is greeted by the charming chirping of the birds...
Z
CHEEEP
CHEEEP
CHIRP
CHEEEP
CHIRP
CHEEEP
HOWL! HOWL! HOWL!
Look up in the sky! There it is!
32

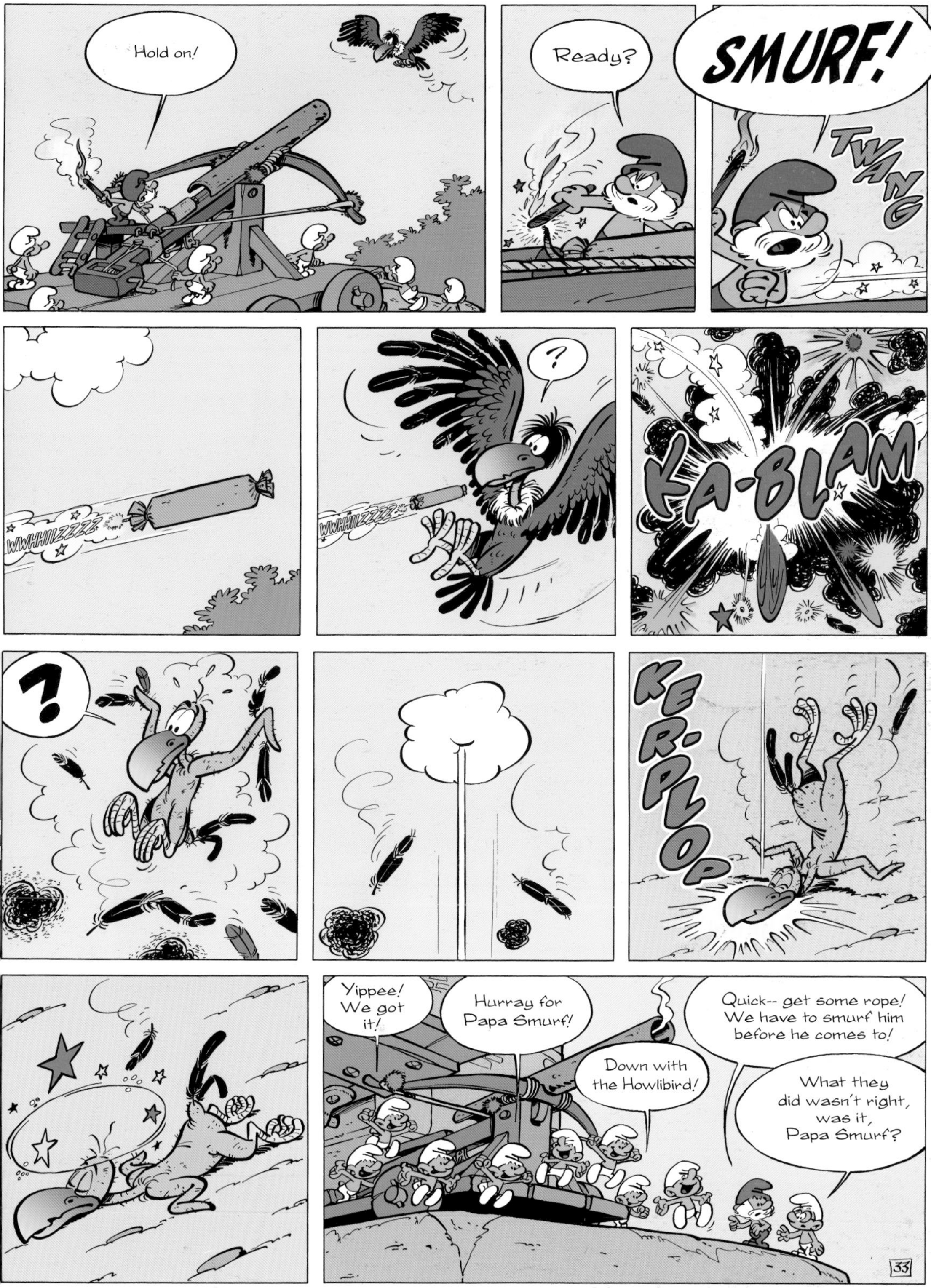

Hold on!
Ready?
SMURF!
TWANG
WWHHIIZZZZ
WWHHIIZZZZ
?
KA-BLAM
?
KER-PLOP
Yippee! We got it!
Hurray for Papa Smurf!
Quick-- get some rope! We have to smurf him before he comes to!
Down with the Howlibird!
What they did wasn't right, was it, Papa Smurf?
33

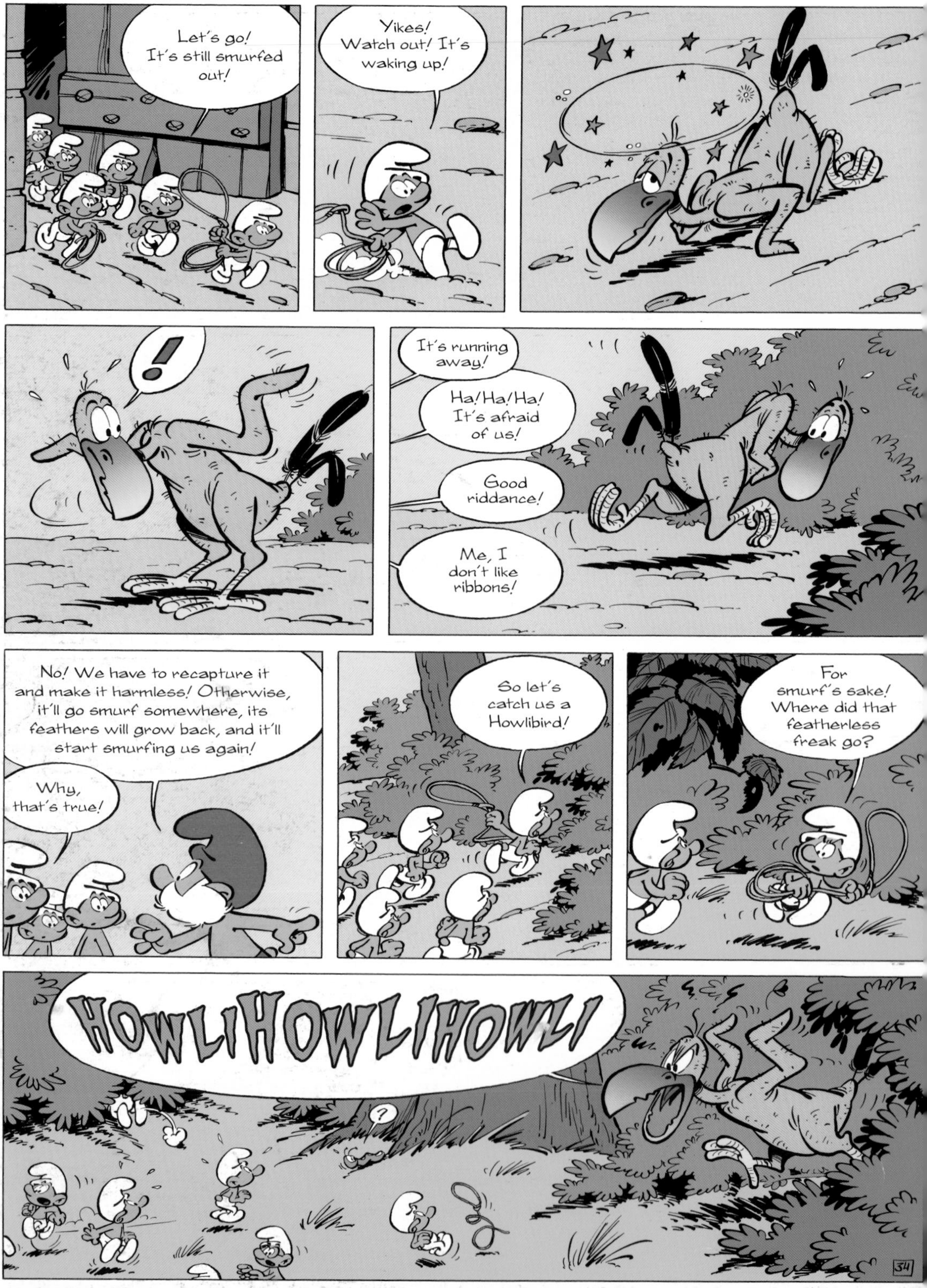
Let's go! It's still smurfed out!
Yikes! Watch out! It's waking up!
!
It's running away!
Ha! Ha! Ha! It's afraid of us!
Good riddance!
Me, I don't like ribbons!
No! We have to recapture it and make it harmless! Otherwise, it'll go smurf somewhere, its feathers will grow back, and it'll start smurfing us again!
Why, that's true!
So let's catch us a Howlibird!
For smurf's sake! Where did that featherless freak go?
HOWLIHOWLIHOWLI
?
34

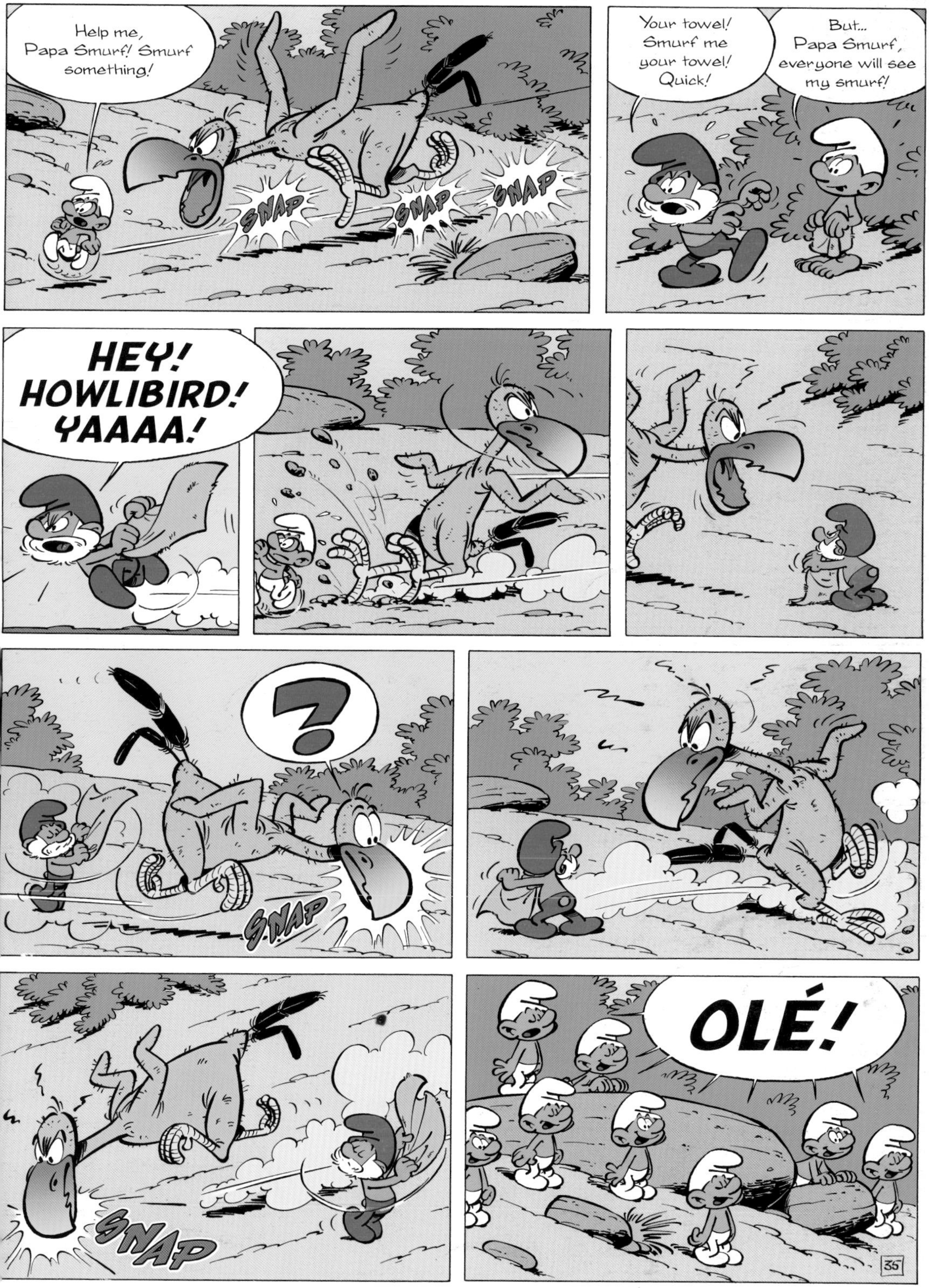
Help me, Papa Smurf! Smurf something!
SNAP
SNAP
SNAP
Your towel! Smurf me your towel! Quick!
But... Papa Smurf, everyone will see my smurf!
HEY! HOWLIBIRD! YAAAA!
?
SNAP
SNAP
OLÉ!
35

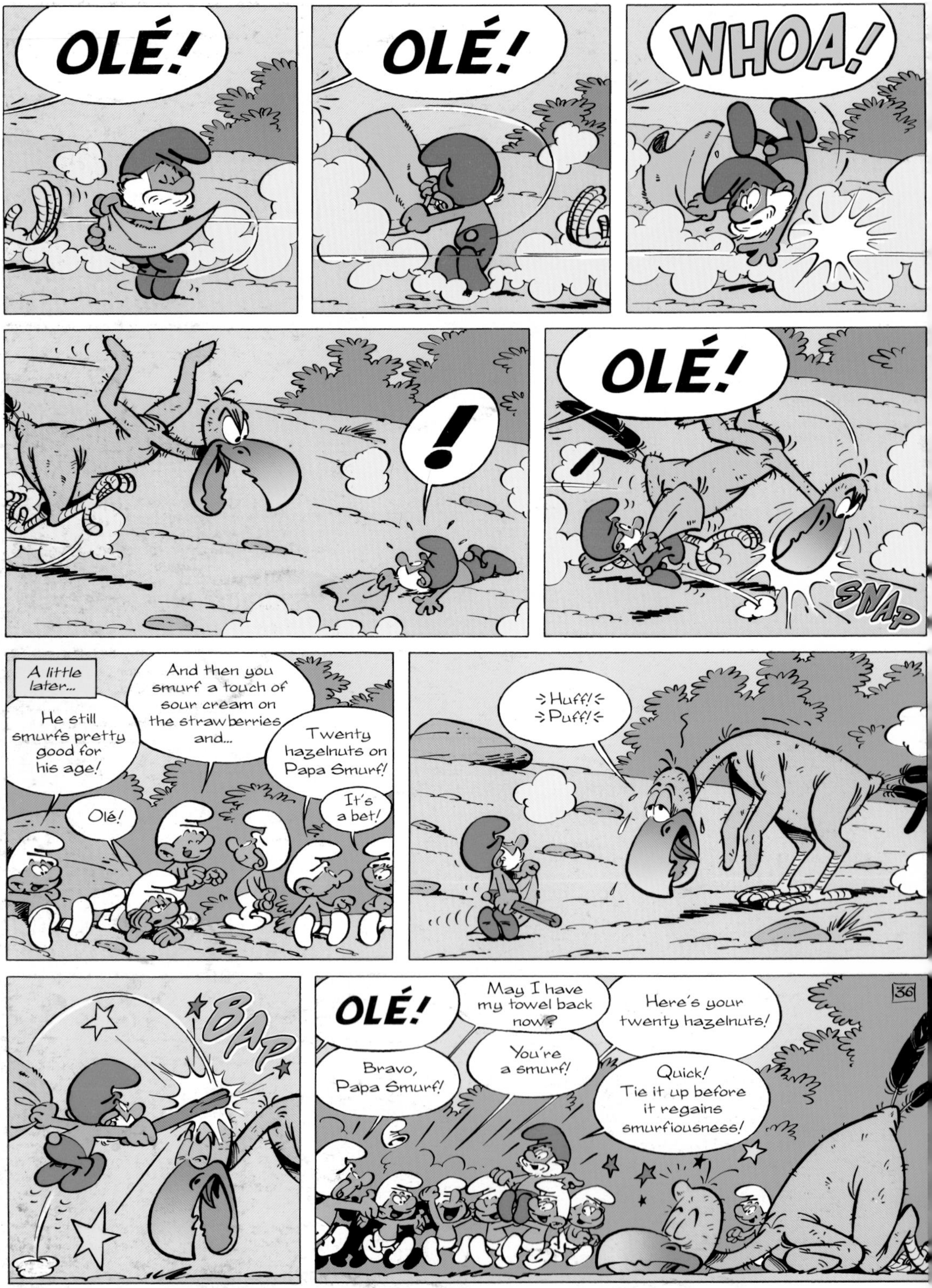
OLÉ!
OLÉ!
WHOA!
!
OLÉ!
SNAP
A little later...
He still smurfs pretty good for his age!
And then you smurf a touch of sour cream on the strawberries and...
Twenty hazelnuts on Papa Smurf!
Olé!
It's a bet!
Huff! Puff!
BAP
OLÉ!
May I have my towel back now?
Here's your twenty hazelnuts!
Bravo, Papa Smurf!
You're a smurf!
Quick! Tie it up before it regains smurfiousness!
36

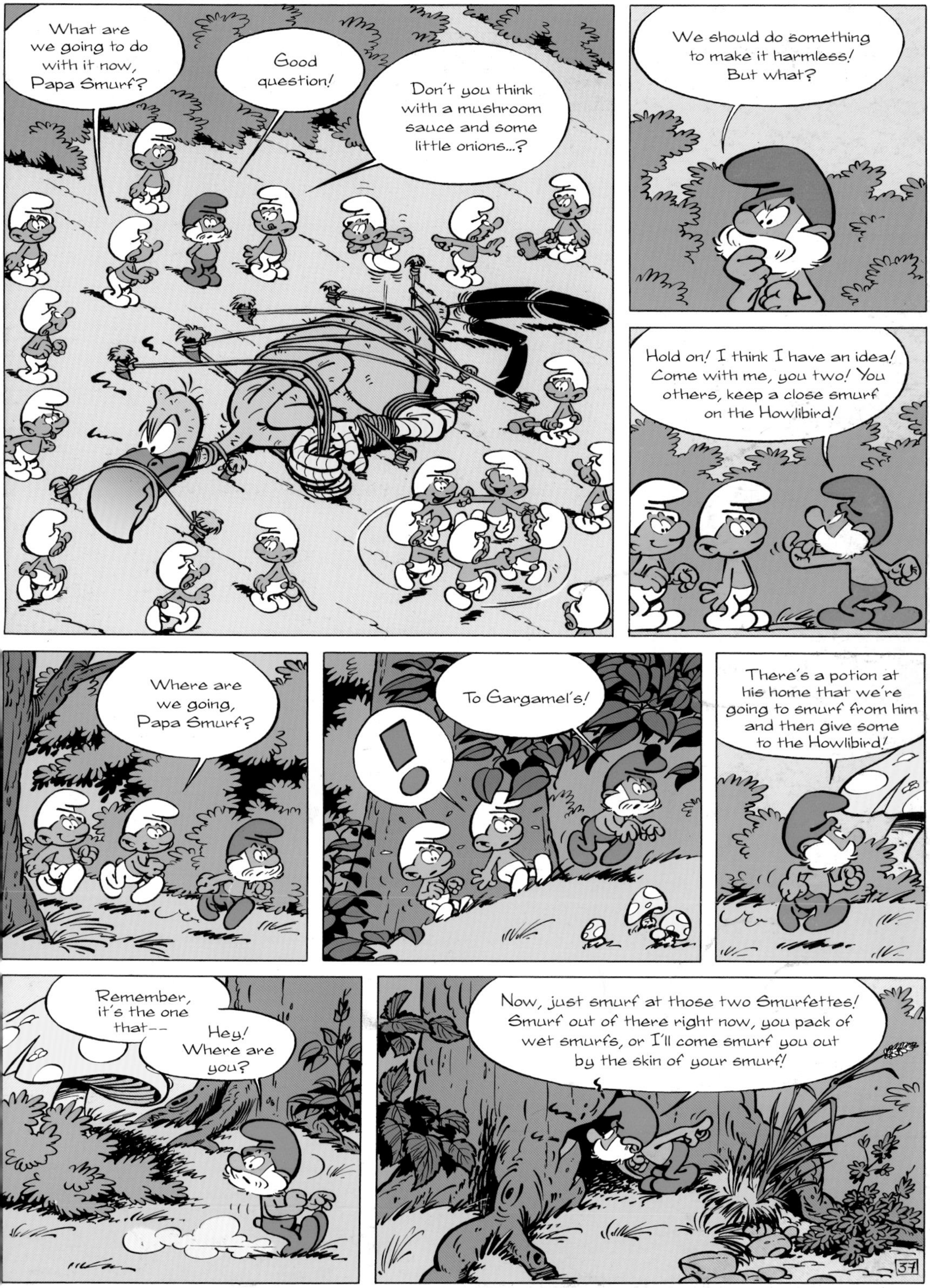

What are we going to do with it now, Papa Smurf?
Good question!
Don't you think with a mushroom sauce and some little onions...?
We should do something to make it harmless! But what?
Hold on! I think I have an idea! Come with me, you two! You others, keep a close smurf on the Howlibird!
Where are we going, Papa Smurf?
To Gargamel's!
!
There's a potion at his home that we're going to smurf from him and then give some to the Howlibird!
Remember, it's the one that--
Hey! Where are you?
Now, just smurf at those two Smurfettes! Smurf out of there right now, you pack of wet smurfs, or I'll come smurf you out by the skin of your smurf!
37

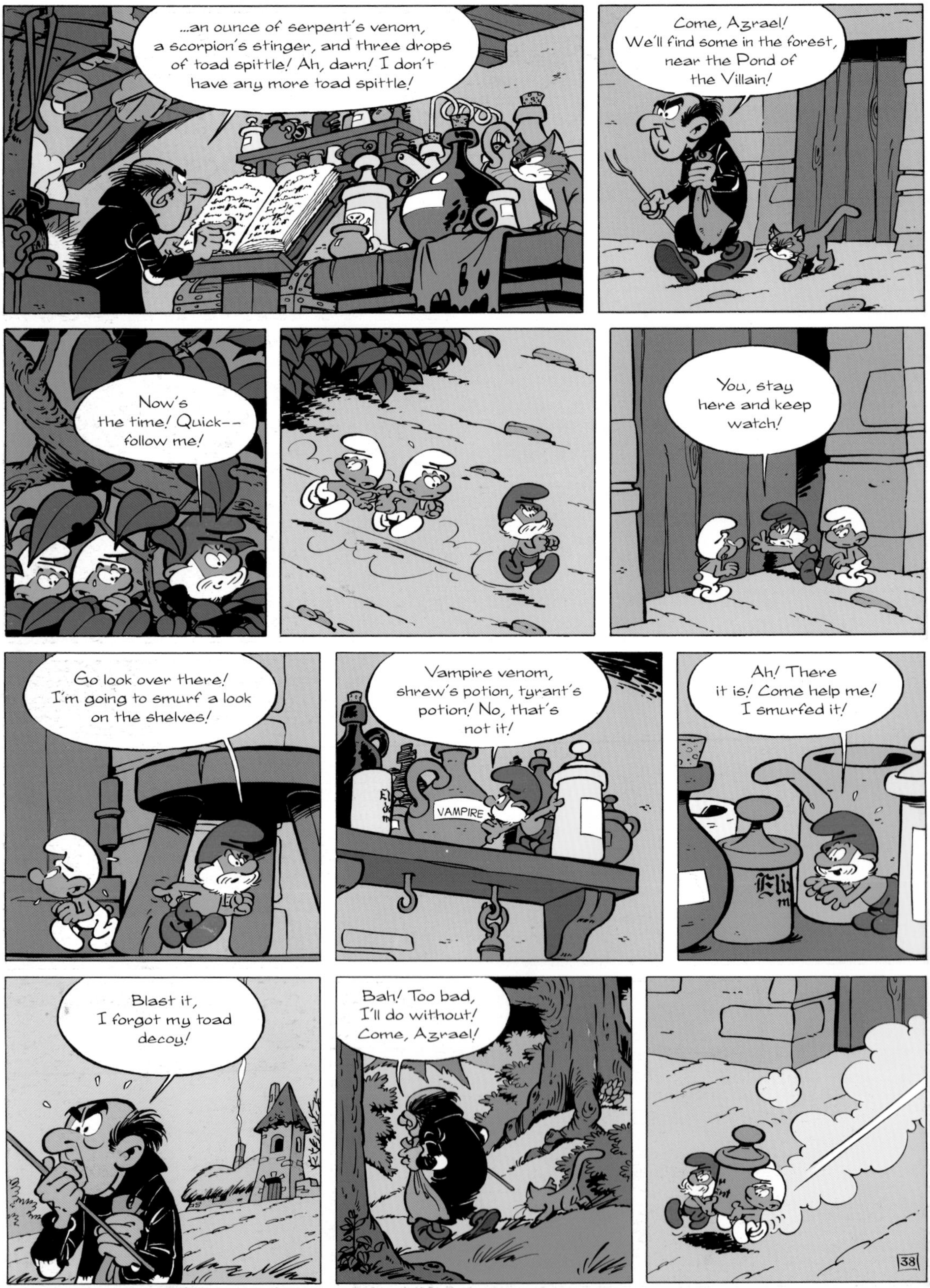
...an ounce of serpent's venom, a scorpion's stinger, and three drops of toad spittle! Ah, darn! I don't have any more toad spittle!
Come, Azrael! We'll find some in the forest, near the Pond of the Villain!
Now's the time! Quick-- follow me!
You, stay here and keep watch!
Go look over there! I'm going to smurf a look on the shelves!
Vampire venom, shrew's potion, tyrant's potion! No, that's not it!
VAMPIRE
Ah! There it is! Come help me! I smurfed it!
Blast it, I forgot my toad decoy!
Bah! Too bad, I'll do without! Come, Azrael!
38

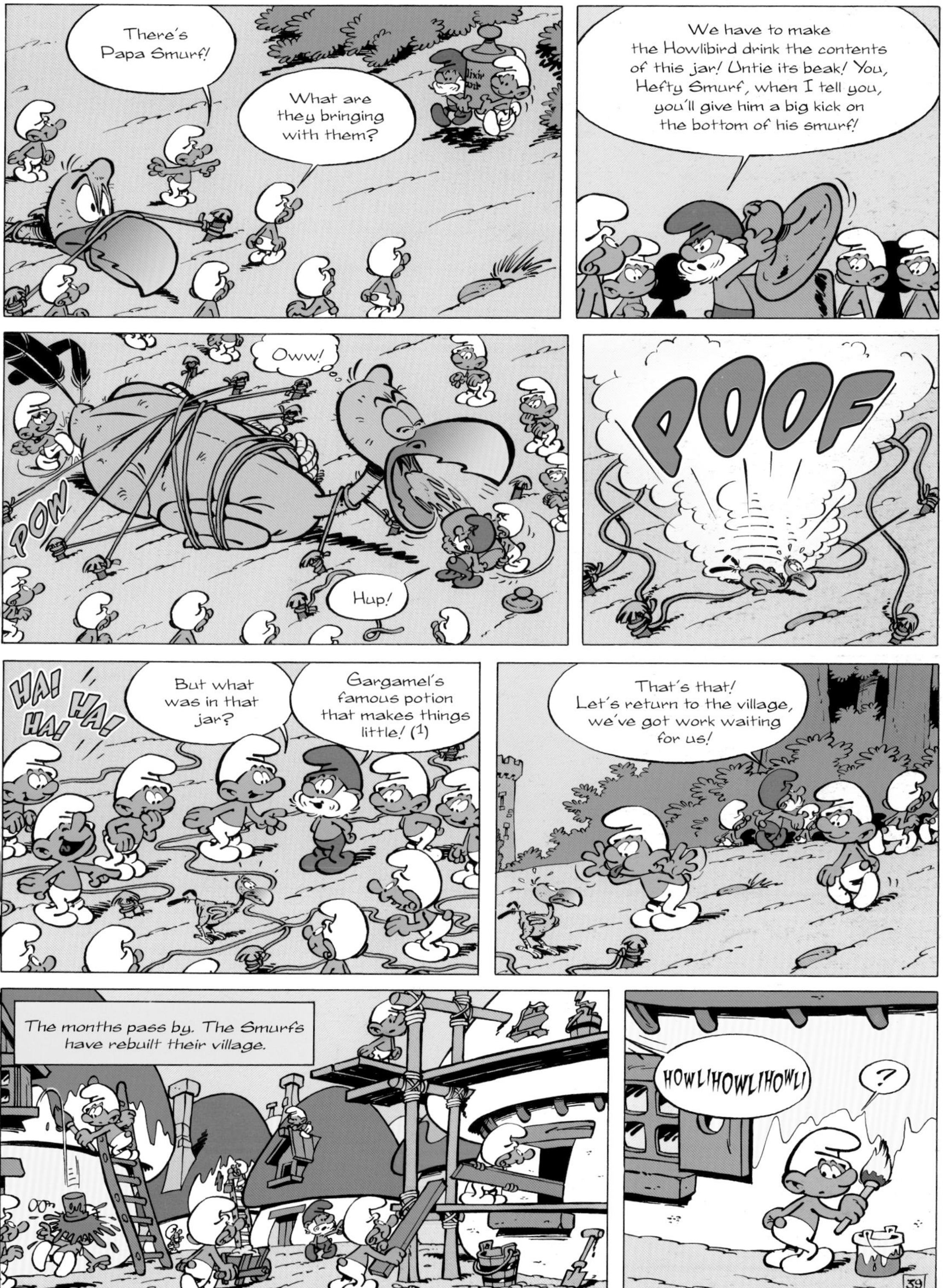
There's Papa Smurf!
What are they bringing with them?
We have to make the Howlibird drink the contents of this jar! Untie its beak! You, Hefty Smurf, when I tell you, you'll give him a big kick on the bottom of his smurf!
POW
Oww!
Hup!
POOF
HA! HA! HA!
But what was in that jar?
Gargamel's famous potion that makes things little! (1)
That's that! Let's return to the village, we've got work waiting for us!
The months pass by. The Smurfs have rebuilt their village.
HOWL! HOWL! HOWL!
?
39

(1) See "The Smurfnapper" in SMURFS graphic novel #9 "Gargamel and the Smurfs" or THE SMURFS ANTHOLOGY Vol. 1.

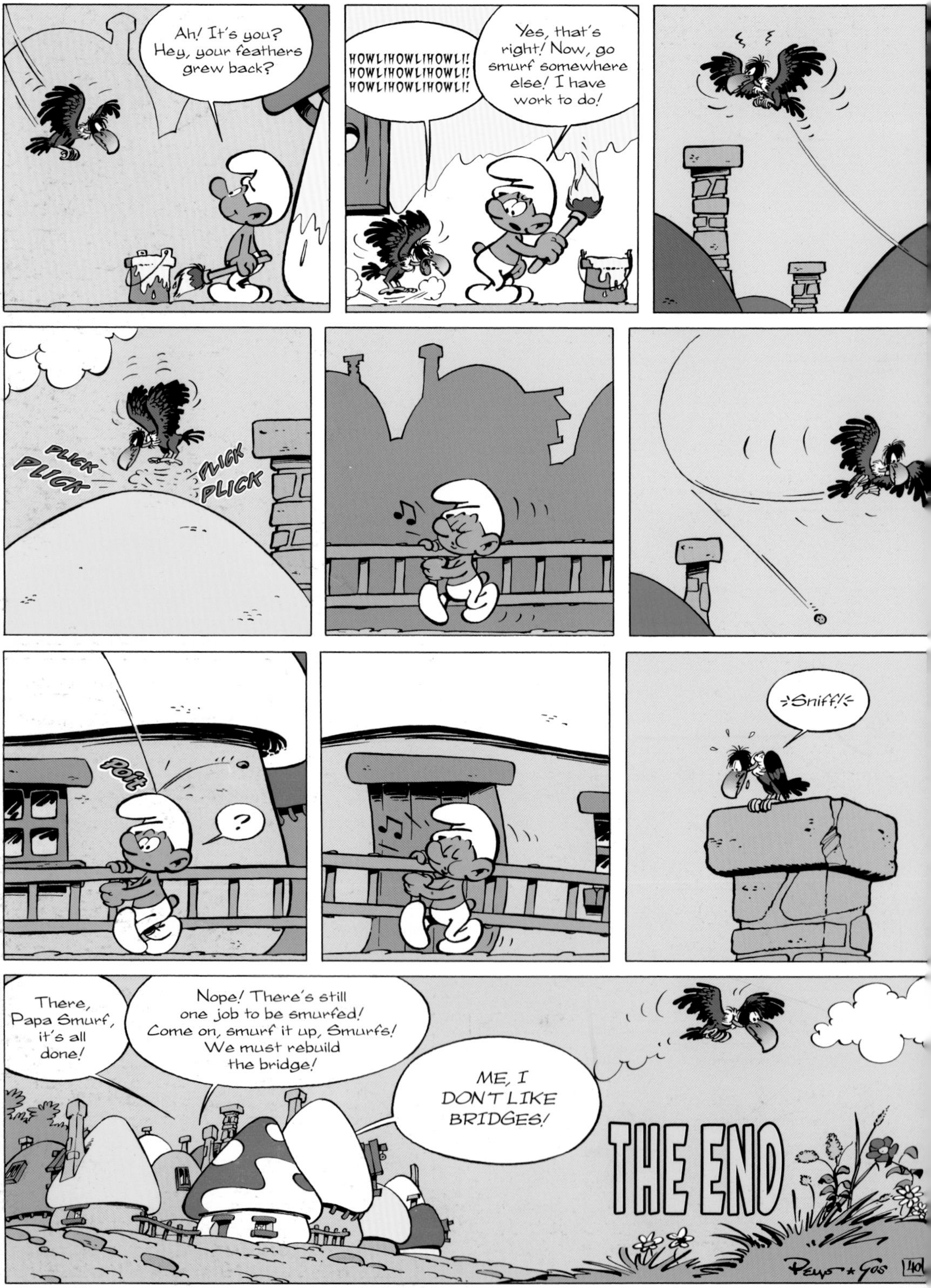
Ah! It's you? Hey, your feathers grew back?
HOWLIHOWLIHOWLI! HOWLIHOWLIHOWLI! HOWLIHOWLIHOWLI!
Yes, that's right! Now, go smurf somewhere else! I have work to do!
PLICK PLICK
PLICK PLICK
Poit
?
Sniff!
There, Papa Smurf, it's all done!
Nope! There's still one job to be smurfed! Come on, smurf it up, Smurfs! We must rebuild the bridge!
ME, I DON'T LIKE BRIDGES!
THE END

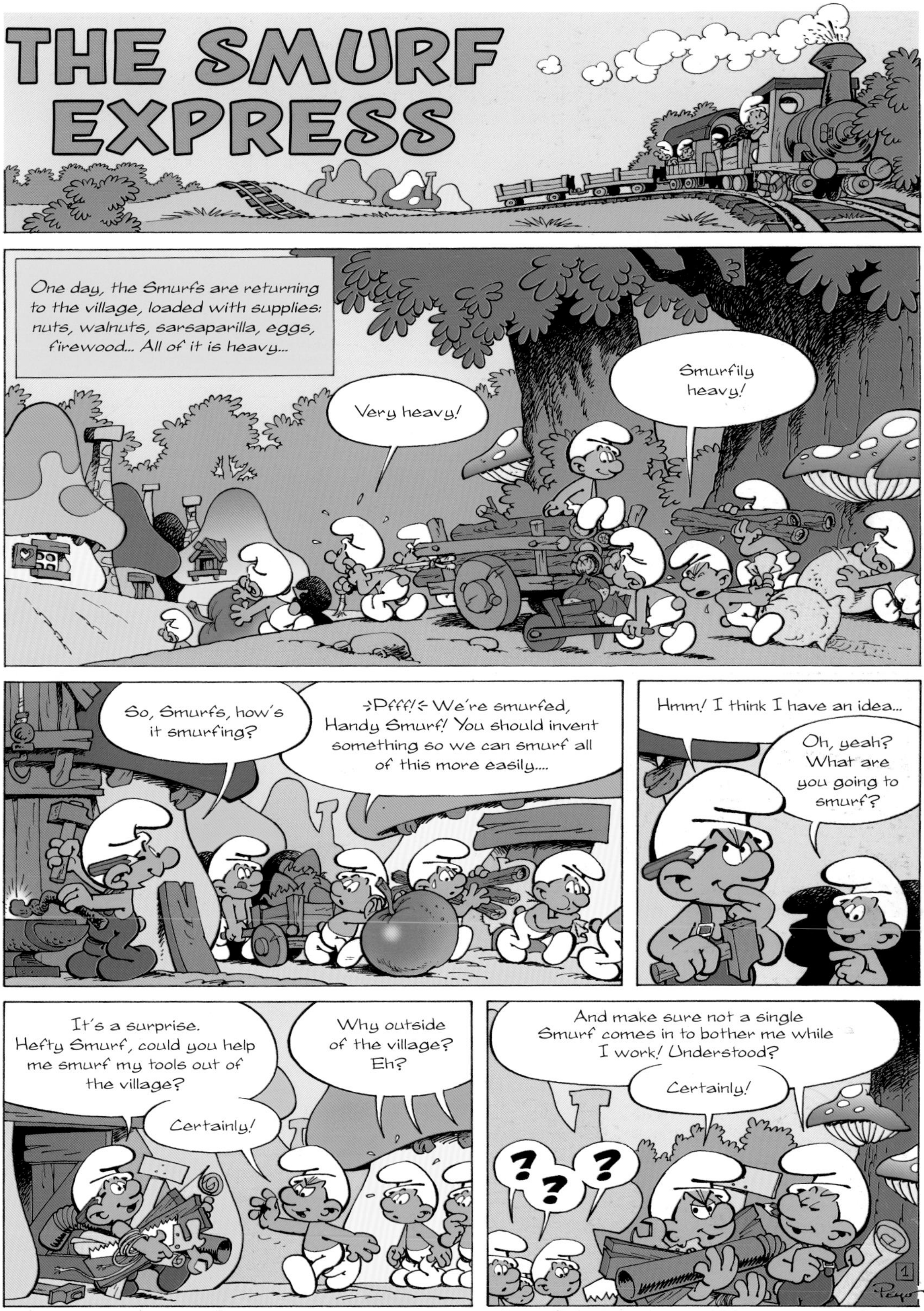
THE SMURF EXPRESS
One day, the Smurfs are returning to the village, loaded with supplies: nuts, walnuts, sarsaparilla, eggs, firewood... All of it is heavy...
Very heavy!
Smurfily heavy!
So, Smurfs, how's it smurfing?
≻Pfff!≺ We're smurfed, Handy Smurf! You should invent something so we can smurf all of this more easily....
Hmm! I think I have an idea...
Oh, yeah? What are you going to smurf?
It's a surprise. Hefty Smurf, could you help me smurf my tools out of the village?
Certainly!
Why outside of the village? Eh?
And make sure not a single Smurf comes in to bother me while I work! Understood?
Certainly!
???
1
Peyo

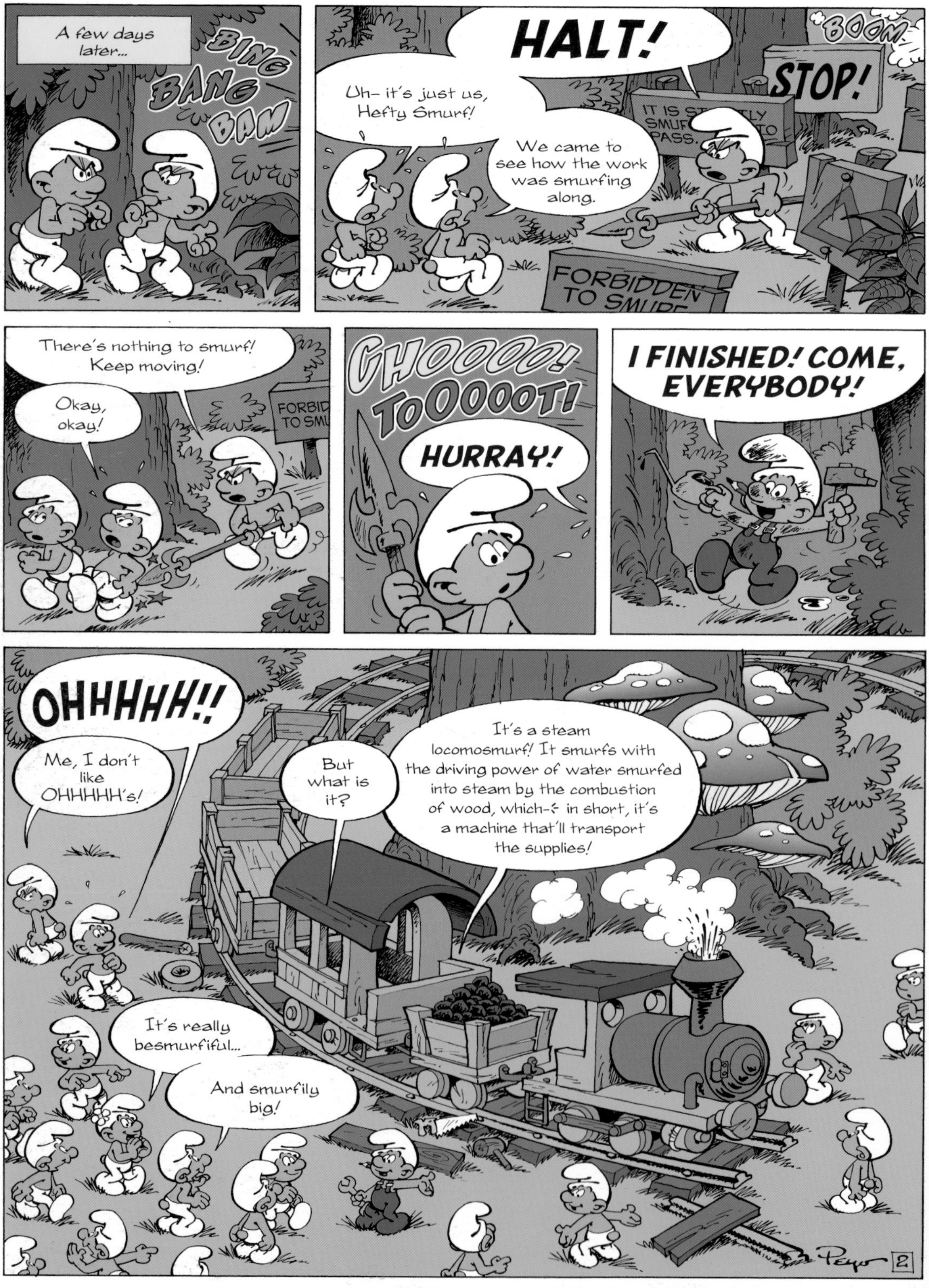

A few days later...
BING
BANG
BAM
HALT!
BOOM
STOP!
IT IS ST... SMUR... PASS.
Uh- it's just us, Hefty Smurf!
We came to see how the work was smurfing along.
FORBIDDEN TO SMURF
There's nothing to smurf! Keep moving!
Okay, okay!
FORBID TO SMU
CHOOOOO!
TOOOOOT!
HURRAY!
I FINISHED! COME, EVERYBODY!
OHHHHH!!
Me, I don't like OHHHHH's!
But what is it?
It's a steam locomosmurf! It smurfs with the driving power of water smurfed into steam by the combustion of wood, which- in short, it's a machine that'll transport the supplies!
It's really besmurfiful...
And smurfily big!
Peyo
2

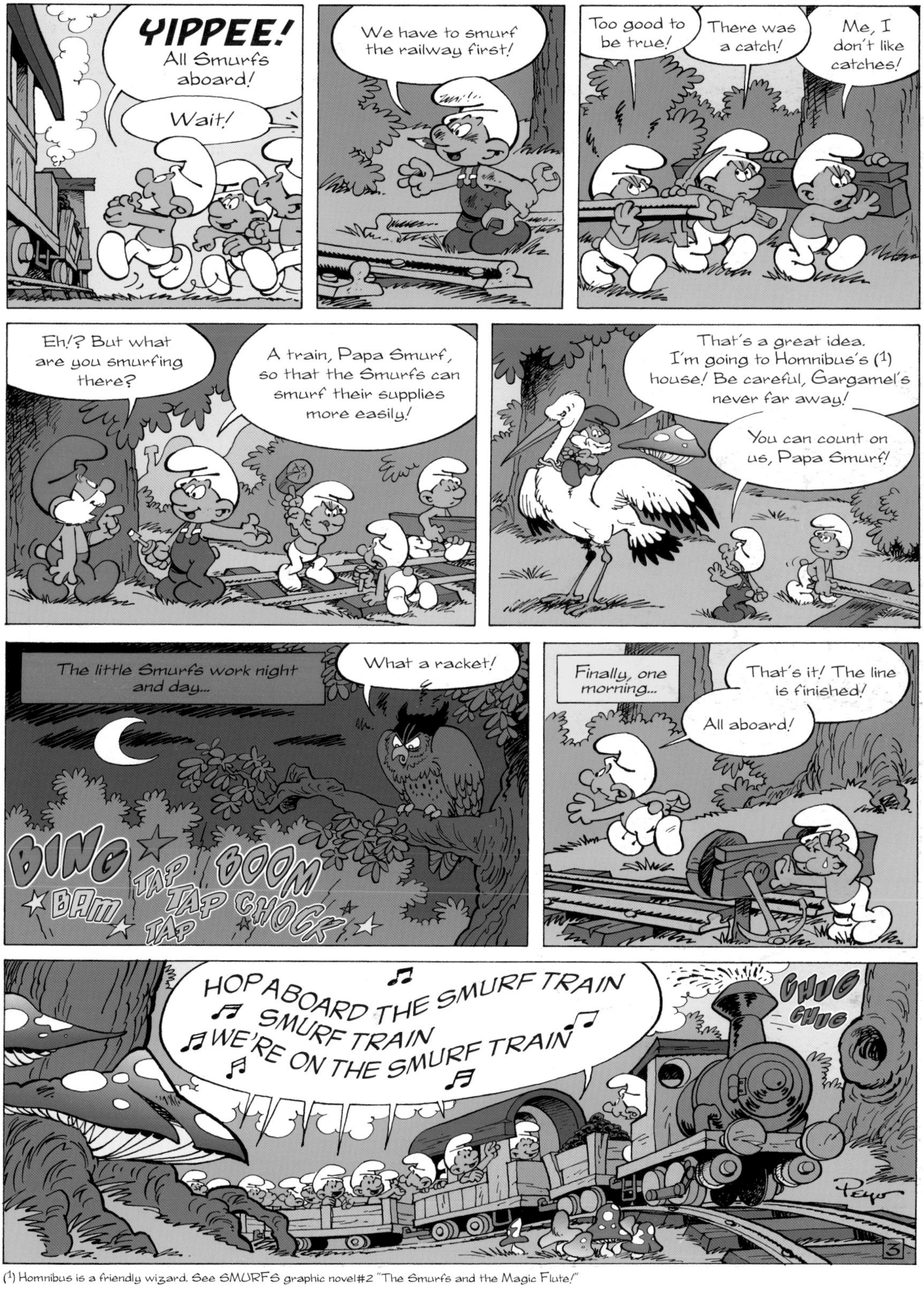
YIPPEE! All Smurfs aboard!
Wait!
We have to smurf the railway first!
Too good to be true!
There was a catch!
Me, I don't like catches!
Eh!? But what are you smurfing there?
A train, Papa Smurf, so that the Smurfs can smurf their supplies more easily!
That's a great idea. I'm going to Homnibus's (1) house! Be careful, Gargamel's never far away!
You can count on us, Papa Smurf!
The little Smurfs work night and day...
What a racket!
BING BAM TAP TAP TAP BOOM CHOCK
Finally, one morning...
That's it! The line is finished!
All aboard!
HOP ABOARD THE SMURF TRAIN
SMURF TRAIN
WE'RE ON THE SMURF TRAIN
CHUG CHUG
Peyo
3

(1) Homnibus is a friendly wizard. See SMURFS graphic novel#2 "The Smurfs and the Magic Flute!"

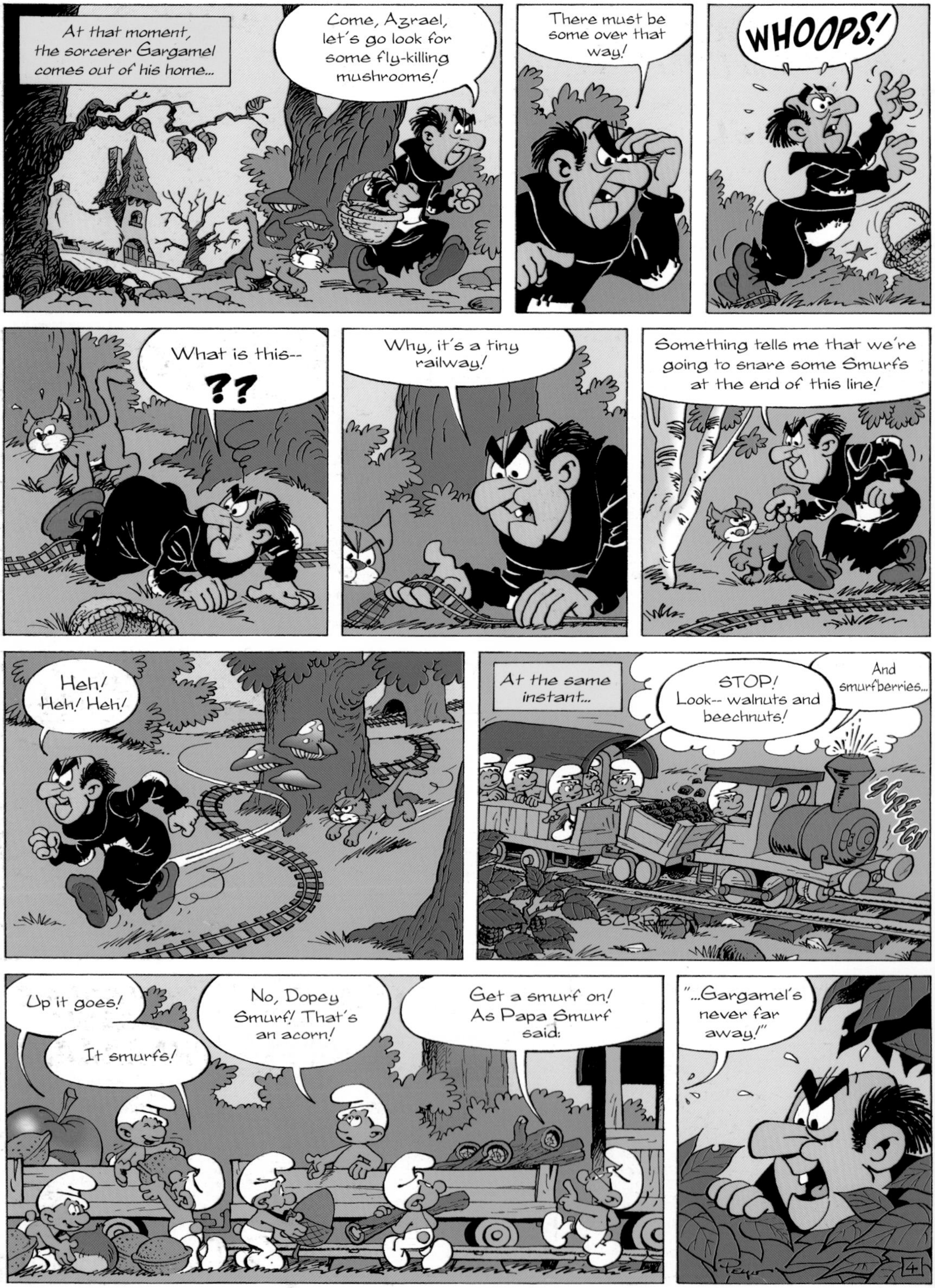
At that moment, the sorcerer Gargamel comes out of his home...
Come, Azrael, let's go look for some fly-killing mushrooms!
There must be some over that way!
WHOOPS!
What is this--
??
Why, it's a tiny railway!
Something tells me that we're going to snare some Smurfs at the end of this line!
Heh! Heh! Heh!
At the same instant...
STOP! Look-- walnuts and beechnuts!
And smurfberries...
SCREECH
Up it goes!
It smurfs!
No, Dopey Smurf! That's an acorn!
Get a smurf on! As Papa Smurf said:
"...Gargamel's never far away!"
4

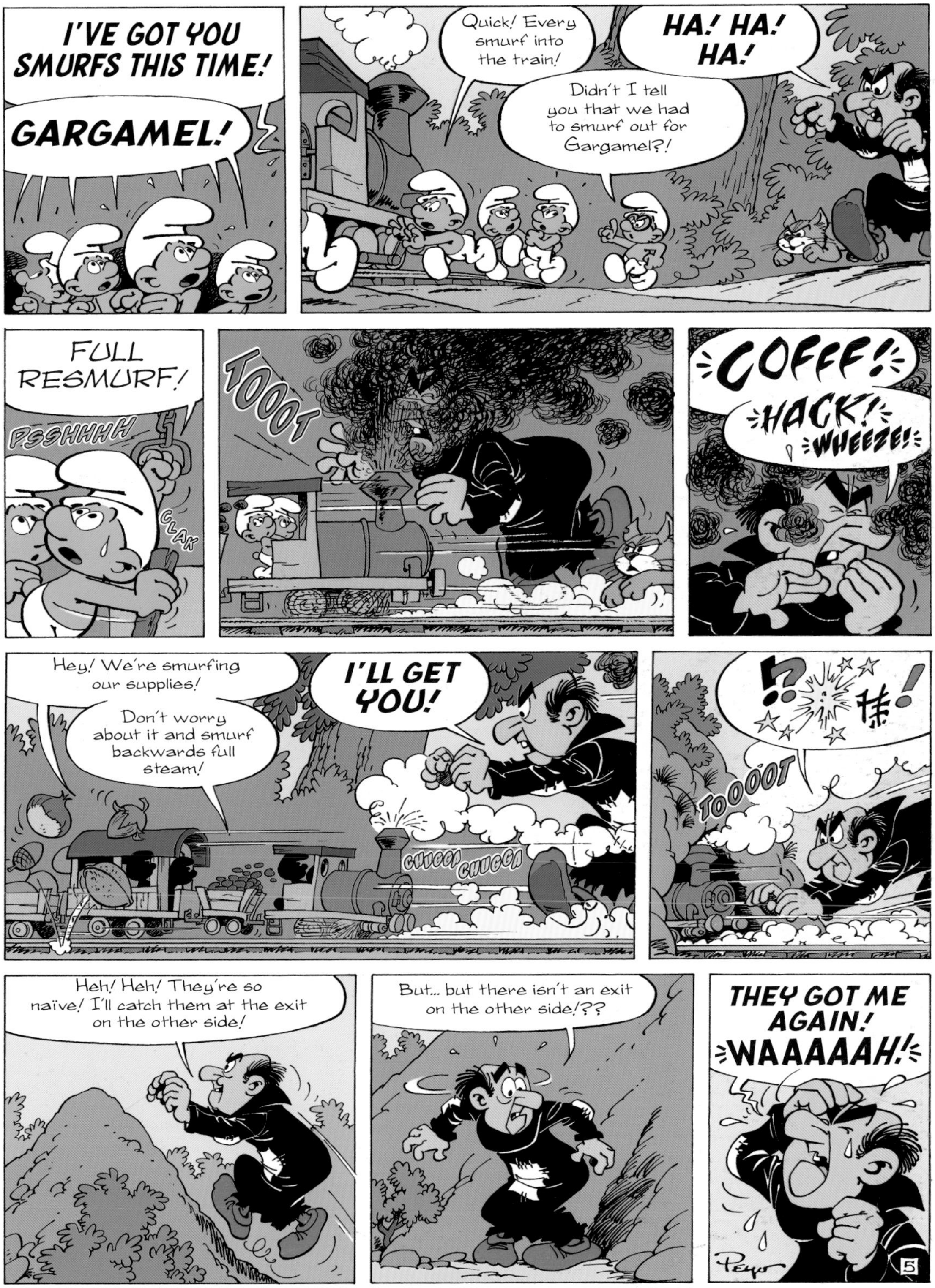
I'VE GOT YOU SMURFS THIS TIME!
GARGAMEL!
Quick! Every smurf into the train!
HA! HA! HA!
Didn't I tell you that we had to smurf out for Gargamel?!
FULL RESMURF!
PSSHHHH
CLAK
TOOOT
COFFF!
HACK!
WHEEZE!
Hey! We're smurfing our supplies!
Don't worry about it and smurf backwards full steam!
I'LL GET YOU!
CHUGGA CHUGGA
TOOOOT
Heh! Heh! They're so naïve! I'll catch them at the exit on the other side!
But... but there isn't an exit on the other side!??
THEY GOT ME AGAIN!
WAAAAAH!
Peyo
5

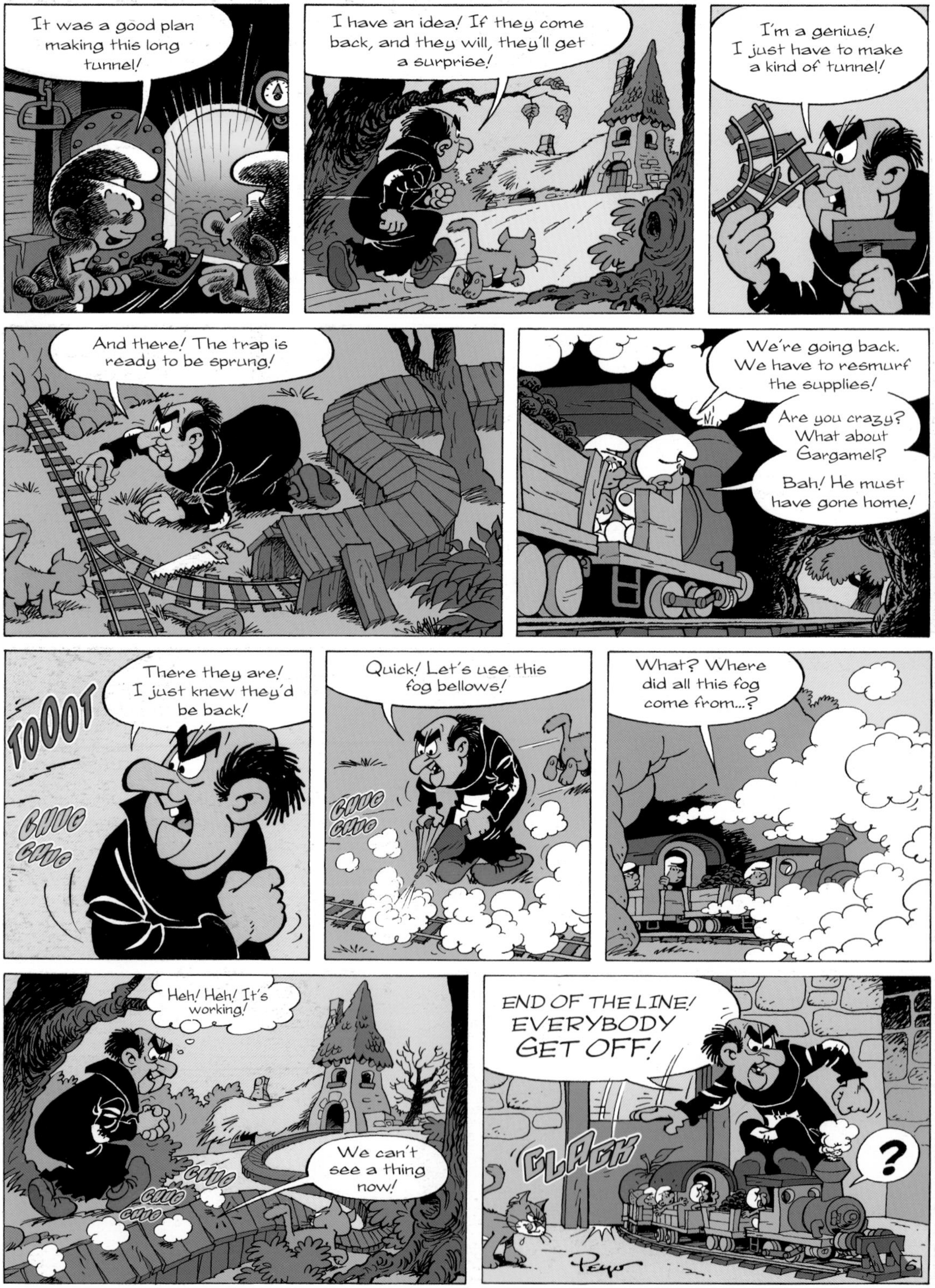

It was a good plan making this long tunnel!
I have an idea! If they come back, and they will, they'll get a surprise!
I'm a genius! I just have to make a kind of tunnel!
And there! The trap is ready to be sprung!
We're going back. We have to resmurf the supplies!
Are you crazy? What about Gargamel?
Bah! He must have gone home!
There they are! I just knew they'd be back!
TOOOT
CHUG CHUG
Quick! Let's use this fog bellows!
CHUG CHUG
What? Where did all this fog come from...?
Heh! Heh! It's working!
CHUG CHUG CHUG
We can't see a thing now!
END OF THE LINE! EVERYBODY GET OFF!
CLACK
?
Peyo
6

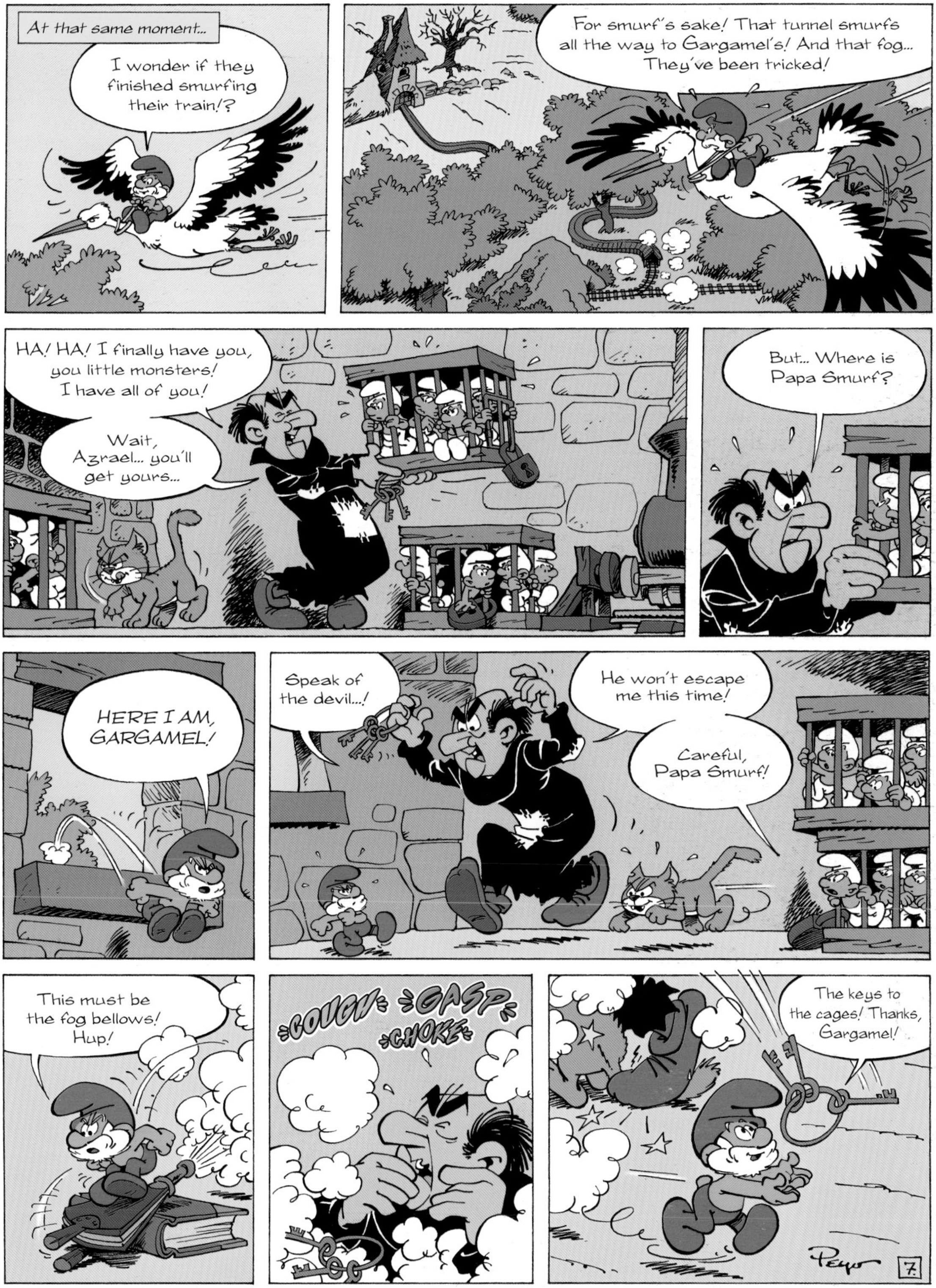

At that same moment...
I wonder if they finished smurfing their train!?
For smurf's sake! That tunnel smurfs all the way to Gargamel's! And that fog... They've been tricked!
HA! HA! I finally have you, you little monsters! I have all of you!
Wait, Azrael... you'll get yours...
But... Where is Papa Smurf?
HERE I AM, GARGAMEL!
Speak of the devil...!
He won't escape me this time!
Careful, Papa Smurf!
This must be the fog bellows! Hup!
COUGH GASP
CHOKE
The keys to the cages! Thanks, Gargamel!
Peyo
7

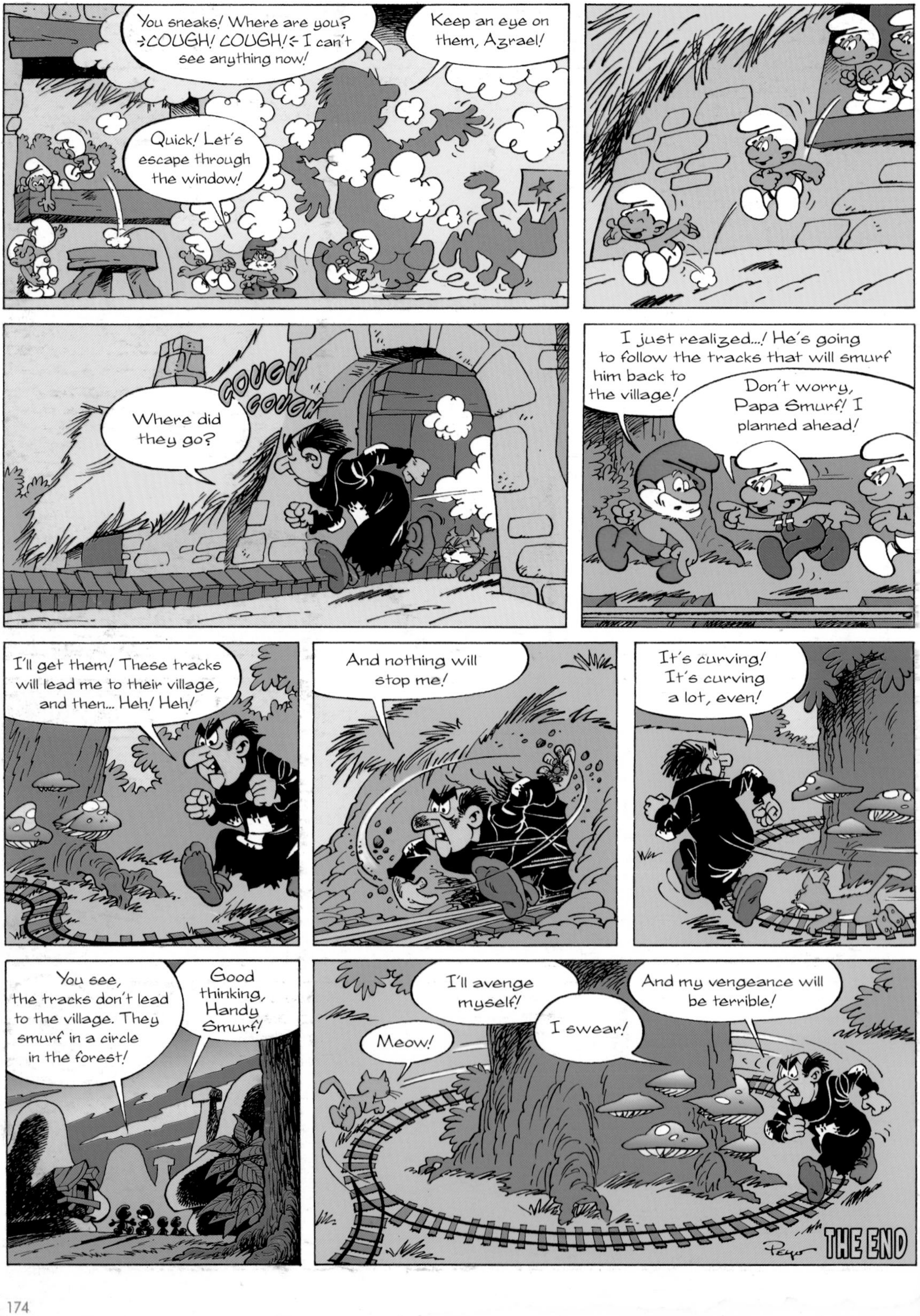
You sneaks! Where are you? ⇒COUGH! COUGH!⇐ I can't see anything now!
Keep an eye on them, Azrael!
Quick! Let's escape through the window!
COUGH COUGH
Where did they go?
I just realized...! He's going to follow the tracks that will smurf him back to the village!
Don't worry, Papa Smurf! I planned ahead!
I'll get them! These tracks will lead me to their village, and then... Heh! Heh!
And nothing will stop me!
It's curving! It's curving a lot, even!
You see, the tracks don't lead to the village. They smurf in a circle in the forest!
Good thinking, Handy Smurf!
Meow!
I'll avenge myself!
I swear!
And my vengeance will be terrible!
Peyo
THE END

YOU CAN'T SMURF IN THE WAY OF PROGRESS

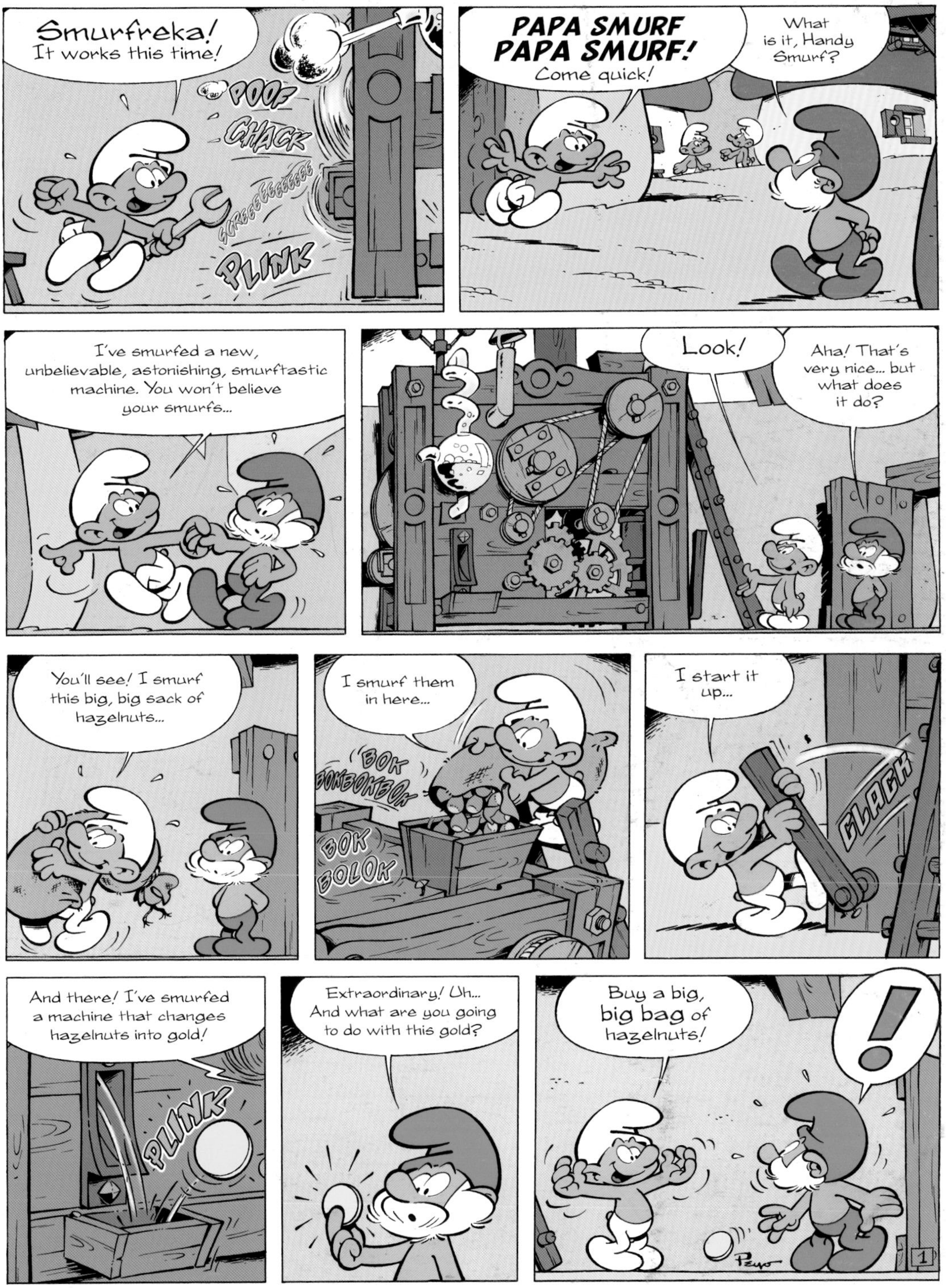

Smurfreka! It works this time!
POOF
CHACK
PLINK
PAPA SMURF PAPA SMURF! Come quick!
What is it, Handy Smurf?
I've smurfed a new, unbelievable, astonishing, smurftastic machine. You won't believe your smurfs...
Look!
Aha! That's very nice... but what does it do?
You'll see! I smurf this big, big sack of hazelnuts...
I smurf them in here...
BOK
BOK BOLOK
I start it up...
CLACK
And there! I've smurfed a machine that changes hazelnuts into gold!
PLINK
Extraordinary! Uh... And what are you going to do with this gold?
Buy a big, big bag of hazelnuts!
!
Peyo
1

WATCH OUT FOR PAPERCUTZ

Welcome to the second edition of THE SMURFS 3 IN 1 from Papercutz, those Peyo-fanatics dedicated to publishing great graphic novels for all ages. I'm Jim Salicrup, the Editor-in-Chief and Gargamel's fashion consultant, here with a few more Smurf-facts to enrich your overall Smurf-experience...

First, this book is being published in 2018, just in time to celebrate THE SMURF's 60th anniversary. If you happen to be anywhere near Belgium, you may be able to attend the Smurfs Experience at the Brussels Expo. It ends January 27, 2019, so you better get your tickets fast from www.smurfexperience.com/en/. Unfortunately, it's already too late to attend the "Peyo: A Retrospective" that was at the Wallonia-Brussels Center in Paris. But don't despair, there's still plenty of Smurftastic stuff still coming your way. In production right now is an all-new animated Smurfs TV series! But that's not all...

As anyone who's seen the most recent Smurfs movie, "The Lost Village" already knows that Smurfette isn't the only female Smurf. We've already published THE SMURFS THE VILLAGE BEHIND THE WALL that featured all-new adventures with those girl smurfs, which is still available at booksellers everywhere, but we're thrilled to announce that coming soon from Papercutz is THE SMURFS THE VILLAGE BEHIND THE WALL #2—featuring an all-new adventure, enticingly entitled "The Betrayal of Smurfblossom."

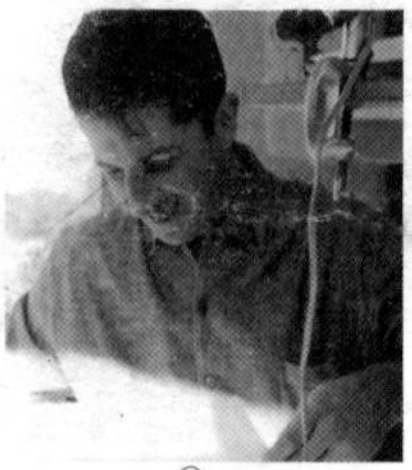
Gos

Of course, I could also mention all the other Peyo graphic novels from Papercutz, such as THE SMURFS ANTHOLOGY, THE SMURFS AND FRIENDS, PUSSYCAT, BENNY BREAKIRON, and more, but instead, we want to include a mini biography about Gos, the cartoonist that worked with Peyo on "The Smurfs and the Howlibird." Over the years Peyo worked with a studio of great cartoonists to help him meet the demand for his comics. Gos was one of those cartoonists. (We want to thank Bas at Lambiek studios for both the bio and photo of Gos.)

Roland Goossens, better known as Gos, was one of the popular artists that published in *Spirou* magazine from the 1970s throughout the 1990s. Born in Thy-le-Château, he was in the professional military prior to his career in comics. He devoted his spare time to drawing and published his first comic story in the military magazine *Nos Forces*. He was in his late 20's when he switched careers and joined Studio Peyo in 1965. He was Peyo's right-hand man on *"Les Schtroumpfs"* (THE SMURFS), *"Benoît Brisefer"* (Benny Breakiron) and *"Jacky et Célestin."* Gos published his first solo short story in *Spirou* magazine in 1966 and helped his studio colleague François Walthéry in the creation of his own series *"Natacha,"* for which he wrote the scripts of the first two books.

Gos left Studio Peyo in 1969 and took over the artwork of the popular detective series *"Gil Jourdan"* from Maurice Tillieux, who kept writing the scripts, in the following year. The collaboration between Gos and Tillieux continued until the latter's unfortunate death in 1979. Gos additionally began his own series, *"Khéna et le Scrameustache,"* that was published in *Spirou* from 1972. This humorous children's science fiction comic, about an extraterrestrial cat and his earth friend, became one of *Spirou's* most popular series.

With adding such alien creatures as *"Les Galaxiens"* to the series, Gos developed an entire universe around his two main characters. Gos got assistance from Yves Urbain and most notably his son Walt in the early 1980s. Walt has focused on the artwork of the stories starring the *Galaxiens* since. After 34 albums published by Dupuis, the series was continued by Glénat in 2005.

We hope you enjoyed THE SMURFS 3 IN 1 #2, and hope you'll pick up our third collection, coming soon. It'll include "The Astrosmurf," "The Smurf Apprentice," and "Gargamel and the Smurfs." We promise it'll be smurftastic!

Oh, and regarding our back cover question "which came first—the Howlibird or the egg?"...the answer should be obvious, "The Smurfs and the Egg" is on page 64 and "The Smurfs and the Howlibird" doesn't start until page 127, so the Egg came first!

Smurf you later,

Jim

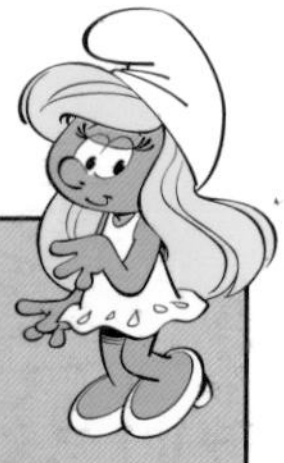

STAY IN TOUCH!

EMAIL:	salicrup@papercutz.com
WEB:	papercutz.com
TWITTER:	@papercutzgn
INSTAGRAM:	@papercutzgn
FACEBOOK:	PAPERCUTZGRAPHICNOVELS
FANMAIL:	Papercutz, 160 Broadway, Suite 700, East Wing, New York, NY 10038